BREAKFAST AT WIMBLEDON

Tor books by Jack M. Bickham

Ariel
Day Seven
Miracle Worker
The Regensburg Legacy

Novels in the Brad Smith Series

Tiebreaker
Dropshot
Overhead
Breakfast at Wimbledon

BREAKFAST AT WIMBLEDON

JACK M. BICKHAM

TOR ®

A Tom Doherty Associates Book
New York

This is a work of fiction. All the characters and events portrayed in this book are fictitious, and any resemblance to real people or events is purely coincidental.

BREAKFAST AT WIMBLEDON

Copyright © 1991 by Jack M. Bickham

All rights reserved, including the right to reproduce this book, or portions thereof, in any form.

This book was printed on acid-free paper.

A Tor Book

Published by Tom Doherty Associates, Inc.

49 West 24th Street

New York, N.Y. 10010

Library of Congress Cataloging-in-Publication Data

Bickham, Jack M.
    Breakfast at Wimbledon / Jack M. Bickham.
       p.   cm.
    "A Tom Doherty Associates book."
    ISBN 0-312-85144-8
    I. Title.
PS3552.I3B7 1991
813'.54—dc20   91-21705
                                                         CIP

First edition: December 1991

Printed in the United States of America

0 9 8 7 6 5 4 3 2 1

Author's Note

The perceptive reader may notice that I have taken small
liberties with the schedule of play at both Wimbledon and the
grass court tournaments immediately preceding it. One or two
other insignificant details have also been altered slightly to facilitate the telling of the story. Except for these details, however,
every effort has been made to make the factual backdrop as accurate as possible. It should also be noted that several actual
worldclass tennis players inevitably are mentioned or appear in
minor roles, but major characters are all fictional, and are not intended to represent real people.

One

SUMMER CAN BE unpredictable in the Montana Rockies. Once I drove into a snowstorm in July. That surprise, however, couldn't hold a candle to the one I got that late May afternoon when Collie Davis showed up, and everything changed.

It was a warm day, with a clear cobalt sky, the sun brilliant against the snow still much in evidence on the higher slopes of the Bitterroots. I was on the No. 6 court at our tennis and golf resort with a group of ten guests, giving them an intermediate lesson. It all felt just fine.

That was when I happened to turn and saw the familiar figure—a slender, slightly balding, fortyish man wearing lemon slacks and a white shirt—standing at the edge of the No. 1 court.

Oh no, I thought. *No, no, no.*

Collie Davis did not make casual visits. He was a career man with the Company, and still active. His days as an overseas case officer seemed to be over, and now he evidently spent most of his time at headquarters in Langley, Virginia. But on three earlier occasions he had popped up in my life with a contract assignment that I didn't want . . . couldn't turn down.

Collie was a good man and a good friend. But I was never glad to see him like this. I did my bit for them a long time ago when I was on the tennis tour. I am a devout coward. I don't want to do any more.

Turning back to my tennis group, I gave them some instructions for a backhand drill and serve and volley practice, then left

1

them temporarily on their own. Heading toward the far end of the courts where Collie stood, I told myself that *this* time, maybe, he would not have a job.

Fat chance.

"Brad," he said with a tired smile that put a hundred sunbaked crinkles around his eyes and mouth. "Don't let me interrupt."

"You already have, Collie."

He stuck out his hand. "I'm sure just being close to your greatness out there will make champs of all of them."

"Sure. Right. What are you doing here, Collie?"

"Good to see you, pardner."

"What do you want, Collie?"

He looked blank, which he was very good at. A casual observer would have figured this weather-beaten, slope-shouldered man for a nonentity at best, possibly one of life's losers. Collie had spent a great deal of time cultivating this nondescript appearance and demeanor. It was one of several reasons why he was so good at his business.

"Why," he asked, "are you so sure I want something?"

"Come on, Collie. No more crap, okay?"

He gave up the act. "Okay. I do want something."

This surprised me. It wasn't his style to be direct. I said, "Forget it. Not interested."

"You don't know what it is yet."

"I don't want to know."

"Let's talk in private."

I looked around. The nearest tennis player was four courts away. "This isn't private enough?"

His eyes could have driven rivets. "I need more than two minutes."

It began to sink into my dense skull that he was in no mood for games. "Let me finish my lesson over there."

"Where can I wait?"

"Go have some coffee on the lodge deck. I'll join you."

He nodded, turned, and exited through the gate in the high

cyclone fencing that surrounded the courts. I watched him head up the curving brick path in the direction of the tall, rambling white frame lodge building. He still had the faint remnants of a limp. I wondered if the surgeons had ever gone back in to get the last of the bullet fragments out.

I went back to my students and tried hard to concentrate on them. I watched their drills for a while, then tooted my whistle. They stopped hitting balls and clustered around me.

"How are we doing?" I asked the guests on the south side of the courts. I focused on a tall, athletic banker from Kansas City, here at Bitterroot Valley for a week. "You're doing better," I told him.

He shook his head. "I'm doing terrible."

"You're hitting with a lot more pace."

"Yes. But I'm spraying the ball everywhere."

"It looked like you're getting it a lot deeper."

"Yes. But too many of them are going long."

Signalling the others to pay attention, I had his partner across the net hit him a couple. Then I stopped them and demonstrated how to prepare the racket earlier, dropping it in a stronger position in order to hit up, across his chest muscles, and attain more overspin. My banker, whose name was Slater, tried it. To his and my amazement he hit a sizzler that rifled over the net and dived in safely a few inches inside the back line. We hit some more to him and he caught on. His grin broadened. In less than five minutes I had made him a happy man.

After that there were other questions: from an attractive middle-aged professor out of Oklahoma who wasn't shifting her weight to get any power behind her forehand drive, and then from several who hadn't picked up the knack of taking the ball early on the return, and finally a tip on dropshotting for a spoiled teenager from Omaha whose ambitious parents had bought him a tennis vacation when what he needed most was a good spanking.

None of them realized I was doing it all with part of my mind at best. My preoccupation—and worry—was about the guy now waiting for me up on the lodge deck. Whatever Collie wanted, for me it could mean only one thing: trouble.

I didn't take time to shower. Still wearing my tennis whites, I checked with the groundskeepers manicuring the gardens between the courts and the downslope location of the pro shop for the golf course, then answered a question for our head maintenance man, then put off responding to some telephone calls from creditors and potential condo investors—with the first unfortunately outnumbering the second 7-2—then exchanged quick pleasantries with a few more guests who couldn't be avoided on my way to the deck. The afternoon sun shone brilliant white against the long, high back and court-side of our wood plank lodge, which looked like the result of a New England Shaker trying to build a Swiss chalet.

It all still felt new to me. I had been here only a few months. Earlier I had imagined I was settled in for a lifetime as a club pro in Richardson, Texas. But when the chance had come to invest in this place with the last of my ill-gotten gains from the tennis tour, I had taken it. Now, along with an old tour pal named Ted Treacher, I was having a fine time except for the periods when I looked too hard at the debt structure and the cash flow, and sheer panic set in.

The massive redwood deck on the back of the lodge was in cool afternoon shade. Collie Davis was there waiting for me, sitting alone at a black metal table on the far edge of the deck. In front of him he had an empty coffee cup and an ashtray with four cigarette butts in it. He got the rivet-gun look in his eyes again when I sat down opposite him.

"So shoot," I said.

"You've done a lot in the short time since I was here last," he observed, unsmilingly surveying the moderately used deck area and other guests sprinkled around the gardens and distant pool area.

"We're making it," I told him.

"You and Ted Treacher are full-fledged partners now? Legally?"

I nodded. "I'm here for the duration. Sink or swim."

"A couple of months ago I would have bet you'd go bankrupt quick, or decide to go back to Texas and be a club employee again."

"Texas is out. I like it here. As to bankruptcy, that remains an option."

He stirred and produced another cigarette.

"I thought you quit," I said, taking one from his pack.

"I thought you quit, too."

"I did."

"Right. Me too."

We smoked. A waiter brought my decaffeinated iced tea. Collie took more regular coffee. Over the nearby quiet murmur of snack-time conversation came the distant whoops of people at play in the swimming pool. A hawk wheeled out of the golf course woods to our west, spiraling against the camouflage brown of the distant mountains and then turning back in a long, slow arc against the vivid blue sky. I felt tense, waiting for Collie to get to the point, but I was damned if I would oblige him by asking. Sometimes you put your pride in the strangest little maneuvers.

Collie stirred, finally. "I haven't spotted Ted."

"He's in Helena today, signing a contract for some more roof repairs."

"And your lady?"

"You mean Beth?"

He did a double take. "Who else would I mean? —Yes. Beth Miles. The beautiful, smart, sexy lawyer-lady who probably saved your sanity last year."

I wished he hadn't asked. "She isn't here," I told him.

"Where is she?"

"California."

He became quieter, keenly observant. "For how long, Brad?"

"I don't know. Maybe forever."

He winced, sipped his coffee, put the cup down again with a little clatter. "You still see her?"

"She flies in for a weekend every once in a while. I've been
out there twice."

"Well, then." He brightened cautiously. "Might be all right,
then."

I didn't answer that because I didn't know how. He didn't say
anything. The murmur of nearby conversations drifted around us,
and a mountain bird sang in one of the ponderosa pines downslope
in the gardens.

A lot of people might have expressed sympathy or pressed for
more information. I knew Collie didn't have to do either. For one
thing, he knew enough about my past losses to realize that trouble
with Beth was not something easily dismissed with empty words.
For another thing, Collie had had losses of his own. When they in-
vented the word "loyalty," they studied Collie Davis as a model.
In his quiet way he was the most fiercely loyal and devoted citizen
I had ever known. He had been loyal to his wife, too, until his marriage was done in a couple of years earlier by some combination of
circumstances no one could ever fully understand—fatigue and
long-term stress, maybe, and the kind of vicious, silent erosion that
destroys relationships the way rust kills old bridges. Then he had
met another woman who said she loved him, begged him to break
old ties to be with her, endlessly pleaded, and finally convinced him.
He had made the break and then the lovely lady of his dreams decided he was not so attractive after all, now that he was no longer
deliciously forbidden, and so she, as they say, dumped him. For any
man, such a combination of events would have been devastating.
For Collie it had been very nearly lethal. He had been left not only
alone with himself, but alone with his sense of having been both
a dishonest bastard and a fool.

I had never discussed more than the bare bones of this adven-
ture with him. Much of my understanding had been gleaned from
between the lines. I had seen him at the worst, when his eyes looked
like windows into a smoky glacier. I had noticed, months later, when
he actually smiled again. Now he was far better than that. But the
sadness was still down under there. Maybe for him, as for me, it

would never go away. Maybe we conceal these things and live with them, like broken bones that heal, but ache when the weather changes.

After a while I said, "We might still work it out. You never know."

He roused himself. "Sure. Of course. It's never over till it's over."

"I'm maintaining hope."

"Yes, right."

I was aware of his keen observation. He would *not* press me. But I needed to talk about it. I said, "When we met in the Caribe I was on an assignment, of course, but she didn't know that. I was pretty crazy still. You remember how I was."

His forehead crinkled. "I remember."

"It was like never-never land. I was away from my regular job and she was away from hers. It was . . . magic. Sorry to be corny. But it was. Then I almost got her killed. I don't think she's ever quite gotten over that scare; it made her see the kind of work I've done for you guys."

"Yes," Collie said, signalling one of our waiters for a refill. "But I saw you both here since then. Everything seemed fine. You were both so happy it was disgusting."

"She's got her work at the law firm out there," I pointed out. "She worked like hell to get the degree and catch on with a prestigious firm. It's tremendously important to her."

He watched the waiter refill our cups, and waited for him to leave us before replying. "Just like buying into Bitterroot Valley, here, is important to you."

"I've got everything sunk in this place. I can't leave it."

"And she can't leave the law firm out there? She can't do her lawyerly bit in Missoula or Helena?"

"We've talked about that. —No. It's not the same."

"How serious is her objection to your contract work with us?"

"Collie, you know Beth. My God, there couldn't be a finer, less controlling woman in the world. But after what happened to her—knowing Sylvester might still be out there someplace, waiting for me—she just can't handle it. The fear is *there*. It's poison."

He shook his head.

"What?" I asked.

"This makes my offer much more difficult."

"Well, at least tell me so I can say no."

His eyes got hard again as he focused on the task. "Could you leave this place for a few weeks? If it was really important?"

"Is that what you want?"

"Yes."

"What's the deal?"

He glanced around. *Now,* I thought, would come the beating around the bush, the innuendo, the fishing expeditions, the vague hints and obscure metaphorical allusions, the half-truths, the no-truths-at-all, and all the other stuff they always went through when they wanted you to do a job for them.

He startled me by being direct: "We need you to go to London."

"Why?"

"We want you to play at Wimbledon next month."

It flabbergasted me. "I can't play at Wimbledon! I'm *old* now, Collie, remember? I'm over forty. I've blown my knee out twice."

"They send you an invitation every year, don't they? As a courtesy to a former champion?"

"Oh, sure, I could get a wild card. But I'd be a joke out there against anybody else in the field!"

"You're still in the ATP computer."

"Right! Ranked number five hundred and—"

"We need you."

I stared at him and made some quick, incredulous calculations. "The opener is scheduled for exactly one month from today. To get in any kind of tuneups, I would have to leave next week."

"Right," he said. "And we'll want you two days at headquarters for briefing on the way over."

"What in the hell could *I* do for you over there?"

"We must get someone inside . . . really inside . . . with the players and officials. Watch and be a source of information. You have a unique advantage in that regard."

"You don't have any other player—any current player—on the payroll?"

"No. You know something about the cutbacks, the new restrictions."

I leaned back. "Collie, this is unfair."

He studied me with gunmetal eyes. "We need you."

"Sure," I said sarcastically. "I'm invaluable."

"You might be, Brad."

"Right. What am I supposed to be looking for over there? A terrorist plot to kill one of the players? A scheme to blow up the stadium?"

"Yes," he said.

Two

COLLIE EXPLAINED. He did not go into detail just yet. It was bad enough in outline. I listened with a combination of shock and dismay.

"You've got to be kidding," I protested weakly.

"You know better," he retorted.

Unfortunately, I did.

Stunned, I looked out across my nice lodge deck, at our guests, at the pretty trees and the slope down toward the golf course, and the mountains far beyond. What he had told me was very hard to believe. But I had learned the hard way that the craziest stories usually turned out to be true.

I turned back to him. "I don't see how I can help."

"Go. Play. Watch."

"There's got to be more to it than that."

"There will be more detailed instructions. Those are being formulated now."

"There *must* be better people to handle something this bad, Collie!"

"Hey, I couldn't agree with you more. But—"

"Then get somebody else."

Collie sighed and leaned back in his chair. "It may come as a great surprise to you, Brad, but a lot of people at Headquarters would like to do just that. You aren't universally admired back there, you know. You did some nice work for us when you were on the tour. Nobody has ever questioned your loyalty. But you've gotten

10

some reputation as a loose cannon. You tend to go off on your own, like you did in Belgrade—"

"Then why not—"

"*Because*, goddammit, how many of our people do you think we can get inside the Wimbledon tournament on a moment's notice? You're a former champion. You're *it*. I told you that."

"I need more information."

"I can tell you some of it."

"I'll need time to think."

"My plane leaves Missoula early tomorrow afternoon. I can give you till morning."

The prospect of doing another job for the Company was not my idea of fun. Especially not now. I had been part owner of Bitterroot Valley Resort only a short time, and it was still touch and go, whether the total investment I had made with my partner, Ted Treacher, was going to start paying off or go right down the tubes. I don't overvalue my importance, and I knew that Ted might manage fine without me for a short time now. But when you've got everything on the table, you don't like to walk away from it.

On the other hand, Collie Davis was not given to exaggeration. After another hour of conversation with him, I knew my choice was going to be very difficult.

"As a newspaperman might say," he began, "I won't bury the lead. Here it is. SAS has solid evidence that terrorists are planning something around the time of the Wimbledon tournament next month. We've got satellite and other data indicating some, ah, unusual weapons-type systems headed for, or already in, Northern Ireland. The Brits' Anti-Terrorist Group is having cats; can't track anything down that's more specific. We need somebody inside, somebody with some experience, a player."

"What would a player accomplish?" I demanded.

"Watch a couple people we think need watching."

"Because they might be involved? *Players?*"

"Maybe involved as potential terrorists, yes. Maybe one player could also become a target."

I thought about it. "A wild card invitation for somebody like me is a courtesy, Collie. They might not even let me play if I tried."

"They'll let you play. We've taken care of that."

"I don't want to go over there and get humiliated in my old age. I don't see what I could possibly accomplish anyway."

"Brad. There isn't anybody else with your experience and cover. SAS is in this. MI5. Anti-Terrorist Group. Us. You can wear your journalist's hat, too. —Do you want to sit in front of your TV late in June or early in July and watch a handful of fanatics kill thousands of people?"

That was hitting below the belt.

A long time ago I was a college tennis player, quick and happy. Then came Vietnam and a long time in a hospital and a divorce, and much of the happy went away. Later I got rehabilitated from the Vietnam wound, if not from the divorce, and tried my hand at bigtime tennis. If you have some God-given ability and enough luck—and work hard enough—sometimes you can make it. I could move and I had some luck, and always figured that the one thing my opponents could not do was work harder than I did, all day, every day. I did well.

About the time I moved onto the professional men's top ten list, a gent approached me and asked if I could do something quiet and superficially innocent for him and his organization during my upcoming trip behind the Iron Curtain as a member of the Davis Cup team. He showed me credentials that didn't leave me much leeway to say no without feeling like I was letting down my country.

The first assignment wasn't much, just passing a paper. Naturally I felt like 007 anyway. After that I did some other routine things, still not absolutely sure which secret agency I was working for. Later there wasn't any doubt, and the first time I blew out my knee, they even treated me to some of their kind of training in Virginia during the long rehabilitation period.

That was long ago too. I went back on the tour and, running

after a ball on the theory of no pain no gain, blew the same knee out again, only much worse. This time I tore the anterior cruciate ligament, which is the kind of injury that has decked a lot of NFL ends and running backs. I would be able to play again someday, the doctors said. But the knee would never be strong again and I would need a heavy brace.

For a while, actually, I felt like I was through with everything. After Vietnam and the divorce I had invested my whole personality in my tennis. If you had asked me in those days who I was, I would have given you my world ranking and current earnings for the year. If you had insisted that you wanted to know *who I was*, I would have been puzzled, inasmuch as I had already given you my entire identity and reason for life.

We make a big mistake when we totally commit to a life goal. Of course that is what we are told to do, and maybe high achievement is not possible without that kind of single-minded dedication. But the trouble for many of us is that we get self-dedication mixed up with self-definition. When I blew out the knee for the second time, and was no longer a world-class player, I found that what this left me being, in my own eyes, was—nothing.

It took a while to get over that, grow up a little. Finally I found a pleasant enough tennis club pro job in Richardson, Texas. I invested my money—most of it badly in Texas oil and gas before the big bust—and started doing some freelance writing for the tennis magazines. I assumed I was through with the Company.

I wasn't. It was not long before Collie Davis visited me the first time and asked me to go somewhere and do something that my name in tennis would facilitate. I went and did it because I felt like I ought to, being an American with very old-fashioned ideas about my country and what I owe it as a citizen. Since then I've helped out on other occasions.

It's no big deal. I've been lucky once or twice. Otherwise maybe I wouldn't be here at all. Still, whenever they ask me to do something for them, I get this feeling that they must be hard up if they can't find anybody better qualified.

So I was by no means eager or happy about this thing. I wanted to stay home. When you've been scared as often as I have, you know you're a coward. But the more Collie told me, the more I got that sinking sensation which said I had to go do it for them.

"I'm going to sleep on it," I told Collie finally.

It was an evening when I was supposed to call Beth. Direct-dialing from my cabin in the woods, I got through to her on schedule. We visited about this and that. She was excited about a case she was researching.

"I might work late Friday night," she told me, "but I can get that crack-of-dawn flight out Saturday and spend most of the weekend there with you." Her voice changed, then, getting happy and ironic. "That is, if you want me."

Hell, I've got to tell her about it. "That would be great, Beth, but we'd better stay loose on that for a day or two. I might be going on a trip."

"Oh?" Her tone changed, and not for the better. "Not trouble, I hope?"

"No," I told her, and went into my liar configuration. "It's really pretty nice news. I got a wild-card invitation to play at Wimbledon next month."

"Oh?" She sounded cooly suspicious already. "Haven't you gotten those before, in other years since you were champion?"

"Well, yes. But my knee is better this year, and I've been thinking. It might be a good way to raise some money for the resort. If I can sell shirt patches and do some work for the magazines, and maybe even ESPN or NBC, commentating."

"There's no way I could go with you, Brad, the way this case is shaping up out here."

"Oh. I see."

She paused. Then she said, "Or maybe you weren't inviting me."

"Well—"

"Maybe," she cut in, using her lawyerly tone, "this is an assignment?"

"Oh, I certainly haven't accepted any *assignment.*"

Couldn't trick her. "But maybe you're going to, Brad?"

"Beth, I don't know where you got that idea. I—"

"Okay. It's none of my business anyway, right?"

"I didn't say that, Beth."

"When will you be leaving?"

"Well, if I go, in just a few days. By the weekend."

"All right, Brad."

It was miserable, hearing this tone in her voice . . . feeling everything slipping away from us. I said, "Look. I'll call back Friday, let you know all the details."

"I may not be here. Some of my sources are down near Malibu, and I may be down there."

"Saturday, then."

She paused. Then: "I don't know. Some of the gang from the office might come down late Friday. Since I'm not coming to Montana, I might decide to weekend down there with them."

"I see. The office gang, you say?"

"Yes. Pat and Shirley. Janis, probably. And David. You remember David."

Yes, I remembered David. We had met on my last trip to visit Beth. Thirty-one years old. Six feet plus. Golden hair and a face that even I recognized was handsome. Why he wasn't in the movies was beyond me. With his slow, insolent grin he had put a proprietary arm around Beth and pronounced himself and his colleagues "inordinately proud of the gutsy little girl."

Yes, David. Die, David.

"Well," I said now, "I'll try to call. If you're gone, I'll ring you later."

"From London?"

"If I go, yes."

"I hope you have a fine time, Brad." She sounded wistful, sad.

I imagined her sitting by the pale telephone in her bedroom, the soft light behind her hair.

I said, "I hope you decide to come back home for the weekend, so we can talk."

"I've been thinking a lot about things," she replied in more her lawyerly tone. "It isn't healthy to narrow your friendships too much—put all your eggs in one basket. I mean, that's how I got devastated once before, thinking my whole life revolved around one person. So I need to spread out, build more interests."

It made perfectly good sense, and it terrified me. "Well, I guess as long as you leave room for me."

"I'm not supposed to take it as rejection if you go off and do some of this . . . special work, Brad. Certainly you should have that kind of freedom, and so should I. Right? —Right?"

"Of course," I told her. The sweet howitzer of reason and feminism, rolled onto the parade ground to develop personality . . . or to erect a bullshit philosophical excuse for selfishly screwing around?

After a bad night, I met Collie again early for coffee.

"Nobody would try to blow up Wimbledon," I told him.

"You've heard of the URA?" he asked.

"I think so. They're the radical part of the Irish Republican Army. Right?"

"More or less. There's a terrorist element in the IRA, and then you've got the wing that tries to win improvements through political action, public relations, that sort of thing. Then you've got the URA. More radical. Then you've got two or more splinter groups inside the URA, more radical yet. By the time you get that far out, you're dealing with people capable of just about anything."

"And that's who's involved here?"

"We think so. A splinter group of a splinter group, probably. Very small. Which is one of the reasons they're so hard to catch. They make the mill-run IRA radicals look like altar boys. They were involved in the bombing that almost got Margaret Thatcher a while back. Might have had something to do with the jumbo jet that blew up last year. A lot of terrorism is blind, random, aimed at creating havoc in a hated society. These people we're talking about here go beyond hate to something that's hard to imagine. They're even suspected of assassinating several younger officers in the Irish Republican Army itself on the basis that the victims weren't active enough."

"If they're that crazy, why doesn't the main body of the IRA take them out?"

"Nobody knows who they are."

"You said it's a small group?"

"Possibly a dozen. Certainly no more than that. They may be smaller now because, a few months ago, they apparently suspected someone inside their own ranks as a possible traitor. There was a purge. Three probable members blown up in a car just south of Belfast; another one found shot to pieces in a rooming house basement; another beheaded—"

I started. *"Beheaded?"*

Collie nodded humorlessly. "The head was found stuffed in a train station toilet. They never have found the body."

"These sound like nice people, Collie."

He ignored that. "Our Brit friends have heard enough to believe the target this time is definitely going to be Wimbledon. It would be just wonderful, from the crazies' point of view, to do something spectacular there. After all, the Wimbledon tournament is the oldest and greatest—a source of great Brit pride—and the world is watching."

"Put some of the royal family in their box," I added, "and it's even better from a terrorist standpoint. —Okay. What are they planning?"

"That's where you come in."

"You mean you think *I* might find out?"

"You go. You play. You commentate. You attend the functions. You're around the players and officials."

"Play blind man's bluff."

Collie lit another cigarette. "By the time you get over there and in position, presumably, we'll have more for you to go on."

"Why is the Company involved in the first place?"

"They helped us when that Maoist asshole was driving around the eastern half of the United States, buying parts for homemade bombs. We reciprocate." He exhaled smoke. "Also, there will be a lot of American citizens in the Wimbledon stands, as always. We take a dim view of their getting murdered. The FBI will be involved in a small way, working out of the embassy, too."

I took a minute to absorb it. Then I remembered something. "You said something about a player being involved?"

He nodded. "Sean Cork."

"Impossible."

"Why?"

"Sean Cork is one of the rising young stars in world-class tennis. Don't try to tell me somebody like that would risk a millionaire career to help a handful of crazies."

"No. You misunderstood. Cork may be one of the targets."

"*Why*, for God's sake?"

"He's from Limerick, but he has relatives in Ulster. He's been outspoken on Brit and European TV about how the IRA and all its offshoots are bad for everybody. He's blasted the official British policy, too, but the government doesn't hold a blood grudge the way the URA does."

"Then Sean Cork may be the central target?"

"Might be. We don't know. That's for you to help us find out."

I groaned and took one of his cigarettes. In recent months I had been training a lot harder—running distances at this Montana altitude—and had cut my smoking to near zero. But the idea of mayhem at Wimbledon shook me. I love that place. I've seldom entered a church and felt emotions like those it stirs in me.

"Are you going?" I asked.

"Not at the start."

"Later?"

"Maybe. We guess an attack would be timed to coincide with weekend or holiday TV coverage worldwide."

"The time our TV comes on with their Breakfast at Wimbledon coverage over the weekend?"

"That's our guess."

"Is there a basis for the guess?"

"If you agree to the contract, you'll come to Headquarters on the way over. Maybe at that time both of us will learn a lot more. I wasn't sent here to brief you—just to see if you'd go."

We sat there on the deck under the beautiful sky and looked at each other. I knew he was thinking the same thing I was.

I waited, but he would not mention it. So I had to.

"You know," I said bitterly, "what else I'm thinking about."

"Sure. But it's no big deal."

"Right. Just my cowardice."

"Yes, you always were a terrible milquetoast, Smith."

"You bastard. Do I have to say it?"

"Yes."

"All right, then. —Sylvester."

"Ah, yes." Collie grinned crookedly, the way he sometimes did when it was in no way funny. "Our friendly KGB assassin who always seems to be spooking around the edges of bigtime operations."

"And who also has come within a hair of killing me, twice," I pointed out.

"Hum. —Well, I checked on that aspect. We have no word of him whatsoever."

The words were dragged out of me. "He's got to be around somewhere."

Collie shrugged. "Sure. He got away from us on St. Maarten and then he got away from us here. But he was not a well man when he was here, Brad. I think I might have hit him with one of my shots that night here, too. We're assuming he's back in treatment somewhere. Or possibly he's been assigned some obscure, nondemanding job while he builds his health back and possibly gets some additional facial surgery."

"You can assume what you want, Collie," I told him. "But if he's in London, I could be walking right into his arms."

"Sure, and a meteorite might fall out of the sky right now and kill both of us. Or we might leave here and get run over by a truck. Or a little bit of cholesterol might stick in some artery in your head and turn you into a drooling vegetable for the rest of your life. What do you want? A written guarantee?"

"I don't want to go someplace where I'm tempting fate with him again."

"Are you scared?"

"You're damned right I'm scared of him!"

He sighed. "My opinion, Brad, is that he's alive, inside the Soviet Union, not operational in any significant way. My added opinion is that the Soviets don't need any more trouble. They wouldn't let Sylvester go after you now if he was alive and well and in the next room. My other added opinion—based on some evidence—is that they don't want terrorism at Wimbledon any more than we do. These crazy groups tend to be an embarrassment to them these days. Every time there's a terrorist incident anywhere in the world, the level of tension everywhere goes up about six points on a ten-point scale. Not to mention some of the terrorist activity they've had to put up with lately inside their own borders. —So no, I don't think you have a thing to worry about. There is simply no chance they would risk an incident by letting Sylvester anywhere near you."

I thought about it, and, mortified by my weakness, tried to salvage something. "Of course if he did come after me I could handle him just fine."

"Of course," Collie said, picking it up instantly. "Then we could give you a medal."

"Oh, not more medals, Collie."

"Yes. You do have a closetful of them already. I forgot that."

"Sure."

"It must be a drag, being such a hero."

"Well, somebody has to do it."

"Indeed. Also, there is the matter that you can probably make some money doing TV commentary while you're over there, not to mention the magazine articles you can probably sell, not to mention that I am authorized to tell you that you can name your own contract price on this one—not to mention that I know you guys are financially strapped here right now, and can use every dollar you can lay hands on."

"You mean," I said slowly, "if I demanded, say, seventy-five thousand dollars—plus all expenses—it would be approved?"

"You are so smart. You really catch on fast. So when can I tell them you'll arrive in Washington for our tête à tête?"

So there it was and I was committed.

Collie left for his plane in Missoula. I started right away making the necessary calls. In London, officials were pleased. My magazine contacts thought a first-person account of my return would be a good feature, and one editor suggested some color work in another piece. My pals at ESPN said fine. Bud Collins thought it might work out, and at any rate we would meet at the Cumberland in London and talk about it.

For a tournament my conditioning was marginal at best. But I had increased my daily workout pace in recent weeks. I was playing or practicing about two hours a day, with another four hours on the courts with students, moving around and hitting additional shots. In the weight and training room I had been getting in almost an hour before breakfast, and doing the running four evenings a week. In the high air that was plenty for me. I felt good. With the heavy canvas-and-plastic knee brace on, my leg felt strong.

If I had anticipated playing several long matches over there, I would have worried. But I didn't. Self-deception no longer came easy as it applied to my tennis. I would try hard and give it all I had, and almost certainly be taken out in my first match. But probably the weather would be cool, and I thought I could go four sets without going into a state of physical collapse. Maybe.

I telephoned my partner, Ted Treacher, in Helena and told him I wanted to go to London. He caught on at once and promised to be back within two days. That situation clarified, I got busy making reservations. Arranged some business matters. Called the corporate offices of my former sponsors, taking advantage of a two-inch item in *USA Today* about my return to Wimbledon after an absence of almost ten years. I didn't know anybody at Converse any more, or at Yonex. They were polite and said they would get back to me. Bill Roberts was still at Prince. He still had the needle.

"Yeah, nice item, Brad. I notice they identified you as the guy who played one of the greatest matches ever in the year when you lost to Borg in the finals. Too bad they didn't mention the year you won the singles at Wimbledon, or the two doubles trophies."

"You can't have everything," I pointed out.

"But the rest of the piece was right, then? You really are going to go play in it again?"

"Looks that way, Bill."

"Want to use our new wide-body racket?"

"I wouldn't mind . . . if the money is right."

"You have an agent these days?"

"I need an agent about like a vampire needs a sunsuit."

"Boy, that's a good one. That's funny. Have you got a writer or what? Let me write that down . . . 'like a vampire needs—' "

"Bill—"

"I'll send you a piece of paper. Look it over and sign it, mail it back. No problem."

"How much will you pay me?"

"I have to ask upstairs, Brad. It will all be in the letter. I promise to have it in the mail by tomorrow noon, air express. For you former military guys, that's twelve hundred. Or maybe I should explain: the little hand will be pointing straight up and so will—"

"Thanks, Bill. I'll watch for it."

So things started to shape up very, very fast, as they had to. Already I felt time pressure.

From the playing standpoint, the pressure tightened Friday. That was the day Terry Carpoman called from Paris.

"You really coming over?" Carpoman yelled, his drawl pronounced even over the hiss of long-distance circuitry.

"Over where?" I yelled back.

"Over here! Over to Europe! To England! For Wimbledon."

"Planning to, Terry."

"Great! Listen! When?"

"A week from tomorrow or Sunday. June three or four."

"How about partnering with me for the doubles?"

"Where?"

"At Wimbledon, of course."

"What happened to Kurt?"

"You didn't see the item? He tore his back up in Rome. We had to forfeit. I'll have to pass up the doubles in the French, but I could get you and me in at Wimbledon."

"I'm rusty, Terry."

"Hey, I remember how you moved around and hit the ball the last time I saw you play. I'll tell you what. I'll get out of Paris right after I've won the singles. Meet you in London. We can practice and enter at Beckenham or Nottingham, or maybe the Stella Artois, and get real good and used to grass again. Then we'll tear 'em up when Wimbledon opens the week after that. What say?"

That was Terry Carpoman: . . . *"after I've won the singles."* A weak ego structure was not one of his problems.

His offer was flattering. I was tempted. Playing with him might be fun. He was one of our brightest young stars, a rising meteor: big, strong, good-looking, quick, talented, intelligent. In another year's time he had a chance to become America's best, if he had luck and worked hard and started learning to curb a crazy temper.

But in recent months, from what I had seen on TV and read in *USA Today*, Terry was not curbing the temper. It was getting worse. He had been a wild man in Rome. I wasn't going to need additional problems in London.

On the other hand, being in the doubles would give me more opportunities to maneuver around and keep my eyes open. And maybe I was holding back just because he was one of the young ones, the new millionaires. They berate the officials and linespeople—mostly volunteers working their fanny off strictly for love of the game—they make obscene gestures at the crowd and shriek gutter talk that would embarrass a Marine, and then they whine if they're asked to play in more than a half-dozen tournaments a year because they're far too busy giving meaningless exhibition matches, bilking the rubes. The money has gotten insane. The players have become a law unto themselves. Carpoman was typical, a spoiled baby, a bully, a petulant vulgarian. But he was no worse than most of the pampered slobs on the tour today.

And he did offer that extra operational advantage.

I said, "I hope you remember I'm at least fifteen years older than you are, Terry, and I've still got a bad knee."

"Listen," he yelled back. "I saw you play recently on that ESPN thing. You ain't dead yet. With your savvy and my power we'll kill 'em!"

And, I thought, a lot of people detested Terry Carpoman. Finding a new doubles partner on short notice—one who would put up with his shenanigans oncourt—might not be easy. Quite possibly I represented the bottom of his barrel.

I said, "So you think you could carry me?"

"Sure! And besides, man, who else am I going to get on this kind of short notice?"

"Well, there is that."

"So let's do it!"

I hesitated, then decided. "Okay. Why not?"

"Great! I'll see you in London and let you fondle my cup from the French."

Ted Treacher got back from Helena later the same day with good news about our roof repairs and some loan money. I filled him in on some of the details on the tennis side. I didn't have to say much more. Ted had been involved on the periphery of the Belgrade operation in 1987. His eyes narrowed, showing he understood there was more involved in my plans than an aging ex-champion's ego trip.

"The doubles as well?" he said, suntanned skin crinkling around his eyes. "Is your life insurance paid up, old chap?"

"It better be," I told him.

"Not to worry, chum. I'll handle things here while you're gone, and if you could contrive to win a match or two, the publicity for the resort could be wonderful."

"I don't think we'd better count on that, Ted."

He raised his wine glass. "A toast. To geriatric tennis and the Wimbledon cup!"

"We have nothing to fear but our opponents," I agreed.

Ted smiled crookedly. "And ourselves."

Our glasses clinked.

That night I tried to call Beth, but got only her soft, slightly distorted voice on her recorder. So they were in Malibu, I thought. She and superstud.

I finished packing and, like Santa, made a list and checked it twice. Had two stiff drinks and went to bed. In the night, had one of those dreams about Sylvester. One of the bad ones. He had an AR-15. And in this dream he wasn't alone. He had this obvious IRA guy with him, a tall, black-haired Celt wearing a bulky dark green sweater and black pants, and carrying an Uzi—a cliché straight out of my imperfect reading of Jack Higgins. When they both started hosing me down, I awoke with a shuddering spasm that sat me straight up in bed.

I tried Beth repeatedly through the rest of the weekend, and got the same recording. By the first of the week I was being childish and petulant, and didn't call any more. On Tuesday I drove to Missoula and flew out, my first destination being Washington Dulles. My briefings at Langley were scheduled to start Wednesday afternoon.

Three
Elsewhere
Tandragee, Northern Ireland

THE OLD TRUCK crept up the muddy country road through a bleak, cold drizzle. The weight of a glistening pile of manure on its flat bed made it rock ponderously from side to side as it rolled through deep ruts.

Upon reaching a break in the hedgerow, the truck braked and made a slow, aching turn into deeply puddled driveway that led up a low, barren hillside to a small house and barn. A sheep dog came from somewhere and barked excitedly.

A low fence made of rotting scrap lumber enclosed a small, freshly plowed garden plot between the house and the barn. The truck groaned to a halt in front of the fence. The engine shut off. The driver's door opened and a short, thin, bandy-legged man wearing a torn blue navy coat and black, hip-high rubber waders clambered down. About fifty, the man had rain-wet black hair plastered to his narrow skull, a large nose, close-set eyes, a stubble beard. He reached back inside the cab, pulled out a wool stocking cap, and jammed it on his unlovely head. It made his ears stick out.

He started through the mud toward the front stoop of the little house. As he did so, the front door opened and a plump little woman of indeterminate middle age came out, huddling under a shawl thrown over her head and shoulders.

"Mother of Mary!" she called in a reedy, friendly voice. "I never expected to see you on a Saturday, and especially in this kind of unfriendly weather, Mr. Squirrel Henry!"

Squirrel Henry snatched his cap off his head, pulled back his

26

lips in a grimace of a grin, hopped sideways from one foot to the other, and bowed quick, nervous little bows from the waist in a paroxysm of obsequiousness. "Never too bad a day to serve a loyal customer, Mrs. Malley! My pleasure, fer sure, fer sure! A stitch in time saves nine, ya know!"

Mrs. Malley smiled back at the little man with all the warmth and admiration good folk saved for honest workers of a station in life even humbler than their own. "Well, Mr. Henry, you can see the garden plot is ready for you!"

"Yes, ma'am! Yes, ma'am! I can surely see that with these old eyes, and I've got a load of the finest sheep manure right here for you, as you can see—and tell with your own nasal apparatus, too, I daresay!"

Mrs. Malley glanced at the load. "And you'll be dumping it and spreading it both, as you've done in other years for me? At the same price?"

"Mrs. Malley, it will be my pleasure!"

The woman went back into her house, shutting the door firmly against the cold, the rain, and the unmistakable aroma that always seemed to accompany Squirrel Henry whether his lorry was loaded or not. Henry got busy at once, and did not pause until half the heavy load had been shoveled over the garden fence and then pitchforked into an even layer all over the bare wet ground.

Mrs. Malley came to the door this time with her change purse in hand, and carefully counted out the coins into Squirrel Henry's filthy hand. She hurried, although she tried to hide the fact. The aroma was seeping steadily into her home.

"Is that correct, Mr. Henry?"

"On the button, Mrs. Malley, on the button! A pleasure doing business with you as always!"

"I'll call again, Mr. Henry."

"And I'll be forever grateful when you do, Mrs. Malley! Just remember my slogan: 'Squirrel Henry's my name, an' sheep poop's my game!' "

The lady colored and giggled simultaneously. "Mr. Henry,

you're a caution! Shame on you, now!" It was impossible to disapprove of good old harmless Squirrel Henry.

"Good day, lady! Thank ya again! Good day to ya!"

And off Squirrel Henry went, whistling an old tune.

Squirrel Henry drove slowly from Mrs. Malley's place to another farm a little farther out. Here the proprietor had wintered many sheep in his close-in pasture and the big old barn. There was sheep manure aplenty in both. Squirrel Henry chuckled, joked, lollygagged around, and tirelessly shoveled up enough to pile a great wet mountain of the stuff on the flatbed of his truck.

He paid the farmer with the very coins given to him by Mrs. Malley.

"That's generous, Squirrel, I'll say that fer ye. I'd be after payin' you to be haulin' it off fer me, now that I ain't farmin' any more. Can't hardly imagine yer payin' me fer it."

"No, Richard, no. No, no, no. I know my business, an' fair is fair. Just remember my slogan, Richard. 'Squirrel Henry's my name, an' sheep shit's my game!' "

Leaving his customer laughing, as he usually did, Squirrel Henry then drove slowly, harmlessly, deeper into the sparse, rain-cloaked countryside. He made it a point to drive through an intersection where he knew the British army often had some manner of roadblock, and sure enough a dozen soldiers had a barricade up. Squirrel Henry stopped and bowed and scraped and said his slogan, grinned, chuckled and practically danced a jig, and was waved on through.

What a funny old man, the soldiers—some of whom had seen him often before—agreed. What a silly, harmless old fart, that Squirrel Henry. They shook their heads at life's wonderments and went back to their lorries.

An hour later, with darkness coming on and the rain still steady, Squirrel Henry pulled into a wooded area far from a main road. He parked at the appointed spot and lit up a cigar.

A few minutes passed. Then two younger men materialized out of the underbrush, each carrying an armload of guns heavily wrapped in thick brown plastic, and sealed with waterproof tape. Squirrel Henry shoveled tunnels in his load of wet manure. They inserted the packages in the tunnels. He covered them up again.

"An' will the really important shipment be comin' soon, then?" Squirrel Henry asked.

One of the men nodded, unsmiling. " 't'won't be long, Squirrel. You be ready, now."

"Oh, yes. Fer sure, fer sure."

Nobody made any jokes.

London

Dull, steady rain pounded against the thick windows of the massive Soviet Embassy at 10 Kensington Park Gardens. Gray evening. In the second-floor office of P. K. Mikanyan, ambassador to Great Britain, ugly brass floorlamps with naked inverted bowls cast harsh light over the high ceiling, doing nothing to dispel or even soften the gloom. The great stone fireplace that dominated one wall of the massive office yawned a chill black.

A fire might have gone far toward making the room seem warm and even cozy, but Ambassador Mikanyan was of the old school: sour, cautious, suspicious, thrifty. The interior of the great three-story structure was as bleak as its concrete exterior, which was covered with white stucco that yielded not an iota to any architectural decoration that might have softened its appearance behind a forbidding, block-long stone wall.

One standing joke, based on the ambassador's notorious paranoia, was that he feared fireplace wood delivered from the local market might contain clever electronic bugs. Old-timers, who sometimes referred to the ambassador behind his back as Scrooge, had a simpler explanation. Mikanyan was simply stingy. He always kept things under budget, and if that required freezing your ass during the long, beastly British springtime, well, there was always the Siberian option.

Mikanyan, sixty-six years old, jowly, liver-spotted, almost totally bald, had had a cancer operation in 1988 and had lost almost fifty pounds since that time. Seated behind his huge, talon-footed mahogany desk, he looked lost under the padded shoulders of a suit that had been fashionable when he first wore it in 1963.

The ambassador was studying a thin sheaf of communications documents on the desk before him. His banker's-type desk lamp had been lit and it cast cruel light onto him and across the faces of the three men waiting patiently, seated in ancient, red velvet-trimmed straight chairs across his desk:

Mikhail Gravitch, senior cultural attache and in reality chief Resident of the KGB in London;

Eduard Lemlek, a "legal attache" charged with internal security in the embassy, and a member of the RCP, a secret branch of the Russian organization that roughly parallels America's FBI; and

Yuli Szulc, a lank, sickly-looking second-tier Legat, duties unspecified, who once had operated in the United States under the code name "Sylvester, and had other names, as well."

It was still in the room. The damned British rain drummed distantly.

Mikanyan continued to read for a few minutes. None of the three facing his desk so much as stirred an eyelash. Some said the ambassador went through this act to test men's patience and respect; others theorized that he did it simply out of senile cruelty. At any rate, there was nothing to do but endure it.

A corner clock struck the hour, the chimes old and a bit out of kilter, so that the tune did not ring true. Mikanyan stirred, closed his folder, and looked up at the men he had kept waiting.

"I am informed," he said in a slow, halting voice, "it is most important that the matter of the rumors of terrorism continue to be pursued diligently. At the same time, it is equally important to maintain maximum security around our investigations. Is this your understanding, Mikhail Gravitch?"

Gravitch, a powerfully built Armenian of forty, showed no expression on his square face, darkly shaded by fine, dense black stubble that careful shaving, morning and evening, could not keep under control. "Steps have been taken, sir."

"And the reports? Are the reports going out in good order?"

"Yes, sir."

"And promptly? Promptness is very important in maintaining our reputation for efficiency."

"Schedules are being met or exceeded, Mr. Ambassador."

"Many reports," Mikanyan insisted. "I want to be sure at least six reports each day are dispatched on this matter."

"Yes, sir," Gravitch said without intonation or expression.

Eduard Lemlek, seated next to him, stirred. Lemlek was a slender man given to pearl-colored suits. He had straw-colored hair going thin on top, and the finest small white teeth. He was always pale, winter and summer. "I have issued several internal memoranda, Mr. Ambassador, concerning security handling of this general topic. My procedures are outlined in your morning briefing folder."

"Yes, yes," Mikanyan nodded. "Very good. Very good, Eduard. You will continue to apprise me of the situation on a twice-daily basis."

"Maximum cooperation," Lemlek said.

The ambassador looked up from the closed folder. "Eh?"

"Maximum cooperation," Lemlek repeated, no expression whatsoever showing on his bloodless face. "I need not remind the ambassador that spreading terrorism could endanger even our embassy, here. Maximum cooperation between all offices is mandatory to assure our own security."

"I am sure," the ambassador said, "Comrade Gravitch is cooperating fully."

Before Gravitch could speak, Lemlek said, "Certain reports are being withheld from distribution to my office."

Gravitch's face darkened and he turned sharply in his chair. "You're getting all you need."

There was a moment's pause. The ambassador, face twisted in consternation, appeared unwilling to intervene between his contentious officers. The fourth man in the office, Szulc—who had operated under the assassin's code name of Sylvester for so long that he often thought of himself by that name—remained still as a statue, his pale complexion appearing almost to glow white in contrast to his dense black beard.

Finally Lemlek spoke: "I need everything, Comrade Gravitch."

"Well, you won't get them. Some reports are beyond your need."

"I require—"

Gravitch lost his temper. "Operate your kindergarten shop, Lemlek, and let us professionals handle the real business."

Lemlek shrank. "Why outburst in such a manner at *me?*"

"I weary of your perpetual harping."

"I only follow procedure!"

"You only do all you can to advance your own case for promotion!"

"Gentlemen," the ambassador said, alarmed. "Please desist!"

Both men silenced at once, Gravitch dark with frustrated rage and Lemlek palely smirking.

"Reports will be routed according to standing protocol," the ambassador said sternly. He reached inside his oversized coat and gently rubbed his chest, a gesture he had shown often in recent months, and one that had spurred rumors that his cancer had returned. "If, Comrade Lemlek, you believe your office has been overlooked in the routing, to the detriment of internal security, you will prepare a complete written report."

"Yes, Mr. Ambassador," Lemlek said, while Gravitch glowered.

"As to you, Comrade Szulc," the ambassador said, turning his gaze to the ashen man who had sat silent and impassive until now, "I am authorized to inform you that a change of assignment is forthcoming through Mr. Gravitch. You are released of temporary in-house duties to which you have been assigned in recent weeks. Mr. Gravitch will inform you of your new assignment."

"Yes, Mr. Ambassador," Sylvester said quietly. As usual his face betrayed nothing. The harsh desk light revealed the faintest, finest network of blue-white lines around his eyes and nose, the only evidence of agonizing reconstructive surgery that his new beard did not conceal.

"Discretion is mandatory in your work," Mikanyan went on. "This is true at all times. However, it has been made clear to me— and I must make it clear to you—that no one is to exceed his assigned parameters of duty by so much as a millimeter during this perilous time. Do I make myself clear?"

"Yes, sir," Sylvester said quietly. The ambassador's words were about as clear to him as the Thames at this time of year, but that was not unusual.

"Good," the ambassador said with the relieved air of a man who had just dealt, and successfully, with a weighty and complex matter. "Now, gentlemen, allow me to review with you the latest report on cultural exchange programs and their tendency to be used by the unscrupulous for espionage purposes."

The meeting seemed as interminable as it was one-sided. On two more occasions the simmering tension between the taciturn KGB resident and eagerly sycophantic Eduard Lemlek almost flared into open conflict. Sylvester sat impassive, shoulders sloped. An acute observer might have noted that he seemed to hold himself too still, like a man unconsciously trying to avoid movement which might exacerbate intense physical pain.

The meeting concluded at last. The three officials left the ambassador's cavernous suite. In the long, echoing tile corridor beyond the door, Gravitch steamed toward the east end of the building. Lemlek caught Gravitch's arm, turning him.

"What now?" Gravitch snapped. His face was a thundercloud.

"We must discuss the ambassador's concerns at once," Lemlek said, chill and controlled as a chameleon. "If you will be more cooperative, a report from my office may not be needed."

"My orders are clear," the KGB Resident retorted.

"As chief of internal security I must insist on more information. The rumors of a major terrorist outbreak continue."

"Lemlek, your job is inside these walls. This matter is outside your purview!"

Faint splotches of pink on Lemlek's bloodless cheeks betrayed the pressure he felt. But he held his ground stubbornly, a stiff statue. "In matters of anticipated terrorism, internal security must be fully informed. But of course I do not desire to cause you extra work, comrade. If you will come to my office now, you can perhaps dictate—"

"Don't issue instructions to me, son of a pig!"

Lemlek jolted back a half-step. His close-set eyes betrayed a flash of spiteful rage, the look in the eyes of a small dog yapping through a fence. "Failure to cooperate must be reported."

Gravitch stared down at him an instant, and Sylvester thought the KGB Resident might resort to his fists. Then Gravitch shuddered and controlled himself. He turned to Sylvester. "Come," he grunted, and steamed off.

Sylvester followed him in silence through long corridors, past a security checkpoint, finally to the wing that housed the KGB's "cultural affairs" offices. Gravitch's suite was deserted at this late hour except for a young corporal, a code clerk, at work on a computer in the front area. Gravitch led Sylvester into his inner office and closed the door.

"The swine!" Gravitch exploded. "He will rub his nose in the ambassador's ass once too often in my presence, usurping authority that isn't his, and I will go all the way to Moscow if I must to have him disciplined."

Sylvester lit a cigar. His hands trembled, another sign of the suffering—physical and emotional—he had undergone in recent months. "I agree that Comrade Lemlek's reasoning is obscure—"

"His line of reasoning is to undermine my authority and promote himself. If this is typical of the new breed, heaven help us!"

"His kind of detail work may be useful in rooting out leads to the terrorists," Sylvester pointed out.

"His kind of detail work is pig shit," the KGB Resident fumed. "We have serious problems here. We have no time for his kind of manipulative swinery . . . his constant maneuvering to make himself look good. That is why I confronted him in the ambassador's office. Now, exposed for the dog he is, he will be forced to restrict himself to his proper work, and stop interfering in mine."

"What about that report he may write?"

"It was only a threat. He will write nothing."

Sylvester knew how obsessive ambition worked. He thought it unlikely that Lemlek would cease and desist. Competition between the services was endemic in embassies like this, and Lemlek was the kind of man who paved his road to promotion with the bodies of better men he had betrayed. But bureaucratic maneuvering was not a matter of real interest to Sylvester; he let it pass.

Still fuming, Gravitch walked to a cabinet whose opened doors revealed a small bar. "A drink?"

"If you please, yes."

The KGB Resident poured two stiff vodkas, handed Sylvester his glass, sat at one end of a long leather couch, and signalled Szulc to sit facing him. The vodka, fiery and good, curled in Sylvester's belly.

"Now," Gravitch said finally, asserting steely self-control. "About your health."

"You have seen the latest medical reports, Mikhail."

"Yes, yes, and the psychological evaluations too, and all the rest of it. I am asking now how *you* view your recovery process."

Sylvester spoke carefully. "I am well."

"Your injuries on St. Maarten were extreme. A lesser physical specimen would have died. Yet you crawled three miles, hiding in the brush, made contact, lived through the transfer to the submarine, clung to life until you reached the hospital in Havana."

Sylvester allowed himself a thin smile. "It was not pleasant, but it was acceptable—considering the alternative."

"It was unconscionable, after all you went through, for them to return you to duty as soon as they did. You should never have been given that assignment in the U.S. state of Montana."

"It was not so bad." Sylvester tasted his bitterness. "I only regret it did not turn out better."

"You were fortunate as it was. Now, I know your formal physical rehabilitation program is complete. The reconstructive surgery at home, and later at the spa-hospital in Zurich, appears a great success. Now that you have spent the last weeks inside the embassy while allowing your beard to grow full, I doubt anyone in the world could recognize you." The KGB Resident allowed himself a wintry smile. "It is a magnificent beard, my friend. I congratulate you."

"Thank you."

"Has your health improved as rapidly as your beard has grown? You appear near normal strength again. Is there still much pain?"

Sylvester decided to lie. "Nothing of significance."

Gravitch nodded grimly. "Which is to say, it is bearable."

"Yes."

Gravitch refilled their tumblers before resuming. "I recognize how you have chafed under the routine here at the embassy. Higher authority has wished to give you adequate time for physical and emotional rehabilitation—and of course for changing your appearance with the beard—before inserting you again."

"And also," Sylvester pointed out, "to allow you and others time to observe me for signs of psychological instability resulting from my injuries and disgrace in America."

"There was no disgrace in America."

"I failed in my mission."

"It was bad luck—could have happened to anyone."

Sylvester's face flushed. "I was bested by an amateur. My years of building cover, first at Syracuse and then at Notre Dame, were lost. I came home in a basket. More recently there was the Montana assignment where I failed again. That is not disgrace?"

"That is bad luck. Bad luck is not disgrace."

Sylvester's simmering frustration and bitterness almost got out.

He caught them just in time and waved his hand. "It is of no consequence."

"Precisely. Because—as the ambassador just tried to make clear—we need all our resources on this one. Not only is it contrary to our own political interests to have terrorists running amok in the world, it is also dangerous. The *last* thing we want is some kind of terrorist activity during the Wimbledon tournament. Terrorism knows no national boundaries."

Sylvester inclined his head to show understanding. "We have too many madmen in the world. They would like to see chaos everywhere."

"Precisely. Every civilized nation has a stake in thwarting terrorism—reestablishing some kind of sanity. These savages know no restraint. They give our business a bad name. They make it too dangerous. Some of those beasts would kill anyone!"

Gravitch paused, then went on. "This kind of terrorist activity must be stopped and punished wherever it appears. Whatever is being planned for Wimbledon must be stopped. For *all* our sakes. And—I might add—our efforts in this direction will necessarily involve stepped-up observation and analysis of British and American counter-terrorist procedures. We can learn from this."

Sylvester relit his cigar. The smoke felt good. "Why are you telling me this, Mikhail? I did not understand what the ambassador was saying to me, or why I was in the meeting. I have been doing scut work here. Do you already know my new assignment? Does it have to do with Wimbledon?"

"I have your assignment. Yes. And it does have to do with the terrorists. But not in the way you might expect."

Bad news, Sylvester thought. Being broken gently. He waited.

"You are being activated," Gravitch told him, "for an assignment perhaps below a man of your background and talents. But it is necessary."

Sylvester waited, aware that his heart rate had increased. He had ached for a return to true field work.

Gravitch began to explain. Sylvester's moment of elation faded, to be replaced by grim acceptance. Northern Ireland. Under cover. Looking for leads—any kind of leads—to the rumored terrorist strike.

A nasty piece of work. A nasty prognosis. In a nasty place.

"You accept?" Gravitch asked at last, after more than an hour.

"Of course." Sylvester did not hide his surprise. "I am a professional. I follow orders."

"The IRA is filled with self-trained radicals, many of them unstable. They sometimes kill on slightest suspicion."

Sylvester nodded.

The KGB Resident leaned forward for emphasis. "We want information, not dead bodies."

"I will try to restrain my maniacal homicidal tendencies, Comrade."

"God damn it, Yuli, I am merely advising caution."

"Yes, sir."

"But we have no time for months of slow progress. We need results."

Sylvester smiled humorlessly. "Rush forward cautiously, then."

Gravitch's head jerked up, almost angry. Then he saw the humor. "Yes. Precisely."

"I understand."

The KGB resident leaned back. "There is one additional matter."

"That being?"

"You have no doubt seen both the news items and our own internal reports. Brad Smith has accepted an invitation to play in this year's tournament."

Sylvester's pulse stirred again, this time sickly, with rage. He hid it. "I have seen the reports."

"Obviously Smith is coming as a CIA plant, to try to help root out what is going on, who the terrorists have inside, where and when they plan to strike. We have our own man inside, of course. It is to our advantage for Smith to go about his business without interference, just as our man will do."

Sylvester watched his superior and said nothing.

Gravitch met his eyes with sober intensity. "Therefore, Smith will be left alone."

"Of course," Sylvester replied quietly.

"You agree?"

"Of course."

"We believe our man inside will be accorded similar treatment."

"Of course," Sylvester said for the third time.

The room fell silent except for the distant drum of the continuing night rainfall. Nothing more would be said, because to belabor the obvious would be not only unprofessional but insulting. Sylvester had managed to see some of his own files, and knew of the psychological profile suggesting he might still be consumed by hatred for Brad Smith. Smith had not only embarrassed him professionally and twice thwarted his official duties; he had caused Sylvester more physical suffering and disgrace than anyone should ever have to go through. But none of that would be mentioned directly. Unless Sylvester showed some sign of extreme stress, it would be assumed he understood that revenge was now quite out of the question.

You will see no stress signs from me, Sylvester thought with bitter satisfaction.

Gravitch continued to study him for what seemed a long time. Finally the chief resident smacked his tumbler onto the coffeetable and got to his feet. "Come into the briefing room. We will commence at once. I want you to fly to Belfast tomorrow."

Sylvester obeyed, carefully keeping his face calm and neutral.

Inside, however, he was a volcano.

The assignment would provide even better cover for the revenge he had already set up for Mr. Brad Smith. It had been difficult to slip out of the compound often enough in the past few days to arrange everything. He had done that—all was in readiness—but he had worried that Gravitch—and possibly others—would link him to what happened to Smith almost as soon as it happened.

But now it would be more foolproof. Sylvester did not have

to be anywhere nearby when his plan was carried out. Now no one would possibly trace anything back to him because he would be in Northern Ireland on Monday—the day after tomorrow—when Brad Smith died.

Langley, Virginia

Tom Dwight sat at his desk deep in the bowels of the headquarters building, scanning the latest classified reports pertaining to the operation they had dubbed *FIRSERVE*.

They told him nothing.

Everything was being done that could be done at this time. Dwight felt sure about that. But his chill deepened whenever he allowed himself to brood about all the possible suspects, all the possible means of wreaking havoc at a public spectacle like Wimbledon, all the places where security might slip up.

Doggedly he reviewed some papers again, looking for something he might have missed. He didn't find anything.

Someone rapped on the frame of his open door. He looked up. "About time."

The man who walked into the room was near Dwight's own age, late thirties or early forties, trimly built, wearing a neat but nondescript business suit and tie. J. C. Kinkaid had brown hair turning gray, and eyes the color of asphalt. He did not look happy.

"Coffee?" Dwight asked him.

"I prefer to live a while longer," Kinkaid said, sitting in the chair that faced his superior's desk.

"So what did you think about our briefing with Brad Smith?"

Kinkaid's face smoothed over to show nothing. "It went well."

"What do you really think?"

"Brad will be valuable. With him inside, staying close to Sean Cork, we might have a real advantage."

Dwight frowned. "I said, what do you *really* think?"

Kinkaid raised anger-filled eyes to his superior. "I agree with

Collie. I think it was totally unnecessary and horseshit not to tell him about Sylvester."

"We don't know for certain that that guy we saw around their embassy *is* Sylvester."

"That's rotten. We should have at least leveled with Brad— told him Sylvester *might* be over there where he's going."

"Tell Brad about a suspicion concerning Sylvester," Dwight said, "and he spends more time looking behind his back than he spends on the case we're interested in." He poured more rancid black coffee from his red-and-black Thermos. "Why worry him?"

"Why?" Kinkaid shot back, aghast. "What if Sylvester decides to have a go at him over there?"

"Look. A new cultural attache or something checked in at the Soviet embassy. A man from the Brits' Home Office saw him once, and said he looked skinny and pale. His official papers don't describe what we know about Sylvester. Why assume he *is* Sylvester?"

"Because he might be. And there's a little more evidence than that, Tom, and you know it."

"Presumptive. All presumptive. We don't *know.*"

Kinkaid tapped his fist lightly but definitely on Dwight's desk. "We should have told Brad anyway."

"No need," Dwight said tonelessly.

"Not even for Brad, who might get his ass shot off?"

"Oh, I don't think the Russians will allow that. I think Brad will be perfectly safe."

"You know from staff meeting that I disagree."

"Yes, but *you* know what the intention analysis specialists said. Nobody is going to let Sylvester run amok. The Russians don't want terrorism over there any more than we do. They'll keep him in line."

Kinkaid stubbornly shook his head. "I still don't buy it."

"Are you letting personalities cloud your judgment?"

"No! You know me better than that, and I think a remark like that is goddamned uncalled for."

Dwight's lips curled in the slightest wry smile. "Just testing."

"Well, you can shove your 'testing.' I'm just saying it isn't good procedure to send a man like Brad over there not knowing the real score."

"Exception noted," Dwight replied, the crispness in his voice betraying the fact that he had lost patience. "The decision has been made."

"We won't change it?"

"No."

"We lied to him while he was here for the briefings, so we keep right on lying to him after he gets to London tomorrow?"

"You do have a way with words," Dwight said. "Now are you sure you don't want some coffee?"

Four

"MR. SMITH? Mr. Brad Smith?"

I turned and looked down at the little man who had spoken to me in the echoing bustle of London's Victoria Station. It was morning here in London, June 4, a precious three weeks before the start of play at Wimbledon, and my flight from New York had robbed me of a night's sleep. Still, I looked at the stranger with surprised interest. No one had been scheduled to meet me.

I have read that schizophrenics have a distinctive odor to their sweat, traceable to methylhexanoic acid. Science has not told me so, but I think there must be some other substance excreted by people whose lives have been marked by failure. Such people emit a sour, acidic smell, the work of a few molecules, perhaps, and so primitive that it communicates on a psychic level I cannot understand. It comes from a rotting spirit and it is not pleasant and I have seldom sensed it, but I sensed it now as I looked down at the little man who had tugged my coat sleeve.

"I'm Smith," I told him.

He was short, pudgy, sad-faced, with watery eyes. His dark flannel suit had never been in style and perhaps it had never been neatly pressed. His white shirt was gone to gray and his pale red tie looked like it had been tied and retied a thousand times: the knot was considerably darker, from dirt, than the rest. He was bald on top, with a bushy fringe of kinky, yellow-gray hair and watery eyes made huge by gold-framed eyeglasses that looked as thick as ice cubes. His face was tracked and crossed by a million miles of broken capillaries. He

43

had a gold tooth and a gold pocket watch and he seemed infinitely tired.

"Allow me to present myself," he said in his small, furry voice. "I am Clarence Tune."

For a second I had the dismaying thought that he might be my contact after all, might represent some change in plans. But he hadn't given the verbal bona fides. "What do you want?"

He pursed his lips as if embarrassed. "If I might have a few words with you, sir."

"Look. I just got off an airplane and the BritRail connection in from Gatwick, and my body doesn't know what day—or night— it is."

Tune grasped my arm in an apologetic way. His grasp was surprisingly strong. He tugged at me, trying to draw me away from the hubbub near the tourist information desk and toward a quieter part of the station. "If you would just indulge me for a few moments, sir, I would be very, very grateful. Really."

"Who are you?"

Flustered, he glanced at some of the people milling around us, then reached inside his baggy suit coat and took out a thin leather wallet worn shiny. Flipped it open, showed me the credential inside. The British are good at credentials. Putting the crown and everything on them makes them beastly impressive, don't you know.

My surprise heightened. "MI5?"

He hastily put the wallet away again. "A few words alone, sir, in private, if I may. Perhaps I could provide transportation to your hotel, or meet with you there at your earliest convenience."

Hands across the Atlantic was all well and good, but I was in no mood to let this sad-eyed little man convey me into the crazy London traffic. "Maybe later. —But why?"

"Of course, sir, of course," he said, bobbing and weaving nervously, like an old fighter reliving a bad round. "Perhaps at your hotel, then, after you have settled in? Say, in two hours? In the tearoom on the lower level?"

"You know where I'm staying?" I asked, incredulous.

"Yes. Please, sir."

"Look. Why don't you just say what's on your mind? I'm just a tennis player, over here for Wimbledon. I don't know why I should—"

"Mr. Smith," Tune cut in, his rheumy eyes momentarily like agates, "I really must insist on that brief meeting. I will await you in the tearoom, in two hours' time. I urge you to cooperate. My agency has information of grave concern to both of us."

"Information?" I was starting to get really impatient.

"Yes, sir," he said. "If you please, sir. We have reason to believe an attempt is to be made on your life. I will await you, sir. May I count on seeing you then? Good. Thank you, sir." He turned and waddled off into the crowd, and was gone.

There is nothing quite as likely to focus your attention as being told your life is in danger. Finding a taxi and riding toward the Cumberland Hotel at Marble Arch, I reviewed what I knew about my assignment so far. And tried to figure out where Clarence Tune might be coming from.

My briefings in Virginia had been thorough, but as usual I had flown on to New York and my overseas connection with as many questions as answers. I didn't know if they had alarming holes in their information, or were withholding things again on some crazy "need to know" basis that nobody in my position could ever hope to understand.

What I now knew was essentially this: a British undercover operative, a member of the SAS, had penetrated deeply enough into an IRA splinter group to pick up strong hints of a major terrorist operation at or near the Wimbledon tournament. Mysterious plans—unspecified—were being advanced. "Shipments" had been made somewhere near Belfast, with more movement of "materiel" expected. Key operatives—like everything else involved, unspecified—had been moved into unknown positions.

All vague, but enough to get the full attention of England's

Anti-Terrorist Group. As a consequence, MI5 had assigned fifteen additional operatives to the investigation, and British army intelligence—notoriously secretive about its activities even to the point of withholding information from fellow services—seemed to have moved in additional manpower as well. Israeli intelligence was in the act at the other end of the presumed supply line, but had nothing of significance to report.

On our side, a new KH12 satellite had been reprogrammed to provide closer scanning of areas near Belfast and the Irish coast that might be significant. So far, the 40,000-pound spy camera platform, capable of resolution down to objects only inches in size, had reported nothing that the rows of Cray MP-48 supercomputers found interesting.

The Brits' original tip had been confirmed, however, through other sources. One of our Rhyolite satellites, listening to microwave telephone talk, had heard the Russians talking about it. Other of NSA's space birds were watching ports in the Persian Gulf region and Libya; some pictures showed trucks taking something out of one of Khadafy's "fertilizer factories."

But it was a morass in northern Ireland—cliques within factions within secret cells of anonymous splinter groups, and not even the top leaders of the IRA could know with certainty who was doing what sometimes, or exactly why. The URA was bad enough, but even these radicals had maverick cells that were worse, and uncontrollable.

The Sean Cork connection was tenuous. I knew Cork by reputation as a young, fiery, immensely talented teenager who some said would pass Boris Becker and Andre Agassi within a year or two. Intelligence agencies were interested in him because both he and his pretty wife had family in Northern Ireland, and after a cousin was injured in an IRA ambush of British soldiers, Cork had held an emotional press conference where he condemned all terrorism and called on everyone in Ulster to forsake violence.

Not much of a speech, really—I had seen a tape of it at Langley during the briefings—but radicals don't like anybody but themselves to be issuing proclamations. There had been threats on Cork's life. He had hired a bodyguard, but otherwise didn't seem to take any precautions. His kind of public life made them practically impossible anyhow.

My job was vague: play tennis and do my other tennis-related things, get as close to Sean Cork as possible, keep my eyes and ears open, and feed detailed daily reports to a Company contact who would get in touch with me soon after my arrival. I had a memorized list of verbal bona fides—sort of key words to use in initial conversation to identify myself and assure myself that the other person was who he said he was. I also had some other detailed information, nothing great. In addition I was supposed to remember the faces of dozens of known or suspected terrorists whose grainy, blurry photos had been dragged out of CIA files and spread across tables in front of me.

Not a lot of data and not a lot of specific guidance. But they seemed to think I might have a chance of contributing to the effort, so here I was. And I had known there would be surprises of some kind. But I hadn't anticipated a Clarence Tune talking about my life being in danger.

Taking a London taxi toward the hotel, I felt irritable about the vagueness of my assignment and Clarence Tune's disconcerting warning. I had called Beth again from Virginia, and when she had heard where I was, she made the Company connection and turned ice maiden on the phone. Add to this my feelings about coming back to London for a Wimbledon where some kid was going to wave his magic composite racket and turn me into a pumpkin, and the resulting mood was dark.

There had been some great times here in London during the pre-knee days. Once, during one of the grass court tournaments that precede the big one, I fell in with some of the Aussies. A number of them were long in the tooth by then, but they knew how to party. On one memorable night we looked up after "just a few beers" to see daylight at the windows.

Panicked, I climbed out of my chair and headed for the door.

"Where are you off to, mate?" one of them, maybe Laver, asked.

"My room! It's daylight, and I play at two. I've got to get some sleep!"

"Never go to sleep at this hour. Worst thing you can do. The trick now is to keep going."

I thought they were crazy. I rushed to my room, slept almost four hours, then went out and played like the hung-over zombie I was, losing to another Smith—Stan—in straight sets.

Two of my all-night drinking buddies played too. Both cooly demolished their opponents.

"Didn't you sleep at all?"

"Nah! Like we told you. We rented motorcycles and took a little spin down south a bit, and then we got into a little dancing with some sweet things from Chelsea. When you've been up all night you've got to keep the motor running, mate. It's your only hope."

A long time ago. We go along, taking it as it comes, and then one day we look up and it's a new decade and we don't think *anything* could make the motor run the way it did in those days.

The Cumberland is a nice hotel, quite large, and I like it. I just wish it didn't look quite so Miami Beach. Reaching there, I dealt with the desk and the bellman in record time, getting confused as usual with the mental gymnastics of doing currency conversion in my head, then briefly checked out my room. The Prince people had delivered my new rackets, and there was a message from the Nike man saying my contract—and shoes—were waiting at the London office. I took a couple of paranoid precautions before going down to the vast restaurant. I found sad Clarence Tune seated alone in a dim, far corner, looking like a time machine throwback to the Charles Dickens era that the restaurant's decor tried to evoke.

He stood and smiled uncertainly as I joined him. "There you are, sir, Mr. Smith. Oh, good. Excellent. Thank you so much for your promptness."

I sat opposite him. "What's it all about, Mr. Tune?"

He signalled a waiter. "May I suggest the Earl Grey, sir?"

I nodded wearily. "Fine. Whatever you say. Let's just get on with it."

Tune happily gave the order to the waiter, then turned back to me with the bright stare of a rabbit. "It's awfully good of you, sir."

"What's it all about?" I repeated.

"First of all, Mr. Smith, my superiors are well aware of your previous work for a sister agency in the United States."

"I don't know what you're—"

"Of course, of course. At any rate, your work in connection with the Lechova case in Belgrade was widely publicized, and it should take no great feat of counterintelligence analysis to guess that your presence here for the Wimbledon tournament, after so long an absence, might somehow be connected with intelligence work. —Especially, sir, I might add before you deny it again, in view of our common concern about possible activities at that tournament. Do you follow me so far, sir?"

I stared at him and refused to answer. He had the most amazing face, like bread dough worked to the point where it glistens. His smile was almost impish and my first whiff of failure about him seemed at the moment less intense. I didn't know what the hell to make of him.

"Yes," he said, showing his gold tooth again. "Quite so. Now. It occurs to my superiors that, *ay*, your mission here may be to observe from within the tournament infrastructure, and *bee*, our antagonists might be just as quick as we to observe this possibility, and *cee*, they might for that reason view you with some alarm and determine to remove you as a complication, and *dee*, although your Chief of Station may be quite willing to risk your life in this manner, it would be dreadfully embarrassing for us if you—who to the general public are a revered figure in Wimbledon history—should be callously struck down. *Very* bad for morale, not to mention our reputation for staying on top of things, don't you know."

He paused and watched, brightly alert and cheerful, while the waiter delivered my tea and some little cakes in a basket. The waiter went away.

I said, "You said you had reason to believe my life might be in danger. Do you intend to tell me about that, or are we just going through more of this Watson and Holmes business?"

He stirred a disgusting quantity of cream into his tea. "Do you know the name Ivor McWilliams?"

"No."

He shrugged. "Perhaps a silly question. No reason why you should know him. Well. Mr. McWilliams is a convicted thief with a history of violence against his victims. He is presently free on parole. Although he spends some time pretending to be an automobile mechanic in Marylebone, he has in fact no significant knowledge of automotive mechanics nor any visible means of support."

"Is this supposed to interest me, Tune?"

"Mr. McWilliams's wife, Abigail, is originally from Northern Ireland, where her two brothers, Patrick and David, remain. Both are suspected of links with the IRA. We believe that Mr. McWilliams has been assigned to *ay,* keep you under close surveillance and/or *bee,* assassinate you."

"Any basis for that idea?"

"Yes. One week ago Mr. McWilliams came into a sum of money. Five days ago, the same Mr. McWilliams won employment here."

"Here? At the Cumberland?"

"Yes. In building maintenance. Which of course gives him access to virtually all portions of the physical plant."

"You have a picture of him?"

"Yes." Tune dug into his inside coat pocket again and slid a grubby snapshot across the table.

I examined it. Prison photo. Grainy and harshly lighted. Nobody looks good in those things, and McWilliams looked as bad as most: unshaven, hair down his neck, large broken nose, deep-socketed eyes, prominent Adam's apple.

"He looks somewhat better now," Tune told me, "and he sometimes wears a brown wig."

I slid the picture back across the table. "If your suspicions are so strong, why haven't you arrested him?"

Tune's soft chin fell. "We have his home under surveillance, of course. But on what charge could we arrest him, my dear man?"

"Christ. —I assume you've passed all this information on to, uh, proper American authorities?"

"Yes, of course, I am assured that has been done. In addition, however, out of an excess of solicitude, I have been instructed to give this information directly to you, as the alleged intended victim, and to maintain close contact with you during your entire stay in Great Britain as an additional security precaution."

I almost groaned. This was great; this was all I needed: someone like Tune, shuffling around in my tracks.

I protested, "I think I can take care of myself."

"Oh, I am sure you can. You appear to be a wonderful specimen, and I am aware of your background. Tell me, Mr. Smith: are you armed at the present time?"

"Hell, no! Don't you Brits take a very dim view of that sort of thing?"

"Oh, certainly. Of course. But I am surprised, rather. I secretly admire the American infatuation with firearms, to tell the truth. I suppose it goes back to your American West. Ah, how I love your western history! Your western flicks! Randolph Scott! Alan Ladd! John Wayne!" He coiled one pudgy fist on the table, thumb and forefinger cocked like a gun. "That scene with Gary Cooper in *High Noon!* —I rather hoped you *were* armed, sir. Two guns, even. I would have been reassured, given the circumstances. I would have told no one, and called you 'Two-Gun,' in jest, of course, don't you know."

"Well," I said through my teeth, "I'm no Two-Gun. And I'm just not that important generally. I'm afraid you're going to be wasting your time."

"No problem, my dear Mr. Smith. No problem at all! And you

needn't worry, sir, about your importance. You may not be. Actually, my assignment to your case is probably proof that you're not . . . in the cosmic scheme of things, I mean. I am incalculably far down the list for promotion or any other form of advancement. This is a wonderfully exciting posting for the likes of me, but if it were of any great import at all, I can assure you that *I* would never have been given the assignment!"

By the time I got rid of Clarence Tune and had returned to my hotel room, my irritation and anxiety had temporarily overpowered the jet lag. I unpacked a few of my things and checked my equipment bag to make sure the airline baggage handlers had not taken out part of their grudge against the world on my stuff. Then I set up my lap computer and tiny printer and made sure they hadn't been garbaged in transit. The hard drive booted right up, and two background pieces I had written in Washington were ready to print out. Most journalists do it—prepare some material before a tournament or whatever. I had never felt quite right about it. But I was going to be hard-pressed to play tennis, keep an eye out for monkey business, and play journalist, too. Having a couple of thousand words ahead of time would ease the pressure a little, and protect the journalist part of my cover.

While I checked things out, however, my head was buzzing with worries and theories, all probably paranoid.

Ivor McWilliams . . . Ivor McWilliams. . . . Well, wonderful. My so-called cover had not been expected to stand up to close examination, but the boys at Langley had assured me that my real history in professional tennis would make my Wimbledon trip seem reasonably legitimate. In my meeting with Dwight and Kinkaid I had been convinced—almost—that nobody would pay much attention to me because the radicals were few and they couldn't possibly have the analysis facilities or manpower to pick me out of the small army of people assigned to the counter-terrorist effort.

"Not to worry, Brad," Dwight had told me with his usual maddening professional cool. "Your assignment comes under the category of extra insurance."

Except that Wimbledon meant too much to me. The idea of coming over here and getting run off the court—made a fool of—worried me.

And somebody had been mistaken about my cover, or I had been conned again. MI5 was onto me, and Clarence Tune was going to be a pain in the nether regions. Ivor McWilliams might be in the hotel for some other reason entirely; for all I could know, the man might even have inherited the money Tune's people had noticed.

Or maybe not.

I prowled around my hotel room and made some tentative decisions, then did some more of my 007 stuff that embarrasses me to talk about.

Want a way to see if anyone opened your luggage while you were gone from your room? Get a Chap Stick. Daub it on the zippers or snaps of your attache case or purse, your toiletry kit, your suitcase. If someone comes in and pokes around, they break the waxy seal.

I daubed my shaving kit and then hauled out my thin, Spanish leather briefcase, the one I always take overseas with me. I still had a couple of magazines and brochures in the case. Leaving these inside, I used the Chap Stick to lay a pasty bead on the ends of the side zipper. Then I slid the briefcase under the bed.

After daubing more of the Chap Stick on the interior hinges of my suitcase and the latches on my equipment bag, I smoked a cigarette, considered my options, and rode to street level in the elevator.

The day was bright, with a chill, sunny sky. I crossed the street corner, reminding myself to look in the wrong directions for oncoming traffic, and walked a block to a pay telephone. The air felt good and it was getting warmer as the afternoon progressed.

When they picked the dates for Wimbledon more than a century ago, they picked the late-June starting time based on weather records. Historically, late June and early July represented the period most likely to provide clear and sunny weather for play. Unfortunately the weather pattern has changed in a hundred years. Now there are often nice days early in the month like the one today, and again later in the summer, but the spring rains seem to fall with dismaying predictability later in June and early in July, during Wimbledon. I could be glad for the weather today, anyway.

At the telephone kiosk I paused long enough to mentally rehearse what I needed to say. Then it took a minute or two to figure out the damned British telephone. They're not that different, but I get confused easily when the currency is different, the dial tone doesn't sound right, and it's hard to tell whether an instrument is ringing at the other end.

I got through the money-inserting and dialing business just like I had more than one brain cell. There were some funny high-pitched noises. Then a woman's voice, contralto, answered. *"Yes? Who is calling, please?"*

"Virginia?" I said. "This is Monte." I heard the tiny click of the recording device switching on. "I've arrived today. I expect to meet the family at eighteen hundred local. Everything has been squared away."

After the slightest pause the woman responded. She had a very nice voice, cool and mature: *"Thank you, Monte. It was nice hearing from you."* The connection broke off.

We were operating on the rule of minus two, but that still left me plenty of time to catch a taxi for Covent Gardens.

The cafes in that area had dragged out their sidewalk tables to catch the warming sunlight. By the time I got there, many of them were packed. People milled everywhere, flocking to the open air pavilion area in the center of the park with its stands of arts and crafts. Some of the usual street players had started up near the church grounds, and had drawn a crowd. I picked up a couple of brochures in the park and then went to one of the cafes and stood around a while, waiting for a table. After being seated, I ordered tea and got busy looking like any other tourist, studying my free advertising and *Boardroom Magazine* street map.

It was nice, despite my tension. I thought about Beth and how much fun we could have had here. I could have brought her. She wouldn't have had to ask any questions. I would have had some time for sightseeing.

That was all in the realm of the abstract now, of course. Clarence Tune's appearance made me almost glad Beth wasn't along, possibly getting herself in danger again by being in my company.

But that didn't make me feel any better about our estrangement. The plane ride had been lonely. For so long there hadn't been a woman in my life. Then one had come to the periphery of my existence and learned just a little about my connections with the Company, and rapidly distanced herself. Next had come those few precious months with Danisa Lechova. And she—partly because of *my* influence on her life—had been murdered by Sylvester. Now Beth Miles was gone, too.

I tried to tell myself she wasn't definitely *gone*—that she was just thinking it over, and we would figure out a way to get our lives back together. But there was a creeping despair. Maybe I was never going to find a woman willing to put up with me and my life. I could live alone just fine. I didn't need anybody to make me feel whole or adequate. But I didn't always like it. And damn: I missed Beth.

What do you do when quite suddenly the trust and optimism aren't there any more? One day you look into her eyes and there is only sunlight. You look again a moment later and you can't see the eyes at all because the snake-lids of disappointment have slid down over them. *My fault*, you think and try to fix it. *Her fault*, you think, and watch her try to fix it. *Our fault*, you both agree, and then circle and bow and falsely chuckle at one another, both of you—who yesterday were as comfortable together as the fingers on your hand—suddenly as awkward and contrived as oldsters visiting Arthur Murray for their $5 introductory lesson. Finally, in desperation, you come to the truth: *no one's fault.*

But the truth is a despair-filled thing, and I was not ready for that stage quite yet.

I finished fussing with my maps and brochures and watched passersby. A few couples, waiting for a table, pointedly stared at me. I didn't look their way any more. Some time passed. Businessmen in conservative suits mixed with pretty professional women and little shop girls in their minis. Some of the tourists were easy to pick out by their inappropriate dress or cameras. There were a lot of Japanese again this year. The Germans came later in the summer when their companies said You *vill* take a vacation, *schnell!*

I watched two young women approach the cafe from the south. Both in their late twenties, and well worth noticing. Legal secretaries or something of the kind, possibly barristers. But there was nothing fusty about either of them. The blonde was loose-haired, her rimless glasses and gray suit failing to make her look dull in any way. The other girl struck me more forcibly. She was really extraordinary, tall, lithe, dark-haired and long-legged, wearing a mauve jersey dress and medium heels. She had strong facial features, a little like Mariel Hemingway, and the way she swung her legs and clung to the small purse clutched under her arm said no nonsense. Zesty good health practically leaped out of the way she moved.

As they started past the cafe, she looked directly at me, meeting my eyes. Caught staring, I glanced away. When I glanced back, she was coming between tables directly toward me, her blond friend in tow.

She stopped at my table, beaming down with a pretty, uncertain smile. Up close she was almost overwhelming. "Hi! Pardon me, but aren't you Brad Smith, the former Wimbledon champion?"

People at nearby tables overheard the question. I was flattered. You don't get recognized often when you're old enough to be in the historical index of the tennis anthologies.

"I guess I am," I told her.

She turned to her blond companion. "See? I told you!" She swung amazing emerald eyes back to me and extended a capable hand devoid of jewelry. "I'm Linda Bennett, and this is my friend,

Marcie Westmore. I saw you play at Orlando last year. We were on the same redline bus to the special products reception, but I didn't get a chance to say hello."

Ah, so. I stood and shook hands with both of them, aware of the scrutiny of some of the people nearby. "I remember seeing you, I think. Wasn't that the night of the tournament semifinals with standing room only?"

Her eyes changed fractionally as she took in my part of the bona fides. "Exactly. Gosh, this is wonderful!" She hesitated and gave a good show of uncertainty about where to go next. "Marcie and I were just strolling by, looking for a place to rest our feet. I know it must be irritating, having people accost you all the time, but I couldn't resist. It really is a small world!"

I pointed to the empty chairs at my little table. "Lots of room here, if you'd care to join me."

"Oh gee, I don't know!" She frowned at friend Marcie. "What do you think?"

Marcie grinned and sat down. Lady Linda pretended to be flustered and excited as she followed suit. She produced a tennis magazine. "Maybe, if it isn't pushing our luck . . . could I possibly ask you to autograph this for me?"

I went through that part of the charade, too, and they ordered Cokes, which the waiter brought promptly. We kept talking tennis trivia, lowering tone, and nearby people lost interest and returned to their own conversations.

That was when Linda leaned fractionally closer. "Marcie is fine. She's a clerk in the office. What's happened?"

I told her about Clarence Tune and his story of Ivor McWilliams. She made it a point to smile brightly and nod as if I were telling a particularly amusing story about my alleged tennis exploits.

"This man Tune is certainly not in any of our plans," she said when I was through.

"I didn't think he was."

She turned to Marcie and said louder, "I have tickets to two of the early days." Then back to me, quieter: "I'll report and get back to you."

"You might ask a couple of things for me. One: can they get Tune off my back, or do I have to figure out a way to live with him? Two: is this guy McWilliams serious, or is Tune blowing smoke? Three: do I proceed as planned, or does this mean I'm already blown out of the water?"

She nodded, her eyes showing she understood precisely my predicament. She was as quick as she was beautiful and I wondered if I would ever see her again.

She said, "I'll convey the questions."

"You might also tell them a theory I have," I added. "You might also tell them I'm somewhat irritated about it."

She watched me cooly. "What is it?"

"I think maybe we have some inter-agency jealousy going on here. I think maybe the Brits are not real happy with the heavy-duty effort they've detected by our people, and for all I know by the FBI's so-called cultural attaches as well. I think maybe the MI5 interest is in making sure I don't accomplish anything, and the MI5 scrutiny has somehow gotten the attention of the people managing this guy McWilliams.

"Or," I added, fuming, "maybe something else is going on here. Maybe I've been set up as the rubber decoy here to attract attention while the real surveillance operations go on somewhere else close to the tournament."

"I'll pass on what you've said," she replied with cool detachment.

"And if it's not too much trouble I would like some answers."

Her eyes showed how she retreated behind them. My unprofessional pique had disappointed her. Whatever personal interest there might have been, it was now gone, flushed away by the floodtide of my amateurish self-pity.

"I'll pass it all on," she repeated. Then she turned to Marcie. "Are we ready, dear?" Back to me, "We really must be running along. Thank you *so* much! It's been wonderful!"

Gushes. Handshakes. Stirring and tremble of healthy, vibrant girl. And then they were on the way out. I noticed that I wasn't the only man in the place who watched them all the way.

Now for a little while there was nothing to do but wait—and hope that what I was waiting for was not some even nastier surprise.

Back at the hotel everything was normal and undisturbed. I smoked one of tomorrow's quota of cigarettes, took a short nap, and whanged out a sort of generic tournament preparation piece for the *Times* back in New York. The messenger took the printoff away for delivery and I showered and shaved and went below-decks to the hotel dining room where I had such a miserable, watery, tasteless, expensive stew that I figured it must be authentic English cuisine. Checked for messages at the desk and found none. Went back to my room again nursing a headache.

The maid had been in and turned down the bed, leaving me two small, foil-wrapped chocolates on my pillow. Somebody else had been in, too, and had disturbed all my Chap Stick burglar detectors. Nothing was missing, but the search had been thorough. Too bad scuts like me never carried anything helpful to searchers.

I smoked some more, worried, worked off some of the tension with isometrics and pushups, showered again, and turned in. They had not told me as much as I had wanted to know during the briefings at Headquarters. I was reminded of a time not so long ago in Belgrade when I had no idea of what I was really getting into. I got up and restlessly looked out my room window, but management had thoughtfully provided me with a view of an interior roof and another wall.

Later, in bed again, I thought more about Beth. We had been together—if you call a long-distance relationship being together—for more than a year now, since our magic meeting on St. Maarten. My work in Montana and her law practice in California would never, perhaps, dovetail. Was it ending between us? I didn't want that. But Beth—and even Montana—seemed a universe away.

I thought then about Linda Bennett's vivid green eyes, and how her body had moved. Clarence Tune's man, Ivor McWilliams, spooked around the edges of my consciousness. But I was not very worried about him yet. Not as worried as I should have been.

Five

WHEN I AWOKE early Monday morning, it was with a stiff back and a sore knee. The back I could attribute to Sunday's airplane ride across the Atlantic, and it would loosen up. The knee ached because too many doctors had stuck knives in it, trying to fix it, and it would never be right again.

The newspaper outside my door carried quarterfinal results in the French Open. Sean Cork had beaten Yannick Noah in one match, and Michael Chang had shocked my doubles partner-to-be, Terry Carpoman, in another. There was a grainy picture of Carpoman raging at the umpire. The caption said he had been penalized two points for code violations.

In the lobby I checked for messages and found a telephone memo saying Terry had called, and would arrive early in the afternoon. There was nothing from the embassy and nothing from Clarence Tune. I had breakfast and took a walk in a misting rain which made it all seem very London.

Movement loosened up the knee. I took it easy, strolling down through the eastern edge of Hyde Park almost as far as the Achilles statue, then meandering west. Despite the intensifying drizzle there were tourists and birdwatchers out along the Serpentine. My London Fog windbreaker proved to be misnamed, and the rain went right through the shoulders, making me start to get chilly. I kept on going, trying to sort out some thoughts about Clarence Tune, Linda Bennett, my assignment, and of course the tournament. None of the thoughts felt organized and I didn't push it. I had to be here, be visible, meet players. Especially Sean Cork. And try to establish some kind of quick friendship with him. Otherwise, my instructions were dismayingly loose. Past experience had taught me not to press, start asking too many questions. All that could accomplish was blow my cover.

I wished for Beth, here with me. She would have liked this, I thought. I realized that I didn't even know if she had ever been to London. There was a lot we didn't know about each other. *Right, Smith. Start trying to follow that line, start trying to convince yourself that maybe the whole thing was a mistake and you don't want her in your life any more. Then after you've convinced yourself of that, you can start trying to believe that eating regularly isn't important to you either, or you don't have to breathe.*

I took a different mental tack, telling myself it might be better that she wasn't here; there was a chance the job could get dangerous because terrorists liked random acts of violence.

And there was always Sylvester. If he was around, Beth was damned sure better off somewhere else.

The guys had insisted they had no knowledge of Sylvester's whereabouts, and certainly no hint that he might be in England, or even in western Europe. Rationality added that he would have absolutely no stake in terrorist activity at Wimbledon, or in any vendetta against Sean Cork. Nevertheless, walking, I had the faint prickly sensation of someone at my back somewhere.

For he would come. If not here, somewhere. If not today, tomorrow. Our lives were interwoven now, and although we might be half the globe apart, we moved like dream-creatures, drugged insect victims rotating slowly with the wind inside the sticky strands of our own lethal web. He had killed my Danisa, and had almost killed Beth as well as me. I had smashed his face beyond recognition, shot him, made him go over a cliff that would have killed any other man. It was more than hate or fear or revenge that twisted around us, holding us in our deadly spiderweb dance. We had each taken the other to the brink, and neither of us could ever rest well, knowing the other was somewhere out there, awaiting his next chance.

Sanity and logic had nothing to do with it now. We simply *were* for one another, tied, moving through the dance we neither designed nor controlled. One day, one of us would be free. But that could be only when the other was dead. Nothing less would work.

A hot shower and change of clothes felt good when I returned to the hotel. After lunch I went to the lobby to await Terry Carpoman's arrival. I didn't have to wait long.

He jangled in about 1:30, turning heads in the lobby. Everything about him was calculated to turn heads. Tall, lank, deeply suntanned, with studiously unkempt blond hair to his shoulders, he wore white canvas slacks, sky-colored lightweight sweater, and pale blue deck shoes. A half-dozen gold chains gleamed in the furry pelt that puffed out of the top of the sweater's vee neck, and the gentleman also wore an earring. He had about two days' growth of golden facial stubble, a cocky grin that lit the lobby, and a gorgeously tall and dramatic Mrs. Carpoman on his arm.

He spotted me the moment he walked into the place. He waved. "Brad!" And started over.

Halfway across the lobby, out from somewhere skittered two Brit teenagers, colorful little birds with yellow-green-red-blue hair, miniskirts, high tight black laceup boots, and a half-mile of rings and bracelets. They intercepted the Carpomans, giggling and holding out small green books and ballpoints. Carpoman promptly went berserk. He knocked one of the autograph books out of one girl's hands. "Get the hell out of our way! What makes you shits think you can invade my privacy?"

Mrs. Carpoman—I remembered her name was Alicia—caught his arm and said something soft and nervous. He hurled her arm away and started on across the lobby, leaving the two birds staring in shock.

His face when he reached me was brutally red. His eyes danced around. The hand he held out to me shook. "Damned little nuisance bastards! Can't you ever have a moment's privacy? —Hello, Brad. When did you get in?"

"Yesterday," I told him. I turned to Alicia, who looked pale and upset. "Hello, I'm Brad Smith."

She was awfully pretty: dark, with large eyes and mouth, and a flair for winter colors in her slacks, blouse and neck scarf. A diamond that had to be three carats glittered on the chain nestled between her breasts, the engagement ring and wedding band showered sparks, and her wristwatch was one of those large Louis Vuitton world-time watches that cost a lot more than the light truck I drive back home.

"I'm happy to meet you, Brad," she said huskily. She turned to her husband. "Darling, I *wish* you would control your temper. You're getting worse all the time."

He refused to look at her. "Blow it off."

She stiffened. "I'm going to our own hotel and then I'm going shopping."

"Do me a favor, for once in your life. Try not to spend more than I'll make when I win the singles title."

Pretty mouth set in anger, she turned and stormed out.

"Goddamned woman is more expensive to keep than a B-1 bomber," Carpoman growled. "Jesus! Let's go have a Coke or something, and talk."

We went to the tea room. More heads turned. We got a table and ordered soft drinks.

"Glad you're here, Brad," he told me, nervously drumming his fingers. "We need to start practice together pronto."

"Okay, Terry. Fine. Incidentally, I'm sorry about the French. That clay—"

"I got screwed at the French. Screwed!"

"Is that so?"

"Yeah, but I don't want to talk about it. Listen. I've already made some arrangements. We've got a court at a club out beyond the Queen's Club today."

I was startled. "Today?"

"Shit, yes. Why waste time? This is serious. We need to do a lot of work together as a doubles team. I want to kill some of those high-falutin' sonsabitches out there. Damn, if I had to lose in Paris, I should have done it earlier. Now it's too late to get in Beckenham. Screwed again. I've entered us at Nottingham next week. We ought to cruise in that one, get several wins under our belt. The money can't touch the Stella Artois or the Scottish Grass Courts, but we need the matches we can get, going through a weaker field."

"You might have asked me before entering us, Terry," I pointed out.

His color brightened, the crazy temper flickering dangerously. "Have you got a complaint about it?"

"I just think you should have asked me first."

"I thought you were a pro, not a fucking prima donna."

"Right," I said. "Forget I said anything. You're right, of course."

He didn't seem able to sit still. His eyes darted around like he felt paranoid. He shuffled his feet, rolled side-to-side in his chair, drummed his fingers on the tabletop, scratched his ear, blew his nose, tasted his Coke, cracked his knuckles.

"You look in pretty good shape," he told me. "We get our tactics in order, we can win this thing."

His grim ambition worried me. "That's nice to think about," I said carefully. "But I'm almost twice your age, Terry, and some of the reflexes just ain't there any more."

He glared. "If you aren't interested in winning, then forget it. Fuck it. I mean right now."

"I'm interested in winning," I said. My face felt hot. "I'm just being realistic. You'll get my best shot. If my knee holds up and we get a good draw, I'll be just as hot for a trophy as you are."

"Okay, then! We'll win it."

"Doubles was a finesse game when I won in the doubles at Flushing Meadows, Terry. It's changed since then. Like golf. It's a power game now."

His jaw set and a muscle clenched and relaxed, clenched and relaxed, in his cheek. "Right. I've got the power. We'll kill 'em."

I gave up on trying to make him be realistic. "I'll give it my best shot. I don't know how to play any other way."

He flushed with angry pleasure. "Damned right! —Listen, I've *got* to win this thing. The singles for sure, and the doubles if you can hold up your end of it. It's not just the prize money. It's the endorsements. I need more endorsements. Hell, I've got a winning personality, right? All I need is a major like Wimbledon, a title I can really cash in on. Jesus. It's halfway through the year and I haven't even topped five hundred thousand yet. And you know what the expenses run. What the tax bite is. I've got to get *going.*"

"I'm with you," I told him.

"Good. Let's shag out of here and go find those courts. How soon can you be ready? I've got a rented limo waiting to take us. You ready now? Let's go."

I got and then we got. The private club was less than an hour's drive away in the chauffeur-driven Mercedes limo. By the time we got there it had stopped raining and the sun peered through broken dark clouds.

Terry had reserved one of their grass courts and we had a handful of members in the bleachers, shivering bravely in the thin sunshine. For a moment I flattered myself that they were waiting for us, but then I saw the TV people and recognized Chris Evert and Jimmy Connors taping a playing strategy piece for the network's sidebar files.

At the appointed time we took the court to work out against each other for a while. I wore tennis shorts and a sweater, with my bulky knee brace strapped on over silk long johns, because the warm-ups wouldn't fit over the brace. We got heated up and played a few games while I started trying to get accustomed again to the speed of grass. The knee made it impossible to slide properly into shots to my left, but I compensated fairly well. Terry began hitting out with his notorious reckless ferocity, and I sent up moonballs, lobs, dinks and undersliced dropshots in an effort to hold him at bay.

As the workout progressed, it came clearer to me that getting back to proficiency on grass was not going to be easy for me. You have to get lower to the ball on grass, take it on the rise, bend your knees a lot more. My bulky brace didn't lend itself to that. In the singles it would be all right, I thought: with luck I might control the pace, keeping the game near my decrepit tempo. The new rackets are so powerful that you can hit endlessly from the baseline. And I already expected to get creamed in the first round anyway. But Terry Carpoman's power game and manic behavior would not make finesse doubles possible, and he had already made it clear he expected a lot more from me than a graceful demise. I worked hard.

After an hour we took a short break and talked doubles tactics. Terry, not at all to my surprise, did most of the talking. It didn't bother me. He reminded me of the years when I had been at the top of my game, with all those wonderful reflexes of youth percolating to perfection, and I thought nothing could hold me back, no one could beat me if I was on my game, nothing bad could ever happen.

Despite my earlier demurrers, he talked power doubles, the kind that's played nowadays at the highest level. When I was among the world's best, there was considerable finesse and touch in even the best doubles competition. But more and more today, doubles strategy has become more physical: blast the serve, power the volley. Wham bam, end of point.

"When you're serving, Brad, if the first one goes in, I'll poach a lot on the second return. Sometimes even on the serve. When I'm serving, I figure you can fudge maybe one step, but you don't need to move too far. They'll probably try to take the alley on you some, and you need to conserve your energy. Most of the time we'll leave the intimidation to me. Now when we get a short ball, naturally if you've got the obvious overhead you'll take it. But if I'm in position and I call for it—"

Ah, how well he had it all figured out, his tactics bathed in that golden glow of overconfidence. I was the heady old veteran with bad legs, and he was the power. I would play the clever angles and make sure to spin my first serve in, and try to set him up for the killer-diller shots at net. He would cover more than his half and take some chances to rest me, shouldering well over fifty percent of the pressure.

It was all theory, and all kind of insulting, but that was okay. He seemed half-crazy with his plans for Wimbledon. I had never seen anyone quite so driven, frenzied, on the brink of being out of control. And I had seen lots of people driven almost mad by this game. So I didn't argue with him. I let him tell me how we would power our way over people.

I felt sad about it, however. I have always had a special place in my heart for doubles. It's a different game out there than singles. Only at the lowest levels of proficiency do you see doubles partners playing what looks like two singles games stuck loosely together. Everything in quality doubles is coordinated movement, anticipation, partnership, and angles. Unless one player is having a really terrible day out there, the margin between winning and losing is even finer than in singles because the team aspect tends to balance off any individual's superiority. The best singles players seldom make the best doubles partners for precisely that reason: they think their own game, and not the partnership; the idea of sacrificing for the pair is foreign to the way they have to think in order to survive singles matches on their own. Our finest doubles teams are composed of players whose names very seldom show up past the quarterfinals brackets in the singles, and some of the best don't often compete in tournament singles.

I like doubles more and more, and not just because I'm becoming an old party. Yes, there are fewer long sprints and exhausting rallies. But I like bridge better than chess, too. The teamwork in doubles—as in bridge—has a fascination entirely of its own. There aren't any lone rangers in quality bridge competition, and there aren't any in good doubles, either. In a quality match, you become aware of a fascinating gridwork of intangibles: your partner's position and which way he seems to be leaning, the way he moved the last time in a similar situation and your knowledge of whether he tends to follow a set pattern or consciously mix up his reactions in a given situation; his strengths and weaknesses if any, how he's playing today and even on the last few points; the game, set and match situation; which way things seem to be turning, where your opponents are on the court, what they've been doing, what they might expect, how they interact, the condition of the balls, the weather, the light, the wind, the playing surface, the stringing of your racket, how well you're playing and what's been working (or not); and always the angles: precisely how deep are you for this backhand, and how many feet or inches do you have down the alley, how close is the nearest opponent to the line, can the other man cross over, what's the angle if you try crosscourt and what will happen to your partner if your shot goes a little high, is there any opening whatsoever for the preferred return up the middle, if you lobbed well could both of you get in to net before their return, and if it works well that long, what angle will *they* have, and what's the angle to the center, what's the angle behind your partner if he crosses over, what's the angle long to the far corner, what's the angle between them over there and is one a step back, what's your best angle if you hit and then have to volley from your shoetops. I love doubles. Sometimes I finish a high-intensity doubles match more exhausted mentally than physically, but still totally drained. In singles, in the old days, I got into a zone sometimes when I was simply there, and playing. In doubles my mental work is so strenuous and continuous that the level of absorption is overwhelming.

Given all that, I listened carefully to what Terry Carpoman had to say, and it all sounded just wonderful in theory. Which didn't surprise me. Terry had gotten incredibly erratic in terms of his personality, from what I had seen so far, since the last time we had spent any time together. But I knew he was not just some talented idiot; he knew and had studied the game, even its history, far more than most.

"Now, look, Brad. I've rounded up a couple of collegians. They play together a lot, even in some tournaments. Let's go back out there and meet them—it's time and they should be here by now—and have a practice set with them."

He didn't ask if that was what I wanted to do, so I did it.

The two kids waiting for us, indolent grins on their faces, were the type you look at and think, *Uh-oh!* Tall, thinly muscular, with good bodies and good equipment and the kind of movements that speak of coordination.

Terry introduced us. The dark-haired lad's name was Simms, and the bulkier partner's name was Hershizer.

"Okay," Terry told us. "You gents can serve first. We'll call our own lines. Just a nice, friendly set for grins, right? But don't expect us to take it easy on you!"

They didn't.

They were up for us.

They were quite good, and clearly had played together forever. Or at least forever in terms of what that is when you're twenty years old. The dark, curly-haired one had a very nice Australian service that you either took early or you went back to the fence for, in order to catch that high bounce. This spinning shot gave him ample time to rush the net every serve, which complicated matters. He had a backhand he could count on. His partner, craftier, seldom got out of position at net, and disguised his intentions well.

They held serve and then took us to deuce on Terry's serve when I blew two volleys. We hung on and the score went finally to 5-5. Hershizer called one of Terry's alley shots wide and Terry had a screaming, red-faced temper tantrum. Both the kids looked truly shocked. Embarrassed, I calmed Terry down enough to continue. He lost his temper again in the twelfth game and broke one of his rackets.

His play deteriorated. He started double-faulting. Then he netted a couple of easy volleys. The kids noticed, and started playing him. Miserable, I began to poach at more unexpected times. My knee sent up messages that it didn't appreciate the treatment. But then I got on a small tear and hit a dozen really excellent crossing and alley shots, and we eked out a precious service break on Simms. Then I managed to hold serve and we pulled it out, 10-8.

When we shook hands at the net, Terry was still acting crazy—

sullen, twitchy, hostile, like the world was against him and he *knew* it.

"Goddamn it!" he snarled at me in the showers. "We stunk the place up!"

"We got together a lot better as we went along," I pointed out. "On that poach of yours, where I crossed over behind you because I wasn't quite up there yet—"

"Yeah. That was a stupid fucking thing for you to do, Brad. I'm glad you recognize that. If you don't do better, we'll get our ass killed at Nottingham and Wimbledon both. Shit!"

I studied the red frustration all over his face. "Want to look for a new partner?"

"No. I don't think so. I don't know. No." He groaned. "Look. I shouldn't have said that. I'm just tight. Forget it. Okay?"

"Okay, Terry. Sure."

What accounted for a sea-change in a man's personality? Carpoman had once been a hard-driving top amateur with a tendency to argue a few line calls, but no serious problems with his emotions. A decent young man. That side of him had just peeked out for about five seconds. But most of the time he seemed half crazy now. Why?

I supposed that the pressure of the life itself could do it. Big-time tennis has wrecked some men's and women's lives, reduced them to husks. Did the beauteous Alicia's expensive habits explain things?

I was still listening to him fuss at me, and thinking about this mystery, when we left the lockers and headed out toward our waiting limo.

Which was when I spotted the familiar dumpy figure standing nearby. That brought me back to reality.

"Wait a minute, Terry," I said. "Somebody I need to speak to."

He stopped with bad grace. "Hurry it up, all right?"

I walked across the enclosure to the crumpled little man in a gray suit much too heavy for the afternoon temperature. He smiled uncertainly as I approached.

"Clarence," I said with quiet disgust, "you don't have to trail me *everywhere.*"

"No, no, not at all," he said worriedly, his eyes following a pair of sweet-legged juniors paddling the ball back and forth nearby. "No problem at all, sir. I enjoyed watching you, as a matter of fact. I say, you men really strike the ball with ferocity, don't you? Such power! Such speed! I am suitably impressed. On the court you really are a Two-Gun, aren't you, now!"

I shifted my duffel bag, made heavier by the sweat-soaked knee brace. "I really wish you didn't choose to follow me. How did you locate me here anyway?"

His pie-dough face wreathed itself in a pleased grin that displayed his gold tooth to its best sunshine advantage. "Clever, eh?"

"Clarence." I took the lapel of his wool suit. "Don't do this. Don't trail me. You're smart enough to know that you might draw more attention to me—make it even more unlikely that I can ever accomplish a damned thing over here."

He reached up casually and enclosed my wrist in his fingers. He closed his hand. It felt like powerful robot-fingers around my wrist. Very gently, he removed my hand from his lapel, then released me. "Oh, I'll be discreet, sir," he said in his usual gentle tone. "Believe me."

Reassessing him, I rubbed my wrist. "Try harder to be discreet, okay?"

His mobile face saddened. "Pardon me, sir. I merely wish to carry out my assignment. Mr. McWilliams—"

"I can't have you blowing my cover just because your people have spotted a two-bit thief in the neighborhood."

Hell, was he going to cry? "I shall endeavor to remain further in the background, sir. Now if you could discuss with me your plans for the next few days, it would—"

"I've got somebody waiting for me over there. We'll have to talk later."

He absorbed this information with the sad stoicism of a habitual gambler who has just shot craps again. He tipped his hat. "Yes, sir. Of course. Perhaps this evening?"

"I'll try."

"Yes, sir. Thank you. Good day." He turned his back on me and wobbled away.

I joined Terry and we motored back to my hotel. Early evening was coming on. I was reasonably worn out but pleased by how my wind and my knee had held out. Terry wanted to have dinner and talk some more. I made an excuse to get out of that.

I went to my room, leaned my rackets against the dresser just inside the door, took another shower and put on fresh clothes, and took some Tylenol for the knee. Then I rested a while. Still no message or signal from the big people.

I was flat on the bed, eyes closed and brain in neutral, when the soft tap sounded on my door. Wondering whether it was Terry or the beautiful lady named Linda or (I hoped not) Clarence Tune or (most likely) the maid, I got up and thoughtlessly unlocked and opened.

The face was familiar. Mr. McWilliams looked a lot like his jail pictures.

The pistol he shoved in my face was a brand with which I was not familiar.

It was ugly, though, and heavy-looking, grayish metal, with a shape almost like a truncated pyramid in front. The silencer looked shiny and new.

Seeing that much took less than a second. McWilliams didn't give me any more time. His lips twisted and he squeezed his hand convulsively. I actually saw the hammer start back. *So he was stupid—it was a semi-automatic you had to shoot double-action on the first shot unless you had cocked the hammer.*

Which gave me part of another second.

I reflexively jerked my hands up the way you'll do when someone throws something at your face. Both hands cracked his wrists, knocking the gun upward. It made a nasty, muffled puking sound and shot fiery particles in my face. Plaster showered down from the ceiling. McWilliams, sobbing an obscenity, stepped back a half-step and aimed at my midsection, convulsively clenching the gun again.

Nothing happened. I blinked and he looked down at the gun. Its action gaped open, a thick, spent 9 mm. cartridge stuck up at an angle, pulled from the chamber but hung in the extractor.

"Jesus, Mary and Joseph," he muttered, and actually tried with both hands to clear the jam.

Two of my nice boron rackets still leaned against the dresser just inside the door. I grabbed one and hammered it down across his wrists. He bellowed, the gun hit the carpeted floor of the hallway, I swung again and missed, and he decided to get the hell out of there.

He ran down the hall to my right, headed for the stairwell sign at the far end. I dropped my racket and picked up his gun. Either he or the drop had freed the mechanism. I snapped a shot after him and the pistol went off satisfyingly, blowing a nice hole in the wall about six feet behind him as he ducked through the exit doorway. Ears ringing, I tried to fire again. Nothing. The gun had jammed again.

Awkwardly trying to get the hot, spent cartridge out of there, I half-ran to the door at hall's end. I wasn't really thinking. But in a tennis match, or on the golf course, when you get your opponent on the run you don't go passively to the locker room so he can rest, plot new strategy, and come back another day.

I had just enough sense to pause before opening the stairwell door. Didn't hear anything beyond. Tore part of a fingernail off, but got the spent cartridge out, and saw the slide go home, chambering a fresh round.

Unless McWilliams had another gun, the advantage now seemed to be mine. I was still running on impulse anyway, not taking time to think things out. I jerked the door open and saw dingy, empty metal stairs, bare walls, no hiding place. And noise of feet on the stairs somewhere below.

I headed down, one floor, a second, then a third. Below me somewhere a door slammed. *Above* me somewhere a door slammed, too, and somebody started down after me. Maybe there had been two of them. Maybe I was sandwiched. Maybe—

No more maybes. I couldn't stay *here.*

A few flights farther down, I realized I had reached the basement. I came to a dead-end corridor, one steel door firmly closed, the other ajar. The open one had a metal sign on it. *MAINTE-NANCE*, it said. That made sense; hadn't Tune said McWilliams worked for the hotel? I hauled the steel door open.

Inside, another corridor, dingier. Bare concrete floor. Dust. The sounds of electric motors and things humming away nearby. Otherwise, deep silence. Had I guessed wrong? If so, I had missed any chance I might have. If not, I had to be careful.

At the end of the short corridor I met two more doors. Again only one was unlocked. Beyond the doorway the sound of motors was a lot louder, and I could see the corner of a squat, heavy piece of machinery of some kind. It had round corners and metallic bulges and it was painted a bright, ugly green.

I slipped the door open a few more inches and risked a peek, keeping my head back as far as possible. A row of the green monsters marched along one side of the room, which had a high ceiling laced with pipes, tubing and electrical cables. To my right, three more big widgets, looking like inverted metal icecream cones, sprouted webs of cable out the top. The room smelled of electricity and oil, and the floor vibrated. Maybe it was the central heating system, maybe power for elevators and other automatic equipment, maybe something else entirely. Didn't matter.

Inside the room the hum became a steady, sullen roar that made my skull vibrate, hurt deep down in the ear. A malevolent, all-penetrating noise I didn't like for the additional reason that it masked slight sounds of movement. Two steps into the giant room, alongside the first of the green monsters, I stopped in my tracks and realized how easy it would be for McWilliams to be standing in the little alley between two machines, a lethal wrench in hand. *Oh-oh, I don't like this any more.*

I hated to back up, though. Only an idiot could fail to appreciate that I was still alive by the hairline margin of his prior stupidity and my good luck. My reactions had been fast and correct, but a smarter assassin would be pouring his tea by now and I would be a pile of rapidly cooling meat. Next time he might be smarter and/or my year's quota of luck might have run out.

I realized how out of breath I was, how sweat-slippery the pistol was in my hand, how scary this was. *Make up your mind, idiot.*

At that moment the door behind me slammed against the wall. I spun.

"Don't shoot, Mr. Smith! Don't shoot!" Clarence Tune, eyes startled eggwhite wide behind his thick glasses, held both hands over his head, making his baggy suitcoat flap. "It is I, sir!"

I lowered the gun. "Christ, Tune! Don't you ever—"

Behind me—again, but this time somewhere deep in the machine room—footsteps scuffled. I swung back around to see McWilliams racing from behind a generator, heading for a back door only six feet from him.

"Stop!" I yelled, badly surprised again.

He didn't so much as veer. He grabbed the doorhandle. *Shoot or let him get away. Which?*

No time to philosophize. I aimed and fired.

To my considerable surprise I hit him. The bullet knocked him violently into the door just as it had started to open, crashing it shut again. He collapsed onto the concrete floor, made one grotesque, violent flopping movement, and lay perfectly still.

"Oh, dear, oh dear," Tune murmured, pressing past me and taking the gun—jammed again—out of my hands with a deft twisting motion that brooked no argument. He walked slowly to the end of the room where McWilliams lay. Looked down. Knelt gingerly and reached down to probe for McWilliams' carotid.

I stood where I was. Shock and disgust sludged through my veins.

After a moment Tune climbed back to his feet with what seemed an infinite weariness. Turned, fixed me with those sagging eyes. "He could not have gotten away for long, Mr. Smith. It really would have been an aid to us if we could have questioned him."

"Is he dead?" I asked, my voice husky.

Tune looked down at the automatic in his hand as if he had never seen one before. "I daresay you really are rather useful with one of these."

"Is he dead?" I repeated. Stupid question. But one always hopes.

"Oh, yes," Tune said softly. "You plugged him dead-center, Two-Gun. You really did."

Six

Elsewhere

Londonderry, Northern Ireland

EUGENE O'CONNOR WALKED into the grimy coffee shop up the street from the textile mill at exactly eight o'clock Tuesday morning. He found his co-conspirator, John Mudd, already waiting for him at a table in the corner, with a view of the street through a dingy window. Only a couple of other workers were here at this hour.

O'Connor slouched across the nearly deserted room and took the vacant chair facing his friend. He raised a dirty hand to signal the old man who owned the place. "Davis! Coffee if you please!"

O'Connor was seventeen years old, tall, lank, adenoidal, with a lantern jaw, hair the color of watermelon meat, and pale blue eyes that always looked like the light hurt them. He was wearing his factory clothes, dirty overalls and filthy gray cap.

O'Connor leered down the considerable length of his nose at Mudd, his friend. "John, me boy," he said, mouth gaping in a wolfish grin. "A fine good morning to you."

Mudd, also seventeen and like O'Connor a longtime dropout, gritted his teeth in an agony of apprehension. Also wearing dirty work clothing, he was as short as his friend was tall, as lumpishly overweight as O'Connor was thin, pale, his yellowish hair already thinning at the forehead. He had small, close-set eyes that had once garnered him the nickname of Piggy.

"Keep quiet!" Mudd whispered fiercely. "Keep yer voice down!"

O'Connor's lantern jaw hung stubbornly in the grin. But he

78

did lower his voice radically, and now it had a menacing edge: "Who's to hear anything bad outta me, Piggy?"

"Don't call me Piggy," Mudd whined.

"Then don't be actin' like a Piggy, if you don't want me to be callin' you Piggy, Piggy."

Mudd shuddered violently, a characteristic reaction when his emotions threatened to overwhelm him. "Goddamn ye! D' ye want people starin' at us in here?"

O'Connor started to reply, but then leaned back with insolent ease as the owner of the shop, an old man known only by his first— or last—name, limped over with coffee, cream and sugar. "Thank you, Davis, my man, thank you exceedingly, sir!"

The old man set his lips in irritation but said nothing, and limped back to his counter.

O'Connor watched him go. "Old bastard wouldna look at us like that if he knew what we're about to do."

"Keep yer voice down, keep 'er down!" Mudd implored. Miserably he began cracking the reddened knuckles of his pudgy left hand.

O'Connor leaned forward, conspiratorial. "The stuff is packed in the suitcase?"

Mudd's tiny eyes swiveled nervously around the room. "Sure. Sure. All ready."

"Fine. My stuff's ready, too. I'll be leaving as planned, then, on the evening shuttle."

Mudd nodded jerkily. "I foller tomorrow." He sipped his coffee, shakily dribbling some down his chin.

O'Connor studied him with unconcealed disgust. "And we meet again Thursday afternoon there at the shop off Lambeth."

"Yes. Yes." Mudd continued to let his eyes slide nervously around.

O'Connor tried to buck him up: "The hardest part is over, Piggy. We've got the guns and we've got the plastique. My friend will have the van for us. All we got to do now is observe our feller, and know when is the right time and place to strike."

"Be quiet, be quiet," Mudd whispered in agony.

O'Connor glanced around. "Nobody can possibly be hearin' us. Try and relax a little, Piggy! The only damn thing that could git us caught now is your infernal scarededness!"

The thought seemed to penetrate Mudd's dense skull. He actually squared his plump shoulders a bit and twisted his face into a ghastly imitation of a smile.

"That's better," O'Connor told him, grinning back. "We're just two pals, havin' a cup before we go home after the night shift. Right?"

Mudd's eyes glazed. He tried to insert his index finger into his right nostril. "I'm scared."

"People think we're shit," O'Connor reminded him. "From the time we was in school, people told us we were shit. Now they treat us like shit, they look at us like shit, they talk to us like shit, we *are* shit. Whose fault is that, but the filthy prots? Who never had 'ny right to be here in Ireland. Who caused the death of your beloved father, Piggy—your very own father! Have you forgotten that?"

Mudd squinted and focused. Thought processes made his face twist and grimace. "I remember everything."

"Then," O'Connor went on, repeating the spiel, "along comes a man like Sean Cork. An Irishman. A tennis player. One of our own. And what does he do? He blathers about keepin' the peace. He acts like we should *surrender!* And what does anybody do about the traitor? What does the IRA seem to be doing? What does the URA? Or *anybody?*"

Mudd frowned, trying to remember. "Nothing?"

"Nothing!" O'Connor repeated. "Nothing! But after we get done, Piggy, by God the traitors like Sean Cork will know their money an' their glamor an' their fancy words can't protect 'em! An' do you know what we're gonna be when word gits out that we're the ones that struck a mighty blow, Piggy? Do you know that?"

Mudd nodded swiftly. "Hero. Us. Heroes."

"That's right, Piggy. Goddam IRA and everybody else will

have to look up to us then. They'll *all* regret thinking we're scum, thinking we're just dumb shits. We're gonna be heroes! Us! An' we're doing it all on our own, without no help from nobody!"

Langley, Virginia

J. C. Kinkaid and Collie Davis walked into Tom Dwight's office. Dwight, his desk covered with photographs and printed matter, looked up at them with all the good humor of a waked-up bear.

"What's happened now?" Kinkaid asked. "Brad hasn't—?"

"No," Dwight snapped. "The Brits are going to keep McWilliams' death quiet. So Brad is still all right on that score, and we've taken new steps. That isn't what we need to talk about."

"What, then?"

Dwight shoved some of the photos across his desk. "Look."

Dwight nodded. "It has legitimate uses, too, of course. One of our 'friends' must be re-selling it to people like Khadafy."

Davis pointed to the photo. "If all this is thiodiglycol, there's enough to manufacture—"

"Plenty of death," Dwight interrupted.

The silence in the room extended. Outside somewhere a telephone could be heard ringing. It went silent as someone answered it.

"Where did this stuff go?" Davis asked.

"We don't know."

"Don't know!"

"We think the ship sailed to Greece. We think this stuff was off-loaded there. We further think it was then flown to someplace in West Germany. We also think its final destination point was to be Belfast."

Kinkaid looked blankly at his superior. "Well, then, no problem. Re-aim a satellite. Notify all our people. This much stuff can't be carried into Northern Ireland in a suitcase, for God's sake. We can intercept it."

"That might be a possibility," Dwight countered, "except for the timing factor."

Kinkaid and Davis looked at Dwight, then at each other.

"Oh, brother," Davis muttered finally.

Kinkaid grimaced. "All right. I'll ask. How long did it take somebody to fish this stuff out of the computers and recognize what we might have seen? —When were these pictures taken?"

"Three weeks ago," Dwight said.

"Hell! Then by now, the stuff could be—" Kinkaid stopped.

Dwight grimly finished the sentence for him: "Anywhere."

Seven

"MAYBE," LINDA BENNETT told me cooly Wednesday morning, "you should just calm down and trust COS to know what we're doing."

"That would be easier," I told her, "if I had any confidence the Chief of Station or anybody else *did* know what we were doing."

A frown momentarily tightened her pretty brows. But she was good; the sign of impatience was gone as quickly as it had come. "Everything is under control."

"Right. But *whose* control?"

"Look, Brad. COS is not a kid. He's experienced in these matters. We have a plan laid out for us by the planners back home."

"Nobody had Ivor McWilliams in the plan."

"That's still being evaluated."

I gave up. She was cool and I was still stressed out after Monday night's attack. I felt a little ashamed of myself. But Linda and COS could be cool easier than I could. Looking right down the barrel of a gun is not your basic pleasant experience. Killing a man is worse. Much worse.

She idly stirred her tea. I noticed, not for the first time, what beautiful hands she had: long, gracefully tapered fingers, red-tipped, but with a look of competent strength about them. We were in the tearoom of one of the smaller hotels not far from the Cumberland, and at this midmorning hour we had only a lone businessman halfway across the room and a middle-aged couple farther away for company. The lone man looked too preoccupied and possibly hung over to notice us at all, and I had heard the couple speaking Italian. So

83

at least our meeting seemed secure, and to a casual onlooker would have looked like the usual thing: the aging former tennis star following up on a chance meeting with a beautiful younger fan, probably hustling her every way he could think of.

Bigtime tennis players—even has-beens like me—never had a problem finding available women. When you're an athlete, the women find you. They tend to be everywhere and, because they're often of the type to whom physical appearances and mythology are everything, they tend to be stunning. The predictable roster runs from 14 to 60 with youth predominating. But I once heard about a wealthy lady from Hialeah almost old enough to draw Social Security who still had enough of her looks left—and was so outrageous both in her pursuit and the things she did after she got her prey's undivided attention—that her list of conquests read like the opening bracket of a major tournament.

So maybe Linda Bennett looked like part of that passing parade. She had done nothing today to emphasize herself. Her dress was almost severe, a plain gray with long sleeves and medium length, and her heels were of medium height. She had done her hair simply, so that it fell loose and virtually without curl. Little makeup, again no jewelry. Despite all that, she was dramatically lovely: tall, lissome, her large green eyes striking, her long legs fetching whether she willed it so or not. And I had done my part to look the role of a fading sports roue by coming to our meeting in dirty Adidas, sloppy gray sweats, and a rain jacket that hadn't been very neat even before it crossed the Atlantic at the bottom of my suitcase.

"As I told you," Linda resumed, "we stick to the original plan. When Sean Cork arrives, you strike up a friendship if you can. You watch for any sign of trouble around him. You saw all the known terrorist mug shots. You might spot one of them. In the meantime, the McWilliams incident is being analyzed, but no one believes his alleged attack was connected directly to any organized terrorist group. His psychological profile—"

" 'Alleged' attack" I interrupted. "Are we now questioning whether he did or did not try to blow my head off?"

She flushed at that. "No. Slip of the tongue."

"Which may reflect a prevailing attitude?"

"Christ." Her eyebrows knit in irritation. "Are we ever paranoid!"

I was perversely pleased to have finally gotten her goat. So, since I was feeling crabby and contrary as hell—my usual reactions to being deeply scared—I backed off: "Sorry. None of it's your fault."

She regained control. "Let's review. The night before last, this man McWilliams made an amateurish attempt on your life."

"I hope you won't think I'm being a prig if I point out that amateurs often succeed."

"Granted, Smith," she sighed, disgusted with me again. "It was a serious attempt and he bungled it and you got lucky, but none of that changes the fact that you might have been done in."

"Let us not use euphemisms. Let's just say 'killed.' 'Done in' might mean anything. If the gun had worked properly, my brains would not be here where I like them best, but probably in a lab bucket somewhere."

She colored. "Killed, then. Yes. You were very heroic, and we all realize how honored we all should be simply to bask in the radiance of your wonderfulness. Now will you please give me a break?"

"I want a gun."

"I can ask, but you know what the answer will be."

"Ask COS anyway. Tell him I'm being an asshole."

"I can tell the truth, you mean?"

I didn't answer that.

She ticked off some points for me. "We have no evidence he was with the IRA, or hired by the IRA, or even sympathetic to the IRA. Our British cousins have no evidence either. He was given some money by a source none of us have been able to identify yet. Either he was an absolute maniac who picked you out because you were easily identifiable as a celebrity of sorts from pictures in the press, or he was acting as a contract killer. Which would explain the money. Our investigation makes him a penny-ante thug who probably went crackers during his last jail term and picked you out of the papers to kill as a sort of mad gesture against society. 'Spoil Wimbledon for some people,' et cetera." She paused, awaiting my reaction.

"Okay," I said. "I don't buy it, but go on."

"Thanks to MI5 and their clout with the police, McWilliams's death received absolutely no publicity of any kind. His family knows, of course; they buried him this morning. But nothing got out to the general public. So—if our line of theory is correct—your job inside the tournament really hasn't been compromised in any significant way, and you're to press on with it."

"Recognizing, of course," I pointed out, "that if you're wrong, the people who sicced McWilliams on me will try again."

She ignored that. "Two additional operational decisions have been made. Number one, there is a lot of concern and puzzlement about how MI5 so quickly identified your real reasons for being here, and what they're really up to with this assignment of Clarence Tune to be your shadow. A lot of your assignment concerning possible terrorist activity is essentially passive, but it's felt we might learn more, and more quickly, if you can turn Tune's assignment to our advantage. With that in mind, your instructions are to cooperate with him in every possible way. Snuggle up to the little guy. Talk to him about the case. Watch for slips; encourage them. Be alert if he happens to drop any other names. We think he's somehow trying to use you. So let's have *you* use *him*. Take him to dinner. Get an invitation to his house if you can. Anything. Let's see if there's something there that he—and his masters at MI5—might know which we don't."

"Lovely," I groaned. "So all I've got to do is befriend the albatross."

She ignored that, too. "Number two," she went on crisply, "it's been decided that the usual signal system might not provide sufficiently quick and continuous contact between you and Drake—or Kinkaid when he gets here. Also, on the off-chance that the McWilliams incident *was* part of a larger scheme, COS wants another operator near you at all times. Therefore, they want you and me to follow up on that chance meeting we had at the cafe, and this tête-à-tête, in case anybody observes it."

I studied her expression, which I couldn't read. "Do you want to spell it out for me, please?"

Her eyes swept up and met mine, and I saw in them an expression I certainly had never seen there before. "Yes," she said briskly. "We've started a little scenario here where I'm the sports-crazy female fan who spied you by accident at the cafe and practically went out of my mind, I was so thrilled. I'm unattached, my usual visible job is as a computer networking specialist outside the embassy, and I really do love tennis. You're unattached, you're here far from home, and I approached you." She paused and looked across the room at nothing. "So. We start seeing each other more openly. From all outward appearances, we start to become . . . attracted."

"Oh."

She turned those amazing eyes back to mine. "So I can . . . be around a lot. You see?"

"So," I said, "I snuggle up to Tune, and I—" I stopped and thought better of it. She was too nice for the cheap shot. "—I spend more time with you, as if we were really hitting it off."

"Yes."

"Any ideas of how we start?"

"Yes." Brisk again. "We have dinner at the hotel tonight. Contrive to let me meet the Carpomans and possibly some of the others, if they'll be around."

"Some will, but not many of the top players. Some are still at the French, of course, and some are playing at Beckenham this week."

"Okay. At any rate I ought to go watch you practice tomorrow."

"Fine," I said, feeling somewhat more cheerful. "And I hope all this leads to my actually getting some information that will help."

"It better," she said, and looked grim for an instant.

"Did that look mean there's new information?" I asked.

"It seems they now think a large shipment of mustard gas, or the stuff to make it, is in Northern Ireland. Anti-Terrorist Group over here has reported possible sighting of two known members of the URA near London. Sean Cork received another illiterate—but very explicit—death threat in the mail in Paris. He'll never live to see Wimbledon, it said. Let's order more tea."

Walking back to the Cumberland alone, I felt my mood sink a notch lower. I had tried to pry something further out of Linda, with no results. I knew she probably didn't have much more anyhow. You work in these things and they tell you only as much as they think you have to know to carry out your part. Sometimes I believe they tell you even less on the theory that you might learn more if you're wide open to *any* possibility because you don't focus narrowly out of preconceived ideas of what might be important. You've heard of the blind leading the blind? Precisely.

I didn't feel good working this way, although I had done it before. And on a scale of one to ten, my time since Ivor McWilliams had been a minus six anyway.

Clarence Tune had moved with astonishing swiftness after giving me the unwelcome information that my single shot had flown too true. He had told me to go back to my room and I had obeyed him. There I tried to make an emergency call to let the embassy know what was going on, but my line was mysteriously dead. Within thirty minutes two plainclothesmen from the London police had been in the room, with Tune and two other men accompanying them. There was a lot of questioning. Once or twice Tune's more authoritative companion had stopped it with a statement such as, "Well, gentlemen, we can really dispense with that line, can we not?" or "That will be enough in this vein, eh?" The big man from the Home Office making sure we didn't talk about security matters. Then they all went away except for Tune, who stayed right with me, murmuring inane small talk and calling me Two-Gun once more before I told him to shut the hell up.

We stayed in. He wouldn't leave. I had a drink and then a lot of drinks. Then I got sick. He clucked and looked sad and watched the telly. I felt like a fool, among other things.

I also felt like a murderer.

Rationality told me that a big, stupid clown I knew nothing about had come to my room with every intention of blowing my brains all over the ceiling, and that when I had shot him a few minutes later I had been acting in response to that. By most civilized standards I had been justified.

"Justified" had nothing to do with how I felt, however.

I knew that Tune and his superiors—like my own faceless controllers—bitterly regretted my fatal shooting of McWilliams. If he had been taken alive, they might have gotten invaluable information out of him. Corpses don't make good witnesses. So from their point of view I had simply screwed up. Regrettable. Press on.

What kept playing back in my mind's eye was the way he had straightened convulsively, then pitched forward in a heap, his life breathing out of him in one ugly convulsion. I hadn't known him; there was no sentimentality in my feelings about him—no wondering when he had gone wrong, whether he had ever wept over the death of a parent or child, no speculation about what kind of universal passions we had shared, unknowing. My reaction was simpler. I was a living creature. He was too. I killed him. The bullet had shattered his spine and sent a massive impact shock wave through his body, rupturing his heart and brain. One instant he had been a man like me, and the next he had been *nothing.*

I think people with religious faith make better killers for a cause. They can always summon a principle, invoke a scripture, recite a parable, stand on a righteous justification. Even more important, they can always cite a higher cause and trust in a greater power. The philosophy reduced to its meanest cruelty in Vietnam: *"Kill 'em all; let God sort 'em out. "*

What did you do when you didn't have a sackful of certitudes handy? Even worse, when there was no way you could delude yourself into thinking he might have gone to a better place, was "out of his misery," had been punished for transgressions, was part of some larger scheme? Where did you find bogus consolation when you felt reasonably sure that this life was *it,* that there was no God up in the sky or anywhere else except maybe somewhere inside your own momentary consciousness? How did you forgive yourself when you had ended a life if you felt pretty sure that there wasn't anything or anywhere or anytime else, and that what you had taken from a man was all he had ever had, or ever would have had?

I had not expected Ivor McWilliams when I accepted the assignment. I had not expected this. Once before, on an island called St. Maarten, I had killed a man. That had been in direct self-defense, and his death had been as much because of accident as because of anything done by me. So I had been able to square that one . . . after a while.

Perhaps I would get square with myself some day about shooting McWilliams in the middle of his back as he ran, defenseless, like a scared rabbit. I didn't feel that way at the moment.

So the operation was just getting under way and I was already sick of it and sick of myself as well as my part in it. *Damn the Brits and Northern Ireland,* I thought, *and damn the Catholics and the Protestants, and damn all irreconcilable conflicts, and damn people for being so stupid, and damn Collie Davis and all his kind, and damn me for playing with them.* What did I expect to gain? Who did I think I might help?

Well, welcome to the real, grownup world, Brad Smith. You killed a man. Stop sniveling. Get with the program. Act like a man. When the going gets tough, the tough get going.

My father's voice, as clear inside my head as if he had not been dead—and *finished, out of existence forever*—lo these many years. Why don't their voices die when they do? Why do they have to achieve the only kind of immortality any of us will ever have by becoming a witch-voice inside the heads of their kids?

When I finally slept that night, with Clarence Tune still collapsed in my hotel room chair, staring at some bizarre, unfunny Brit "comedy" on the telly, it was as much the whisky as anything else. In the morning, however, the sun was shining outside the hotel and

Tune acted bravely cheerful, and I listened to the ghost voice of my father in my head, then had a shower and tried to get with the program. My morning workout with Terry Carpoman went better than the first one. My bad knee bent better and I got more low ones back. He got violently angry only once and did not sulk long afterwards.

After lunch the knee ached seriously. A long whirlpool soak helped. I met with one of the advance men arranging the U.S. audio feed for the British video that would be sent by satellite back to America. A dismaying distance across the city, Wimbledon officials had a downtown press conference to talk about stadium and court preparations and plans for bracketing. Wearing my press hat, I attended. Then went back to the hotel, hauled out the laptop computer, and did a short—and I hoped light-hearted—piece on Evert and Connors, together again for the network shows.

It was clear by that evening that nothing was going to come out about Ivor McWilliams. Brad Gilbert, Tim Mayotte, Horacio De La Pena and a couple of other players showed up at the hotel. Those of us without an entourage met for dinner and fretted about transportation, the food and prize money distribution. Ostentatiously putting my notebook on the table so everyone would be sure I was playing journalist, I asked some questions, but not too many. The guys cooperated with good nature and gave me some useful quotes.

Later the candy was delivered to my room along with Linda's handwritten note effusively thanking me for being so sweet when we met at the cafe. In response I made the telephone call from a public phone and got my summons to the next afternoon's meeting with her. That was the meeting I had now just finished.

Back at the hotel I found Terry Carpoman pacing around the lobby like a player on the bubble, waiting to see if he got a seed. He bounded over to me, gorgeous young body making the blue sweats look like sweats ought to look in motion.

"You're late!" he complained with a frown. "If we're going to get in another workout, we've got to get moving!"

"I didn't know about another scheduled workout, Terry."

His jaw fell. "I told you this morning! Goddamn, Brad, you're acting like you don't *care* if we win this thing!"

I didn't remember his saying a word about it. Realized he probably had, and I wasn't paying attention. "Sorry," I told him. "Met a lady and I guess my mind was elsewhere."

He continued to look blank, digesting that. Then he filed it and leered. "Life in the old goat yet, right?"

"Right."

"Well, go get your stuff and let's haul ass, if you can still walk."

I got and we hauled. We put in a long workout and I felt my timing starting to sharpen. It requires months of the most intense preparation for even the greatest athletes to come back from a layoff. Even John McEnroe took a long time to return to anything remotely resembling his old form after a long layoff. I was never going to get back to anything approaching real tournament readiness again. But recent months of running in the mountains, and long hours on the court, had gotten me far readier than I had any right to be.

Sean Cork, out of the French now, still did not show up here.

Late in the afternoon, Clarence Tune tapped on my door and entered diffidently after I unlocked. He looked older and tireder, and so did his suit. "A word with you, sir?"

"Do I have a choice?"

With a deep sigh he sat on the end of my bed. The reek of failure spread out through the room. "About Mr. McWilliams."

I didn't say anything.

"It seems," Tune said reluctantly, "we have a modicum of information concerning the person who gave him the mysterious money prior to his attack on you. We wish to discuss this intelligence with you—compare notes, as it were."

"What do you think I can tell you?"

"Well." He almost writhed with discomfort. "It has been suggested, sir, that an *exchange* of information might be useful. Which is to say, we provide you with what little we have, in exchange for which you might provide us with some data that might be of use to us."

"What kind of data?"

"That, sir, I don't know. You see, sir, we really have no idea what you know and what you do not know."

"Well I can answer that, Clarence. I know very, very little. I've been dropped in here cold."

He took that in and thought about it. He looked, if anything, sadder. "Well, then," he said at last. "Let me brief you on our information about Mr. McWilliams and the man who gave him money, and we shall see if there is anything at all you might contribute. Needless to say, all of us might benefit greatly if we could identify this man and apprehend him."

"Needless."

"All right, then." Tune took out his battered old notebook, flipped dog-eared pages. Columbo after his Social Security kicked in. "It seems that our man observing Mr. McWilliams' neighborhood saw Mr. McWilliams twice meeting a person at a pub not far from his flat. On the first occasion the stranger sat beside Mr. Mc-Williams at the bar, and they had a pint together. On the second occasion, they again had a pint, and talked quite a long while. Then a few days later, our informant happened to notice the same gentleman—this time driving a small delivery lorry—taking a package to Mr. McWilliams's flat."

"Same man for sure?" I asked.

"Yes, our informant is quite sure it was the same man."

"Not a known police character?"

"No, sir. Allow me to describe the man for you. There is always the possibility he might, ah, appear in your vicinity. Also, my superiors suggest the remote chance that you would recognize the description."

"Go ahead."

He sighed and consulted his notes. "The gentleman is described as of rather average height, perhaps five feet, nine inches.

Quite thin. He was wearing heavy work shoes of the type that can be fitted with thick soles to bolster height. He has dark hair, quite long. A dark beard, very full. Which could have been a disguise. Very pale complexion. Perhaps he has been ill recently." Tune looked up at me expectantly.

"Doesn't sound familiar," I told him.

"One more item, then, sir. Our observer heard his voice—although not the words he spoke—in the pub. Our observer was struck by the man's voice. He described it as very soft, rather high-pitched, almost feminine, in contradistinction to the man's otherwise quite-masculine appearance. He said the voice was very distinguishing, almost a woman's voice, very quiet and singularly high-pitched, perhaps with a slight lisp."

Tune stopped and looked hard at me. "What is it, Two-Gun?"

"What?" I said.

"What is it?" he repeated.

"Nothing," I told him.

It couldn't be. It just couldn't be. It had to be a coincidence—or a trick in my mind growing out of the old nightmares.

But sitting there, feeling Tune's watery eyes bore into me, I chilled.

Coincidence?

Mistake?

I wanted very badly to think so. But I didn't.

The description of the unidentified man's voice was too good—too accurate. I had never heard more than one voice as unusual as the one just described. It was a voice I would never forget.

It belonged to the KGB assassin who had twice taken me to the edge: Sylvester.

Eight
Elsewhere

London

SYLVESTER'S THURSDAY EVENING shuttle flight from Belfast landed
on time at Heathrow. He rode the train into Victoria Station, then
took a taxi into Mayfair, where he lost himself—and any possible
surveillance—for almost an hour. Then he hailed another taxi and
went directly to the embassy in Kensington. It was dark when he
arrived in answer to the Chief Resident's summons.

Inside, still brushing raindrops from his trenchcoat, he met
Mikhail Gravitch in the KGB official's inner office.

Gravitch, his shirtsleeves half-rolled, paced the floor. "Information: a man named McWilliams made an attempt on the American's life," he began.

Sylvester played dumb. "The American—?"

Gravitch glared at him. "Smith! Brad Smith!"

"This is news!" Sylvester exclaimed. "The man succeeded, I
hope?"

"The effort was bungled. McWilliams was killed. Smith was
unhurt."

"Unfortunate," Sylvester said.

Gravitch stiffened. "Unfortunate, you say? When the policy
of keeping hands entirely off Smith has been made abundantly
clear?"

Sylvester made an elaborate shrug. "I assume we had nothing
to do with it. But am I to pretend I would not be pleased if Brad
Smith died?"

Gravitch smacked a big fist into his open palm. It made a sur-

95

prisingly sharp, nasty sound. "God damn it, Yuli! That pig, Lemlek, tried to file a report to Moscow suggesting someone from this office might have been involved in the attempt on the American. He mentioned no names, but his draft was filled with references to threats to our internal security due to uncontrolled activity by one of our own people. You *know* who he was referring to."

Sylvester maintained his stoic calm. "You were able to stop the report?"

"Yes. *This* time. But the swine will try again, perhaps through the diplomatic pouch." Gravitch stopped pacing and fixed Sylvester with a baleful stare. "You *assure* me you knew nothing of the attack on Smith?"

Now it was time to don the mask of outraged innocence. "Of course I did not! I went to Ulster as ordered. I have been there this week, getting a place to stay and a part-time job in a bakery—laying the groundwork to carry out my assigned work!"

Gravitch studied him with narrowed eyes. The KGB Resident was clearly uncertain.

Sylvester added stiffly, "I would welcome Brad Smith's death. All I would hope, if someone said he had been killed, is that they could also tell me he died only after a long period of suffering. But your orders were clear. If I am ever again going to get new assignments worthy of my talents, this damnable blot on my record must be expunged. I have to prove I am as reliable as always. —Mikhail! It would be professional suicide for me to disobey your orders in this matter—to let personal vendetta threaten my chances of full reinstatement and reinsertion into the U.S."

"How do you explain this man McWilliams's assassination attempt?" Gravitch's voice had moderated somewhat, and although it was still tinged by suspicion, Sylvester's carefully planned responses seemed to have made him less certain. "Who else would hire a scoundrel like McWilliams to kill Smith?"

"I don't know. But if I had wanted to trick you and have Brad Smith killed, *I* would not have gone to an amateur!"

"Who, then?"

"How am I to know that, comrade? Someone in the IRA itself. Or for all you have told me thus far, how do we know this man— his name?"

"McWilliams."

Pretending to forget the name, Sylvester thought, had been a nice touch. "McWilliams. Yes. —How do we know McWilliams did not pick Smith out of a newspaper photograph, and waylay him on the street in a clumsy attempt at freelance robbery?"

Gravitch turned and walked to the window, staring out into the inner courtyard. "The attack did not take place on the street."

Sylvester said nothing to that. Another good trick, he congratulated himself. He waited.

When Gravitch finally turned back from the window, his expression had changed again. The anger had faded, to be replaced by an implacable calm. "I had to be sure, my friend. You understand that."

And you are no more sure than you were when I walked in, Sylvester thought. *But you are at least uncertain. So now you will pretend reassurance. And scrutinize every move I make, watching for a telltale slip on my part.* "Of course, Comrade Gravitch. It is of no consequence."

Gravitch walked to his desk, sat down, flipped open his box of Havanas, and offered it to Sylvester. The two men admired and clipped their cigars, and shared the KGB chief's lighter. Their smoke curled toward the ornate plaster panels of the ceiling high over their heads.

"We will speak no more of it," Gravitch said. "The attempt complicates matters for us in some ways, but that is no concern of yours. Please tell me briefly what progress in Ulster."

When he left the embassy an hour later, Sylvester felt like he had a boat anchor digging its hooks into his intestines. Frustration made his teeth grate audibly. *Damn* the fool McWilliams for his incompetence! Damn Gravitch's suspicions. Damn everything!

Hunching his coat around his neck, he walked south to the far end of the park and then turned east, continuing on, automatically putting space between himself and any connection with the embassy, using various automatic tricks to lose any possible surveillance.

Brad Smith had heaped professional disgrace on Sylvester's head, had caused him almost two years of physical agony, and remained the only living blot on the reputation Sylvester had prized. In his stupid, bungling way, it had been Smith who fouled the Belgrade operation and made it necessary for Sylvester to kill the man who had once been an operative as respected as he himself had been. And it had been Smith again who made it possible for the CIA to destroy the St. Maarten link. Then Sylvester had blundered Smith's murder, and almost paid the price with his own life. For that blunder, Sylvester had his memories of the agony, a permanent pain in his chest, a slight limp, a wholly reconstructed face that burned and ached most of the time.

Sylvester might have found the discipline to let all that pass.

But more important than any of it was another, unassailable fact: Brad Smith was the only enemy alive who might now recognize him.

Not the face, with this beard. But perhaps from the physique and stance. And almost certainly from Sylvester's distinctive voice.

The voice was the one thing completely unchanged about him. The surgeons had been able to do nothing about that. In the right—or wrong—circumstances, Smith might begin to make guesses from Sylvester's body conformations and movements. Given the chance to hear Sylvester's voice, a man of Smith's acuity would recognize the man behind the new face without question.

Sylvester knew that Gravitch—and those above him—discounted this danger. Either they knew they would never again assign Sylvester into an area where he might have the remotest chance of encountering Smith, or they had already decided the risk was too great, and Sylvester would never have a crucial assignment of any kind again—ever.

In either case it was intolerable. Sylvester's life had been built around his training, his fanatic belief in the war against Capitalism,

his value in the fight. The only way he could ever feel sure of significant assignments again was for Brad Smith to be dead.

And beyond any rational explanation was the scalding emotion
in Sylvester's belly, a feeling that he had imagined he, as a professional, could never feel: total unreasoning blood lust. He hated
Smith and would never rest until he was dead. Sometimes, when
he thought of the American, he actually felt his moorings to reality
start to slip—the thoughts and feelings coming at random, with
frightening intensity. Smith had to die. The hate made it so. Sylvester felt he would never be sane again until Smith was dead.

This was the ruling fact of his life, taking precedence even over
his own professional discipline and loyalty. *Smith had to die.*

Thus far, Sylvester thought, he had been lucky. His brief meetings with Ivor McWilliams had not been observed. His cover had
been perfect during the visit as a delivery boy.

There was always a chance, however, that MI5 might question
people in McWilliams's neighborhood. The chance was slim that
someone might provide a useful description of him. But he could
not afford to risk that chance. Brad Smith might be on guard now.
Comrade Gravitch's continuing suspicions must be calmed. Sylvester thought he knew how to ease all these problems.

He was not happy about his plan. The plan involved grave risks.
A dear friend would have to be sacrificed. But Sylvester had learned
long ago that his own security took top priority.

Since his arrival in England he had spent most of his time inside the embassy, letting time help him grow the beard that so
changed his appearance. On the few occasions when he had slipped
out late at night to escape for a few hours the suffocating atmos-
phere behind the embassy walls, he had retreated to a tiny apartment he had rented in a down-at-heel section of Marylebone where
no one would expect a foreign Legat to reside.

Now, however, he needed a new place. One that could be prepared as a stage setting for his plan to persuade Brad Smith and
the British that he was no longer a threat.

Old cautions had prevented him from taking more than a few

absolutely untraceable possessions to the Marylebone flat. It could be abandoned now without danger, without regret, to make way for his survival plan.

He had to act at once, then allow himself to be seen on a shuttle flight returning to Belfast.

Far from the embassy now, he hailed a taxi.

Belfast, Northern Ireland

Billy Daugherty had no hint anything was wrong.

The other four members of the group had already assembled when he walked into the tightly sealed basement room of the house in Lower Falls. A single light bulb glowed on the end of its cord, suspended from the bare wood rafters. Francis Moriarty sat behind his card-table desk of authority, a 13-round Browning automatic pistol serving as a paperweight for a few scraps of paper. The others— Hennigan, Taylor and Boyle—leaned back in straight chairs tilted back against the seep-wet stone walls.

"Billy, m'boy," the thickset, powerfully built Moriarty said in greeting. "Sit you doon."

Daugherty nodded obedience and shook hands with each of them: Hennigan the fish merchant, bloodless-thin, with a fringe of pale red hair remaining despite his age of only twenty-five; the swarthy Taylor, soot clinging to face and bare, brawny arms after his day's work at the steelworks; Boyle a skinny kid of nineteen with angry pimples in eruption all over his homely, big-nosed face. All of them wore rough work clothing and utilitarian caps, and there were no other weapons in sight, although Daugherty knew the group owned many, including a Sterling submachine gun, two Remington shotguns, an old U.S. Army Colt, a couple of Smith & Wesson revolvers, and their pride and joy, a Heckler & Koch MP5. Cigarette smoke blued the air of the hermetic room, making Daugherty's eyes sting.

"Now that we're all here," Moriarty said, folding his hands on the table in front of him, "let's get to business. First, what do we hear of the patrols the last few nights?"

Taylor bit a piece of cuticle from a blunt, mangled finger on his left hand and spit it to the floor. His fingers left new soot smudges on his liverish lips. "Hanrahan and Barker are convinced it's routine."

"Ay," Hennigan chimed in, "they have no' taken anyone in."

"The basta'ds're lookin' for somethin'," Boyle said sharply, angry as always. "It's been quiet. They got no cause."

Moriarty nodded agreement. "They're onto something."

"They've heard the same things we heard," Taylor suggested.

"But we don't know any more than we did," Daugherty chimed in cautiously. He looked at his companions. "Do we?"

"We know the stuff came in. There be too much talk for it not to be so."

"But who's got it? Where?" Daugherty appealed to Moriarty. "How can somebody be planning something this big, and none of us have a clue?"

"Maybe," Moriarty replied, "that's about to change."

Daugherty tingled. "Meaning?"

"There's a meeting tonight. Late. Down at Kirk's. I'm to go alone."

Boyle leaned forward with fierce excitement that made his pimples fiery red. "Then there *is* gonna be a big strike!"

"Don't know," Moriarty told him. "Maybe we'll be learning at this session of leaders."

"Then we'll know something at last! They're drawin' us in! We ain't goin' to be left out in the cold after all!"

"Maybe we're being drawn in," Moriarty replied, "an' maybe we ain't. All I know is there's this session. I'll be going and I'll be seeing. We meet back here later. Make it three o'clock tomorrow morning. I'll hope to have a lot more information for you then."

"I want in this thing!" Boyle protested angrily.

"We've heard the rumors it's big," Moriarty shot back at him. "Maybe we get in an' maybe we don't."

"Why woul'n't we?"

"Because, lad, the fewer know details, the lesser chance they is of somebody bein' a betrayer."

"*I* ain't no betrayer!"

"I know that, lad, I know that. But how many times in the past has they been when somebody turned around? How hard has the SAS and every bloody body else tried to get somebody inside on us? If this is what I suspect, ain't many going to be told nothing. Maybe that's all I'm going arter tonight—orders to shut my yap and stop even so much as wonderin'." Moriarty climbed out of his chair, reached for the Browning, checked it carefully, and shoved it under his belt in back, under his dark jacket. "If the best way for us to help is know little, an' keep shut up, then that's what we do. I'll go see what I see. You boys be back at three and I'll tell you how the ground lays."

He crossed the small room and unbarred the thick, badly warped oak door. It jarred open. From above, beyond another door at the head of the steps, came the sound of children at play. He looked back at each of them. "Whatever I learn—or don't—we maintain discipline. Remember that." Then he went up the stairs and was gone.

The others left at ten-minute intervals, using different outside doorways, as was the drill. Billy Daugherty was the third man to leave.

He walked the alley away from the meeting house, feet padding lightly in thin, oily puddles from the early rain. Overhead, between black angles of old brick buildings and chimneys, the clouds had partly broken and a sliver of moon showed through. Only the bottom sliver was illuminated. A Cheshire moon, they had always called it, the Cheshire cat, grinning down.

Billy had gotten the shivers when he was a tyke, and his daddy told him stories about that spooky old Cheshire moon. His momma had scolded Daddy sometimes for scaring the youngsters, but Daddy had laughed. Daddy had been enormously big and old and fine and wise, and Billy and his brothers and sisters had adored him.

Then in 1977 Daddy had been killed in a spray of gunfire erupting between the IRA and British troops. Billy's life had been changed forever.

That had been far in the north, near Derry, and the family name had not been Daugherty. Convinced that the IRA had been responsible for causing the gunfire that killed his father—destroyed his family and ended his childhood—Billy had run away, dropping from view.

He joined the British army. Later, when his background brought his file to the top, he was recruited into the SAS, the Special Air Service Regiment. More than four years ago, equipped with a new name, a new fictitious background, and even a "family" in County Louth—the man now known as Billy Daugherty had come to Belfast.

It had taken this long to be somewhat accepted inside the Moriarty group. Daugherty still was not fully trusted. Except for two messenger jobs and an insignificant part in a skirmish with British regulars on the streets which he could not have avoided in any case, he had been given no vital duties and told little.

But now, with Moriarty excited about a possible major attack in or near London some time in the not-too-distant future, Daugherty was picking up more information.

The little he knew—and had already passed on to his control—suggested that he might be close to something very big indeed. He knew his earlier reports had galvanized widespread activity in the south.

But he didn't know enough. They needed—cried for—more.

And tonight might be his chance.

Walking the black alleys alone, Daugherty knew the safest bet lay in returning to the meeting place at three as instructed. Possibly Moriarty would tell them everything—or all he knew, anyhow—then.

But the meeting at Kirk's would have other ringleaders there. Daugherty might recognize some of them.

He knew he could not get very close to Kirk's, an old pub in a section wrecked by fighting two years ago. Sentinels would be everywhere. He had to count on learning the facts from Moriarty at three. But one three-story building, gutted and deserted, remained amid the rubble less than five hundred meters from Kirk's. Daugherty thought he might be able to sneak up on the ruin and see something with his night glasses, hidden inside his shirt, from there.

Risky, yes. Lookouts would be all over the area. But Daugherty knew every crevice of the area. He knew he could get close, at least. Then, given the slightest sign of sentries, he could turn back.

Daugherty plodded on, silent in the black, mentally fuming, torn between his sense of duty and a shuddering, primitive fear.

Go! ordered the voice of duty. *Your fear doesn't count! You could learn things of tremendous importance about what they plan!*

Stay away, stay away! the other voice cried in his mind. *They will catch you and kill you. Nobody could ever accuse you of cowardice for staying away from such a risk.*

Daugherty did not know what he would do. He knew time was running out, and felt impatient anger at himself.

Then he realized where he was, and stopped in his tracks.

All the time he had been agonizing, his footsteps had been carrying him unerringly into the section of the city that centered on Kirk's.

So he had made the decision without realizing it. The voice of duty had won.

Daugherty shuddered.

London

"Thank you, sor," the old lady murmured, practically drooling as she folded Sylvester's pound notes and buried them deep in the pocket of her filthy apron. "It isn't often gents pay a month in advance, but it surely do make life simpler alla way around, don't it."

"It does indeed, Mrs. Jarvis," Sylvester said with a smile. "I shall plan to move in tomorrow, if that's convenient."

"Oh, indeed it are, Mr. Timmerman, indeed it are. You'll enjoy it here, you will. It's a nice, quiet place, and we run a clean house here, my hubby and I, we don't put up with no loud shenanigans, we don't."

"Good night, Mrs. Jarvis."

"A good night to you, Mr. Timmerman!"

Sylvester left the ratheap East Waterloo building, managed to find a taxi, and rode to the Waterloo tube station. He rode across the river to Charing Cross, where he used a public telephone. His luck was good. Motard himself answered the telephone.

"Pierre," Sylvester said, making his voice warm and hearty. "This is Max."

"Max!" Pierre Motard's voice rang with pleasure and surprise. *"How fine to hear from you, my good friend! You received my last letter?"*

"Yes," Sylvester said. "It was fine to hear from you again, my good friend!"

"Tell me! You are in Zurich?"

"No. I am calling from London, my friend."

"Ah . . . ? There is a problem? Your health has . . . ?"

"My health is excellent, Pierre. I call because I have had some unusual good luck. I have come into a small amount of money, my friend. —No, let me correct that —I have come into quite a lot of money, and a wonderful assignment from my brokerage house. Pierre. I am calling because time is short if we are to take advantage of this stroke of good luck. You remember how often you have expressed the desire for a reunion?"

"Yes, of course, but—"

"Pierre, this is the perfect time. Why should we wait longer to see each other again? I want you to come to England. Now."

"But—"

"Pierre, I am to embark in a few days' time on a driving tour of more than a dozen British communities. Included will be Stratford, and the area around Stonehenge. Also later both Bath and Portsmouth. With my new wealth, I can pay for everything. It will be my pleasure! Come at once, my old friend! We may never have such a fine opportunity!" .

There was a long, shocked silence. Sylvester let it extend, bridling his impatience. He had maintained contact with Pierre Motard for more than a year against just such an eventuality. Now the fool had to say yes.

Finally the voice came: *"It is very sudden, Max, and my work here—"*

"Let the work wait, Pierre! This is a once-in-a-lifetime! — Pierre! You saved my sanity for me in Zurich! Allow me the joy of doing this in a token of repayment, I beg of you!"

"Well . . . ," the voice came back finally, *"I suppose they could do without me for a week, perhaps . . . and God knows I have always yearned to see more of your England . . . and to see you again, my beloved friend—"*

"Then it's done!" Sylvester cut in, making his voice sound warm and glad. "Let me call you again tomorrow at this hour, my best friend! Make immediate travel arrangements. I pay for everything. The sooner you can arrive, the earlier we can make final plans for our grand tour of the islands! You must arrive by Sunday at the latest. Saturday if you possibly can!"

When he finally left the telephone almost fifteen minutes later, Sylvester was soaked with nervous sweat. He was going very fast. Nothing must go wrong. He would practically have to be in two places at once if this was all going to work.

But he had known for a long time that such an eventuality might arrive one day. The possibility was the only reason he had maintained contact with the sentimental clot. It could be made to work.

Poor Pierre.

But he was stupid, and deserved no consideration. Sylvester's security came first.

Belfast, Northern Ireland

The night had grown darker, almost as if an evil blackness radiated out of the rubble-littered streets. Clouds now covered the moon. The night had become chill, somber. Jagged edges of broken rooftops stood against the faint sky light like monster tombstones. Daugherty crept along the foundation of what had once been a schoolhouse, and knelt to peer ahead in the darkness.

Bombed-out houses and cratered earth pocked the nightmare landscape ahead of him. Perhaps a hundred meters farther on stood the hulking black of the three-story building, once a brewery. Nothing moved. Daugherty could not see Kirk's from where he knelt, but he knew he might be able to use the night glasses even as far away as the last bombed-out wreckage that stood between his present position and the taller ruin.

Sweat stinging his eyes, Daugherty knelt without movement for more than fifteen minutes, straining to detect the slightest movement anywhere ahead.

Nothing.

Far beyond the impenetrable empty black that hid what was left of Kirk's a few city lights shone faintly. The edge of the wrecked area was more abrupt on the north side, Daugherty knew—which meant more danger of discovery over there. More sentries would be posted over there than over here.

He hesitated, still watching for some telltale sign. An owl called, and another answered. There was no other sound.

I do not want to do this, Daugherty thought. *I can justify playing safe. Better some news than none. Live to fight another day.*

But then his training rebelled. *Coward!* it shouted.

He glanced at the luminous dial of his watch. Almost midnight.

The meeting might already be under way. He had to decide *now* whether to creep forward or slink away.

One of the owls called again. Daugherty decided. As before, the stern voice of duty won out.

Daugherty made absolutely no sound as he crept slowly forward, staying tight against the crumbled masonry of the old wall of the school. He had to hurry across the remains of the street separating the school ruin from the cratered moonscape beyond, but it was so black he knew no one could observe him. Tension made his breathing irregular, raspy in his chest. He fought to keep that quiet.

Now he had reached a point halfway to the taller ruin. He shrank down against the jagged mass of a fallen building stone and opened his jacket to remove his night glasses. The zipper made a tiny chutting sound. With slippery hands he unfolded the glasses, leveled them toward Kirk's out there hidden in the vast darkness, and began to scan.

A voice right behind him made him jump in terror: *"Ah, Billy boy, so it was you all along."*

Moriarty's voice: burry-soft with sadness.

Scalded by terror, Daugherty dropped his glasses and lurched to his feet. Rocks tumbled under boots. Men appeared all around him. Hands grabbed his arms, pinioning them. He got a glimpse of Moriarty standing in the gloom, face hidden by his cap, hands jammed morosely in his pockets.

Arms swooped over Daugherty's head. The thin wire looped around his throat and tightened. *Oh no it isn't possible this can't be happening there has to be a way out it's*

The wire cut through.

Nine

LINDA BENNETT WAS late Friday evening. I fumed around in my room, remembering Terry Carpoman's angry departure for Nottingham without me, and the more recent telephone call to Beth in California. She had been too quiet, too polite. I had hung up feeling worse rather than better.

It was almost ten o'clock when someone finally tapped on my door. I was a lot more careful this time about finding out who it was. It was Linda, the one I had been waiting for.

She walked in, sleek-looking in dark linen slacks and a white shell. "Sorry I'm late."

"Me too," I told her. "Carpoman went nuts when I wasn't ready to drive to Nottingham a few hours ago."

She sat on the couch and crossed long legs. "From what you've said, he goes nuts at the slightest provocation."

"We play up there in just a couple of days, Linda."

"Sorry."

"So what's the verdict?"

"We were waiting to make sure. Sorry. The answer is no."

"COS won't supply me with a gun?"

"That's right."

"After what I told you about Tune's report that shows Sylvester is probably here?"

"COS considered all that. The answer is still no."

"Britain's gun laws?"

"He checked with Langley. You're not current on handguns."

I swallowed the sarcastic comment that came to mind. Not that I had really expected them to say yes. They're sticklers for the regs. I hadn't been through the Company's handgun course for more than three years, so I wasn't currently qualified, so they wouldn't have issued me a sidearm if I had been Horatio alone at the bridge.

"No problem," I said aloud.

She smiled. "At least you asked."

"Right, and now I know I have to get one some other way."

The amusement in her eyes died. "No, you won't."

"Watch me."

"That's a total disregard for procedure."

"So is getting shot at, Linda."

Now I had disappointed her and she went cold. She got back to her feet. "Grow up," she snapped, and turned away from me.

I watched her angle across the deep carpet center of my hotel room. Despite the slacks she was wearing fetching high heels. She had great legs, in case I didn't mention that before. At the corner table on the far side, beside the matched chairs, she picked up my pack of cigarettes and used a hotel match to light one. The angry silence between us hung thicker than her smoke.

I had told her what I had learned from Clarence Tune, and my suspicions about Sylvester. She had taken my information and request away with her. Then I had had to wait until now.

"COS," she told me, "has not seen the report your man Tune seems to have mentioned. However—"

"COS should get it, then," I cut in.

"*However*, no data exists to support your contention that Sylvester is in London, or anywhere, for that matter."

"Bullshit."

She did not reply at once. Silently she smoked in quick, manlike puffs. Her impatience also showed in the way she fervently tapped one foot on the carpet. I thought her impatience was equal parts anger and frustration and seething, breathing girl. This was supposed to be business and she was hacked at me and it was no time for monkey business. For all that, watching her, in the aftermath of the frustration of the call to Beth, I felt a need gathering, heating, deep in my belly.

She told me, "Further checking will be done. In the meantime, there seems to be no reason for alarm. You're to feign cooperation with Tune and continue your assignment. COS says he wants you to expedite contact with Sean Cork."

"Tell COS I'm working on it. Cork will be at Nottingham tomorrow."

"Okay."

I walked close to her to pick up a cigarette of my own. Had to reach across her to get to the pack on the table. She didn't budge. Our bodies faintly brushed. A jolting psychic spark leaped between us. Catching my breath, I looked into her eyes. They dilated.

Neither of us spoke. She took a half-step backward.

I lit my cigarette.

"Look," she said finally. She had to clear her throat before going on: "There can't be anything to this Sylvester idea you got. COS would level with us on something that serious. And this is a URA operation—if there *is* an operation. The Russians would want no part of the thing."

"If Sylvester is around here," I told her, struggling to pay attention to business, "the terrorist plans become incidental to both of us."

She absorbed that and thought about it. Then: "I tend to believe COS. That Sylvester isn't here."

"You can afford to believe that, Linda. It's not your rear end on the line."

She flinched angrily. "Damn you! Just because you're so attractive, does that give you a right to ambush me every time I let my guard down a little?"

I was astonished. "Hey. Sorry. I—"

Someone rapped sharply on the room door that opened onto the corridor. Both of us jumped.

Touching my fingers to my lips, I walked over and stood beside the door. "Who is it?"

His voice came sad and apologetic. "It's Clarence Tune, sir. I do beg your pardon, but we must have a few words."

I looked at Linda. We both knew without saying it that Tune might start guessing our real working relationship if he found her here like this. What to do?

She made her decision about the same time I came to one. She hurried soundlessly past the big bed and went into the bathroom, silently closing the door behind her.

I unlocked the hall door and opened it. Tune, his wrinkle-wrecked suit coat over his arm, came in with the look of a tired beagle. He smelled of sweat along with failure.

"What is it?" I asked, relocking the door.

He peered around quizzically. I realized how smoky the room had gotten with two of us puffing away. "Sorry," I said. "A little nervous."

He moved closer to the sitting area table and his eyes dropped to the ashtray where one of the butts had lipstick on it. Damn. He looked away again just as quickly. "I'm afraid, sir, I've been asked to follow up on something of earlier today."

I decided my only line of defense was to bluff. "At this hour? Hell, Clarence, do you know what time it is? I've got to get some sleep!"

"Yes, sir. I understand, sir, and I am deeply sorry. However, there has been a, ah, rather unfortunate break in one of our pre-existing information links. Which has caused my supervisor to urge that I follow up on this without delay. It will take only a few moments, sir."

I made a great show of being disgusted. "Go ahead, then, if you have to."

"Yes, sir. Well. When I mentioned a description to you earlier, your reaction indicated that you might recognize some aspect."

"No, I certainly did not recognize anything—"

"If that is to be your official position, sir," he cut in with great sadness, "then fine. We shall say no more about it. However, please be aware that all our forces are looking for the man at the present time. And judging by your earlier reaction—the one you didn't have, of course—it would seem to me that you might very much like to see said suspect in custody. Now if you will just reconsider, sir—"

"Clarence," I said, "there's nothing to reconsider. I—"

The doorway of the bathroom opened. Both of us turned our heads. I am not sure which of us got the greatest shock. Linda, wearing only tiny black bikini panties and a brazen black spiderweb of a bra, walked out.

"Darling," she said, looking around as if unaware, "I can't find—" Then she looked up and stopped abruptly, a hand going to her breasts, as she pretended to see for the first time that I was not alone. "Oh! Darn! Sorry! I didn't hear—"

I recovered enough to go along with it. "We won't be long, Linda."

She made a small moaning sound of acute embarrassment, turned, and fled back into the bathroom. The door shut firmly.

Clarence Tune looked like a man who had just seen a miracle. I felt near shock myself. Linda had covered for us just fine, promoting our "relationship" in the process. What shocked me was how she had looked. I had known she was beautiful, but the vision who had just come and gone was incredible.

"Sorry, Clarence," I managed after a few seconds. "The lady—"

He removed a grayish handkerchief from his pocket and dabbed his filmy forehead. He actually looked pale. "Yes, sir. Of course. Well. I see I have really interrupted something. I . . . uh . . . about our earlier colloquy?"

"Clarence, I have no idea who your mystery man is, and that's straight."

"Yes. Well." His eyes darted around. He was still shaken. "I . . . uh . . . yes. Well. If that is your position." He straightened his battered tie and cleared his throat. "We can discuss this . . . further . . . in the morning. Perhaps."

I walked him to the door. He more or less staggered out. I relocked.

The bathroom door opened again and Linda, just as near-naked and stunning, walked out. At the coffee table she bent for another cigarette. She was vastly amused. "Poor little guy! I thought he was going to have a heart attack."

"Me too."

She chuckled. "I could see that. But he would have noticed the smoke and the cigarettes. Better for him to think smutty little fantasies about us than to wander into a hint of the truth."

I stared at her and then looked away and couldn't decide what direction I was supposed to look. Her long, shapely bare legs drew my eyes like magnets. The wispy bra strained under the burden of beautiful breasts. My hands itched for her.

"Hey," she said, sitting on the edge of the bed and crossing her legs. "Have I embarrassed you?"

"Oh, hell no. My face is always this color."

She chuckled, vastly amused. "This is no more revealing than a swimsuit."

"Sure. Right."

"And it accomplished a purpose with friend Tune."

"Yes."

She looked up at me. Her smile changed. "It accomplished a purpose with you, too, I think . . . huh?"

I backed away from her. "I think you'd better get dressed and get out of here."

"No one would think anything about it, Brad. Officially, I mean. It's part of the act we're supposed to be building. I'm supposed to be your groupie."

"You'd better get out of here, Linda," I repeated.

She was no longer smiling. Her expression had a solemn hunger in it. "Listen to how you sound. Your voice. I don't do this sort of thing, and you don't either, or your voice wouldn't sound that way."

"We haven't done anything, Linda."

She refused to unlock her gaze from mine. "Not quite yet."

"I don't know what you're talking about."

"Brad." Her voice was huskier, the need speaking. "It's happened. We both feel it."

I didn't say anything. Pulse hammered in my throat. I couldn't keep my eyes off her.

She said, "I don't have to leave here tonight."

"No. You need to get dressed and get out of here."

"No complications. Just—"

"*Go*, Linda, God damn it!"

"Really?"

I looked at the ceiling. "No. Yes. I mean yes."

She uncoiled those legs and stood. If she had come toward me, all my wonderfully brave ethical decisions would have gone straight through the floor like a reactor melting through to China. But she didn't come toward me. Soundlessly she walked into the bathroom again and closed the door.

When she came back out a few minutes later she was fully clothed.

We looked at each other foolishly, like two fighters in the sudden post-adrenaline cool after a match.

Then she grinned. "Wow," she breathed ruefully.

"Well said."

"I'm not through with you yet, buster."

"Say good night, Linda."

She came over and gave me a swift peck on the tip of my nose. "Good night, Linda."

I stood in place, fondling my whisky, and she let herself out. I locked the door behind her. Her perfume lingered in the air. The room looked like a hotel room without her in it. Shaky, I started trying to figure out precisely what kind of idiot I had just been.

Ten

Elsewhere

Belfast, Northern Ireland

EARLY SATURDAY MORNING, Sylvester trudged several blocks from his Belfast flat to use a public telephone. He called his assigned number in London.

"Yes?" the neutral male voice answered.

"This is Joe Greene," Sylvester said, "and I am calling about my progress on the Irish linen accounts?"

"Yes," the voice replied. "Have you completed making both the credit and consignment calls?"

"No," Sylvester said. "There was some sales resistance. All is well, but under the circumstances I will not return to the home office today. I will remain on the road until the first of the week."

"I understand, Joe." Was there the slightest hint of relaxation in the operator's tone? "When will we see you?"

"I will report again early in the week."

"All right, Joe. Thank you for calling. We will await your next sales report."

"That's correct. Goodbye."

Sylvester left the public telephone kiosk feeling almost like his old self.

It was good to be in the field once more. He was proceeding with extreme caution and in fact had not yet accomplished anything in terms of identifying even the most tenuous lead to whatever the IRA might have planned. But just being under cover, and at risk, stirred his blood—made him feel alive again after months of suspended animation.

In the two days since moving a few carefully planned items into his new, cheap walkup in London, he had been in Belfast. When his plan came to its conclusion, searchers would find only what he had planted for them to find in the room. His real passport and handful of valuables resided in a safe at the embassy, his cash in a bank deposit box rented under still another fictitious name.

Sylvester's "official" lodgings in a hotel not far from the Soviet embassy had not been used in weeks. For all practical purposes he had vanished from the globe.

He had worked hard in Belfast, assiduously making himself visible in what the analysts believed to be some of the right places, watching, seeing some possible contacts being made—and waiting. Ordinarily he might have returned to London again this weekend to report, just to keep Gravitch happy. But the telephone call had covered that, telling them he would stay in Belfast and continue being a good little boy.

Which of course he had no intention of doing.

He took a taxi to the airport and caught the British Airways shuttle for London. He sat in a seat near the back of the plane and kept to himself behind a newspaper. The flight was not heavily booked. Family members and a few weary businessmen scattered around the cabin. No one paid any attention to him, which was fine. He was quite well aware that he had started a new and potentially deadly game—not just a double game now, but an identity within an identity within still another identity, and a course of action within the course of action his Resident had ordered—within another course of action still.

All risky. All necessary, if he was to throw the surveillance off the trail and get a chance at Brad Smith.

London

Late Saturday afternoon, J. C. Kinkaid got off a flight at Heathrow and was met by a slight, balding man wearing wrinkled cotton slacks, bulky gray sweater, and a dark windbreaker: Ed Grossman. They walked to the parking, where Grossman had left his small Ford. The two men exchanged few words until Grossman had reached M4 and fallen into the dense flow of traffic.

"Flight go okay?" Grossman asked, expertly moving along at maximum speed.

"There wasn't a bomb on board, if that's what you mean," Kinkaid told him.

"And you were almost on time. Great luck so far."

"It's a hell of a time to fly across west to east. I feel like lunch and it's already starting to get dark."

"You'll feel grand tomorrow after not being able to sleep more than three hours tonight."

Kinkaid decided that was enough small talk. "So where are we?"

"It's second and long. Martin is still in Londonderry but doesn't have a clue. Our people scattered around town hear *nada*. The new update from the Brits says they don't have anything useful either. Did you read the new stuff on their loss of a man up there before you took off?"

Kinkaid experienced a small, nasty sense of surprise. "No. What happened?"

"Another service had a man in pretty deep. Something happened. They discovered him somehow."

"The IRA did?"

"Or the URA. Whatever."

"What happened to him?"

"His body was found a couple of nights ago on a garbage heap in Belfast. They found his head last night, bobbing around near the shore of Lough Neagh."

"Christ."

"That's what we thought, too."

"Where do we go from here?"

Grossman neatly passed a gleaming luxury car and slipped in behind a small bus, then switched again to get an open lane several car-lengths ahead. He patted the Ford's plastic dashboard. "It always makes Suzie happy when we pass a Jag or a Mercedes. That's a good girl, Suzie. You just keep perking along, hon."

"Where," Kinkaid repeated, "do we go from here?" He felt herky-jerky nervous inside and he had a headache and his fingers and ankles were puffy. "What about Smith?"

"Well, he hasn't done much of anything useful since he slew the villain at the hotel. But he's about to contact Cork. We can hope."

Kinkaid ignored the sarcasm. He knew what some of the field pros thought about using someone like Brad Smith. They hadn't seen Smith's records, and couldn't know some of the good work he had done in the past. His shooting of a possible source of crucial information was generally considered cowboy stuff; McWilliams had been unarmed and fleeing when it happened. Nobody considered what *they* might have done if they had just had a pistol shoved up their nose.

"Where is he right now?" Kinkaid asked.

"Nottingham. Little grass tournament."

"He's playing the doubles with Terry Carpoman?"

"So I understand."

"Cork is there?"

"On the way. He finally lost in Paris, so maybe Smith can catch up with him now and start doing us some good."

Kinkaid felt his patience slip. "It's hardly Brad's fault that Cork kept winning over there."

"Hum."

"What *else* do you have in the way of good news?"

Grossman changed lanes again. "There's the matter of Sylvester."

"That report was nothing but hearsay," Kinkaid pointed out. "The flimsiest sort of stuff."

"Yes, I agree. The Brits haven't made the Sylvester connection as far as we can tell. But nobody matching the description of that delivery driver has been seen again in the neighborhood. So they think he—the anonymous face—may have been tipped off."

"How?"

"Unknown."

"What does Brad say about it?"

"Oh, as recently as a day or two ago he was quite convinced that the description fit Sylvester, and he created all sorts of minor furor. Two calls for extra meetings. Asked for a handgun."

"Was a weapon provided?"

"Of course not."

"How did he react to that, if you know?"

Grossman smiled, his face wrinkling in the subdued white glare of the traffic. "Said he would get his own."

Kinkaid didn't say anything to that.

Grossman observed, "You don't seem surprised."

"No."

"It doesn't worry you, that your man promptly went into a panic and started yelling for firearms?"

"I doubt that he was in a panic," Kinkaid bit off. "Also, I happen to know what's happened between him and Sylvester before, and what Sylvester is capable of. Asking for a gun makes good sense to me."

"At this end of the operation," Grossman said portentiously, "we tend to believe Sylvester is dead or incapacitated inside Russia somewhere."

"Do you, now," Kinkaid said.

"Yes. Think it out for yourself. Unless your man Smith lied about that earlier encounter with Sylvester—"

"He didn't lie."

"Then Sylvester is still far from well. Any earlier activity on his part would have been emergency callout. There's nothing from the Russian perspective that would make the present situation an emergency for them. No normal person would be back on duty in London at this time."

"Don't you guys ever read the reports?" Kinkaid asked. "Sylvester is *not* your normal person, for Christ sake!"

Grossman was not impressed. "Our analysis still says it would be absurd to think he might be around here."

"Right," Kinkaid said through gritted teeth.

Grossman passed a Fiat and another small bus. He patted the dash again. "Wonderful, Suzie. Atta girl, hon."

Near the border, Northern Ireland

"Roadblock," Lyle grated, leaning forward in the passenger seat of the old truck to squint at the lights ahead.

"Now Nedwin, now Nedwin," Squirrel Henry said soothingly. "It's na a problem. Calm yourself." He downshifted expertly, babying the aged lorry into second gear. "We got nothin' to be hidin', now, do we?"

Ned Lyle stared anxiously at the older Henry. The bright lights of the army roadblock, now coming nearer fast, etched his weather-beaten face in anger. "There's never been a roadblock right along here like this!"

"I said *calm yourself, man,*" Squirrel Henry repeated. This time there was a slight edge in his voice. "They wouldn't be findin' nothin' if they looked fer a year. Now just let me handle the talkin', an' you just be a friendly, ignorant farmer, eh?"

Lyle grated his teeth audibly, but subsided. His sudden angry fear smelled like vomit inside the truck cab. Squirrel Henry started applying the miserable old brakes to the truck, and was rewarded by the usual scream of metal against metal, and not much else in the way of results. He liked to joke, Squirrel Henry did, that he ought to rent the truck for fires. It would need no siren, he always said; all the driver had to do was touch the brake pedal and he would be heard for miles.

Henry began whistling tunelessly between his broken front

teeth to show Lyle that he was calm, and there was nothing to worry about.

In truth, Henry did not like it at all.

For one thing, it was a *big* roadblock. Inching the old lorry up toward the white-and-black wood barricades, Henry could see three big troop carriers parked back in the dimness away from the floodlights, plus a couple of cars, plus a communications lorry. It looked like several dozen British soldiers lined up along the road behind the blocks. They were heavily armed—no surprise there—but they were paying a lot more attention to business than he had often seen them do at such times late at night.

Well, no help for it now but to bluff it through. Henry stood on the brake pedal and got it stopped a few feet from the barricade.

Two soldiers walked up on Lyle's side of the truck, two more on Henry's. He cranked the cracked window down, letting in the wet night chill.

"Good evenin', sojers! Nasty night fer bein' out!"

The noncom in charge did not smile. "Your name, sir?"

"Squirrel Henry's my name, an' sheep shit's my game!"

The noncom jerked. "What?"

"Sheep manure! That's my game—my business! I go an' pick 'er up an' I go an' haul 'er someplace else fer a garden! Got me a nice load on right now, fer a sweet little widder woman down near Ardee. Maybe you know her. Name's the widder McLoughlan—"

"All right, all right. You on the other side. Your name?"

"Jamie Kelly," Lyle said, his voice a croak of tension.

To his relief, Squirrel Henry saw that none of them picked up on that. For, as Lyle spoke, the soldiers on both sides of the truck caught their first whiff of the overwhelming stink wafting from the rear in the backlash of wind caused by stopping.

"Both of you step out," the head noncom said with the expression of a man wishing he were somewhere else.

Squirrel Henry climbed down, keeping up a continuous stream of chatter. Lyle kept quiet as ordered. Henry kept on yapping, about the imaginary widow McLoughlan to the south in the town of

Ardee, about the weather, about sheep and their proclivity for producing manure of the highest garden quality. The stink from the
high, wet pile in the back of the truck started getting truly wonderful, and the soldiers hurried their inspection of his papers.

Sooner than a careful examination would have permitted, the
noncom handed the papers back. He had started looking nauseated.
"All right, Mr. Henry. Please proceed carefully."

"I will indeed, sarjunt! I wouldn't wanna tip over an' lose all
this grand fertilizer, after the sheep worked so hard makin' it, now,
would I!"

The soldiers lifted the barricades back. Still grinning and talking, Squirrel Henry climbed back into the driver's seat, waited for
the ice-pale Ned Lyle to get in beside him, then started the old lorry
again, got it in gear, and creaked across the border with many waves
and giggles.

In the back, buried under the sheep manure, the four fifty-
gallon drums of thiodiglycol rode heavily, lashed to the wood floor
of the old truck. Squirrel Henry whistled a happy tune, pleased with
himself and idly wondering about the ultimate destination of all this
stuff he had been hauling, and how they intended to use it. But he
was canny. He was not curious enough to ask. People who asked
those kinds of questions tended not to attain old age.

London

His feet like lead weights, Clarence Tune trudged up the dark,
familiar street of the dreary neighborhood so close and yet so far
from fashionable Sussex Gardens. Soon his street would be leveled,
perhaps, to make way for expansion of the pretty area to the south.
But by that time, with luck, Tune figured, he would be dead.

Intent on the problem the American Brad Smith had handed
him, Tune scarcely noticed the young thugs lurking in a doorway
across the way, or the prostitute who swung her heavy hips as she

approached him and then, recognizing him, slumped on past without bothering to display her usual storefront eroticism.

Reaching his building, Tune dug his well-worn brass key out of his coat pocket, inserted it in the heavy old lock, and entered the downstairs hall. Something—a rat—made a furtive scurrying sound. Intent on the Smith dilemma, Tune ignored the rat, too, and climbed the stairs.

The smells of mildew (generalized) and cigar smoke (Mr. Parks) and meat stew (Mrs. Eiffelman) permeated the second floor landing. Tune unlocked the door to his rooms and entered, gratefully closing the door and relocking it in total darkness. He sighed. Then he turned the antique wall switch.

An overhead chandelier—dirt-crusted glass danglers and a dozen grayish imitation glass candles, half of them burned out—blinked yellowly on. The light shone over Tune's sitting room, about a dozen feet square, faded floral wallpaper walls, dark overstuffed Victorian-style furniture, a yellowish fringed lamp on a round table with the shade askew, paper blinds drawn at the bay window in front, newspapers and magazines scattered around amid the wreckage of several weeks-old frozen dinners. Tune removed his coat and did not bother to hang it up, but instead draped it over the end of the sofa. As he turned, his cat Shane slunk out of the bedroom and meowed at him, rubbing against his pant legs.

"Hello, Shane," Tune said wearily. "Hello, pretty cat."

Shane, a fat old tabby with pale eyes and a generally sour disposition, awarded him with a purr followed closely by another, sharper meow.

"You must be out of something," Tune said, turning from the bedroom door to enter the tiny kitchen and grope for the switch.

The light came on in the kitchen to reveal peeling white-painted cabinets and a sink and drainboards that looked like an army had camped in it. A fat black roach ran across the top of some dirty dishes and dove to safety in an open cereal box. Shane walked around and around, meowing piteously. Tune examined the food and water dishes on the floor beside the litterbox. The dirty pale blue dishes were empty and dry. The surface of the litter in the box was studded with dozens of bullet-sized black turds.

"Oh, my, yes, I see," Tune murmured. "Well, yes. You poor thing, Shane. You poor dear." He refilled the water dish, found the box of catfood in the cabinet and filled the food dish too, and watched approvingly as Shane dug in. *Should change the litter, of course. Do it tomorrow.*

Tune walked back into the living room. *Should clean the house, too.*

Do that sometime.

Tune's unmade bed filled the bedroom. He got out of his rumpled black suit, carefully hanging it on a hangar, and decided he could wear the shirt another day. Must be thrifty, but must look one's best. He put on slippers and a shapeless red flannel robe and went back into the living room again.

He was incredibly tired.

It was a relief to have Brad Smith gone to the tournament for a few days. Staying up with him—trying to get something out of him—had worn Tune to a nubbin. But when Smith returned, his highly unusual request must be dealt with. And now, after today's meeting with his superior, Tune felt even more pressure.

After more than thirty years in the service, Smith represented a very big assignment for Tune, and he felt the weight of its responsibility. He wanted very badly to show the commander that he was a better operative than they had ever given him credit for being. He knew that assigning him to Smith was tantamount to saying Smith was not viewed as very important, and he had half-expected them to put a better (i.e., younger) man on him after the McWilliams business. His superior today had been blunt about that. *"We are short on manpower, Clarence. It simply has to be you. We have no one else, you see."*

And thank you kindly for the vote of confidence, commander.

Tune sighed again and poured himself two ounces of brandy.

In the old days, Agnes had had the brandy poured when he came home full of stories and vigor and dreams of how he was going to knock the world into a cocked hat. In this very room. Tune could close his eyes and still see her standing by the sunwashed front windows—sparkling windows then—with her smile and the tremulous look of love in her eyes.

So long ago . . . so long ago. She had been gone more than ten years already.

Sipping his brandy, Tune sat on the couch after moving his coat aside. He closed his eyes and saw Agnes and missed her still, loved her still. He thought about how long it had been. Then he thought about the day's meeting with his superior. Agnes would have been outraged if she were here, and he told her the things the inspector said—his patronizing attitude—Agnes would have been furious.

It did not feel good, being spoken to as Tune had been spoken to today. A small bit of him was furious, too. *How dare you talk to me that way! I've given you my life!* But he knew better. He knew he had never done much.

Maybe . . . a very, very small voice inside him said . . . they were wrong about Brad Smith. Perhaps he would assume a larger role than anyone expected. Certainly his unparalleled request of Tune hinted so. Perhaps the assignment would yet give Tune a chance to show his mettle.

And wouldn't that be grand, Agnes?

Shane wandered back in from the kitchen and hopped up on Tune's lap. Tune stroked him gently, but forgot and stroked too far back behind the front shoulder. Shane turned and bit him on the forefinger, drawing bright, painful blood. Tune reached out to slap back in retaliation, but as usual the cat's reflexes were faster than his, and Shane had already jumped to the floor and shot out of sight somewhere.

Tune sucked the wound and used his other hand to reach for the book beside him on the couch. He opened it to his mark and started reading. He was not sure he could concentrate on the story, as bad as his day had been and as worried as he was.

He stared at the words, replaying the commander's dry, insulting instructions. He replayed, too, the startling conversation with Brad Smith:

"Clarence, I want you to help me."

"Yes, sir? What would it be?"

"I need a weapon. A gun."

"A gun, sir?"

"A handgun. An automatic, if you can come up with one. A revolver will do. Ideally, a 9 mm."

"But surely, sir, with your resources—"

"Clarence, I'm asking this as a personal favor. No one will ever know. Will you help me or not?"

Tune had murmured that he would have to think about it . . . did not know if it were at all possible, sir.

Of course it was possible. Hidden deep in the wall panel behind the kitchen cabinets Tune had four handguns that were strictly secret and decidedly illegal, even for him. There was the Webley .455 he had carried out of the army with him long ago, and the 1911 .45 ACP given to him by his American friends in Berlin after that operation there in 1966, and the Smith & Wesson .38 revolver— all nice, functional weapons, lovingly maintained. There was also the .380 Beretta he had taken off the body of the jockey killed in Soho years ago, but it had a broken spring and other internal calamities.

"You've got a gun or two, Clarence. At least a throw down. I'll return it when this is over."

A throw down—a gun kept to toss down beside a man you had shot and killed, then found to be unarmed. Yes. Tune had kept the Beretta for just such an unlikely happenstance. It surprised him slightly that Brad Smith knew about throw downs. But possibly Brad Smith knew about a lot more than Tune had been able to get out of him. Perhaps Smith's station chief had refused him a weapon on some stupid technicality, like his not having a signed paper showing he had qualified in a CIA course within the past two years.

The British, after all, were not the only ones cobwebbed by bureaucratic regulations and paperwork.

But it was not an easy decision for Tune. He worried about Brad Smith—Smith's safety. But he also worried about his own personal, professional risk involved in giving Smith any of the handguns. If the office ever learned that he had such weapons—much less had provided one for someone like Smith—the commander would have his testicles on the flagpole.

What to do . . . what to do? Tune was torn on his dilemma. With another sigh he tried again to escape into his novel.

He was just getting to the good part: Powder Valley was about to experience some of its worst trouble ever.

For a few pages, he read automatically, not really registering what Pat Stevens was saying on the page. Fragments of the afternoon meeting with his superior played over and over against a backdrop of the old, perpetual sadness about Agnes; in his imagination Tune made brilliant ripostes and showed the inspector the quality of his mind—how he had been underestimated and mistreated over all the years. The conversation with Brad Smith kept wanting to rerun, too. *"You've got a gun or two, Clarence."*

Of one thing Tune felt sure. The commander had underestimated Brad Smith's possible role in what lay ahead. Smith could be important; he could find himself—and Tune—in the crucial center of things. And if that happened, Tune might prove himself at last.

Nothing was more important than proving himself at last. But Smith wanted a gun. . . .

Still reading words and not content, Tune slipped to another obsession: his impending retirement. They would not let him continue in service much longer; what would he do then? *Did it really matter if he gave the man a handgun when he was so close to the end of his service anyway?*

The problem seemed insoluble. For the third or fourth time, Tune started the chapter over.

This time he succeeded. The words formed pictures. The novel caught him. His attention focused on the page. Against the distant sounds made by Shane in the kitchen, scratching furiously around

in his overladen litterbox, Tune was transported back to the old
West, riding along, headed for danger, respected, confident and in
control and happy, ready for any fate.

Ramsgate

It was quite late in the evening when Sylvester drove into
Ramsgate and parked not far from the docks. The hovercraft from
Calais had been in for hours.

Walking into the vast, deserted terminal building, however, he
spotted his old friend Pierre Motard dutifully waiting for him: a man
of his own height and weight, sitting alone on one of the bare
wooden benches in an empty section of the building, his small suitcase beside him on the bare concrete floor. Motard sat slumped inside his trench coat, an oily brown paper bag on his lap. As Sylvester
approached, not yet seen, Motard dipped a hand into the bag and
took out a piece of brownish chicken and began gnawing on it.

Sylvester walked closer. "Pierre, my friend!"

Motard looked up and dropped the chicken leg back into the
bag. A broad smile transformed his long sad face. He got hurriedly
to his feet, wiping his greasy hands on his coat. "Max!" he cried.

They shook hands. Sylvester threw an arm over Motard's shoulders. "I regret my lateness, my good friend. How was the trip?"

Motard's sagging eyes shone. "Oh, it was grand!" His English
had a heavy overlay of French accents. "From home I rode the *Ra-
pide* to Paris, and what a fine ride that was! The weather was clear
and fine to Calais and I saw many wonderful sights. Then the hovercraft ride here—what speed! What excitement! I would not have
believed it possible!"

Sylvester smiled like an indulgent uncle. Motard was such a
fool. But that made Sylvester's plan possible.

"Come," he said. "My car is not far away.—Here, my friend.
Let me take your bag!"

They walked together, leaving the terminal building and proceeding toward the car. Pierre Motard chattered happily about all the grand sights he had already seen, and how wonderfully he anticipated the few days ahead, traveling in Britain with his dearest friend. Sylvester made the proper replies, assuring Motard of his undying affection.

After initial treatment for his chest wounds and broken bones in Moscow following the St. Maarten debacle, Soviet doctors treating Sylvester had still been confronted by the problem of his shattered face. Brad Smith's attack with a tennis racket had broken his jaw in two places, displacing several teeth. In addition, his second or third blow had caved in the bone under and beside Sylvester's right eye, smashing his nose and the upper bridge of his mouth at the same time. After escaping the immediate area, Sylvester had lain in agony for four days, hidden in a toolshed on the outskirts of Philipsburg. Gangrenous tissue in several deeply lacerated areas of his face had stunk hideously by the time he was finally gotten off the island at night.

Emergency treatment onboard the submarine had helped, and the doctors in Moscow had worked heroically. But their first concern had been simply to save Sylvester's life; while focusing on his chest wounds, they had surgically excised rotten facial tissue and set bones without regard to how he might look later. As one doctor had later explained to Sylvester, "We were not certain there would be a 'later' for you, don't you see."

Later, when it was clear Sylvester would survive, the question of his appearance had to be faced. Not a vain man, Sylvester nevertheless screamed for the mirror in his hospital room to be removed. His one horrified glance when bandages were removed had shown him a gargoyle: a ghastly, purplish ruin of a face that reminded him instantly of the classic old American movie about the hunchback of Notre Dame. Sylvester could not abide it; he was so ugly and misshapen that he would never again be able to face anybody, much less ever resume his work.

The doctors conferred. Decisions made. "You will be transported to Switzerland, where the finest facility exists for reconstructive surgery. No effort will be spared."

The private hospital on the heights overlooking old Zurich specialized in cases that would have been pronounced hopeless a decade earlier. Burn victims predominated, but the broken survivors of war and major accidents were there in large numbers. As part of the entry examination, every severely disfigured patient—and that included just about all of them—was subjected to a complete psychological evaluation in an attempt to determine how strong was the patient's will to fight and live—a gauge of the patient's likely ability to withstand the long agony of reconstruction.

Sylvester's entry profile showed profound depression and overwhelming, unfocused rage. His psychological prognosis was guarded.

Treatment began nevertheless. After X-ray and other examinations, a new facial appearance was designed by an artist working with the surgeons who would do the work. The sketches were then translated into lifesize plastic head models, which were in turn scanned into a computer, where Sylvester's internal and external injuries were transposed onto present facial models as well as the final projection. The surgical team then prepared an "intervention modality" menu—a list of the operations that would be done, in the order in which they would be performed.

Nineteen such procedures were forecast.

After the fourth procedure—the deepest and most extensive to date—the medical team became more concerned about his mood. He spoke to no one. He refused more pain-deadening medication than any patient on record, arguing that he needed his mind because it was all he had left. His food intake fell off radically and he lost weight.

The doctors thought they were losing him.

It was at this time—partly at the psychologist's behest and partly on his own—that Pierre Motard appeared one day in Sylvester's room. At the time, Motard walked with a slight bent, left shoulder lower than the right, and his face was a series of smooth planes, its tight white surface transmarked by a thousand very fine, very

faint pink tracks: the healing signs of his own reconstructive sur-
geries.

"You must have faith, my friend," Motard said.

"Faith?" Sylvester repeated, his voice shaking. "Look at me.
They dig and cut, and I am still a monster."

"They will repair everything. Trust them."

"You are insane! You can't know what it is like!"

Motard smiled sadly, tightening all the little scars fading on
his face. He took some pictures out of an envelope he had brought
with him and handed them over.

Sylvester looked at them—and recoiled violently.

"*Oui,*" Motard nodded. "A former student at the university
blamed his failures in life on a failing grade I had given him, resulting in his dismissal, years before. He was mad. He shot me twice
in the chest, once in the shoulder. I fell unconscious. He battered
my face with the gun, then poured petrol on me and set me afire.
When the authorities broke in moments later—killing him instantly—they were amazed to find life in me at all."

Motard paused and reached down to gently squeeze Sylvester's
shoulder. "I know you were in a similar accident of fate. Our injuries
were remarkably similar. That is why I am here. To tell you I have
been through it. I *do know.* And I know you can make it!"

The former professor's visit had helped. Sylvester caught hold
of himself by the nape of the neck and vowed to try harder. He
forced himself to eat and exercise despite the ongoing pain. Perhaps
partly as a result, the next surgical procedure went better.

In the months that followed, Pierre Motard came back again
and again. He brought books and little presents. He gave more of
himself to Sylvester than any person could have been expected to
give.

The two became fast friends—or as close as anyone could ever
be to Yuli Szulc, alias Joe Greene, alias Max Swinman, alias Sylvester.

Sylvester recognized then—and knew now—that Pierre Motard had been instrumental in saving his sanity. Not only had they

gone through amazingly similar incidents; they were nearly the same age and build, with a common interest in European history and literature. When they parted at the hospital more than a year after their first meeting, they looked at one another out of faces curiously similar: smooth, waxen, regular, with those thousands of tiny scalpeltracks beneath the surface, visible only on the most minute examination.

"I thank you," Sylvester had said that day, clasping Motard's hand.

Motard, always something of a sentimental fool, grew wateryeyed, and impulsively pulled him into a brief, rough hug. "We are brothers!"

Since that time Sylvester had not seen Motard, and had replied to few of the Frenchman's effusive letters, and then briefly, with surface politeness. But now he was glad he had had the foresight to maintain that minimal contact.

He put Motard's bag in the back of the rented Ford, then unlocked the passenger side for his friend to get in. Walking around the car, he got behind the wheel and drove out of the lot.

"What is our first destination?" Motard asked excitedly.

"First we return to London," Sylvester told him. "I have some papers I forgot. Then we will be on our way."

"Our next stop, then?"

"Toward Bristol first, I think."

Motard rocked forward and back in his seat with excitement. "Ah, Max, Max! I will never be able to repay you for your generosity! To have such a tour ahead—and to share it with you, my dearest friend!" Motard reached over to squeeze Sylvester's shoulder in an old, familiar gesture of solidarity. "Brothers under the skin! Remember?"

Sylvester remembered, all right. He owed Motard everything.

Sad, in a way, he thought, that it had to be ended in the way he planned to end it just a few kilometers ahead.

But, after all, Motard had an empty life, meaningless, lonely, dull. He would not be losing much, really. —And hadn't he said a dozen times, in his excess of sentimentality, that he would gladly give his life for his wonderful friend Max?

The killing would be quick and painless. In view of all Motard's help and devotion, Sylvester owed him this kindness.

Eleven

DESPITE COMPETITION FROM other grass court tournaments, the Nottingham tournament had drawn some good players. Driving there at the crack of dawn Sunday, I felt myself tightening up, thinking tennis for almost the first time, really, since I had arrived. Wimbledon was just two weeks away now. That fact beat in my mind. Whatever else was pressuring me, it was *Wimbledon* in two weeks.

Wimbledon is so special that it's hard to talk about it. When I won the singles there, and later the doubles, it was such an achievement—such an emotional passage—that nothing will ever surpass it. All of us have such moments in our lives, I think: a few minutes or hours that, even as we are living them, we know will never be forgotten. We hoard these few times, and burnish them, because we know they will never come again, and may never even be approached for their luster in the storehouse of our memories.

All my Wimbledon dreams had been bigger than life, treasures. They were so grand that I had resisted the thought of returning in recent years, even as a spectator, sensing that any renewal could only taint the past with the corrosion of now.

In taking this assignment, however, I was not just returning to watch. I had to *play*—in the singles because I had the wild card, in the doubles with a man I didn't much like because that would give me additional opportunities to observe events and other players. I did not look forward to the playing. I would give it hell, sure, just as I had been doing in practice and as I intended to do at Nottingham. It's the only way I know to operate. And in the Walter Mitty

135

area of my mind there were those fleeting delusional pictures of me
out there in the finals again—"the Smith Miracle," the papers
would call it—and of course since it was a wild fantasy anyway, I
would win the big cup.

But no rational person could expect that, or anticipate more
than a desperate effort on the part of the old gent, maybe just
enough to avert total humiliation . . . the obscuring of all the old
memories by the crud of present ineptitude.

Even if I had been younger and more tournament-sharp, too
many other things were going on to allow the kind of concentration
required for top performance. The incident at the hotel—the memory of that gun muzzle staring in my face—was still sharp, and I
felt shaky when I remembered. Keeping up my journalist's cover
work required daily attention, scrambling around for short interviews that would not only satisfy the *Times* in New York but provide
fodder for the magazine pieces to come. I worried about Beth.
Linda . . . the way she had looked in my room that night . . . tugged
at the edges of my mind.

When I arrived at the Nottingham club, however, I checked
in with tournament officials and learned I had run into some luck.

A harried, middle-aged club officer named Marcus Conway
met me. "Sorry, sir, but we can't say when you play, or whom, quite
yet. Rain delays at Beckenham had caused us to have some late with-
drawals and changes."

"I guess," I told him sympathetically, "that means bracket
changes for you?"

Conway heaved a sigh. He looked drawn, grayish, strung out.
"Indeed, sir. The tournament committee commences meeting
within the hour to redraw the brackets almost in their entirety."

"I'll just check in," I told him, "and look up my doubles partner."

Conway's face twisted. "That would be Mr. Carpoman, I believe?"

"That's right."

"Yes." Another sigh. "Mr. Carpoman is at the main building,

I believe. He is *very* distressed about the delay in the draw. —Has he spoken yet with you about the possibility that you and he might withdraw in protest?"

Damn. "No. I just got here. Look. I'll go talk to him. Maybe I can calm him down. I want to play here. I think he does too."

"Yes. Well." Conway put on the stiff upper lip. "Mr. Carpoman has been rather unpleasant about it, sir, actually. When we told him that your doubles draw would likely stand as originally scheduled, he became . . . ah . . . agitated."

"What would that draw be?"

Conway fussed around in the bottom of the attache case on the card table in front of him and came up with some sloppy, penciled and erased and re-penciled bracket sheets. "That would have you playing Paul Annacone and Christo Van Rensburg." He looked up from the sheets, blinking at me.

I almost grinned. Annacone and Van Rensburg were a formidable doubles team. Terry had had cats because he was looking for a first-round setup.

"They're tough," I observed.

"Yes, sir," Conway agreed with an apologetic tone. "Actually, Mr. Smith, we have little choice on that matter. We have, however, attempted to balance off the difficulty of that draw with the way we hope to redraw the singles pairings."

"And those would be—?"

He consulted more dog-eared sheets. "At the present, those would have Mr. Carpoman meeting Mr. Pugh, and you facing Mr. Taylor."

"May I look?"

He handed the sheets over.

On the basis of his year so far, Terry Carpoman was seeded third here, behind Brad Gilbert and Sean Cork. Possibly out of deference to my past, the planners had kept me off the bottom of the seed chart, ranking me in ahead of the antique Pablo Rinaldi and a fourteen-year-old from Chile named Sanchez. Terry's first match was presently scheduled to be against Taylor, whom he ought to handle easily, but his second was against Alexander Volkov of the Soviet Union, who could beat anyone on a given day. I was paired against Pugh, then Gilbert, and it would take two more miracles after that if I was to go far enough to get oncourt with the person I most wanted to meet, friend Cork.

"Look," I said to Conway. "What would you think of making this little change?" I drew some arrows on the roughdraft pairings.

He stared. "You would rather start against *Cork?*"

"I admire his style of play, and I want a hard test at once," I told him.

"Well." He was flabbergasted. Maybe no one had ever before asked him to arrange a *tougher* pairing. "This is . . . unusual, sir. To say the least."

"If you could arrange it, however," I said, "I could make a most strenuous attempt to convince my partner to take the doubles draw as it stands."

"Let me make certain I understand," Conway said, looking at me like he thought I was mad. "If we give you a harder opening singles match, you will try to convince your doubles partner not to withdraw?"

"That's right."

He rolled his eyes heavenward. "I believe it can be done, sir."

Hoofing it up to the main building, a grand old castle-like structure with ivied stone walls and rounded corner turrets, I considered the best tactic to take with Carpoman. By the time I walked into the spacious old lobby, I had it figured.

Good thing.

"Goddamn!" His nasal voice rattled across the vast tile floor. "It's about time you got here, Brad! Have you heard what these people are trying to *do* to us?" He came charging over, creating a scene, a red-faced maniac in pale blue sweats. "Shit, I'm not taking this! I'm withdrawing us from the doubles!"

"No," I told him, "you don't have to do that. I've fixed it."

He looked blankly at me, a tic leaping on his cheek. "You did? What? How?"

"Can you imagine?" I said. "They had us down against Annacone and Van Rensburg—"

"Yeah! Right!"

"But they were *about to change it,*" I added before he could
speak, "In our most important tuneup before the All England, they
were going to weaken our draw and make us look like a couple of
wimps. Can you imagine that?"

Poor Terry's face went as slack as a wet bedsheet. "Uh—"

"I told them," I charged on, squeezing his shoulder for emphasis, "that we aren't going to be known as a couple of front-runners
that play patsies. How would *that* look? I ask you! —And how much
useful work for Wimbledon would we have gotten, playing a couple
of clowns not worthy of your abilities out there?"

"Well," Carpoman said. He licked his lips. His eyes looked
dazed. "Yeah. Sure. Uh—"

"I struck a deal with them," I added. "To get them to *guarantee* us a decent first-round doubles match that wouldn't disgrace our
reputation, I agreed to accept a change in the singles draw. For myself, I mean."

"You had a good draw," he said hoarsely.

I grinned and clapped him on the back. "Well, to keep us an
honorable test in the doubles, I did a deal with them. The way it's
going to be now, I open against Sean Cork."

"Cork!" Carpoman actually staggered back a half-step. "Cork
will kill your aged ass!"

"I know, Terry," I said, oozing sincerity. "But the honor of
our doubles team is more important. Playing with you—that's the
only chance I have of getting anywhere. Having a good test here
in doubles is worth *any* sacrifice I might make on the singles side."

He just looked at me. He was absolutely stunned.

"What a BS artist!" Linda said on the phone an hour later.

I didn't share with her a tentative disturbing conclusion I had
reached about Terry's erratic behavior. I hoped I was wrong. If I
was right, it could mean that he—desperate, driven, erratic—might

fit into the dark side of my mission. If I was right, he might be capable of anything, even selling out to terrorists.

The final brackets came out as I had anticipated. As Sunday wore on, more players and their entourages arrived. Terry and I got in some practice against a couple of Brazilian kids. I took it easy, Terry was his usual manic self, and we didn't keep close score, so it was all right. I thought they beat us.

In the evening a couple of other oldtimers like myself, Stan Smith and Arthur Ashe, checked in. We did brief interviews, and then Arthur suggested turnabout—him interviewing me for his HBO tape. I agreed, and later had a good visit with Fred Stolle and Cliff Drysdale. Play was scheduled to start very early Monday morning, and no one stayed up very late. I kept an eye out for Sean Cork, but was disappointed. Word came that he would arrive early Monday, in plenty of time for his match against me. After watching an abortive, nasty spat between the Carpomans—over money, of course—I turned in.

So on Monday I finally came face-to-face with Sean Cork, the man I had come to meet and watch.

I was already in the locker room getting ready, and matches were under way outside on six courts. A morning shower had delayed things.

Cork came in looking harried and taut.

A tall kid, bone-skinny, with fiery red hair and a complexion splotched by sunburn patches under his eyes, he jangled in with two aides in tow. One was a beefy, slow-moving gent who had "bodyguard" written all over him. The other was the dour, wizened little Charles Finneran, a really oldtime player who now functioned as Cork's trainer.

I had met Finneran a dozen times. But his eyes skimmed right over me as he looked around the locker area. "Crummy accommodations! I shall speak to the tournament committee about this at once."

"No," Cork said with weary resignation.

"But first no complimentary automobile and now no privacy!"

"Finny, be quiet."

"But surely they can't expect us to share space with every riff-raff in the hemisphere!"

Sean Cork went pale. He turned and caught Finneran's arm in a vise-grip that hurt, judging by the trainer's expression. "Just carry the bags, Finny, and be thinking about the problem! I don't need your damned big mouth around here!"

Finneran pulled free and rubbed his forearm. He looked pouty. He was good at looking pouty. "Yes, sir, Mr. Cork, sir."

Cork stared at him a long moment with the expression of a man plagued by demons. He turned to the other man who had entered with him. "Weiss, you can wait outside."

Weiss stood well over six feet tall, and his tight black tee shirt showed off arms and torso muscles that would have looked more at home in one of those weightlifting shows where the steroidy darlings grease up and posture for the judges. He had no forehead.

"Sure you'll be all right, Mr. Cork?" he rumbled.

"Yes. Fine. Out with you, now."

Finneran and Weiss headed for the door. It closed behind them. A profound silence fell over the locker room. I messed around with my knee brace. A couple of other players left the room. Sean Cork, silent and frowning, began unstowing some gear out of one of his duffelbags and packing it into a locker not far from mine.

I kept dawdling, waiting a chance to catch the eye of "the Limerick Lion." He didn't look much like a lion today. He looked tense, withdrawn, shaky.

I finally managed to make eye contact with him.

"Hello!" he called, soft and friendly. "You're Brad Smith, aren't you?"

I sauntered down. "Guilty."

He pumped my hand with youthful enthusiasm. Up close he was even younger, and he seemed sincerely pleased to meet me. His eyes brightened with teenage energy. "This is an honor, sir! It really is! I'm Sean Cork. I want you to know you were one of my heroes when I was growing up! Now I understand we play in a little while. Wow!"

Being beheld as an historic artifact never cheers me much, but he seemed sincere. "You're having a fine year, Sean."

His face twisted. "Fine year?" Then his expression changed. "Oh. You mean oncourt."

"Bad luck in Germany, but before that—"

"My timing is off," he said with boyish candor. "I don't know *what* the hell is wrong. I've been trying to work on it. Maybe I'll get it straightened out here."

"Hope so, Sean." I grinned at him. "But if you make some unforced errors against me out there, you won't hear me complaining."

"My God! You'll probably kill me!"

I hesitated, making sure, but there was no sarcasm in him at all. My impression of his youth and naiveté intensified. This man— this high-ranked world-class player, political symbol—and maybe terrorist target—was a kid. Younger than his age, even, because so much of his life had been lived between the lines of tennis courts . . . so much of a boy's normal growing-up experiences walled out by the narrow concentration on a game. I began to like him. I also began to feel a little sorry for him. His body was nineteen, his off-court maturity was closer to fifteen, and his problem was ageless: too much too soon.

I told him, "I just hope we have a decent match."

He frowned, worried. "Maybe we could visit later."

"Sure. I'd like that."

He gathered his rackets and started for the stadium door, then turned back with an afterthought. "Your finals match against Borg was one of the greatest I've ever seen. You had him. You *had* him. All you had to do was make that little dropshot. He would have never gotten to it. A little dink. I wake up in the night sometimes, and I've been playing a championship match and I've just missed a little shot like that. God." His eyes drifted off. Then they came back. He tried to brighten. "I have a tape of that match between you and Borg. I've played it a hundred times. You were great then. I think about that match a lot."

"I think about it some myself."

He went out, and in a few minutes I followed.

It would be pleasant to relate that I went out and got his full attention by drilling him in straight sets. Actually, I surprised myself by playing far better than I had expected. He played loosely, hitting a lot of balls long and wide, not because he was trying too hard but because there was obviously something wrong with his racket preparation and follow-through. But I was still the one who got drilled, 6-4, 6-4, in an hour and ten minutes.

"That was a good match!" he enthused afterward, a new look of respect in his eyes. "You really hit some good shots! That was great! Playing my childhood idol! Fantastic!"

"Thanks for the workout, Sean."

The worried frown returned. "Did you notice all the balls I hit wild?"

"I remember a few."

"I've got to get that worked out." He looked around. "Did you see my man Weiss in the stands?"

"No, but then I wasn't looking for him."

The frown deepened, became haunted. "He's supposed to be there. Close. —Did you notice those rough-looking guys seated almost directly behind the end judge? Didn't look like tennis fans to me."

I played dumb. "What else would they be?"

He stared into his private world for a few seconds, then remembered himself. "Nothing. —Nothing, of course. —Well—listen, you're not leaving the club or anything, are you?"

"No, Sean, and I'd enjoy having a good visit with you. What say we get together at your convenience?"

"That would be grand! My wife, Kitty, would like it too. She's your biggest fan. She says you were the best of all the old-timers."

"I'll look forward to hearing more about that, too."

*   *   *

Linda Bennett arrived on schedule, looking so beautiful that I had to concentrate to avoid staring.

"What's your room number?" she asked, and I told her.

"Darn," she said. "We're at opposite ends of the building." Then she brightened and gave me an ironic, inviting barrage from those eyes. "Of course I could always *get* to your room pretty fast . . . or you to mine."

I didn't answer, and tried not to think about it. I thought about it.

Late in the day, Terry Carpoman easily won his first singles match. He was hardly delighted. "I played like dogshit! If I don't do better tomorrow, the Russian will have my ass."

That didn't happen on Tuesday. He won his second singles match early in the morning. I watched that, and Sean Cork's match, from the stands. Terry played like a man possessed, booming in sixteen aces as he took out Volkov in straight sets. It was the kind of good, hard match you want early in a tournament: never in doubt as to the ultimate outcome, but a solid workout. Neverthless, Terry threw a temper tantrum. My suspicions grew.

Sean Cork played like a ghost—silent, no sign of emotion, no hint of exertion showing through his amazingly smooth-flowing movements. He played well within himself, still hitting loosely, frowning a lot in irritation with himself.

Even so, he was amazing, much better than he had been against me the previous day. It was easy to see why some rated him the next No. 1. He returned serves for winners that few players would have laid a racket on. He was so confident in his reflexes that he often crept up inside the backline, the way Andre Agassi likes to do. Then he took the ball so early, and blasted it back with such force, that he virtually removed the other player's presumed service advantage. His court movement was exceptional: both quick and anticipatory. He had a classic service motion of his own, with fireball results, and the poor Russian soon was standing a full twelve feet behind the backline and still failing to get the best ones back.

Cork could play the baseline game. The only sign that he was having timing problems could be seen in the way he stayed back there on many points when his fireball returns provided perfect opportunity to move in and attack. His backhand had a classic beauty, whether he was hitting them with overspin to a corner or undercutting the ball to change pace and bounce pattern. He could hit the forehand with extreme power or a cunning little sidecut that made the ball veer and die with an unpredictable hop.

Late in the match, when Cork seemed thoroughly warmed up and started his normal grasscourt net game, his power really asserted itself. His drives from the baseline set the Russian up again and again, and Cork moved to net with fluid grace and as much speed as anyone I had ever seen. When he hit an overhead it sounded like a howitzer blast; the results were similar, too.

With all of this, it was clear to me that his timing problem was not all in his head. Toward the end, although the outcome was not seriously in doubt any longer, he hit more balls long and wide. Watching, I thought I saw the problem. I wondered if worry about terrorist threats had started the slide into bad hitting habits, perhaps by robbing him of some of his concentration and court time for practice.

Often I saw him look into the stands. Finneran, his trainer/coach, and the hulking Weiss both sat up there where he looked. But he wasn't looking at Finneran for tacit encouragement. His eyes always went to Weiss.

So, I thought, the threats on his life were in his mind after all. It was apparent he was doing his best to banish them. But sometimes good intentions and mental discipline are not enough: the distraction *will* come through, and you carry it in a corner of your mind like a nagging headache. Sean Cork had his death threats in the same way I had Sylvester, always there on the edge of consciousness, an aching darkness.

I liked the kid already. In today's cast of spoiled millionaires, he was less affected and more decent than any I knew. There was a boyish sincerity in him that seemed almost too good to be true, but it was true. I saw some fans approach him for autographs and he seemed sincerely surprised that anyone would want an autograph from *him*. I wondered if he had similarly misjudged his fame earlier, when he made his remarks about the trouble in Ulster. Maybe he just hadn't realized that anything he might say could be taken seriously.

It rained in the afternoon, washing out the doubles. My knee was grateful.

That night some of us got together for a drink. I met Kitty Cork, who lived up to her reputation as a totally unaffected and bewitching beauty. I caught a little frown around her eyes on several occasions, but didn't find even the remotest chance to mention that she seemed worried. The threats hanging in the air from the north, I thought, were taking a toll on this really nice couple.

I admit I also spent some time looking over my shoulder. Sylvester was back in my thinking. Clarence Tune was nowhere in evidence, and I almost wished for him. I had decided that if he didn't come up with a gun for me, I was going to start talking about an imagined avid interest in hunting. Maybe I could then rent a shotgun with the story that I intended to do some sport shooting somewhere.

"You have a nice start on cozying up to the Corks," Linda Bennett observed late that night.

"Anything new on the terrorists?" I countered.

She shrugged pretty shoulders.

"You're a big help," I told her.

She gave me an ironic battery of eyes. "I strive to please."

That line I left right where she had placed it.

In the morning they used extra courts to make up the doubles matches, and Terry and I went out to face Annacone and Van Rensburg. I did my damnedest, and naturally Terry was a wild man out there, but they still waxed us, 6-4, 6-3. Terry had a temper tantrum in the locker room afterward and broke two rackets.

"That's all right, that's all right," he fumed later at the inn.

"They got some lucky bounces and you didn't look very sharp." He scowled at me. "Were you *trying?*"

The question startled me. "Yes, Terry, actually."

"I got the impression you might be saving yourself a little. On a couple of points you were really slow getting to net, and Paul was hitting those dinks back at your feet. If you weren't trying, it's all right. I mean, Christ! You're no spring chicken. I understand. You've got to save yourself some."

"That's very understanding of you, Terry. Thank you very much."

"Just let me know when you plan to coast a few points, man. I'll try to cover a little more for you."

"All right, Terry. You're very considerate."

His awkward expression of camaraderie turned into a scowl. "You've got to work on your serve."

"Terry, I'll sure try to do that."

I spent a little more time with Sean and Kitty Cork. The talk was all of tennis. I liked them. They were sweet kids. She obviously adored him. It was mutual. I wanted to hear about the death threats and his political views, but no opportunity presented itself. I felt that I was accomplishing my primary goal, establishing a real friendship. So I told myself to cool it and be patient.

On Thursday afternoon Terry was scheduled against Gilbert, and I wanted to see that. I was up in the stands by myself, watching them warm up, when someone dropped into the seat beside me, the one I was saving for Linda.

"I'm sorry," I said, starting to turn. "But that seat—" I stopped.

Clarence Tune, mournful in his dark suit despite the warm afternoon sun, sighed and clucked regretfully. "It's I who should apologize, sir. I am very sorry to inform you of this, but it really is imperative that you return to London with me at your earliest possible convenience. Something quite extraordinary has happened."

*   *   *

When Tune gave me the outline of what had happened, I left
the bleachers and went with him after leaving a note for Linda. On
the drive back toward London, Tune told me more.

Two nights earlier, a man had been found dead on an isolated
side road near the intersection of A20 and the Ring Road outside
of London. Everything pointed to a hit-and-run accident. The back
of the victim's head was smashed, and bits of automotive-type paint
peppered the indentation. There was also a small puncture wound
in the lower back of the kind that might be made by an ornament
on a car's hood—pardon me—bonnet. One side of the man's body
was severely abraded and his clothing torn, markings consistent with
the scrape marks and bits of blood and tissue on the pavement near
where the body was found.

Accident examiners theorized that the victim had been walking
close to the edge of the narrow, curving lane. Worse, he had been
walking with the direction of potential traffic. A car rounded a curve
close behind him (so the report theorized) and struck him squarely
in the back, the bonnet ornament piercing the lower back in the
instant before impact tossed him over the car, smashing his skull
as he was hit by either the top front edge of the vehicle or a side
pillar. The body then was tossed onto the pavement, where its velocity caused it to bounce several times before skidding to a halt.

Investigators who measured skid marks, distances from the
curve to likely point of impact, etc., wrote that the driver of the
death car probably had had less than one second to veer to avoid
the walker. After the blow, the driver had panicked and kept on
going.

A bulletin went out promptly, seeking reports on vehicles with
recent front-end damage. Repair shops were notified. In the first
eighteen hours after filing of the report, more than a dozen drivers
with crumpled fenders, bumpers or bonnets were pulled over and
questioned. Two repair shops called in repair jobs to be checked.
None of this investigative work led anywhere.

It might have ended there, another accident report left to mildew in a file, except that the victim carried no identification of any

kind, only a scrap of paper with an East Waterloo address and the name of a woman written on it, and a key that evidently was for the door to a flat. When officers went to the address to check further, they learned more.

The name on the sheet of paper was that of the woman who operated the building. Examining the key found in the dead man's pocket, she found the tiny letter on it which indicated one of her units. She told investigators that she had rented the room to the gentleman only a few days earlier, and didn't know anything about him, but he seemed a quiet and decent sort, and he had paid in advance. She provided the name her renter had given to her, but had no other information.

Clucking about life's sadness, she went with the officers to the room, where they conducted a painstaking search.

They found little: two old suits and some shirts and ties hanging in the alcove off the bath, some underwear, socks and handkerchiefs, shaving articles, a couple of old newspapers, a battered suitcase. Nothing appeared at all helpful until one of the investigators happened to notice a magazine tucked under the bed. A Russian-language magazine.

That stirred interest. The searchers went over everything a second time. This trip through, they found a crumpled used airline ticket, the carbons indicating a Lufthansa flight from Budapest to Frankfurt to London, including a stub indicating that the passenger had gotten to Budapest earlier on a flight out of Moscow. Taped to the back of a picture on the bedroom wall they also found two current Swiss passports with two different names and the photograph page of each blank.

At this point a tight lid of secrecy had been clamped on everything.

Bigger investigative guns were rolled out. They found one more scrap of evidence: in the trash container behind the building, the soggy remains of a vehicle rental form. When that was checked out, it turned out that a man fitting the corpse's general description had rented a delivery van on the day a witness had seen a man fitting the corpse's general description make a delivery to the home of Ivor McWilliams.

At this point, dead ends had started appearing with dismal regularity. But someone remembered Clarence Tune's report about my reaction to description of the deliveryman. Tune was called in. "And here I am, don't you see. Taking you back to London, sir."

I watched the grubby London outskirts roll by the dark windshield of his car. A wisp of hope curled inside me, but I could not afford the luxury of noticing it. I maintained the feeble deception: "I don't see how any of this has anything to do with me, Clarence. So a bum got run over and killed. I'll humor you. But if you're thinking it might be someone important—"

"Well, sir, you do see how it could have been the man who hired Ivor McWilliams, don't you, now?"

"I suppose that's possible. But—"

"And you do see how the items discovered around his room tend to indicate a Russian connection . . . and possibly something sneaky underfoot?"

"That's your kind of business, Clarence. Not mine."

"*Yes*, sir. Of course, sir." Tune actually sounded put out with me. "Nevertheless. We know and you know that you have had two nasty scrapes with the fellow usually coded 'Sylvester.' —No, no, please let me talk, sir. We shall be there in a few moments and it saves so much time if we do away with the ritualistic denials. Thank you, sir. Well, then, there is a theory afoot that your 'Sylvester' was in London and up to something, and may indeed have tried to hire McWilliams to do you in, as it were. He then moved from his usual digs, wherever they might have been, fearing possible identification by our people. And then he was killed in what really may have been a random accident on the roadway."

"What," I demanded while I cast around for what I should really say, "would somebody like Sylvester be doing out on a godforsaken road?"

"I'm sure I don't know, sir. But that's where we believe he was—and that is who we believe our corpse is, actually. Or was."

"And I'm supposed to go to this morgue and take a look."

"Quite. Yes, sir."

"And say whether it's Sylvester?"

"We should hope you could do that, yes, sir."

I decided to give up the deception that hadn't worked anyway. "Clarence. I haven't seen the man for a while, and then only fleetingly. He could have changed his appearance again. I don't hold out a lot of hope that I could positively identify him, and I don't hold out any hope that this is him, either."

"Yes," Tune said. "Well. Quite. But if you *might* identify him, we have to have a go, do you see?"

I didn't answer that. The prospect of actually being able to identify Sylvester—to see him stone cold dead, and know he was off me forever—made me feel slightly feverish with excitement. I had been so afraid of the son of a bitch for so long. Had hated him so much, and imagined that one day we would face each other again. . . .

Tune slowed the little car and wheeled it up to the iron gates of an imposing stone compound. I read a prison name plaque on the cornerpost. Tune showed the guards a credential and the gates were opened and we drove through. We angle-parked in front of the largest and tallest of the massive gray-black buildings, and got out.

I felt more shaky. I wanted it to be so. Oh, how I wanted that.

Tune went up the granite steps of the building. I followed.

"He looks so natural," people say. Or: "He looks like he's just sleeping," they tell one another as they stand before the casket. But it is always a lie. A dead man is a waxen figure. The pallid chill of the face of death is a mockery of what was.

The man-form naked on the still cold slab in the London morgue might have been Sylvester. All you could say with certainty was that he was dead.

Hoping, I forced myself to study him carefully under the cold glare of the cruel overhead light.

He had been a solidly built man with muscular arms and shoulders showing signs of weight loss from earlier days. He was the right size. His hairy chest showed the bluish pucker of a fairly recent and very ugly gunshot wound above the right nipple. His body fur masked other possible older scars. Out of his dense bush of genital hair protruded a wrinkled bulge of genitals that must have once been his pride and joy. His thick neck and blunt skull might have been Sylvester's. The sunken, wide-set eyes were a match. But the slightly flattened nose and wide mouth, twisted downward in the death grimace, were those of a stranger.

Tune pointed toward the face. "The severity of the blow to the back of the head may have caused some contortion of the facial features."

I didn't say anything. *How could I be sure?* Because I wanted so badly to be sure, I kept staring . . . studying.

Tune cleared his throat and spoke again, very softly, the way people often do around the dead. I wonder if people fear they'll wake them. "Rigor mortis, or the preservatives, have brought these out." His soft tones echoed in the concrete silence around us. "I have been assured they were invisible prior to the death process. Very fine work, I am told."

I couldn't see what he was talking about until I leaned closer.

Near-microscopic little tracks—the faintest blue and pink on the waxen surface of the skin around the eyes, nose and mouth, betrayed old reconstructive surgery. There were many, many tiny lines, hinting at how extensive the surgery had had to be.

"No telling what he once looked like," I said, standing up. "Before this."

"Indeed not," Tune said.

"How old was this plastic surgery? Any guesses on that?"

"Less than two years old."

"I see."

Tune watched me. I was through. He nodded to the attendant, who re-draped the corpse. We went alone into an adjacent lab, a

large cold room with bare tile floors and walls lined with closed steel cabinets. I shivered.

"So," Tune said. "What think?"

"It could be Sylvester," I told him.

"Could you possibly be more definite than that, old chap?"

"He's the right age, the right build. There's the old chest wound; that matches, too. The face—I just don't remember him looking like that."

Tune thought about that. He looked disappointed and tired. "He could have had more surgery. And there is the distortion caused by the severity of the blow to the head."

"Yes," I conceded. "Or this could be a man who just happened to have similar old injuries."

"Highly unlikely coincidence, don't you think? Especially considering the items found in his room?"

I took a deep breath, trying to maintain a pessimistic attitude. "We can't be sure."

But a slow hope was building inside me. I had to be careful, I had to be cautious, I could not allow myself to draw a conclusion based on hope. But Tune was right: all the other evidence fit what we knew. There could have been more surgery. The blow to the head could have caused distortion. My memory could be faulty. This man was clean-shaven, and Sylvester had had a light beard in Montana when I saw him last, for such a brief time.

I thought the chances were no better than fifty-fifty that the corpse in there was my old nemesis.

But hope is very powerful. We can convince ourselves of almost anything. During the days when my first marriage was already dead, I convinced myself that the reality was otherwise. Elizabeth's icy contempt, I told myself, was merely tension. Her repeated mysterious absences were only her way of asserting her own personality with innocent diversions. The cool nausea of despair in my gut was only a symptom of my failure to be understanding enough, to achieve the kind of trust in her that someone so wonderful deserved. Sometimes the most insane self-delusion seems better than the chill puke of reality.

Tune stirred, bringing me back to the present. "It would make a very nice item in my file, of course, if I could report a definite identification. The commander would be *very* pleased with that."

"I don't know how I can say that, Clarence. I can't leap to a conclusion, here."

"Oh, but I say. If a man rides into town alone, wearing a thin glove on his right hand, with his sixgun belted low, and he matches the poster description of a noted desperado, wouldn't the local sheriff be justified in 'leaping to a conclusion' about him? In *High Noon*, wasn't Gary Cooper justified in 'leaping to a conclusion' about—"

"This isn't a goddamned western movie, Clarence!"

He took that in, stood silent a moment, then heaved another sigh. "Let us review the circumstances."

"Not necessary, Clarence. I know you want a positive ID. You think I don't? It's *impossible*. Sorry."

"You're sure of that?"

"I'm sure that I'm *not* sure. Right."

Tune slumped. "Oh, dear." He looked bleak. "Disappointing."

He offered to drive me back to Nottingham but I was too tired, and said I would head back there early in the morning. He drove me to my hotel in silence. It was very late. But my brain was going Mach 3. It was just too much coincidence. Our operation surrounding Wimbledon might still be an unholy mess as far as I could be aware, but maybe I had just had Christmas, birthday and a visit from the Easter Bunny all on the Fourth of July. It was all I could do to maintain a somber demeanor for poor Clarence.

He stopped to let me off curbside.

"About the gun," I said.

He peered at me, eyes invisible behind the thick glasses. "You still believe that might be necessary?"

"Yes."

"Oh, dear. I had hoped otherwise."

"Maybe it's Sylvester down there. Maybe it isn't. I can't take the chance."

"Yes. Well. . . ."

"What's your answer, Clarence?"

He rocked in his driver's seat, exquisitely worried. "Very well. You shall have it."

"When, Clarence?"

"As soon as I can manage it, sir."

"*When?*"

"Soon, sir!"

"Thank you."

He sniffed. "You're welcome, sir, I'm sure."

Twelve

I MADE A call to the contact number at the embassy, identifying myself as Uncle Harry, saying I was at my hotel and wanted Aunt Harriet to call me back at her earliest convenience. I expected somebody to call and set a meeting place. Instead, a little over an hour later, somebody knocked on my hotel room door.

I went to the door but didn't open it. "Who is it?"

"Kinkaid."

I opened up and J. C. Kinkaid came in, removing a plastic raincoat that streamed water onto the carpet. He looked tired and hassled. "This better be good, Smith."

"It is."

He looked around. "Where's Linda?"

"I left Nottingham in something of a hurry. Unless we wanted to blow her cover with Clarence Tune, she had to stay behind."

"Not a good idea to separate like that. Her orders were to stick with you."

"I'll turn in my merit badge."

Kinkaid tossed his light-weight coat over a chair and turned to face me, hands on his hips. He was wearing khaki pants, the lower legs black with rainwater, soaked loafers, an aged-looking white Banlon tee shirt. "Is this what you needed? Somebody to crack sarcastic jokes with?"

"Tune came to Nottingham to pick me up to identify a body."

The signs of weariness vanished. "Whose?"

"Maybe Sylvester."

Kinkaid scowled down at his wet shoes, then fished for a cigarette in his pants pocket. "You'd better tell this slowly, and leave nothing out."

I did. Kinkaid smoked two cigarettes, interjecting quick questions that convinced me he was as surprised as I had been.

"Holy shit," he said when I finished.

"My sentiments exactly."

He paced. "If this is true—if it's really Sylvester—it removes one big major, major complication."

"You don't seem very surprised that it *might* be Sylvester."

He looked quizzically at me.

I explained, "You guys denied the possibility that he might be around."

He stood motionless, a thin man of medium height with asphalt-colored eyes that revealed nothing. "It wasn't my idea."

"But you did have some reports that made you think he might be around?"

"Nothing very convincing. Don't get pissed off."

"You guys screwed me again, J.C."

"No, it was decided you didn't need to know."

"Didn't need to know!"

"It wasn't my idea."

"Well, I'm mad about being lied to, as usual. On the other hand, if you people did have hints Sylvester might be in London, then maybe there's a better chance that that corpse down there is him."

"You couldn't make a positive ID?"

"It doesn't look a lot like I remember him. But time has passed. The body build is the same. The scars seem to match what would be expected. The locals found incriminating stuff in his room. Clarence said the force of the killing blow to the head could cause distortion of facial features."

"So it could be him."

"Yes."

Kinkaid watched me closely. "You want to believe it's him."

"Oh, hell yes."

"We will definitely check this. I hope it pans out."

"Needless to say, I'll be waiting to hear your conclusions."

He nodded. "In the meantime, you carry on with the assign-ment."

"I've gotten closer to Sean Cork. I've noticed something in his tennis right now that's bothering his effectiveness. I plan to mention it to him—discreetly—and maybe get closer by giving him a little coaching."

"Great. You're to stick with him and keep your eyes and ears open."

"I'll do it. But it doesn't seem very specific."

"Well, you studied those mug shots at the office."

"Yes, and I understand what I'm to do if I spot any of those IRA faces."

"Okay, fine."

I found a cigarette and lit it. "Anything else?"

He surprised me: "Yes. You ever hear of Melville Oldham?"

"The Brit millionaire who brews beer and races cars?"

"That's the one. He's also a big tennis buff. Every year he in-vites players and their ladies up to his country home the last full weekend before Wimbledon. Then he rents a house for Wimble-don's two weeks down near the club, has a lot of tennis guests in during that time, too. —He hasn't invited you to the country place this weekend?"

"I haven't heard anything about it."

Kinkaid lit a third cigarette. "Cork and some others are going. Get an invitation to go too."

"What," I asked, "if I can't?"

"*Do* it. We want you close to him out there. It might be a grand place for an attempted assassination."

"I'll try," I promised. "What can you tell me about Oldham?"

"He's out of the brewery business. He has connections in Northern Ireland, where he's trying to start some kind of motor car business. He used to collect beautiful young wives like he does cars, but he's got an American girlfriend right now he really seems to like."

"How old is he?"

"Sixty-five. He stopped racing motor cars on his last birthday. He's sinking a fortune into the Northern Ireland car-building thing. Has other interests, too, but none that are interesting to us."

"Politically active?"

"British taxes were just eating his lunch in the brewing business, and when he sold his beer interests, he issued a big blast at Margaret Thatcher's government for, quote, failing to halt the spread of Socialism in Britain, unquote, and, quote, wasting our national treasury and the lives of our young men in a bottomless pit in Northern Ireland, unquote."

I studied Kinkaid. "You don't think *Oldham* is in with terrorists, surely."

He shrugged.

"I'll get an invitation if I can."

"You can. He likes champions, present and past."

"We'll pull Linda Bennett back for the weekend," he added. "We'll need her here to help check out this body in the morgue. We're short-handed as hell, as always."

"Okay, so I'm on my own?"

He grinned crookedly. "Just you and your shadow, Clarence Tune."

I was aware of my disappointment, and that irritated me. I didn't want to feel that I was getting to where I liked having Linda around. "No problem," I lied.

We talked a few minutes more about the watchful state of all the security forces in and around London. The vague picture I got was of uncoordinated officers falling over one another, and nobody turning up anything. Assumption: a terrorist incident during Wimbledon was still on. Evidence: none new. Progress: zero.

*   *   *

After Kinkaid left, I paced the room a while. Then I did my time zone calculations and figured I could still catch Beth at her office in California. The call, surprisingly, went right through the hotel, the overseas operator, AT&T longlines, and even the receptionist at Beth's law firm out there.

"Brad?" she said, disbelief in her tone.

"Hello from London," I said. "Wait a minute. I'll stick the phone out the window. Maybe you can hear Big Ben."

"Is something wrong?"

"No, not a thing, babe. I'm playing at Nottingham and getting into better shape."

Her voice relaxed slightly. "I was worried something might have happened."

"No," I lied. "Nothing."

"And your . . . other work is going all right?"

"Sure. Nothing to it."

Pause. Then: "So why have you called, Brad?"

I was incredulous. "Because I miss you . . . wanted to talk to you—hear your voice."

She sounded strained and remote. "That's very thoughtful of you. Thank you."

I tried to pretend she was not acting weird. "So how are you?"

"Just fine. I'm in the middle of a trial. Tax evasion. Very interesting, complicated as hell."

"Hope you win."

"Thanks. We've got a shot."

And suddenly we didn't have anything to say to each other.

We were hung up, stymied by the disagreement over my CIA connection, our inability to work out a workable compromise between my new life in Montana and her law practice in California, the gulf that separated every practical aspect of our lives from the way we both felt absolutely perfect and inevitable whenever we were together.

I said, "I sure wish you were here."

She didn't say anything to that.

"It's been raining some, but we've gotten in most of the matches. Wimbledon is just a little over a week off now, you know."

"Yes. I know."

"And everything there is fine?"

"Yes. Busy."

"My knee is holding up pretty well. It's interesting, being back on grass."

"I'm sure it's fun."

"I've been playing with Terry Carpoman, you know. He's a wild man. He has changed so much in the last few months, Beth. It's incredible. He loses his temper at the slightest provocation. He's really unstable. He and his wife fight constantly. It's sad."

"Yes. Well, things happen, you know."

I cast around. "And you're okay?"

"Oh, yes. Fine."

"Do you hear anything from Ted in Montana? Anything like that?"

"No, nothing."

"Is there . . . anything else I need to know?"

"I can't think what it might be, Brad."

And I couldn't think of anything more to try.

She said, "Well, Brad, it was sweet of you to call. I guess I'd better run."

"How's the weather?" I persisted miserably.

"Oh, fine. Just fine."

"Well, it's warmer than normal here, but we keep getting these showers."

"Oh."

"England's weather is funny."

"Yes."

"Sunny one minute, rainy the next."

"It sounds odd, all right."

"But you're okay, Beth?"

"I'm fine."

"Great. Well. It was good to hear your voice."

"You too, Brad. Good luck."

I hung up and thought about Linda. Maybe, I told myself, it was a very good thing she wasn't within reach right now. I wanted her badly.

Back at the tournament the next morning, I watched Sean Cork lose in the quarters to Jimmy Jimerson, whom he should have beaten easily.

"I don't know what it is," he said afterward in the locker room, where I had made it a point to be waiting for him. "My timing is so far off—"

Finneran, his coach/trainer, held up a fist. "The thing to do, lad, is hit oot! Hit harder! Blast 'er deeper an' get back in the swing!"

I saw my chance. "I disagree," I said.

Both men looked at me, Sean surprised, Finneran angry.

"When your timing is off," I explained, "you don't get it back by overhitting. Besides, Sean, I think I've seen what your real problem is."

Finneran's lip curled. "And yer a coach now, too, I suppose?"

"Be quiet, Finny," Sean said. "Go on, Brad."

"It's easier shown that told," I replied. "And I might be wrong. But get us some court time and we can hit some practice balls, and I'll show you what I mean."

Finneran snarled, "An' naturally yer qualified to coach him, since he beat yer ass off oot here the other day."

Sean colored. "Finny, bug off." He turned back to me. "Are you going to Melville Oldham's this weekend?"

"Haven't been invited."

"He has courts. I'm leaving shortly. What if I asked him about inviting you?"

I pretended uncertainty. "If it wouldn't be intruding—"

"God, no! As a former champion, you're just the kind of person he most enjoys! The fact that he hasn't invited you already has to have been a simple oversight! —Look. Let me check it out and get back to you. Then if you'll come up for the weekend we can rally and work on my game. It would mean a lot to me, Brad." He cocked an eye at Finneran. "I haven't been getting any real help anywhere else, and I'm ready to try anything. —And you'll enjoy the weekend. Melville throws a great party."

"I'd be glad to come along," I said.

"Fine! I'll check and get back to you within the hour!"

Back at the main building, I found a note from Linda in my mailbox. It said a friend in London was ill, and she was returning there at once. So COS had recalled her for the Sylvester probe, just as Kinkaid had expected. I headed for my room, and was intercepted in the lift lobby by Terry Carpoman and the comely Alicia. Both were all scowls and anger.

"If I get you an invitation to Melville Oldham's," Terry said, "you'll come, won't you?"

"I was just talking about that with Sean Cork, and—"

"Because," he cut in brusquely, "we need to practice this weekend, and he's got courts."

Alicia said nastily, "What you need practice on, *dear,* is controlling your temper."

He wheeled on her, face splotching. "You just shut your face, see!"

"*I'm* not going to that country house and sit around all weekend when I could be shopping!"

"You'll do as I goddamn well say!"

"I'll do as I wish!"

"We don't need you going back to London and spending more money. We've got to economize right now, goddamnit! How many times do I have to tell you?"

She stamped a pretty foot, and diamond pendants bobbled. "I'm sick of hearing you talk about acting like we're impoverished! We have plenty of money! All you have to do is stop acting like a crazy man, and get control of yourself and win some tournaments!"

"We're not buying any more expensive frou-frous! You're staying right here with me, and we're going to Oldham's for the week-end!"

"We'll see about that!"

"I'm the man and you'll do what I say!"

Alicia's pretty mouth twisted in an ugly sneer of contempt. "Too bad the only mannish thing you're capable of doing these days is shout and bully people."

Terry went white. "Shut up, or I'll—"

"You'll do *what?*" she flung back at him. "You haven't been capable of doing *anything* to me for months!"

His hand lashed out and cracked across her face. Jolted backward, she almost fell, tears of shock and pain bolting from her eyes.

Terry turned reddened eyes back to me. "If Cork can't get you an invitation, I can. You'll ride with us. A man will be here within the next hour or two, delivering my new Jaguar. Plenty of room. You'll enjoy it." He turned back to Alicia. "And you're going, bitch. It will be fun, you'll see."

It sounded like it was going to be hilarious.

Thirteen
Elsewhere

London

THREE FIGURES SLIPPED into the alley garage under the cover of darkness. The two seventeen-year-olds from Londonderry, Eugene O'Connor and John Mudd, stood blind in the black interior of the building while their fellow conspirator, Reggie Montgomery, fumbled for a light switch on the bare board wall. He found it, turned it. Light sprang from the open wood rafters overhead, making all three men blink, momentarily dazzled.

Montgomery was older than the two school dropouts from Derry. He was twenty-two. Bone-thin, his dirty dark hair tied in a ponytail, he wore bib overalls and filthy canvas shoes that might once have been white. He had close-set eyes, weasel eyes filled with crafty hatred.

Montgomery, child of a London prostitute and an unidentified father, had been first abandoned at five. From then until he was eighteen, he went through one foster home after another. As a tot he had eaten feces and tried to set his house on fire. Later he had tortured and killed house cats, beaten an adoptive brother into a coma, had screaming fits at school which earned him expulsion, was arrested a dozen times on complaints ranging from stealing candy to clubbing a blind news kiosk operator with a lead pipe. He had "spells," as he called them, which were always violent. Often he did not remember them later.

The one thing consistent in Montgomery's life had been rage. He had never known any other significant emotion. He saw life as a challenge to get even and inflict pain.

His contact with O'Connor and Mudd had been accidental, but he had seen at once that they shared something important. The two mental defectives from Northern Ireland had railed openly about "getting revenge" on some notable public figure to win respect for themselves. They thought they could be heroes if they killed or maimed the right famous person. Montgomery believed they were crazy to think this way, but the idea of helping them excited him. He had played them along like fish in a stream, feeling their delusions of grandeur.

And now he had them.

Mudd and O'Connor began to recover from the sudden bright light. They squinted at the tall, rusty beige van parked under the lights. It looked like one of the rear springs might be broken, and sat right rear down, like a large animal with an injured paw. The side windows—there were only windows in the front doors, the back portion being solid metal—were spiderwebbed with cracks. A headlight was broken out.

"This is *it?*" Mudd groaned.

"How can we use *this* for a getaway car?" O'Connor snarled in disappointment.

"She looks poor," Montgomery said soothingly, "but she runs like a dream. A dream!"

O'Connor strode over to the van and hauled open its back side door. Peered inside. "Can we torch out a hole in this sidewall for a gun?"

"Sure, sure," Montgomery grinned.

Mudd walked over disjointedly, cracking his knuckles. "I dunno, I dunno."

"Shut up, Piggy," O'Connor snapped, and turned his attention again to Montgomery. "If all else fails, we can load the plastic explosive inside and ram his car or house with it?"

Montgomery's grin shone like a wolf. "Sure."

O'Connor paced back and forth in front of the aged van. "All right. We'll buy her from you. The deal as said."

"Yes," Montgomery agreed.

"We got the guns and we got the plastique. Can you cut that hole in the side for us right away? Tonight?"

"Sure," Montgomery soothed. "But what's the big hurry?"

"We said in our note he would never live to see Wimbledon. Wimbledon starts in a week. He'll be here probably the day after tomorrow . . . him and his fancy lady. We're running outta time. He's got to die now. Next week. Wednesday."

Mudd's round face brightened. "They'll know then who they're dealing with, right, Gene?"

"Sean Cork should of never said them things about the IRA," O'Connor said, his head bobbing. "After we destroy him, we'll be the greatest heroes in ages . . . ages! Nobody will ever laugh at us again."

"We'll never have to work again, neither," Mudd agreed.

"It will be the grandest thing we have ever did." O'Connor turned back to Montgomery. "Well. Here's yer money, cash. Now git to cuttin' that hole for us. And we'll be done with you."

"Ah, no," Montgomery said, smiling.

O'Connor looked blank. "You say no?"

"I'll not be leaving," Montgomery said. "You might need more mechanical help. And I want in on this one. I want to see them people die. I like seeing people die."

O'Connor stared at the older man, and his Adam's apple bobbed. Then he looked at Mudd, who blinked. Neither of them had the mental machinery to cope quickly with any change in plans.

"Besides," Montgomery told them. "You need a driver."

O'Connor's teeth clicked like the jaws of a trap. "Yer right. —All right! Yer in! And God bless us all!"

Belfast, Northern Ireland

The Lufthansa flight from Frankfurt touched down heavily in the midst of a steady rainstorm. Rashid Khemin, visiting lecturer on Islamic culture at Queen's University, deplaned with 77 other passengers and waited patiently, along with the others, during the usual customs inspections.

Khemin's battered, softsided suitcase and crated package were given close attention. The inspectors were very polite, and pretended to be casual. But they went through everything, unwrapping the three bundled Islamic icons and inspecting them, too, with great care. Each was a small, ornately framed painting on grass paper, illustrating a truth of Islam.

Khemin, who made frequent trips to Frankfurt to collect artworks sent there by associates in Iraq for use in his lectures, was patient, understanding and friendly during the search.

The inspectors found nothing out of the ordinary. Khemin's visa was duly stamped once more, and he left the airport smiling.

One hour later, securely locked in his room, he began the slow and painstaking process of inserting a thin steel blade into invisible seams in the faded gilt ornamentation on one of his artworks' frame. He worked five hours before he could peel two layers off the giltwork and begin to remove the seventeen ounces of Semtex so carefully packed into hidden crevices—enough plastic explosive to blow an airliner out of the sky, or devastate one side of Wimbledon stadium.

Ten miles away, Sylvester sat in a pub, nursing his pint, listening to the conversations around him. He had overheard a few interesting remarks which led him to believe his background briefings had been accurate, and members of the URA faction sometimes frequented the building. But he had not been able to pinpoint any single local suspect, and his quiet enquiries of other sources had been disappointing.

Sylvester was pleased with his ruse in London. There had been nothing whatsoever in the press about Motard's body. This could only mean that a cloak of secrecy had been thrown around the case by the Home Office. Which could in turn only mean that they had found his carefully planted "hidden" clues, and were at least investigating the chance that the corpse could be Sylvester.

That was good, and meant his trick had worked. Brad Smith would be somewhat less on guard now. An easier target.

But Sylvester needed more information on the terrorists. His plan for Brad Smith had to be dovetailed with what the terrorists planned. And he did not have much time left. Qualifying play for the Wimbledon tournament was set to begin. That meant the terrorist scheme must begin to unfold soon. It was all going to start moving any day now. Sylvester had to be ready to get back to London and start putting his own secret scheme for Smith into operation.

London

The Soviet ambassador, crumpled inside his 1955 suit, fixed Mikhail Gravitch with a baleful stare over the top of his desk. "Moscow is concerned."

Gravitch spoke through gritted teeth. "I am aware of Mr. Lemlek's report suggesting a threat to internal security through my 'unleashing' of Mr. Szulc on the fact-finding mission to Belfast. I sent my own contradictory report, pointing out Szulc's long record as 'Sylvester,' and my conclusion that he is stable and trustworthy."

The ambassador allowed a sigh to escape his caved-in chest. "Moscow worries that Szulc may be unstable despite your report. Psychological studies indicate such instability. Lemlek's reports have added to official alarm. I have been asked to send positive reassurance that Szulc will not attempt to seize upon any situation as a pretext for an attack on the American, Brad Smith."

"I can assure you, sir, that Szulc is following orders. There will be no attempt on this man Smith, and therefore no backlash that might in any way threaten our internal security system or image in the community."

The ambassador fixed Gravitch with worried, watery eyes. "You are certain?"

"Yes, sir!"

Another sigh. The ambassador reached for a pen. "I will reassure our superiors in Moscow. But I must ask you to be vigilant, Mr. Gravitch. If, after our reassurances, Comrade Szulc should attack this man Smith, it would mean not just his career. It would mean mine—and yours—as well."

"I understand perfectly," the KGB Resident replied with all outward appearance of calm.

When he left the ambassador's office, however, Gravitch was in a turmoil of rage and uncertainty. Lemlek! he thought. The filth's posturing and maneuvering for political advantage never stopped. In happier days, Gravitch would have devised a means to terminate him and make it appear the work of some other nation.

That was out of the question now, unfortunately. The only way to beat Lemlek was at his own game. The man must be discredited.

A start on that course would be for Szulc—Sylvester—to perform perfectly, making no violent threat whatsoever to Brad Smith—just as Gravitch had promised. That would discredit Lemlek's dire forecasts. From that point. . . .

But first, Gravitch thought, plunging deeper into worry again, Sylvester had to keep his promises and stay away from Smith.

It crossed Gravitch's mind to recall Sylvester and reassign him to duties inside the embassy. But no, that would look like a feeble, defensive response to Lemlek's reports.

Sylvester, then, despite Gravitch's own hidden misgivings, had to remain on the job in Belfast.

But Gravitch had to devise new ways to assure himself of Sylvester's whereabouts and activities. Not easy. But it could be done, at least in part.

The KGB Resident thought about the outcome if he determined Sylvester *was* plotting against Smith. But his thoughts turned more to his own handling of the information than to disposition of Sylvester. For if the man played into Lemlek's slimy hands by doing as that filth had suggested in his memos, then Gravitch hoped not to wait for official action by headquarters. He would do everything in his power to terminate Sylvester himself.

Fourteen

TERRY CARPOMAN'S JAGUAR did not arrive as scheduled Friday, and it still had not shown up Saturday afternoon when Sean and Kitty Cork invited me to ride to Melville Oldham's country estate with them. We left Carpoman screaming over the telephone at some unfortunate dealer in London, and his wife Alicia grimly looking over priceless antique jewelry in the resort curio shop.

"Terry is not a pleasant fellow," Sean observed mildly as we drove away.

Kitty smiled. "I don't know why he should be surprised. No British subject would be."

"That the car is late?"

"Darling, it's a Jaguar. It will be a wonder if it ever runs long enough to get here at all."

"Ah," Sean crooned, "you're a cruel one, you are."

She smiled at him with loving challenge. "Too cruel for you?"

"Very, very cruel. And heartless."

"I thought you *liked* me heartless."

"Ah! How could you think such a terrible thing!"

"Do you want me to get rid of the leather things, then, darling . . . and all that sort of heartless thing?"

He shook his head in mock despair. "I'm a saint to be putting up with the likes of you. You break my heart, you do."

Kitty's smile was sweetly wicked. "Is there *nothing*, then, I might do to keep your poor heart from breaking?"

171

"Well . . . there might be *some* things."

She wriggled with pleasure. "Tell me."

"Later, m'luv."

"Good," she purred with soft, happy triumph.

I kept quiet because their loving conspiracy put them alone in the universe. I enjoyed their secret codes, their games, the obvious pleasure they gave one another. They matched. I couldn't help but compare their play with the Carpomans' macabre, circling cannibalism. Then I thought of myself and Beth, and wondered if open war was better than suspended emotion and the cavern of ice built by emotional withdrawal.

They lapsed into silence as we motored into the English countryside. The fickle weather had turned again and the sun peered through broken clouds. After a while, seeming to relax more as we distanced ourselves from both Finneran and Weiss, whom he had left behind, Sean told me a bit about Oldham, our host.

It seemed that in 1979, the seventeenth Earl of Callishaw succeeded in doing something several consecutive generations of the family had been working on. He, along with his two equally useless sisters, finally managed to use up the last of the money. After the Earl fatally shot himself in a bungled attempt to gain sympathy, his sisters tearfully kissed their polo ponies goodbye and moved to Birmingham. The old castle, the manor house, and approximately 200 acres of rolling woodland were placed on the auction block.

British authorities were interested for museum purposes. Melville Oldham outbid them and moved in.

"He lives in a fifteenth century castle?" I asked.

"No," Cork said over his shoulder. He paused while he steered his rented Fiat around a slower car on a stretch of roadway so narrow that our rightside wheels bit deeply into the shoulder, scattering gravel and dirt. "The castle is in a very bad state of repair, don't you know. He restored the manor house and surrounding grounds. Lives there modestly . . . for a man of his means."

"It sounds like Oldham's place is a fortress—the kind anybody would be safe in."

Kitty Cork leaned an arm on the back of her seat to look at me. "Why do you say that? Who's needing a fortress?"

"It was just a remark," I told her.

"Ah, Kitty, luv," Cork sighed. "It's no great secret that our enemies in Ulster would like to see harm come to us. If I didn't know Melville's place *is* like a fortress, do you think I could have risked leaving Weiss behind us, now?"

Worry twisted her face and she turned back to the front. The set of her pretty shoulders was painfully tight. Cork said to me without turning, "You had heard of the URA threats, I suppose?"

"Something, yes," I said. "But I didn't take them seriously."

He didn't reply. I saw his jaw muscles tighten.

"Do you?" I prodded.

"They're maniacs. They and their threats are to be taken very seriously indeed."

"But you play all these public matches. You expose yourself to danger constantly."

"What else can I do? Am I supposed to let them scare me into a hole, where I can never play tennis again, or make a living?" His voice cracked with tension. "A man can't just *hide.*"

"Some people do, Sean."

"Well, not me. —Besides," he added, glancing at his wife, "I don't think they follow up on many of their threats anyway, now, do they? I bet in reality we're perfectly safe . . . perfectly safe."

It sounded good and brave. But I didn't think Kitty was fooled. Possibly that was because Cork's words sounded so much like some of the things I had tried to get Beth to swallow when we talked about me and the Company.

The next thing she said confirmed my suspicion. She turned to look over the top of the seat at me, and her remarkable eyes were worried. "All Sean said was that the violence should cease. Is that so bad?"

"It doesn't sound bad to me," I told her.

"They're vicious." Her voice shook a little with scared revulsion. "We've gone on. But it's living in constant fear . . . never knowing when someone will jump out at you, or a bomb will be laid, or you'll hear the sound of the gunshots too late. Really, you have no idea."

I almost smiled at that. "I'm sure I don't."

"It's never-ending," Sean picked up, steering around another curve in the roadway. "That poor land. The poor people. On *both* sides. Of course, given my background, I tend to side with the Catholics. Isn't that ironic? The few little things I said—they angered the IRA and their subgroups more than the British army. And if I *had to* take sides, I would be wanting, finally, to join the IRA myself."

"But you won't do that," I said.

He snorted humorless laughter. "They would love that. They could hang my head from a lamp post for certain."

Kitty shuddered. "Don't talk that way."

"If people could just *try*," he said wearily, shaking his head. "There has got to be a way to work things out. The damned dumb British government should never have created the situation long ago. Never. But they never learn, do they. They—the British and your country, America, did the same thing again when they created Israel. How can you expect to move a new population into a populated area, by force, and expect there to be peace? It's mad!"

"You're for the PLO, then, too?"

He groaned. "No. I'm for peace. I'm not for the British army and I'm not for the IRA, and I'm not for the PLO and I'm not for the Israeli occupation of the Golan Heights. All I *ever* said was that people have to try to get by the old hates, all the old stupid mistakes, and work with what exists *now*, and find *some* way to stop the bloodshed."

It was a naive speech. A young man's speech. That I agreed with it only made me feel old and worn, because my own hopes of ever seeing sanity in either region had long since passed.

Sometimes there may be no solution to a problem. When England decided long ago to support a pro-Empire Protestant colony in the north, a step was taken that all the pleas in the world for moderation cannot make peaceful. It's hardly a unique situation, this bastardization of a territory by "diplomats" who think they are smarter than history. *"Sorry I'm late for the meeting, gentlemen. You say you're having trouble deciding where to create a new country as a buffer? That's no problem. I thought about it while shaving this morning, and the solution is quite obvious. May I use your pencil? Thank you. Now, gentlemen, we simply draw a new national border here. . . ."*

I asked, "Do the threats concerning Wimbledon worry you?"

He paused a long time before he replied. "Yes," he said finally.

"But you'll follow your normal pattern away from the courts, and do your damnedest on."

"What else can I do?"

It was my turn not to answer.

After a long time he said, "That's one reason why it's so good of you to come up here with us—help me with my game, if you can. I've been thinking maybe I'm just a coward—just can't handle the pressure. I want you to show me that it's technique, not lack of courage, that's bothering me."

"I don't think it's lack of courage, Sean."

"Ah, but you can't *know*."

"I know," I told him.

"How?"

"You're here. You're not hiding."

The Oldham manor house was a modest little thing that made Harrod's department store look like a boutique shop. Four stories, not counting a possible finished attic, ivy-covered stone, Edwardian arches over tall windows, and a forest of stout chimneys over the red tile roof. Sixty bedrooms, said Kitty, who had read something in a travel brochure. Three thousand square feet in the basement wine cellar alone. Five sitting rooms, two great rooms, one large ballroom and one small, three meeting rooms, one conference room, four offices, staff quarters for eighteen, ten-car garage, seven outbuildings, two pools, tennis courts, four-hole golf course, stables, riding trails, stone and steel fencing with security perimeter lighting and television, etc., etc.

"I guess it shows there's money in beer!" Cork said as we drove up.

Only two other cars, both Rolls Royces, stood in the hugely curved brick driveway in front of the house. People inside knew who we were because we had gone through the identification thing at the manned front gate a half-mile from the house. So it was not a complete surprise that the gigantic oak front doors swung open as we got out of the car, and a tall, handsome elderly man emerged from the house.

It had to be Melville Oldham himself. He was accompanied by two very large, long-haired dogs with friendly grins on their faces. If we had needed further proof of Oldham's wealth, the dogs would have supplied it. Upper class people tend to have large, friendly dogs. Lower class people have large, vicious dogs. The middle class can often be identified by their small, vicious yappers, often with painted toenails.

Oldham came down. He had a self-assured air of authority and wealth about him. Kinkaid had been right: he did not look his sixty-five years. A towering man, perhaps six feet, five, he had wide shoulders, athletic hips and legs, a mane of thick gray hair, craggy features. In pale blue slacks, running shoes, white turtleneck and bulky highland sweater, he looked like someone I would have expected in the senior finals at a major tournament.

"Sean!" he called out heartily, extending a hand that might have palmed a basketball. "Grand you could join us!" He shook Sean Cork's hand. "And Kitty, my dear!" He enveloped Kitty in a bearhug, then turned to me. "It's fine to meet you, Brad. I'm Melville Oldham." He tried to pulverize my hand. "You honor us, my friend! Come in! My man will see to the luggage. Just leave the key in the car. How do you like the little Fiat, Sean? I have one for running about, you know. I love my Jag, but the damned thing keeps breaking down, and one doesn't go to the stationery shop in a Rolls. That's so-called British workmanship for you. Nothing works any

more. I'll have to show you my new Porsche. There's an automobile
for you! Brad! Tell me: has your knee completely rehabilitated? Is
that what's behind your return to Wimbledon after such a drasti-
cally lengthy absence?"

Inside we found guests all over the place. But it was so big it
swallowed them up. Zina Garrison was on hand, along with Betsy
Nagelsen and Natalia Zvereva. Zina said Pam Shriver and Steffi
Graf were outside somewhere, and Martina was expected. Johan
Kriek and Peter Lundgren walked in. I pulled out the trusty reporter's notebook and got a couple of quotes from them, then one from
Boris Becker. Pete Sampras came in. A few minutes later I experienced a soft but definite surprise to encounter Bjorn Borg and his
lady on the terrace, visiting with two younger players from Argen-
tina. Bjorn looked fine and we had a good short visit. It revived
memory of that dropshot I had missed against him so long ago, but
of course neither of us mentioned it.

Some people collect playing cards. Melville Oldham collected
players. Zack Willingham, the great British grand prix driver, was
also among the guests. So were two world-class professional golfers,
a soccer player whom I probably would have recognized if I weren't
so ignorant, and a handful of others in lesser sports. Three or four
British sportswriters had also come by. They stayed together off on
the fringe of things, wallflowers at the prom. We all milled around
and were served a choice of icy white wine or mixed drinks.

There was plenty of time before dark for us latecomers to be
shown around. Oldham did the honors himself, accompanied by a
tall, strikingly beautiful brunette of perhaps twenty-five. Her name
was Dacri, it seemed—pronounced like the drink—and she was
American, from Santa Fe. She had been a TV news reader covering
the great hot air balloon race out of Albuquerque half a year earlier.
Oldham was entered, piloting a balloon decorated to look like a gigantic tennis ball. She asked him a few questions on the air, he apparently asked her a few after the camera stopped rolling, and he
then took her for a ride in his gondola. Love (or something) at first

flight. She had now been living here, as nearly as I could make out, about three months.

Starting our tour of the grounds, we followed Oldham and Dacri out across the courtyard and through the gardens, maneuvering a maze of formal shrubbery, and passed the swim complex with its two cabanas and separate bar and food area. Beyond, turning right along a brick sidewalk that curved under massive old oaks, we passed shuffleboard courts and the little sign that indicated the way to the first tee of "Oldham Acres," and then neared the tennis courts. This part of the estate was densely wooded and rugged, ancient ravines and sharp rocky abutments forming the kind of overgrown badland you might have seen in an old Sherlock Holmes movie. It was when we came around a sharp corner on the path that we could look ahead, over the top of a sharply eroded bluff, and see the old castle.

"Will you look at that!" Sean said with soft reverence.

We would and we did.

Not a lot of it showed above the top of the bluff, but enough. It appeared to be another five hundred yards ahead at least, many tall trees standing out of a deep ravine between it and our position. I guessed there was more than the ravine separating us: probably a small hill and a wood.

Rough stone walls showed to the left, with the kind of notches in the top that might have once been used by bowmen. To the right, a square stone turret, considerably taller. In the center a blocky structure with ancient tile roofing, faded and broken by weather. I could make out rotted wooden shutters at some of the deepsocketed window emplacements, and just the end of some larger wooden structure down low: maybe one end of some sort of footbridge.

In the moment we all stood quite still, looking, I got a small, elemental chill. As a child you read of castles and knights, and later if you're lucky you travel to see some of them. The fortress over Salzburg still awes me. But my own favorite is not that one, or even one of the fairytale castles of France, but the great old enclosure at Berghausen, in Germany, where the first battle ax was thrown more than a thousand years ago. Once, on a quiet Sunday morning, I walked down by the little lake at the foot of the path that leads to one of Berghausen's earliest battlements, and a chill fog lay over the world and I would not have been greatly surprised if one of those medieval warriors had walked down out of the mist to stop me in my tracks. Castles go deep into our childhood, is what I'm trying to say: they're special.

I had never before come upon one so unexpectedly, however, and at such close range. It silently dominated our position. I was struck by the sense of impossible power it must have communicated to its subjects long ago. Its utter silence and isolation did something to me, too. Castles could never originally have been like most of us are forced to experience them today, filled with the sounds of Japanese cameras and American teenagers, the moldy rot in the air overlaid by cigar smoke, perfume, and plastic sandwiches.

"The old castle," Oldham explained unnecessarily. "Quite beyond repair as living quarters, unfortunately. I've had it well fenced to protect it from occasional hikers, and a certain amount of bracing done on the old roofing to keep it from falling in entirely. No one uses it but doves and pigeons."

"Can we go over and see it?" I asked.

"Of course, old man. I'll lay on a walking tour tomorrow, if you like."

We walked on past the bluff, the path descending and taking the castle out of view. We approached the tennis courts. Although it was not yet dark, plenty of daylight left in the evening sky, brilliant lights sprang to life ahead of us as we approached.

"Bit of a walk from the house," Oldham told us, "but the ravine protects from the wind, as you can imagine. Now that everything is lighted, the location does prevent glare-disturbance to people back up the hill who might want to do something else. Although I can't imagine what else they might want to be doing. — Watch your step, here, Kitty. Here. Let me take your arm, it's a bit precipitous here."

They went down, followed by Sean, me, and a couple of others. Dacri, left on her own, glided to my side and linked her arm with mine. "I hope you'll enjoy your stay, Brad." She had a remarkable voice, very low-pitched, so that anything she said managed somehow to sound mildly suggestive and filled with implication. "Melly is thrilled to have you, believe me. And so am I."

After the second it took me to figure out who "Melly" was, she added, "Of all the people we expect over the next few days, *you're* the one I most wanted to meet."

She was clinging to me a lot closer than the rock steps required, and I was trying to convince myself it was the way she was with everybody, a natural flirt. We reached the bottom of the steps and it was darker here with rock walls and vines overhanging the walk where it cut through an old embankment, and she didn't move away from me.

"I want to spend time with you," she added softly.

"I'll just be here a couple days, Dacri, but I bet we get a chance to visit."

"I hope so." She squeezed closer against my arm, her breasts tantalizing. Then, as the group ahead of us reached the brilliant light thrown off the courts, she separated from me. "Later."

What the hell? But there was no time to think about it. We were at courtside.

Where Oldham had a small surprise for us. Instead of the two courts I had been told about, he now had six.

"You can see which are the new ones just completed," he told us, pointing. "Impossible to establish more grass quickly enough this year, but two of them, with the artificial turf, are as close as one can get on short order. The workmen did everything in their power to blend the new in with the old."

Looking down the width of the six courts, I couldn't tell which were old and which new. The paved aprons matched, as did the high mesh fencing and the shrubs and trees around the perimeter, some of them quite old. At the moment all the courts were vacant.

Sean Cork looked across the group toward me. "Brad, we could get in some work."

"First thing in the morning?" I said.

His worried frown deepened. "Could we possibly start sooner? Like right away?"

"I guess I'm game," I said, looking at Oldham.

He shrugged. "Whatever you wish."

Cork's eyes were imploring. Getting near a court, he had reverted to worry about his game. "Now?" he said.

"I suppose we could go back and change, and swat a few, Sean."

"I'd like that," he said grimly.

"Tour is about finished anyway, friends," Oldham said easily. "Here. Let's return to the house by way of this path over here. Different views, you know. Some of the roses are quite nice, I think."

We started back, conversation subdued, footsteps muted by the soft loam of the winding path. Partway back, we came around a curve and found two men standing beside one of the large rose beds. They wore workmen's clothing and caps, and had rakes in their hands, but there wasn't any sign of work being done. They looked up sharply at our unexpected appearance, then quickly got busy with their rakes.

They had their faces averted as we passed them, and nobody else noticed them much at all.

I noticed them, however.

I felt like somebody had hit me in the midsection with a very large hammer.

I hid it as best I could, and it seemed no one noticed.

We reached the house again.

"Change and meet down there in fifteen minutes or so?" Sean asked.

"What?"

"I said—"

I got my bearings. "Sure, Sean. Fifteen minutes is fine."

I went to my quarters, a great and airy second floor room with a canopy bed and massive mahogany armoire and chairs, overlooking the rear gardens. I changed automatically, but my mind was on anything but my assigned Sean Cork.

Only one of the gardeners we had unexpectedly encountered on the path had been a stranger to me.

My memory for faces is fairly decent, and some of the photos they had showed me in the terrorist mugshot book back in the States had been excellent. One of the good ones had been of a terrorist named Mallory. Memory said he was suspected of bombing a theater in York less than a year ago. Twenty people had been killed. Mallory hadn't been seen since, the notes under his mugshot had told me.

But I had just seen him. He was the second gardener.

Down at the courts with Sean Cork, a couple of others rallying nearby and a few perched in the low bleachers as spectators, I had to struggle to pay attention to the business at hand.

"I've got John Twain in the first round," Cork fretted. "Ordinarily I ought to take him. But he played wonderfully the other day when I watched him, and my game is going from bad to worse. I've tried a slight change in my forehand grip and I'm concentrating hard on the motion, but they keep going out. I don't know if it's my follow-through or the pronation or racket preparation going back or *what.*"

He was doing what most amateurs make the mistake of doing when they approach a pro for a lesson: they start right out by telling the expert what the problem is, and what should be done about it. Rather than showing, shutting up, and listening.

I didn't point that out to him. I nodded thoughtfully and suggested we hit a few balls and see, although I thought I had already spotted the problem.

He started pressing instantly, the extra effort tightening his muscles, throwing his timing a micron off. A lot of his drives sizzled by me for clean winners. Too many went long. He overcompensated on a few and netted them.

I called him to the net after we were thoroughly warmed up and used some indirection on him.

"You know," I told him, "Twain really likes to hit that backhand overspin and the forehand drive. All he knows how to do is attack. If I were playing him, I would hit undersliced stuff and dinks and even a few moonballs, taking all the pace off. It will drive him crazy."

Cork nodded glumly. "I've been thinking about that." He hammered the edge of his custom composite racket on the netcord. "But I can't go very far like that! I've got to stop hitting so many balls long!"

"Let's hit a few more balls," I suggested. "But try to hit them easy, okay?"

"Easy isn't going to—"

"Sean. Humor me."

So, with bad grace, he did. Then I called him to the net again. "On your racket preparation, try rotating your shoulders back another inch or so."

What I really wanted him to do was keep his elbow in about a half-inch closer to his ribcage. But I had no doubt that Finneran had already told him that, and it hadn't worked. What I hoped to accomplish was to have him thinking about two other keys—racket preparation and easing up—which would put his elbow closer without his thinking about it.

He tried manfully to do as I had asked. His first forehand, unpressured, zinged over the net and dove safely in about three inches in front of the backline. He raised his eyebrows, surprised and hopeful.

I courtesy-served him another twenty-five. He returned each better than the last. By the end of the twenty-five, he was practically dancing.

"You're a genius," he said, sweat dripping off the end of his nose. "I would have taken months to figure this out!"

I didn't bother to tell him he had it figured out before we took the court. After all, he had been the one who first mentioned racket preparation as a possible problem. You get to be a good teacher by showing them something right after they've started to notice it anyway. That way they seldom get discouraged, they learn at the pace their body will allow, and they think you walk on water because you helped them learn what their muscles already knew, if they weren't concentrating on all the wrong things.

"I think I've got it solved!" Cork told Kitty gleefully as we trooped back to the house. "This man is incredible!"

"We'll work on it some more," I told him. "I want to stick close to you the next few days and make sure you don't lose it again."

"That's so good of you, Brad! How can I ever repay you?"

I smiled. It felt good to think you were doing something right for once. But spotting the known terrorist, Mallory, had tied my stomach in knots. Was Mallory the hit man? Was this the weekend when somebody intended to take Sean Cork out?

Later, after showering and changing, we joined the evening's partying. There were cocktails, some live music by a small British combo that couldn't read music, late dinner, smalltalk. Melville Oldham began to get jovially drunk. Some got drunk in other ways. I circulated, worrying about what I should do about my recognition of the "gardener."

I knew one option was to call London and report it at once. Nice, quick, efficient. But I worried: if somebody like Mallory was here, the estate telephone lines might be tapped. And even if they weren't, a call to London would result in some variety of police swooping down to make an arrest. The hullabaloo would likely end the stay at Oldham's manorhouse for everyone, blow my cover, and thus end any chance I might have of learning anything else.

On the other hand, if I waited and then Mallory tried to kill Sean Cork, was I capable of stopping him?

I couldn't reach a decision. Your bush-league Hamlet at work. I figured I would stay close to Sean right now, and see what developed. Looking for him, I wandered around Oldham's house.

Lights blazed everywhere on the sprawling ground floor, all the doors stood open, and I wasn't the only one drifting around. I found several people in the big recreation room, some of them playing pool and others tossing darts. Nobody in another of the great old sitting rooms, where a fire burned quietly in the fireplace with no one to enjoy it. Terry and Alicia Carpoman had finally arrived—sans Jaguar—and I met them strolling out of a paneled den with big game trophies and African artifacts on the walls. She said it was a great house and she wanted one a lot like it some day. Terry, his brow knit with gnawing ambition, told me we had to practice in the morning, then led her away. His voice echoed back: *"Goddamn it, Alicia, do you have to throw our poverty in my face at every opportunity?"*

The next room I came to, far from the distant noise of the main part of the house, was a library. A fire in here, too, and standing brass lamps over deep leather reading chairs. Walls covered, floor to ceiling, with bookshelves. I investigated. Many of the volumes were predictably old and leather-covered, a thin film of dust on their marbled tops showing they had not been read for a long time, if ever. I pulled a couple of them down, a book by a man named Savage about the history of Somerset, published in 1830, and a very old edition of Shelley. The spine of the Shelley made a nasty cracking sound when I started to open it, and I wondered if it had ever been opened before.

A great many of the books on two other walls were more recent, and obviously had been well thumbed. Oldham, it seemed, read more than books on business and engineering. Although he had a tremendous amount of stuff on automotive engineering and design, as well as brewering and brick-making—his two former businesses most often mentioned with his name—there were extensive holdings in history, especially British history, philosophy, political science, sociology, even religion. His apparently voracious and eclectic curiosity made for strange shelf-fellows: the documents of Vatican II alongside *Das Kapital*, Tocqueville and Hayakawa, Churchill beside Rachel Carson beside Niebuhr beside Goebbels beside a six-volume set on Northern Ireland beside a handbook on Zen. There

were many books of maps, demographic studies, UN documents.
Many of these focused on Northern Ireland too.

There was much more to friend Oldham, I thought, than met
the eye.

"If you see anything that interests you particularly," a voice
said behind me, "please feel free to browse it."

I turned and saw Oldham standing in the doorway, his smile
crooked, a martini in his hand. Everything about him but his eyes
appeared completely relaxed and offguard, slightly tipsy. His eyes
looked like bullets.

"I don't imagine I'll have time to read anything while I'm visiting here," I told him, "but it's a great library. I envy you."

He waved it off. "A vice of mine. I stay active most of the time.
I need only three hours or so of sleep each night. I awake about
four in the morning, summer or winter. I often read until dawn.
I read very fast and there are no interruptions during those hours."

I decided to take a small risk. "You have a lot on Northern
Ireland, I notice."

He didn't so much as blink. "Yes. It's a fascinating area. Tragic.
A bottomless pit. England has so mucked it up now that one won-
ders if there can ever be any solution, short of a forced mass migra-
tion of one faction or another."

"People like to think there is always some solution."

He shook his head, and in this moment I could see how deeply
he felt about the topic. "It's like the Palestinian question. A solution, yes. Everyone wants that. But *how?*"

I paused before answering, and he went on with his own answer: "The only scintilla of hope lies in industrial development."

"Hasn't some of that been tried?"

He ignored me and went right on. "It's poverty that creates
revolution. Industrial development of the right kind, with the right
kind of leadership and local input, defeats poverty. It can be done.
It must be done. The risks must be taken."

I studied him. He had spoken with great force and emotion.

I wondered if I had just heard a part of a speech he had given somewhere.

It also occurred to me for the first time that Mallory might
not be hiding here under false pretenses as far as the owner of the
property was concerned. Was it just possible that Oldham was an
IRA sympathizer?

It seemed absurd. But crazier things had been known to happen. In the United States we had IRA sympathizers who arranged
money and guns both for the IRA.

I said carefully, "It's a complicated problem. Some people, I've
heard, think there isn't a solution."

Oldham smiled and raised his martini glass. "No affair of ours
tonight, however, eh? Are you enjoying your stay thus far?"

I said I was, and we visited about nothing for another minute
or two. I decided it was time to drift back to the main party.

It continued for a while, slowing down. Midnight came and
went. Guests drifted off. I stayed close to Sean and Kitty until they
said they were also turning in. I kept talking and walked with them
to their room on the second floor.

They paused at their bedroom door, their expressions betraying
the uneasy feeling that I was acting weird.

"Well," Sean said uncomfortably, "good night."

"Be sure to lock your door," I told him.

"Surely there's no need here!"

"Sean. Your man Weiss is miles from here. Lock up."

"Oh," he said, frowning.

"Will you?"

"Yes," he agreed.

I waited until they were inside and I heard the bolt slide closed.
Then I went back downstairs.

There were not a lot of people left in the big living room.
Within a few minutes, Melville Oldham said ta-ta and sauntered
unevenly off to bed. I slouched on one of the large, overstuffed velvet
couches near the fireplace, enjoying a cigar someone had pressed
on me, when the formidable Dacri glided over to sit beside me. The

motion opened her slit cocktail skirt over a fetching acreage of bare brown leg.

"I love the smell of a cigar," she said, smiling at me.

"Most people don't."

She inhaled voluptuously. "I think cigars are wonderful. So masculine. I think they're a turn-on."

I watched some of the other few guests talking around the room. There was no one else in the immediate vicinity of our couch, and we might as well have been in the room alone as far as conversation was concerned. I didn't know if I felt uneasy or not.

"I think it's wonderful that you've come back to play again," Dacri told me.

"Well, it was time, I guess. They like to have old-timers show up. Sense of history, et cetera."

"There you go again!" She put a feline hand on my forearm and squeezed none too gently. She was a very strong young woman. "You must *not* denigrate yourself. I saw some of the television coverage of that tournament you had at your own resort in Montana only a few months ago. You played a *fabulous* match against Lendl."

I had to grin at her.

"What?" she demanded archly, not sure whether to be amused or angry.

"I lost," I told her.

She hadn't removed her hand from my arm. I was very aware of the warmth. She now squeezed again, as if unconsciously stressing her point. "We *must* talk about this, Mister Brad Smith, at some length. I have decided your self-image is badly tarnished. You need coaching."

I chuckled. "You're welcome to try, Dacri. Just don't—"

"Good," she cut in. "I'll come to your room in . . . say . . . an hour?" She gave a little shiver. "It will be delicious. I can hardly wait . . . can you?"

Fifteen

I FORGOT WHAT I had intended to say. "I beg your pardon?"

She didn't have to repeat the words because her eyes were saying everything. But she repeated them anyhow. "I'll come to your room. In an hour. It will be quiet by then. Leave your door unlocked. I'll just . . . slip in."

I breathed slowly, letting that sink in. I must be the most naive older gent in the western world. I never cease to be amazed by how some of them leap in and blurt out what's on their mind.

"Oh, my," Dacri said now, her lovely lips curling in a smile. "I've shocked you."

"No," I said.

"I haven't? Good. Then I'll see you in an hour."

"I uh, I don't think so, Dacri," I stammered.

She studied me. "Melly is drunk. He'll pass out and sleep as if in a stupor for about four hours. That's his way, drunk or sober. A bomb couldn't wake him, then he's up and ready to go another day and a half." She paused a beat, letting that sink in, then added, "My bedroom next to his has a lock on the door anyway, and even if he violated all his past practices and tried to find me, he wouldn't be able to. It's perfectly safe for me to leave . . . to come to you."

I began to experience the old civil war, north against the south. This was a stunning, sexy lady. There would, it was clear, be no coyness, no pretense of undying love, no expectation of aftermath. Just fine, thoughtless, lusty excitement.

The south was for that, fervently.

189

Unfortunately the north spoke first: "I'm a guest here, Dacri. Of Melville Oldham. You're his . . . friend."

Her smile held. "You're sweet. But let me explain. Melly knows I might play with someone else. It's part of our understanding. I love him dearly and I would never flaunt my needs or talk about him behind his back or do anything to expose him to ridicule. But my freedom is understood. That's one of the reasons we get along so beautifully." She paused and took a deep, lovely breath. "And I'll see you in an hour."

"No," said the north, scared by the clamor from down south.

Dacri removed her hand from my arm. It felt cold and vacant where her hand had been. "You might want to change your mind," she told me. "I give really great head."

She watched me for an instant and added huskily, "And you would like that, wouldn't you. I can see it in your face."

I lurched to my feet. Looked at my watch. "Look at the time. It's late. Thanks for the talk, Dacri. Time for the old folks to go take their Metamucil. See you in the morning?"

Then I got out of there, not looking back at her, and went straight upstairs to my room like a good little boy.

Once in, however, the good little boy started kicking himself.

What the hell was going *on* here? First Linda, now Dacri. Two tremendously attractive, youthful, desirable women, ready to make love, and the elderly gent *turns them both down?*

Yeah, and then stands in his room with a discomfort not easily assuaged, wondering why.

I didn't understand myself. I was a single person, and God knows I had normal appetites. And God knows Dacri—like Linda before her—had stirred them to a froth.

Don't tell me, I told myself, that you were thinking about Beth Miles. Beth, half a planet away in California. Beth, who would never know a thing. Beth, who wouldn't be hurt by a harmless little tussle in the hay over here. Beth, who might be playing spin the beach blanket with the bronzed surfer boy anyhow. What's the matter with you, Smith? You must be getting old. I almost lean to the theory you're getting senile.

But I realized, examining the painful feelings aswirl inside me, that Dacri's invitation had not been what really stirred me up. She was gorgeous and desirable, but her words had been only a trigger. What she had triggered was the simmering, painful need in me for Linda.

I realized I was angry at Beth, that she wouldn't be here with me, wouldn't come to Montana, seemed to be walling me out. Now she felt a million miles away, and Linda was *here*, and I wanted her more every time I was with her. I wondered what archaic sense of honor held me back.

Disgusted and tired, I went back out into the hall long enough to test the Corks' doorknob, assuring myself it remained locked. Then I returned to my own room and locked myself in, too, then turned off my room lights, the furtive kid making like he's already asleep for the night. Pale starlight filtered through the tall casement windows. I sat on my bed and pulled off my shoes, wiggled my toes, received the small messages from achy calf and thigh muscles, and a sharp twinge from the knee. I was restless, edgy, wide awake. Shelving all my usual good resolutions I fumbled around and found my cigarettes and lit one, then walked to the windows and peered outside.

House lights had been extinguished below, and the indirect garden accent lights had gone out too, probably on a timer. At first everything below looked inky black, but as I stood there smoking my eyes adjusted further and I began to make out the faintest outlines of things—trees, shrubs, statuary. My mind flitted from one thing to another and kept circling back, closer on each revolution to my worry about the bogus gardener, Mallory. I still didn't know what the right course of action should be. I considered doing and saying nothing at least until we got back to London, and then I thought about the likely outcomes if I called my contact number first thing in the morning. Neither plan looked anything like foolproof. I yearned for foolproof. If I guessed wrong, we might lose a valuable source of information. But far worse, we might lose Sean Cork.

I was still turning it over in my mind when a sudden, unexpected movement in the garden below caught my complete attention. I straightened out of my slouch and strained to see more clearly.

A figure—so indistinct in the dark that I couldn't even make out the general profile—had moved out of the pitch directly below my window. The man or woman—no way to tell—walked silently across the decking and went down the three steps into the garden. I thought I saw enough to make out the silhouette of pantlegs on the steps. A man, then . . . except that women sometimes wore slacks.

The figure proceeded a few steps into the garden and stopped near the grayish shape of a tall piece of statuary. I remembered it: a woman, classical, only slightly smaller than life, a cloak draped over one shoulder and flowing down her left side, but otherwise nude. Most places it would have looked phony and ostentatious. Here you knew it was probably a genuine antiquity, freighted in from God knows where at a cost of let's not think about it.

The shadowy figure beside the statue remained motionless. My cigarette burned my fingers. I kept holding it by the filter because I didn't dare move or take my eyes away from that shadow below. The house had fallen quiet now, the lights extinguished, things buttoned up. Something about the way the figure moved below was also hurried, furtive. Whoever this was and whatever was going on, it was no routine slip outside for a final smoke or look at the stars.

The figure moved again, turning to its right as if to face one of the many entrances into the mazelike formal shrubbery. It just stood there. Then I made out the smallest movement *deeper in the dark,* in the opening of the maze: a second person.

They were talking. Whispering.

Just as I had figured that much out, the will-o'-wisp shadow in the shrubbery vanished. My other figure moved—following—and vanished in the same opening.

Christ. What did I do now? Something was up. I needed badly to know what it was. This could tell me if Sean was at immediate risk. But you didn't just go bumbling down halls and stairs and out into the night chasing shadows, did you? That was crazy.

So naturally while I was thinking such fine, rational thoughts I was jamming my feet into my shoes, hurriedly lacing them, easing the bolt back on my bedroom door, peering down the dim, empty hallway, and practically running for it.

Scattered nightlights glowed along baseboards in the lower level of the mansion. I went the way I was surest of not encountering a delay or a mistaken deadend, getting back to the room where the party had been. It was dark, embers glowing red in the fireplace, the smell of stale smoke in the quiet air. Crossing the room, I unlatched the garden doors and slipped outside.

It had gotten cold and damp. Went right through me. I couldn't see much. Closing the door behind me, I moved along the perimeter of the patio, went over the low planter wall at the side and dropped to the soft earth of the flowerbeds three feet below, and hurried noiselessly along the backside of some of the ornamentals to a point near the statue. My heart thumping in my throat, I stood very, very still, straining to hear something. First there was only the deep night silence. Then I made out a slight scraping sound—then a couple more of them—well to my right and almost out of hearing. Shoes on the gravel pathway we had walked earlier on the way down toward the courts.

Guided by starlight and a wispily clouded sliver of moon, I skirted the formal gardens and climbed as quietly as I could through some cloyingly sweet honeysuckle ground cover, coming out on the path fifty feet below. I listened again, but couldn't make out a thing. It felt spooky out here. My skin prickled with the sense that eyes were watching me from all directions. I knew the smart thing to do was turn back. Then, back in the safety of my comfy room, kick myself for being a coward . . . maybe missing a golden opportunity to learn what was really going on.

Well, hell.

I stayed off the gravel path, but moved through the grass and flowerbeds roughly paralleling it, descending toward the ravines below. Stopped often, listening, hearing nothing. Maybe I had gone right by them. Maybe they had doubled back, or were so far ahead I could never catch them. I was in a real mental sweat when I reached the bottom and stopped again, but this time I heard the voices.

Two voices, male, on up ahead, talking very softly.

Sound carries at night, especially in dense cold air like tonight's. I could tell they were on over the hump in the path somewhere, beyond the dirt-and-rock promontory from which we had earlier spotted the nearby castle ruins. If I could climb to the top unobserved, I might be able to look down and see and hear them.

Reassured about where they were, I risked going three-quarters of the way up on the stone steps. Then I left the path and climbed on up through night-wet brush, around some boulders and smaller rocks, and crawled on my belly the last few feet to the very top.

For a second, nothing. Then the voices came so close I almost grunted with surprise.

"Cork is here."

"I know. Ignore him. He's not our worry. The other one is."

"He's being difficult."

"I know that, too. We have to put pressure on him to cooperate."

"What if he keeps on refusing?"

"He'll cooperate. We have to see to that."

"He's no one to push too far."

"We push him anyway."

They were below me and slightly to my left, standing on the path under an outcropping boulder so that I couldn't see them. I had actually overshot them slightly and was now ahead of their position.

I wanted badly to see them. From this range, with luck, I might identify them.

I felt relief about Sean, but the rest of the overheard conversation made no sense. But people did not slip out in the middle of the night and hold a rendezvous halfway to hell and gone in the boondocks, to discuss the weather or the condition of the daffodils. I had come this far and it needed to be finished. Which meant seeing them.

"When some of these people are gone we'll talk to him."

"You'll make him do it?"

"Isn't that the plan?"

"Yes but—"

"You just take care of your part and we'll do ours!"

I moved inch by inch around the side of the boulders that stuck out of the clumpy earth, shielding me from where they sounded like they were below. Every movement set my teeth on edge. I couldn't make a sound now, or I was done for. The earthen edge of the bluff sloped sharply downward at my immediate right, and I had to be careful as hell or I might slip. They were still talking. I was so busy inching around that their words didn't register. Clouds slid over the moon and things got darker.

Still couldn't see straight enough down. Carefully brought up my right knee, got my right foot firmly planted in the soft dirt, started to raise myself, a few inches at a time, to try to see over.

Without warning my right foot went out from under me. Dirt shot over the embankment. My balance went, and my right leg shot out in a split, going over the edge. My weight teetered and faster than I can say it I went sliding over the edge to my right in a shower of loose dirt and small rocks.

I don't know how it must have sounded to them, but to me it was like riding on the inside of an avalanche. I slid, tearing clothes and hide, and bounced over the jagged rocks and plunged free, out of control, for an instant, then landed in shrubbery with all the subtlety of a crashing airplane. Slid and rolled over about six times, and came to a halt half onto the path well beyond their position, on the far side of the bluff, head lower than my feet and partly buried in sliding dirt and pebbles.

To my right—or maybe it would be my left if I got unscrambled—came the sounds of quickly hushed urgent voices and the harsh pounding of running feet. *Shit!*

I rolled over a couple of times, getting off the path on the downhill side. The movement got me to my feet. Everything seemed to be working after I spit dirt and rubbed some of the embedded stones out of my arms. My quarry, now suddenly my pursuers, thanks to my latest outburst of stupidity, had been forced to run all the way around the spiral pathway to get to this side of the promontory. A break for me. But it sounded like they were damned near on top of me by now.

Not thinking, I plunged down the steep path, thinking about nothing but getting away from them. Behind me came a sharp, muted voice. Something made a nasty sound going past my right ear. Rock on the wall beside me exploded into hot fragments that bit my face and chest. The little spitting sound behind me caught up, and the bright metallic sound of metal on metal. A pistol, silenced, a near-miss, the action working for the next shot. I dove off the path into the deep brush.

It must have fooled them momentarily. When you're the one being chased, it's hard to remember that it's just as dark for them as it is for you. Anyway, charging down the hill through the brush and splashing across an ice-cold little creek no wider than the alley on a doubles court, I realized I had put some space between us. That made a small spasm of sanity enter my dim brain: I slowed down a little and climbed the embankment on the other side with considerably less speed but much more quiet.

They were still coming, though. Partway up the embankment I paused to listen, and heard them down below me somewhere: clothing rasping on brush, rocks being kicked loose, heavy breathing. Having no choice whatsoever, I kept climbing.

A couple minutes later I looked up and made out the murky outlines of a stone wall standing in front of me: old blocks of granite, big ones, rough, creepers all over them, and a few tumbled to make a hole. *The castle.*

Any port in a storm. I crawled through the hole and found myself inside one of the corner turrets. I was all the way on the bottom, and looking up reminded me of my childhood when we used to play inside an abandoned silo. But this silo had a hole in its side about ten feet above my head, and starlight shone through.

Given enough cowardice to fuel the old muscles, you can do a lot of things. The turret boulders were huge, uneven pieces broken out. Plenty of hand- and footholds. I climbed the inside of the thing like I knew what I was doing, looked out the big hole, got my bearings, and climbed on out to drop lightly onto a dusty interior wall walk.

So now I was truly inside. The moon was out again and its illumination painted everything the color of skim milk: the top of the wall, another turret, the inside grounds below me, and the old stone walkway from my position to a sort of catwalk around the upper story of the blocky central building to my left. The only hiding place appeared to be that way, so I crossed the walkway and managed to pull myself up onto the ancient clay tiles of the roof. One of them cracked and slid beneath my weight, which was the first inkling I had that maybe I hadn't made the best decision.

They hadn't been far behind me. Maybe they would have heard the tile slide and fall, although the noise probably hadn't really been nearly as loud as my shocked ear said. At any rate I couldn't stay here, spread-eagled on the roof like a spider waiting to be swatted. I scrambled on up the roof, my insides starting those little quakes and panic-gusts that accompany fear of falling from a height. One of many old chimneys or vent flues stuck up, three feet across, stout stone, smoke-scarred from ages of fires inside somewhere. I crawled around behind it and leaned against the stones, fighting for wind, looking back the way I had come. *Jesus, had I just crawled across that steeply sloped, ice-rinky roof?*

Back on the side of the turret I had climbed, a head stuck out of the same hole from which I had emerged. Hidden in the darkest shadow of the chimney, I froze. The head emerged more, and then shoulders, and then a figure climbed out and dropped to the walkway just as I had done.

A second head appeared in the hole.

"See him?"

"No."

"Watch it, I'll jump down."

"No! Go back. He might have gone around the other way. Circle."

The figure in the hole stuck out an arm. Pointing right at me. My guts dropped.

"He could have gone that way."

"Impossible! That old roof wouldn't hold a man's weight!"

Swell. My rooftop hiding place began to look like a trap.

"Are you going around the wall?"

"Yes. I'll meet you on the far side. If you see him, shout."

"Right." The head disappeared from the hole.

I stayed as still as one can get and still maintain heartbeat. My friend on the walkway remained a shadowy figure, unidentifiable. As I watched without moving more than my eyes, he went along the walkway toward the south and vanished into the dark. A few minutes later I caught his movement again on the far side, in the ancient courtyard far below. He crossed the courtyard, ducking into what might have been a few doorways. He appeared to be very thorough.

My legs, cramped under me against the chimney, were just about to agony, stage ten, when the other figure appeared in the courtyard far to the other side. Their two shadows moved together, must have conferred. They were easily sixty feet below me and more than three times that far away in horizontal distance. I just managed to see them around the stones of my hiding place without moving. I was not about to move, pain or no.

They were talking, but I couldn't hear a thing.

Then they split up again, vanished into the bowels of the building. I stayed put.

They could just keep looking, I thought, until daylight arrived. Then my shadowed perch would stand out like a spotlight. But maybe they couldn't stay that long, I told myself; you didn't meet in the dead of night if you could allow the meeting to risk daylight identification.

So I stayed put. And waited.

And waited.

It felt like an hour that passed. About the time I was convinced they had gone, I startled back to alert again. I spotted one of them retracing his path along the top of the walkway toward me.

He reached the point where I had crossed. Stood there for what seemed like about two days, his hands on his hips, unmoving. Staring across at me. I didn't dare to look directly back at him. Maybe human eyes don't reflect light like animals' eyes do at night along the highway, but I couldn't take the chance. I wasn't about to look at them, except with my peripheral vision.

If he managed to make me out, or came across, I was a dead man. Not that I didn't have a plan in mind. But it involved sliding down the roof and going over the side, hoping I could miraculously land right, bones unbroken, after the sixty-foot drop. I didn't like the odds.

After another eternity a second figure appeared on the walkway over there. Again the shadows rendezvoused.

"What now?"

"Don't know. Let me think."

"Who do you think it was?"

"How should I know?"

"Could have been a damned kid. Farmers over that way, have kids that play around here at night sometimes."

"Let me think. Shut up."

Silence. Then more talk, but lower, so that I couldn't make out what was being said. Then they moved. One, and then the other, climbed into the turret and went out of sight, clambering back to ground level on the outside.

It got very, very quiet. After an hour or two an owl called, and another, somewhere inside the castle, answered. I sat hunkered against the old chimney for another eternity, listening to their conversation. It was boring.

When my watch showed almost 4 A.M., I knew I had to do something. Maybe they were perched below somewhere, just waiting for that. Or maybe they had given up. I didn't think they had had any more chance of recognizing me than I had of seeing their faces. Maybe they had persuaded themselves I *was* a neighborhood child, panicked into running all the way home. Maybe they had decided that—whoever I was—I had eluded them and gotten away clean.

Whatever. Daylight was coming. If I had any chance of getting back to the mansion, it had to be while there was still dark.

I clambered on around the roof and let myself down through a hole into a musty attic. Found my way to ground level. Skirted the entire circumference of the castle and spooked back toward the manor house like a Cub Scout playing Indians: scoot from bush to bush, squat and look around, hope the booger man doesn't get you.

Amazingly, he didn't. I got back to the house—as far as I could tell—unobserved. The back doors remained unlocked. I slipped in.

It was still dark inside, but I was shocked to hear soft radio music coming from somewhere. Then I smelled the coffee, which reminded me of Melville Oldham's weird waking hours. I hurried upstairs to my room like an errant husband trying to sneak in past a jealous wife, and breathed slow and raggedly after locking myself in again.

It was after the shower, smoking a cigarette, that a couple of things began to dawn on me:

1—I had failed to make an identification.

2—I had probably alerted Mallory and fellow schemers that somebody had them under suspicion.

Which meant I had blown it, I thought. But on the plus side I now knew Sean Cork seemed to be safe, at least for the moment.

It crossed my mind to slip back downstairs to the telephone and call my contact number immediately. I rejected that option because it meant the risk of someone discovering me, and wanting to know what in the hell was so important that I had to make unauthorized long-distance calls in the middle of the night.

Then, thinking about it some more, I realized I couldn't risk telephoning at any time from this house. Oldham's library shelves of books about Northern Ireland, and some of his anti-Brit comments, began to worry me more than they had before. Was it possible he was so embittered by experiences with British taxation, and possibly foreign policy, that he *knew* Mallory was here—was harboring him? Or could he be the one the two men had been talking about when one told the other he would *"make him do it"*?

Either way, the house phones might be bugged. I could not risk a call.

Whatever the damage caused by my oafish attempt to follow and eavesdrop, it had already been done. The two men were alerted, but they had not recognized me. I decided things couldn't be made any worse by my waiting until I could get to a secure public phone without undue pressure on somebody to drive me away from the mansion.

It was not, however, a pleasant feeling. I felt like a screwup, and momentarily helpless. Not a good feeling at all, but I couldn't shake it all the time I scrubbed my muddy clothes in the bathroom, trying to hide all evidence of that fact that I was no Sam Spade. Sometime during this process, I started remembering the ugly sound of the bullet and the cough of the silencer on the gun that had just missed me, and the slope of that rotten old tile roof. Then the shakes came pretty bad for a while.

Sixteen
Elsewhere

London

WEDNESDAY, JUNE 21: just five days before the opening of the tournament at Wimbledon—where all of them feared terror might strike. Endlessly waiting in the uncomfortable straight chair against the wall of the outer office, Clarence Tune was as worried as anyone.

The office was in an old but impressively paneled and carpeted section of the Home Office administrative complex. Under the watchful portrait stares of former prime ministers, a pretty ash-blond secretary with ice-cube eyes tapped at the keyboard of her word processor. She had ignored Tune for a long time now. Tune felt like he had been here forever, waiting to be summoned into the commander's office. He was depressed.

Thin morning sunlight shone faintly against the closed heavy draperies at the corner windows. The fourth consecutive day of fine weather. The newspapers were full of optimistic talk about the weather and the upcoming opening of championship play, and even staid old London showed faint signs of excitement at this time every year. For Tune the anticipation was not so happy.

Three days ago, on Sunday night, Brad Smith had informed him of seeing the terrorist Mallory at the Melville Oldham estate the previous evening. As a result, on Monday, agents had entered the estate and conducted a thorough search. Melville Oldham had been outraged by the invasion of his privacy, and had threatened all kinds of political trouble. Much worse, Mallory had vanished. On Tuesday a general bulletin had been issued, with no results thus far. Now, on Wednesday, Tune could not interpret a summons to the commander's office as anything but potential bad news. Possibly complaints by the influential Oldham had already started flocking home by way of irritated higher-ups. Whether that was so or not, this was a bureaucracy: *someone* had to be blamed because Mallory had escaped.

Tune sighed.

As if his sigh were a signal, the telephone beeped on Miss Ice-Eyes's desk. She turned from her screen and picked up the instrument. "Yes, sir?" Her voice was soft and discreet, like the synthesized tones of those computers that called to ask you questions about magazine subscriptions or the state of your roof.

She listened a moment and hung up. She looked at Tune. "You may go in, Mr. Moon."

"Were you speaking to me? The name is Tune."

She turned back to her keyboard. "Whatever."

Tune got to his feet. His knees cracked loudly. "Thank you so much." He crossed the room, footsteps muted by the thin carpet, tapped diffidently on the tall oak door, and opened it.

Commander Fairchild had windows behind his desk. The draperies had been corded open. This provided a fine view of a sun-drenched tar roof with circular ventilation stacks and Ultra High Frequency antenna tripods all over it. The commander's desk was large, possibly mahogany, with eagle-claw feet. The chair was dark brown leather. A map of England covered one wall. Except for one wooden filing cabinet and a very small open bookcase, there was nothing else in the room except two straight chairs facing the desk where the commander sat, hands folded on his desk blotter. The commander looked like the actor Walter Pigeon had long ago. He knew that, and cultivated the image with pipes and wise looks down the side of his long nose.

He flicked a finger toward one of the chairs. "Clarence. Good of you to come. Please sit down."

Tune obeyed. He sat on the chair's hard front edge. Had the commander picked these chairs personally? If so, why had he picked the most uncomfortable chairs ever made by man? Had he had the

legs sawed off two inches? If not, why else did the chair put Tune
so low in front of the desk, as if he were an altar boy on the lower
steps, and the commander the priest?

"How have you been, Clarence?" the commander asked in a
neutral tone.

"Fine, sir. Thank you." Automatic meaningless question, automatic meaningless answer.

"Good, good," the commander intoned. He unfolded his
hands and reached to his right to pull a folder over to the center
of the desktop. Following this movement, Tune noticed for the first
time the folded newspaper page and pencil on the edge of the desk.
The newspaper was turned to the puzzle. *The puzzle,* Tune thought,
staggered. *He had me wait two hours while he worked the puzzle!*

The commander opened the folder. "I have the latest reports
on the Wimbledon matter. I note that our men, when they visited
the Oldham estate Monday, found no trace of the suspect reported
by you Sunday night."

Tune licked his lips. They felt like sandpaper. "Yes, sir, correct,
sir."

The commander's marble-blue eyes raised from the folder to
fasten on Tune. "Would you care to speculate on that, Clarence?"

"Speculate, sir?"

"On our failure—again—to achieve any significant progress on
this most distressing case."

"Sir." Tune cleared his throat. "As you know, the American
assigned to my concern, Brad Smith, did not report sighting our
fugitive, Mallory, until he, Smith, had returned to the city. Upon
being informed, I posted the information immediately and called
it to the attention of—"

"Why did Smith not report the sighting earlier, Clarence? It
occurred Saturday, did it not?"

"Yes, sir, it did—"

"Then why did he not report to you earlier than late Sunday
night?"

How am I supposed to know, you idiot? He doesn't work for

us! "Sir, Mr. Smith is not under instruction. As I stated in my report, he worried about possible telephone taps at the Oldham mansion. He stated he could not depart prematurely without worry of alerting Mallory, and he hoped to learn more."

"But he did not learn more, did he, Clarence."

"No, sir."

"Foolish logic on his part."

"Yes, sir."

"Problem would not have arisen if you had been with him."

"Sir, there was no way to get an invitation!"

"You tried?" The commander's eyes riveted brightly on Tune.

Tune was nonplussed. "How *could* I, sir? Melville Oldham's antagonism toward the sitting government and our office is widely known!"

The commander reached for a brier. "You should have thought of something."

Tune did not answer.

"As to Smith," the commander went on, packing the pipe, "We have no assurance that he did not notify his own people at the American embassy before calling you."

"I rather suspect he did, sir."

"Damn it, Clarence! Can't you win this man's confidence better than you have? Can't you control him better? Do we want the CIA mucking about in our back yard, conducting investigations into persons we don't even know about yet?"

"Sir, that's not what happened! I—"

The commander waved Tune silent. "You should have arranged to have the information expeditiously. Mallory was somehow alerted, and we found no sign of him by the time our men arrived. The burden of responsibility for this failure falls squarely on your shoulders."

Stunned, Tune could only stare. How did this pompous idiot think he could have gone to Oldham's mansion with Brad Smith? How did he think Tune could control Smith's actions? By what insane logic could he assign blame to anyone?

But of course Tune did understand.

In the commander's bureaucratic world, blame *must be* assigned. Something *must be* written into the column on the form titled "Responsibility." The highest authority wanted explanations, not reality. Bad luck, human error, or the inevitable complexity of life could not be considered. Something went wrong. Q.E.D., blame must be assigned.

"You have had a long and useful service, Clarence," the commander told him now, riffling pages of the folder. *My personnel folder.* "As you know, we are expanded to the limit with this operation and the Iraqi thing at the same time."

"Yes, sir."

"I personally approved assigning you as liaison to this man Smith. There were those who argued that your record . . . and your time in service . . . might disqualify you in terms of the demands of the assignment. However, I vouched for you." The commander looked up sharply.

"Yes, sir," Tune said.

"There was an apparent attempt on Smith's life, as I am sure you recall."

"I was there, sir."

"Yes. Precisely." The commander's fingernails rapped on the file. "You were there, Clarence. But the suspect was killed. So we got no information. Later we noted Smith's interest in the Irish player, Sean Cork, and sought additional data from you on anything Smith might have learned in that regard. Again, your report noted failure."

The commander sighed. "Now we have this. A known terrorist, a wanted murderer—and your report is generated at least two days too late to produce results."

Tune sat miserable, hands clutching his knees. Where was this going? A dread had begun to put out chill tentacles in his belly.

The commander had the pipe going now, and spoke through a cloud of aromatic smoke. "Clarence," he said quietly, "your time in service qualifies you now for an honorable retirement with full benefits, assuming this office grants credit for accrued sick leave, unused vacation, et cetera. We—"

"But I must stay on until my regular retirement date!" Tune choked. "Sir! You know what it means if a man takes the earliest possible out! It means he was asked to leave. It means . . . ineptitude."

The commander closed his folder and fixed Tune with those eyes again. "I have thought this out carefully, Clarence. You've established something of a relationship with Smith. That should count for something. We are well into the game, here. Wimbledon is about to begin."

The commander paused and puffed, leaving Tune in agony.

Then he resumed, "I have decided, Clarence, that in view of these factors, and your long and honorable service, you should be continued on the assignment."

"Thank you, sir! I can assure you—"

The commander wagged his finger for silence. "But I wanted us to have this meeting to make sure you understand the gravity of the situation. I am a people person, Clarence. I love each and every one of my people. Of all my good qualities, compassion and understanding are perhaps the most notable. But we are all under pressure here. Grave pressure. Another balls-up from you, and I shan't be able to protect you again. You will be removed from the assignment, and I shouldn't be surprised if action were to follow concerning earliest possible separation from the service via retirement proceedings."

Tune stared into the man's glacial blue eyes and felt the cold sink all the way into the bottom of his gut. He wanted to get up and reach across the desk and put his fist right between those eyes. He wanted to—

But of course one did no such thing. Not after twenty-nine years in service. Not when one was loyal.

And filled with self-loathing because one was also as frightened as a mouse.

Tune said softly, "Thank you, sir."

"Don't let us down, Clarence!"

"I won't sir. Thank you again, sir."

"Good man!"

They shook hands. The commander came around his car-sized desk to put a heavy arm over Tune's shoulder, walk him to the door. "Best of luck, Clarence. But always remember: the good men *make their own luck,* eh?"

Tune twisted his face into a meek grin. "Yes, sir! Oh, that's well said, sir! Good day!"

"Good day, Clarence! Good hunting, eh? —Marsha, will you please come in now, and bring your pad?"

Once out on the street, Tune stopped to take a few deep breaths and calm himself. His stomach hurt savagely. He was so sick of being overlooked, denigrated, cheated, treated like a fool. He was as hurt and angry as he had ever been in his life. *If a chance comes, commander,* he thought bitterly, *I'll give you results. You'll have a terrorist's head on your desk right beside your bloody puzzle!*

He had to do better. He saw now that this was his last chance. Unless he could make something happen now, his file would go in a bin somewhere with retirement notations on it that might as well have read *"CASHIERED: FAILURE."*

Something hit Tune's cheek. Startled, he looked upward. The sun had vanished. A cloud had moved in. It had started to rain.

Tune went to look for Brad Smith.

Bristol

Late Wednesday morning, Melville Oldham's driver parked directly in front of the antique art dealer's shop in Grosvenor Alley. A police officer directing traffic at the corner noted the illegal maneuver, registered the fact that the offending vehicle was a Rolls Royce, and carefully turned his back, continuing to signal lesser folk driving the main thoroughfare.

Melville Oldham, bundled in a trenchcoat against the cold rain, hurried across the brick sidewalk and entered the art shop. The tinkle of a bell announced him.

The inside of the shop towered over him: shelving packed with musty old pieces of pottery, bronze and stonework, suspended gilt frames containing paintings ranging in worth from nothing to a small fortune, nooks and crannies and balconies and counters. Oldham spotted two other customers browsing in side rooms.

Behind the front counter, the portly old owner recognized him at once. "Mr. Oldham, sir! Welcome again!"

"Has my appraiser arrived, Durland?"

"Yes, sir! You will find him in the rear alcove!"

Oldham went directly back. He found his man standing in front of a late nineteenth century pastoral scene, a poor piece, as if seriously studying its worth. "Durland" was a short man, middle-aged, with sagging jowls and old-fashioned pince-nez eyeglasses. He looked the role he played as Oldham's rare book appraiser.

"You're late," the man told Oldham.

Oldham ignored that. "Damn you! How dare you put a wanted man on my payroll!"

The man shrugged. "No harm done. He was well away before anyone tried to interfere."

"You had no right! What would my guests have said if they had realized? How could I have answered the charges if your man had been apprehended on my grounds, in my employ?"

"As I said, no harm done, sir."

"And then you make me wait almost three days before agreeing to meet with me!"

The contact's eyes looked coldly hostile behind the meek spectacles. "There was no need for haste. We had no new instructions for you. Now I can tell you that the other people will arrive within the next two nights for removal of the materials from your property."

"No, God damn you!"

The man looked at Oldham with new interest. "Eh?"

"I said no! There won't be any more! I've gone far more than halfway, trying to meet your demands. But you've taken advantage of my trust at every turn, and I've had enough!"

"Meaning?"

"Meaning I'll cooperate no more! I'm through with your bunch!"

"Please do not make such rash statements, sir. And do not be so foolhardy as to move or dispose of our supplies on your grounds, or—"

"Idiot! Even if I knew precisely where you have something hidden on the grounds, do you think I would risk tampering with it? But wherever it's hidden—whatever it is—it will jolly well rot right there!"

"You must realize, sir, that the consequences of such an action would be . . . severe."

"I've invested more than a million pounds in the preliminary studies, but by God it can still be abandoned. I try in every way I know to *help* your people, and I receive back nothing but extortion."

"I urge you to think carefully."

"Tell your people," Oldham said, shaking in an effort to control his towering outrage. "As of this moment, we are finished."

With that, he turned and strode back out of the shop.

London

The rain pounding against the windows of the Soviet embassy on Kensington Park Gardens matched Mikhail Gravitch's black mood. The KGB Resident had seldom been as angry or harried as he was at this moment, facing the bloodless Eduard Lemlek.

Gravitch shook the computer-generated radio copy under Lemlek's nose. "I warned you about this kind of damned effrontery!"

Lemlek stared at the paper, his milky eyes revealing glacial cunning. "But comrade, it is only one of my routine internal security reports."

Gravitch slapped his palm across the pages. "For the third time—the third time!—you have exceeded your authority and cast aspersions on my competence to direct our external activities in Great Britain!"

"I have no idea what you mean," Lemlek murmured.

"You know damned well what I mean, you weasel! —Look here. Look, where *again* you mention Yuli Szulc's outside assignment!"

Lemlek pretended to read with concern, although clearly he himself had drafted the words as part of his ongoing war of nerves designed to promote himself by demeaning Gravitch. "Why, all it says is that we require additional personnel inside the embassy, in view of outside assignments to such as Mr. Szulc."

"And it goes on to say, you bastard, that—I use your own words written here—'delicate outside assignments in volatile areas at this time, using personnel previously on medical restriction, not only deplete manpower available for internal security operations but create potential new problems for internal security,' unquote."

Lemlek met Gravitch's angry stare. The smaller man showed no emotion. "But this is only a fact, comrade Gravitch. Surely you could not ask a fellow security operative to include less than all the facts in his reports!"

"Lemlek, you have done nothing in recent months but raise spurious questions and create confusion. Damn you! I'll have no more of this! If you once more file a report like this, I plan to demand a hearing for both of us in Moscow."

Lemlek's pale lips quirked, almost betraying a smile. "If such a hearing is called, I shall of course be pleased to do my duty and cooperate fully. I am confident any such investigation would vindicate me entirely."

"Maybe," Gravitch bit off. "But just remember one thing, Lemlek. Such a hearing would be conducted on *my* grounds—on Dzerzhinsky Square."

The mention of the KGB headquarters' home address accomplished what Gravitch had hoped: despite his enormous arrogance, Lemlek paled visibly. He took a half-step backward, and his Adam's apple bobbed as he tried to collect himself.

Finally he managed hoarsely, "I do what I believe is right."

Gravitch had made his point. With another glare, he turned and walked out of the office.

Heading back toward his own area, the KGB Resident worried anew about Yuli Szulc—Sylvester—and his assignment in Ulster. He knew Lemlek would seize upon any indiscretion to embarrass him. Sylvester—if he made a single bad move—might give Lemlek the ammunition he needed.

Gravitch entered his own office and pulled up Sylvester's last two brief reports on his computer screen. Sylvester seemed to be accomplishing very little. The thought that had plagued Gravitch previously now recurred: *was Sylvester up to some game of his own?*

It seemed unlikely . . . even mad. But Gravitch remembered those psychological profiles. He had trusted his ability to gauge men, and had sent Sylvester out when more cautious supervisors might have kept him inside a while longer yet. It was the kind of gamble which a man like Lemlek could make much of if Sylvester proved unstable.

Gravitch closed the report file and stared at the blinking cursor on his blank screen. He had earlier devised a plan for keeping closer tabs on Sylvester, but pride in his own judgment and respect for Sylvester's record had prevented his putting the plan into effect. Now, however, with Lemlek increasing the pressure, Gravitch had no choice. The plan would be set into motion.

The KGB Resident pressed an intercom button, summoning his top aide.

Belfast, Northern Ireland

Terrence Dean did not look much like Northern Ireland's most feared terrorist.

At five feet, six, and one hundred and thirty-five pounds, with baldness swiftly eroding his close-cropped curly black hair, wire-rimmed eyeglasses and tiny hands that fluttered like birds when he got excited during a conversation, he looked more like a school-teacher or a music master, or possibly a cab driver. His nondescript clothing—usually plain, cheap dark trousers and a well-worn wool shirt open at the collar—did nothing to mark him.

It helped Dean's chances of survival that no photograph of him existed, and police-type sketches made by terrified witnesses to his few public appearances during attacks on British army units were wholly inaccurate. In the minds of survivors, Terrence Dean was a blurred figure, very large, very frightening, a massive man who moved with the grace of a wild animal.

The witnesses were remembering his power, not his physical self.

Sitting in the basement of the shabby, unremarkable little house with his two most trusted henchmen, Dean field-stripped and cleaned a 9 mm Beretta semiautomatic while he talked. His two aides, Jack Blake and Squirrel Henry, nursed beers and added more cigarette smoke to the dense cloud already graying the tight little room.

"Squirrel," Dean said, "you have enough help to move the gas again this weekend?"

"Aye," Henry nodded, gnomelike in the smoke curling around his head. "Nedwin i'n't smart but he's strong. We can handle it."

"You'll stay in the area, then, afterward. Cruickshank and Moriarty will find you."

Squirrel nodded again. "Ye'll be comin' doon when?"

Dean, ever suspicious, looked up with sharp resentment flaring in his eyes. "You think you need to know my exact plans, do you?"

The older man saw his mistake and paled. "No, no," he said quickly. "I jus' follow orders, Terrence. I don't need to be knowing anything."

Dean turned to the squat, blond-bearded Blake, who sat with brawny blacksmith's forearms on his knees. "The truck is ready?"

"Yes," Blake replied, unmoving and stolid. "It's hid away safe and proper and the paintin's to be done this weekend."

"Good," Dean grunted. "We need to be staying on top of schedule now. The truck is painted and then moved to the other garage. Squirrel, you get the gas trucked in. Jack, you and Cruickshank will get the stuff out of the castle basement and transport it. We meet again Saturday, and then we start the final phase."

Both Squirrel Henry and Blake watched Dean. Neither allowed himself to speak.

"You will know the exact date and time of the attack soon," Dean told them. "I promise you. There are just a few details to iron out yet."

"Whatever you say, Terrence," Squirrel Henry said soothingly.

Dean finished cleaning the Beretta and started reassembling it. His skinny hands moved with lethal precision. "We'll be having another session with Oldham. If he remains stubborn, we have something planned to change his mind. We can't use his castle for afterward, of course, because of Mallory's getting himself seen there, and those Anti-Terrorist folk showing up to search for him. Place might be watched intensely . . . afterward. But he has to let us get the stuff out now."

Again, both Henry and Blake stared, intensely curious. But again they were afraid to ask.

When no one spoke, Dean added, "That's all for this time, then."

Squirrel Henry put down his beer bottle and slowly raised himself to his feet. Despite his short stature, he had to bend slightly to avoid bumping his bushy gray head on the basement rafters. "I'll be leavin' first, then."

"I'll expect a report."

"Aye, ye'll be havin' it."

Dean quickly finished assembling the Beretta. He inserted the loaded magazine in the handle and worked the slide, loading a cartridge in the chamber. Thumbing on the safety, he put the weapon on the table with the hammer still fully cocked. A dangerous way to carry a gun. But all of life was dangerous for Terrence Dean, and accidentally shooting himself was among the least of his worries.

Squirrel Henry got to the stairs leading up out of the basement. "Oh, there is one wee thing."

Dean looked at him.

"About poor Mallory."

Dean's expression did not change, but his voice gained a chill edge: "He'll be on every new alert sheet. He can't help us now."

Squirrel digested this. "He's hidden, then?"

"Yes," Dean said. "Well out of sight."

Very well out of sight, Dean thought.

Mallory had been careless and had become a liability. Captured now, he might have been subjected to the kind of chemical-assisted interrogation that could get out of him all he knew of the operation in progress. Mallory was a veteran, and in the instant last night when Dean trained his Beretta on the man's face, there had been sudden understanding, and only the most fleeting moment of fear.

No one had ever said you might lose your life only to the English. It was understood that betrayal of the fight was cause for execution, and becoming too visible—or knowing too much—might also make you too grave a risk if allowed to keep on living.

Mallory was no more risk now, Dean thought. And no one could question how well he was hidden. The quickly dug grave back in the highland gorse was good and deep, and might never be discovered.

London

J. C. Kinkaid and Linda Bennett met at Walton's, the fine old restaurant bordering Knightsbridge and Chelsea, where the IRA staged a terrorist bombing in the early 1970s. The windows still showed signs of the protective shuttering installed here and at other well-known watering holes during the time when mainstream IRA policy was to hit public places at random.

The two CIA operatives ordered salads and tea, and chatted smilingly, voices low, looking like old friends having a casual moment together.

The conversation wasn't that pleasant.

"Look," Kinkaid said. "He screwed up."

Linda Bennett nodded glumly. "But he did have his reasons."

"He went down to Oldham's place and spotted a hell of a lead, then played Maxwell Smart and alerted the sonofabitch, not to mention almost getting himself killed, and then he waited another day before letting us know about it. Has the dumb ass had a stroke or something?"

"Why don't you ask him?"

"You're his contact. Not me."

"You know he worried about tapped phones, and he couldn't go rushing out of there early Sunday or he would have tipped everybody off that he isn't what he seems."

"Tell him," Kinkaid grated, "he should have called us the minute he spotted that guy, and risk the chance the Oldham estate phones were bugged. Tell him he should *not* have played superspy in the middle of the night. Tell him he should have then, at least, immediately called us. Or even that guy Clarence Tune. Tell—forget it."

Linda studied her colleague's grim expression. "Have we gotten some additional bad news or something?"

"We had a chance to make a contribution and he blew it! Isn't that enough?"

"You've always been one of Brad's admirers, from what I've heard. One screwup doesn't seem to me to justify quite this much mad."

It was Kinkaid's turn to reflect and work on the tea. His cup made a little clattering sound going back onto the saucer. He heaved his shoulders in an obvious effort to relax. "Okay. Maybe you're right. It's just so goddamn embarrassing."

"It's still mainly the Brits' deal, though."

"Granted. I just wish—well, forget it."

Linda decided to try a bit of the muffin. She chewed reflectively. "Any more on that man who might have been Sylvester?"

"Maybe it was Sylvester. Everything seems to fit. Of course we aren't barging in and alienating the Yard or anybody by asking for an autopsy of our own. But Brad—if he really isn't brain-damaged—thinks it might very well have been Sylvester, and everything we know about the corpse fits."

"Anything around the Soviet embassy?"

"Everything looks normal. One face is missing, a guy named Zulk, Sulzak, something like that. But our info is that he's been recalled to Moscow temporarily. So it looks like our friend Sylvester was here on some freelance-type deal, working alone. What he was doing out there in the country that night is anybody's guess. It isn't that far from a small RAF unit. Whatever. Good riddance."

"We can hope." Linda looked at her watch.

"Another appointment?"

"Brad has a doubles practice with Terry Carpoman, and then he and I are going out to dinner with Sean and Kitty Cork."

Kinkaid reached for a cigarette, then thought better of it. "Brad has done a very nice job of getting close to Cork, anyway."

Linda's eyes took on a momentary hard edge. "Glad you can find something good to say about him today."

Kinkaid looked up and slowly grinned. "You sort of like him, huh?"

"Go to hell, J.C."

Kinkaid's grin widened. "But you do like him, huh? Huh?"

"Who?" Linda retorted.

In the slum garage, behind locked doors, Reggie Montgomery gleefully rubbed his hands together. "This is going to be great. This is going to be fantastic, boys! —Boom! And there goes pieces of Mr. Sean Cork all over the street!"

Fat John Mudd squatted on an overturned empty keg and cracked his knuckles one after the other. "We gotta be careful," he said fretfully. "This explosive stuff is dangerous. We got to put it in at the right time."

Eugene O'Connor looked down at his cohort with unconcealed disgust. "We come this far, Piggy—we're *this* far" —holding up two fingers an inch apart— "from being *heroes* of the people of all of Ulster—and you start losing your guts."

"I'm not losin' my guts, damn yer eyes! I just said be careful!"

"We will be," O'Connor said. Then his wolfish grin gleamed. "But now we know where he's gonna be Saturday, and we know about when he's gonna be there. And now we can strike our mighty blow, and oh, how grand it are going to be!"

Seventeen

ON SATURDAY—two days before Wimbledon was to begin—it rained.

"Now we can't practice!" Terry Carpoman raged.

"Terry," I said with all the patience I could summon, "I wasn't going to practice today anyway. I told you that."

"We need it! We're not playing well together! We got a hard draw. The committee is trying to screw us. We should have worked out. All we've had so far is shitty luck. Damn!"

I ducked him late in the morning and went to the doctor, who drew a little fluid off my knee. Then, after hurriedly sending off a short piece to New York on how weather delays might affect various players, I moved out of the Cumberland and into a much smaller hotel in South Kensington.

The move wasn't necessary, but most of the players stayed in that area, and it was where I had stayed the year I won the singles title. Not that I am superstitious. But I don't walk under ladders, either.

My new hotel was off the beaten path. Old, awkwardly restored and on a narrow side street, the Victoria was five stories tall and looked more like an apartment building than a hotel. It was not favored by the more important players and not likely to draw curious fans wanting to gawk at their heroes. It had only sixteen rooms. The ceilings were high, the walls covered by faded floral paper, the plumbing made groaning noises, and the telephones didn't always work. I liked it.

Terry and Alicia Carpoman moved, too. Into the London Tara. Alicia had heard it was the best there was. Sean and Kitty Cork moved into a hotel like mine, and just down the street.

Linda Bennett moved into the room adjoining mine. She was in there about thirty minutes when there came a tapping on the doors that connected the rooms. When I unlocked my side, I found she had already unlocked hers. Wearing a short crimson silk robe sashed at the waist, she came into my side and looked around. She had showered and her wet hair was drawn back tight from her face, making her classic features even more stunning. The short robe revealed long, bare legs almost to her hips.

As she turned back to face me after her examination, she caught me looking. She struck an ironic but nevertheless bewitching pose.

"If you're wondering," she said throatily, "the answer is no."

"No?" I managed, and then swallowed with some effort.

She sat on the edge of my bed and crossed those legs. "I thought maybe you were wondering if I had anything on underneath."

"Oh, Linda, Christ!" I groaned.

"I know you great athletes aren't supposed to leave your competitive edge in the bedroom, Brad," she purred. "But—"

"Just hold it right there," I cut in.

Her expression changed. "Why?"

"Because nothing is going to happen, goddammit, and this kind of stuff just makes me uncomfortable as hell."

She stood, the simple motion supple and sexy, and came toward me. "We like each other. We're going to be here a while. Brad! I'm *not* a chippie. I don't come on to every man I meet. You and I—" And here her expression changed again, and there was no teasing at all— "we're special. I feel that." Her hands teased along my shirtfront. "You feel it too. Why deny it?"

Without consciousness my arms went around her. I bent down and she raised her mouth to meet mine. Our lips had just touched—

it felt like brushing flame—when it happened just like it used to in the worst Hollywood comedies.

In her room the telephone rang.

"Damn!" she muttered, and disengaged to hurry in and answer.

I waited, breathing hard, fuming. I could hear her soft voice, brief replies.

Then she came back, but only to the door. "I've got to go see COS. Some updates on people we might watch for."

I threw up my hands. A brief, rueful laugh caught in her throat, and she closed her door to get dressed and leave. Minutes later I heard her outside door close, and she was gone.

Rain spattered down. I prowled the hotel, waiting for it to be time to go out to the stadium with my gear. The trip was not necessary, but I was being driven by old habits.

I would have something else to think about in the evening. The four of us—Linda and me, Sean and Kitty—were scheduled to go together to a party thrown by Melville Oldham in the evening. Traditionally he rented a house near Wimbledon and entertained throughout the tournament. I wondered if Linda would be back in time for that. I wondered what was going to happen between us later tonight.

After cooling off a while, I tried to make some new decisions. Whatever was going to develop with the terrorists was only a matter of hours or days away now. Both Linda and I needed to have all our wits about us. If there was a chance for either of us to have an impact here, that chance would be diminished if we started playing house—got so caught up and preoccupied with each other that we weren't looking in directions we were supposed to be watching.

And I did not delude myself about the lady named Linda. She had teased. She had a sense of humor. But behind the teasing was something considerably more powerful. She had spoken the truth. I knew she was not the kind of woman who hopped casually into bed with a man. And the look in her eyes—the sharp, hot intake of breath as I finally put my arms around her and bent to her mouth—had spoken volumes.

Neither of us could start something now. If we did, we might be blinded to practically everything else.

Later? I didn't know. But the desire for her was a hot, coiling thing inside me. . . .

I was back in my room a little later when someone tapped on the hall door. I answered cautiously, speaking through the door. "Who is it?"

The furry little voice replied, "It's Clarence Tune, sir. If I might have a word with you?"

Damn and hell. I opened the door. Tune came in. It had started to drizzle outside, and his dark brown suit had waterstains on the shoulders, where his old raincoat had only sieved the water, and below his baggy knees, where a car had splashed mud on him. He looked tired and sad, as always.

"What is it, Clarence?" I demanded irritably.

"Well, sir," he fretted, opening his suit coat and reaching around behind himself, "I have something for you." With that, he produced as pretty a little .38 S&W revolver as I have ever seen.

"Hallelujah," I said, reaching for it.

"Take care, sir. It's fully loaded."

I took the little gun and examined it. I couldn't tell it had ever been fired. It was the detective model, the one with the hammer almost fully buried in the body. The hideout design made the butt considerably too small for my hand, but it felt good anyway. I had a S&W .38 back home. The nice, fat, subsonic bullet did not have the smashing power of a .45, but it was plenty big enough to discourage a person mightily.

I pocketed the weapon. "Thank you, Clarence."

His sad eyes drooped. "I yet believe, Two-Gun, that your need no longer exists, actually. I recognize that you might brush with terrorists, yes. But we have men everywhere. And with your old nemesis, Sylvester, dead—"

"If he is dead," I cut in.

Clarence studied me with mild surprise. "Oh, surely, sir, you don't still doubt that the corpse was he."

I didn't answer him. I hoped the body had been Sylvester. My guts did not tighten now every time I spotted a distant figure with Sylvester's build, and when I answered the telephone now I did not unconsciously brace myself for the sound of his high nasal voice. My mind might say I couldn't count on anything. My emotions said I was rid of him forever. So there was no way to answer Clarence Tune, really. Did I believe Sylvester was dead? No. Yes. Maybe. Old habits are hard to break.

After waiting a long minute or two, Tune told me, "I will want the weapon back, sir, when this is over. And I devoutly hope and trust you will not have occasion to fire it."

"Agreed, pal." He looked so forlorn I put an arm around his shoulders. "You look like you've had bad news."

"No news at all, sir. Except that Anti-Terrorist Group believes several sightings of possible terrorists in the city within the last day or two indicate that we are far from in the clear as to our fears for the tournament."

"Anything more definite you can tell me?"

"I am afraid, sir, there *isn't* anything more definite."

"Damn."

"Indeed, sir." He paused a beat, then: "May I ask your plans for the remainder of the day, sir?"

"I'm going to Melville Oldham's party tonight. —I told you he's rented a house not far from the All-England Club as a home-away-from-home during the tournament, right?"

"Yes, sir, quite. Mr. Oldham has done that for several years, I understand."

"Well, I've been invited, along with most of the rest of the tournament field, I imagine, and I'm going. —Have your people uncovered anything at all about Oldham, Clarence? Anything I should know?"

"No, sir," he said mournfully.

I let that pass. The boys at our embassy, especially COS, had been interested, I had been told, in my observations in Oldham's library. They seemed to think terrorist Mallory's presence there might not be out of Oldham's knowledge. So Oldham—since I had entry to him—had been added to my list of duties.

Was it logical to believe that a beer-brewing, car-racing million-aire would conspire with a bunch of scruffy fanatics to destroy the society that made him wealthy? I didn't think so. But it wasn't logi-cal that terrorists might be after Sean Cork just because he made some idealistic statements, either. Blowing up cafes and trying to wreck airplanes and planting bombs on city streets were not very logical either.

Nothing about this endless war was logical. Occasionally I would catch myself using part of my mind to think about it, what I knew of how it started, all the attempted solutions that had been tried, the role of fanatics on both sides. It just looked hopeless . . . endless. Just keep on randomly killing people forever? More insan-ity. It was all crazy. How was I—or anybody else—supposed to out-guess and thwart crazies?

I tried not to think about it. I had to trust that I was doing my assignment, even though I couldn't see the faintest sign of doing any good at all.

But now my time had run out. Now—Monday—the stadium would fill for the first time this tournament. Some royal family mem-ber or other might be in their special seats any or every day. Sean Cork would be oncourt, in the open, even more frequently. And all the king's horses and all the king's men—if the crazies were clever enough—would not be able to put things together again.

And what in the hell were any of us doing about it except mill around and hope a lot?

Tune's visit had fine-tuned my nerves. Linda said she wanted to make the trip out to the stadium with me, but I wanted to go alone, and did. I stowed my stuff in my locker and fiddled with adjustments on my spare knee brace and then went outside, still alone, and made my way up into the stadium.

Light rain fell as I climbed out of the dark. I emerged on a ramp halfway up and stood behind the railing, looking around. The stadium, rows of dark seats glistening wet, stood vacant. The court below, under tarps, looked dreary and deserted. The dark green scoreboard area showed no names, no scores, and in this instant it was like I might be the last living being on the planet, and had wandered here into a silent, holy place where unimagined rituals once played out. Wind sighed, and then three sparrows darted across the seats near the far end of the court, wheeled sharply against the drear green back wall, and flung themselves upward against the sky, and were gone. I shivered.

As often as I had done this, I had never been here entirely alone. There had always been another player somewhere nearby, or workmen in the stands or oncourt. The weather had isolated me. Looking down, in my mind I could almost hear the *thowck* of ball against racket, feel the slide of a long run and reach for a shot on the extreme sideline, remember the cool, wet discomfort of an early match one year when the grass was still firm and green, or the parched, yellowed, beat-up dryness of a semifinal match after hot days of play and constant use had burned and worn the grass to nothing, and it was like playing on dusty cement. It took me back.

Remembering, my matches here all ran together, a single blurred newsreel, more feeling than fact, with instants of the most vivid total recall: the match against Roscoe Tanner that year when he was completely on his enormous serve, and he had 23 aces in our five sets; the matches with Connors, his blasts to the backhand and completely fearless rushes to net; the early match one year against V. J. Armitraj, a beautiful match where both of us seemed able to hit every shot with balletic grace, and when it was finally over, regretting that this had to end; the days on this court with Arthur Ashe, and the match the London press facetiously—and with total inaccuracy—billed as "the battle of the Smith Brothers," because the draw made it Stan Smith against Brad Smith, with Stan still playing beautifully, but entering the phase of his career where I stood now: with all the very best high points behind me. And of course the indescribable moment of winning, and then holding the trophy up to the stands and thinking, *Nothing can ever be this good.*

But above all, as I knew it would, the memory of that last encounter here with Bjorn Borg came back: the fifth set, the shadows growing long, lungs and legs and mind numbed by more than five hours out here on this court, the score in my favor, 6-4, 4-6, 3-6, 7-5, 5-4 and the crowd almost hysterical, applauding and crying out on every point, Bjorn serving to even the set and falling behind, and then my passing shot that gave me break point, 30-40—the point for game, set, and match, and the championship.

I remembered *everything* about that point: waiting, sweat stinging my eyes, swaying from side to side, thinking, *Just get it back, make him win the point.* And his big, high-hopping, heavy serve, my return crosscourt, his looping forehand deep, my backhand to the deepest corner, his miracle get, my forehand drive, finding reserves I didn't know I had in order to get near the net, his desperation scoop return from twelve feet behind the baseline, the ball dipping low and weak over the net, right in front of me, a perfect setup, a dead ball, calling only for the simplest little dink on my part, a dropshot almost any city park hacker could make nine times out of ten, and Borg so far back out of position that even as he started forward it was surely over for him, and my calm, careful, easy little cut at the ball. And the ball hitting the net cord, rolling along its top for almost a foot, then falling back on my side. Giving him new life. And, after he then held serve, the chance to break me and serve out the set and match and hold the great old cup aloft while I stood there pretending to smile.

There was so much here, for me and for anyone who loved the game. It went back far beyond my memories, and as I stood there, a few of the names and old images, some from faded photographs, trooped before me: Steffi, of course, and Chrissie and Martina and the old lady herself, but also Goolagong and Court, Althea Gibson, Mo Connolly, Louise Brough, Helen Wills Moody, Suzanne Lenbglen. And God, the men who had played for this championship and won, names like Newcombe; Laver; Hoad; Budge; Perry; Tilden; Doherty; Renshaw. Some of them had never played here because their time had been when the tourney hadn't moved yet to Wimbledon. But they were still part of it, the All-England tradition. There was nothing else like it, nothing that could come close.

Birds darted again, bringing me back to myself, standing on the ramp. I shook off the daydreaming. There didn't seem much chance I would get back to Centre Court this time around. I would have to win at least two matches to do that. I caught myself wishing I hadn't started to get old, or that I hadn't blown the knees out. *How in the hell did I get this way?* Yesterday or maybe the day before I was twenty years old, and my knees, like all the rest of me, were indestructible.

Melville Oldham had rented an eighteenth century town house on the corner of two narrow residential streets within long walking distance of the tennis complex. The staid brick house had a small, iron-fenced yard, a rarity for the neighborhood, but the streets were lined with cars on both sides when my taxi arrived, and a lot more cars—other taxis and private vehicles ranging from little Fords to Cadillacs—had things impossibly snarled as drivers tried to find parking. Sean and Kitty Cork, in the front seat of his little car, and Linda and me, in the back, craned our necks looking for a place to park.

"Good lord!" Sean groaned. "We should have taken a taxi!"

"Take a left here on this side street," I suggested.

"You know the neighborhood, eh?"

Linda cooed, "He knows his way around," and slipped a teasing hand between my legs to stroke my thigh.

I grabbed her hand and held it tight. Our eyes met, and hers laughed with pleasure. She looked stunning in the dim light from outside the car.

Sean took a left as suggested, falling in behind some other cars.

We drove a slow block, then another. Up ahead, we spotted a boy signalling cars into a rent lot.

"Looks all right," Sean said, braking. "We can walk from here."

"That's just grand for you to say," Kitty replied good-naturedly. "In these heels, Linda and I will be seeing the trainer for shin splints tomorrow."

"Well, luv—"

"I was teasing, honey. Pull in."

He did. One of the boys in the narrow paved lot waved us into a tight spot. Sean parked, we got out, I paid the boy, and we started away.

"Did you lock it?" I asked as an afterthought.

"Yep." Sean displayed the keys in his hand.

Linda walked close beside me. The mutual desire was heady stuff.

Yard and porch lights blazed all over the front of Oldham's house when we arrived. Sean signed a few autographs for fans on the sidewalk beyond the fence, and then we got in.

A servant standing in the entry hall hurried to admit us. Two rotund older men in poorly fitting business suits, standing nearby, gave us a hard look and then relaxed, seeing we weren't gatecrashers who required prompt escort back to the sidewalk.

Inside we found about thirty other guests on hand ahead of us. I spotted Graf, Connors, Kriek, Flach and Bryne, and far across the sprawling living room Terry and Alicia. Terry looked angry and maybe slightly snooted, and Alicia, as usual, looked like two million dollars in a melon-colored St. Gillian dress and very high matching heels. I waved but stayed away.

Within a few minutes Linda and I had been sifted apart by different conversations, and I was by myself when Melville Oldham came in from another roomful of party to put an arm over my shoulder. "Brad. Good of you to come."

"Thanks for the invitation, Melville. Wouldn't miss it."

He frowned. "Yes. Well, with so many events going on this

evening, no one will stay long, I suspect. But this is a tradition with me, just like my regular seating in the stadium." He squeezed my shoulder with an ample hand. "I regularly have extra seats in my box, old chap. At any time you're not involved in your own competition, do look in on me."

"Thanks," I told him. "I might do that."

Another squeeze. "Yes. Do. Actually, I mention this to very few. But I would enjoy watching a match or two with you at my side. Give me your expert insights, don't you know."

"I'll keep it in mind, Melville. I might spend more time in the players' section—"

"Of course, of course." He winked. "If there's a chill in the air, however, I have a special brew I always bring in my Thermos. Officially, of course, it's hot porridge. Unofficially—well. Come see."

I started to reply, but suddenly his hand fell from my shoulder and I saw him start upright like a man who had been hit by a heavy electric shock. Color left his face. He stared to my right.

I turned and glanced across the room, where I saw a slender, dark-haired young woman in a Banana Republic-type safari outfit talking with a couple of the new South American players I hadn't met. She was striking, with large dark eyes and long hair loose on her back.

"Excuse me, old fellow," Oldham said grimly, and headed off.

I turned as someone else said something to me, but managed to keep my eyes on the scene as my host filtered his way across the room, waited while the dark girl talked with the young Argentinians, then said something to her. She turned and gave him a blinding smile. His expression would have darkened the sun. He said something else and turned and walked toward a doorway which evidently led into another part of the house.

The two people who had buttonholed me were a couple of our younger American players, not quite in the top rank yet, survivors of the qualifyings. I had been half-listening to them. It was pretty familiar stuff:

"Yes, I play Monday, out on Thirteen. Cantaras, from Chile. That old douche bag, he'll probably hit those stupid moonball shots of his, trying to make me look bad. And I hate Thirteen. It's the worst court out there. Totally wrong for my game. I never get a break."

The speaker eyed me with righteous, spoiled indignation, waiting for me to agree. I saw the dark-haired girl separate herself from the South Americans and glide toward the door through which Oldham had vanished. My curiosity mounted.

The other young player standing in front of me said, "Billy, you think *you've* got it bad? They put me on Court Three. I hate it! Everybody there will be rooting for Murphy. And the way he struts around, making his damned pronouncements, it just makes me want to puke! What do you think, Brad?"

I smiled at them. "Maybe the luck will change for all of us. Excuse me." I left them and headed for the doorway that had been used by Oldham and the girl.

When I got there, I found that it led into a hallway that went to another room across the front of the house where the party was also in progress, but in addition it turned back toward the back of the building. I saw lights shining into the hall back there from other rooms. Not seeing my quarry in the other front area, I strolled toward the back.

The first two rooms were unoccupied. I neared the back of the hall when the voices came, first Oldham's, low, shaking with anger:

"No one invited you, goddamn you! I want you to leave! Now!"

The girl's voice replied, softer, but still hearable: *"I'll stay and you will do as you are instructed."*

"I'll have security drag you out!"

"No." Her voice remained soft, implacably calm: *"You will not."*

"Damn you!"

"Are you going to do as we ask?"

Something made a muted clattering sound. Maybe a lamp being knocked over on thick carpet. I saw the shadow in the doorway and just managed to duck into the nearest doorway, a lighted rest-room. As I swung the door closed I got a glimpse of Oldham, his face a storm cloud, churning back toward the party.

This was interesting. Of course it might be only an old girl-friend, back to hassle for money. Oldham's words, and the girl's steely control, made me think it might be something quite different.

Buying time, I washed my hands and dried them carefully on one of the pristine guest towels, then opened the door again. By luck, just in time to come eyeball to eyeball with the dark girl, head-ing back up the hall toward the front. Startled by my abrupt appear-ance, she veered, catching breath, fixing me with those great dark eyes.

"Sorry!" I said, giving her my best oaf grin.

She recovered instantly. Her smile was like a 500-watt flood. "You're Brad Smith. Hi. I'm Rebecca Mavson. An old friend of Melville's."

I shook her small hand, which had metal cords under the velvet surface. "Hi, Rebecca. Nice party, isn't it? So you're an old friend of our host?"

"Yes. I just got in. I wanted to surprise him. And it was fun. He's such a dear man!"

"I bet he was glad to see you."

"Oh, yes. He was simply flabbergasted! *So* pleased!"

We strolled back toward the party. Still testing, I asked, "Are you a big tennis fan, Rebecca?"

"The best there is!" she told me.

"Who do you like in the men's singles this year?"

Her eyes glazed for a nanosecond. "Well. There are so many—"

"I'm betting," I said, "that it will be Arthur Ashe and Ken Rosewall in the finals. Don't you think so?"

"Well isn't that odd!" she beamed. "Those are exactly the two players I've been predicting!"

"Or Becker could sneak in there."

"Well, yes. . . ."

We reached the intersecting hall that led to party rooms. See-ing her start left, I veered right. "I see someone I have to meet, Rebecca. Talk to you again later?"

"I hope so," she told me with another 500 watts.

Interesting. She was supposed to be a dear old friend, but Old-ham had looked like a man who had been gutshot when he churned past my closing door in the back. She was supposed to be a tennis buff, but she didn't know the new players from antiques like me.

Maybe I had just come up with something. Too bad I had no idea what.

I wandered around a few minutes, renewing some acquaint-ances. No sound of forceful eviction came from the main room. I meandered back that way and saw the pretty Rebecca chatting ani-matedly with a couple of our top woman players, and—across the room—Oldham glaring balefully in her direction, but doing nothing more. The gorgeous Dacri appeared and linked arms with him, and his irritation magically vanished. Looking down at the lovely Califor-nia girl, he showed everything in his expression. He was smitten, truly and deeply and well. I felt for him.

I found Linda and filled her in on what I had overheard be-tween Oldham and the lady named Rebecca.

It was late when we left the party. I was not too surprised when a bulky figure detached itself from a lamp post outside the Oldham house and discreetly fell in behind us as we walked away: Weiss, Sean Cork's bodyguard. It felt reassuring to have him behind us.

Sean kept yawning as we strolled the dark street back toward where we had left the car.

"Early practice tomorrow," he said, yawning still again. "I hope I sleep."

I held out my hand, catching a few tiny raindrops. "Looks like it will be Wimbledon weather."

He thought about that, then brightened. "At least it's starting. And I guess that shows the death threat was just some nut, eh?"

"I notice Weiss is along, however."

"Maybe after this tournament we'll have to reevaluate that. A man can't have a shadow all his life!"

We reached the parking lot. Most of the other cars had already departed. We crossed to Sean's rented car. He reached for his keys, then paused. "That's odd, now!"

"What?" I asked.

"I *know* I locked it! You even asked me about it, didn't you?"

It took an instant for me to understand what he was saying. He reached for the door handle on his side and pulled the door open.

"No!" Linda said sharply.

Which was when I caught up. "Sean, get away from the car."

He straightened up, face blank. "What say?"

"Get away from the goddamned car!"

Linda moved, grabbing Kitty Cork and pulling her to the side, around a car parked beside ours. Sean stood there, blank. I rushed around the back of the Fiat and took him by the arm, pulling him away, across the lot, as fast as I could drag him.

"What *is* this?" he demanded, struggling against me.

I caught sight of Weiss running ponderously toward us. I wanted to yell at him to get down, but there wasn't time. Behind us, under or near the car, there was a quick little fizzling sound that turned my blood to ice. I knocked Sean flat. An orange fireball exploded, lighting the brick walls of nearby buildings like midday, and heat and shock washed over us.

Eighteen
Elsewhere

Belfast, Northern Ireland

CLOUDS MASKED THE stars and moon, making the night as black as the mood of the city.

In the flat where Terrence Dean was in hiding, the telephone sat silent. Dean stood staring at it, as he had for more than an hour.

Time was running out and everything was turning sour. Dean was violently angry.

Anger was not a new emotion to him. His entire life had been a fight.

He had always been small, and as a boy he had been forced to choose between living a life as small as his stature or fighting boys a head taller. By the time he was fifteen, every tooth in his head had been knocked out and he had only one functioning kidney. But none of the boys challenged him any more, and two men who had tried were dead. By this time Dean's anger was chronic, a fact of life. His kind of anger, however, was controlled. He had learned early that losing control put you at a disadvantage, like the professional boxer who lost his temper in the ring.

Dean's father had died in prison during a long term for terrorist activity. His mother had not spoken to him in six years. Dean had no feeling about either parent. He had sublimated all his rage into a single obsession: war against the English, whom he saw as invaders, barbarians who had made his homeland a colony for Protestant trash. Dean lived only to disrupt normal life for the English. "I am a peaceful person," he liked to say. "I grant the Prots eternal peace whenever I can."

234

Dean's anger at the moment, watching his telephone, focused on news he had gotten an hour ago. Someone had tried—and failed—to kill Sean Cork, the Irish tennis star. A bomb had been planted in his car, according to Dean's sources, but the job had been done clumsily, by amateurs. Cork and his companions had escaped with bruises. Only a hired bodyguard, running to help, had been injured; he was said to be in critical condition in a hospital near the scene of the blast.

Dean did not care whether Cork lived or died. What enraged him was the fact that the amateurish attempt would put security forces around Wimbledon in a higher state of alert. It would make his mission more difficult.

And now he had to wait for another call, the one that would tell him whether Melville Oldham had yielded to common sense, or had to be convinced. Dean was ready with his contingency plan if Oldham dug his heels in. *Nothing* was going to stop the strike at Wimbledon now, after everything was so nearly ready. And there was absolutely no more time to shilly-shally; the materials hidden on the Oldham estate had to be freed up instantly.

Dean waited, chain-smoking.

Thirty minutes later, the telephone rang. Dean leaped to answer it. "Yes?"

The male voice said: "She called from London. He's being difficult."

"Still saying no to what we require?"

"That is correct. He told her to go to hell."

"Right," Dean said, and hung up.

Going back across the room, he unlocked a small, antique mahogany cabinet and took out a gray metal gadget slightly smaller than a carton of cigarettes: a Motorola handi-talkie taken from a dead soldier and modified to transmit and receive on six illegal frequencies in the 150 MHz range.

Dean turned the radio on, checked the band selector, raised the unit to his lips, and keyed the transmit button. "Standby, standby, over."

The tiny loudspeaker instantly came alive. *"Standby,"* the answering voice said, metallic but recognizable.

"Proceed," Dean said.

"Roger, proceed."

The squelch tail dropped and Dean turned off the radio and hid it again.

A few miles away, in a section of the city filled with empty warehouses and deserted factories, four men left the car in which they had been waiting. They walked out of the trashy alley and down streets starting to turn to rubble after years of bad weather and neglect.

Within fifteen minutes the men approached a well-kept cyclone-type security fence surrounding a long metal factory building. Inside, except for two small security lights on poles, all was dark. The men knelt at the fence and one of them worked a set of bolt cutters. The fencing was spread and the four crawled inside.

Once on the grounds, the men hurried across an open paved area and paused only when they had reached the deeper shadows of the main building. They moved along the wall, crouching again when they reached a metal door to the interior. The leader signalled one of his aides, who produced a big pair of vise grips. He clamped them onto the handle on the door and threw his weight into it. With a groan and then a sharp metallic spang, the doorlock mechanism snapped. The leader pushed the door open and led his men inside, AK-47 at the ready.

Inside, they risked brief flashes of their red-masked flashlights. The great, vaulted four-story expanse of the building—a single room two hundred meters long and half as wide—swallowed up their quick reconnoiters. Except for scaffolding towers looming like prehistoric monsters here and there, and a few scattered toolracks, the entire main area was dusty, deserted.

The leader gave a signal. One man moved to the south, another toward the north. Each carried a small canvas bag. The leader and his remaining man cut across the assembly floor to where they knew the offices were on the far side. Glass tinkled as, bolder now, they broke in.

The offices were bare and utilitarian, mainly housing for old desks and the latest in drafting tables and engineering apparatus. Everything looked dusty under the blips of red light.

The leader and his helper split up and did their work, which required a very short time.

Less than ten minutes later, the four men rendezvoused at the shattered door, conferred in a few words, and got out. They crawled back through the hole they had cut in the fence, split up, and vanished.

One hour later, a timing device of the type available at Radio Shack stores in the United States for 92 cents closed its electronic gates. A current flowed. The explosion that shattered the closed factory building broke windows for three blocks and was heard ten miles away. Fire gushed into the night sky as cleaning fluids and industrial solvents blew, then burned.

The first firefighters appeared on the scene in their outmoded old firetrucks. In the lurid red of the flames they could easily read the black-on-white sign on the front of the building. The sign looked new and nice and it read: OLDHAM SPORTS CARS, LTD. But it was a wooden sign and within minutes it was surrounded by smoke and flame, blackened, and collapsed into the holocaust.

South Kensington

"Mr. Oldham. I trust I didn't wake you?"

Melville Oldham immediately recognized the voice on the telephone. Oldham's bedroom clock showed 3 A.M. He had been expecting this damned call since his manager in Belfast had awakened him with the tragic news an hour earlier.

"God damn you," Oldham said, and began to shake.

"Ah. Then you have heard some bad news, I take it?"

"You son of a bitch! You know damned well what happened in Belfast two hours ago!"

"It grieves us all, sir. It truly does. Perhaps, if you had listened to our advice and our very reasonable requests—"

"Bastard! Murderer! Here I am, plowing millions of pounds into pilot studies and engineering projects to produce a wonderful motor car in Northern Ireland—give some of the poor damned blighted people a decent job and living wage—and do you appreciate it? Do you help? No! Just because I won't take part in your murderous games, you blow up my factory site. You destroy the very project that would bring more good to your people than any—"

"Enough sermons, Mr. Oldham."

"God damn you!"

"Just listen please. I am instructed to tell you that you will cooperate with our associate, the one to whom you were so rude during your party last evening. You will cooperate *fully* with her very modest requests. If you fail to do so, there could be other . . . and worse . . . misfortunes."

Oldham began to shake so hard he felt he might fall. *I am not young any more. This kind of stress can burst an old heart.* "You bastards. You swine. I still want that little slut away from here. I will not cooperate. What more can you do? You've already sabotaged the car plant—ruined my hopes!"

"We can do more, sir. Believe me."

"And I can notify the authorities. Have her arrested."

"No, Mr. Oldham, indeed you will not do that."

"I—!"

"You will *not*, Mr. Oldham, because the next time the building we select as a target might not be unoccupied, as your pilot project building was tonight. The next time, the target could be your house . . . or some store or shop where your little American girl— what is her name? Dacri?—some shop where the pretty Dacri might be visiting."

"You wouldn't do that!"

"Please don't test us, Mr. Oldham. We are going for our merchandise now. If you alarm the authorities, or try to stop us, the next disaster to befall you will be infinitely worse. Good night." And the connection was broken.

London

Shortly after dawn on Sunday, Sylvester sat in a coffee shop where he knew the taxi drivers liked to congregate. Outside, rain misted down.

Wearing a little goatee and pink-tinted glasses, Sylvester listened to the drivers talk. He had been here twice in the past week, and they had begun to accept him as a fixture. Which was what he wanted.

The stuff used to stick on the extra hair itched, and Sylvester felt like a fool wearing it and the stupid glasses. But along with the work clothes and pea coat they transformed him. He did not think even his closest associates from the embassy would have recognized him if—unlikely event!—they walked into this working-class place.

"Joseph!" a friendly voice said.

Sylvester looked up from his stout. His new friend, the taxi driver, stood grinning crookedly down at him.

"Again this morning, Joseph?" the driver asked ironically.

"The woman is a demon," Sylvester said, following up on his assumed persona, the story he had made up to explain his appearances. "She screams at me and throws things, I leave. If this keeps up, or if I do not get a job soon, we will go back to Birmingham."

Chuckling, the driver sat down and signalled for his mug. "You should drive, like I do. There is always the excuse of a sick driver whose place you had to fill, or a long trip. You go home only when you want!"

Sylvester sighed. "Perhaps. —Will you cut cards with me to see who pays for the tea this morning?"

The driver clapped him on the back. "But I will win, as usual!"

"No matter," Sylvester said, feigning the sadness that so amused his new friend. "No matter."

"I enjoy taking your money, my friend."

Sylvester smiled and shrugged.

His plan was moving on schedule.

In his embassy office, Mikhail Gravitch pored over Sylvester's latest reports from Belfast. Sylvester was making no progress whatsoever.

Gravitch pushed a button which summoned an aide. Despite the hour, his lieutenant hurried smartly into the room, every button of his army tunic in place, his flushed Serbian face as hot and smooth as if he had just stepped from a shower and shave.

"Yes, Colonel Gravitch?"

"You will activate the contingency plan calling for continual surveillance of the American," Gravitch ordered.

"Yes, Colonel!"

And if this is the wrong move . . . or an inadequate precaution. . . , Gravitch thought, *then my career will be over.*

Sunday night, inside a small automotive garage on a back alley near Soho, two men in gas masks carefully turned the valves on a series of tubes and hoses that connected their farm truck's load of drums to the bulbous, white-painted tanker truck parked beside it. A compressor chuffed steadily, assisting the transfer. While the two masked men worked, three others, assault rifles in hand, guarded the locked doors.

It required several hours. Finally the job was finished, the pressure gauges checked, the valves all closed and double-checked. The compressor, with a coughing sigh, chuffed to a halt. It seemed quiet.

The two men removed their masks. One was Francis Moriarty. The other was his assigned top aide, a hook-faced man named Cruickshank.

The two men did not know each other well, but they did not try to hide the sweaty scared look on their faces now that the masks were off. Transferring the gas had been scary enough. But the really hairy part was just starting.

The truck had its bogus company name emblazoned on both sides: *TOPS PETROL.*

"Then we can move it on signal?" Cruickshank asked. "I can notify Terrence?"

Moriarty nodded.

Eight miles away, in another garage, Eugene O'Connor shook his fist in the face of Reggie Montgomery. "You said you knew how to plant it!"

"How was I to know they would notice?" Montgomery whined.

"Now we have to do it the other way!"

John Mudd, hunched miserably on his overturned keg, looked up with tears in his eyes. He had been crying all night. "Maybe we oughta just go home, Gene. Maybe we done our best—"

"Imbecile!" O'Connor screamed at him. "We still got the guns. We still got the grenade. We still got the van. Reggie has got us these new explosives. We're going to get him this time—tomorrow night!"

Nineteen

MONDAY, AND WIMBLEDON weather: misting rain beyond the car windows, people hurrying along the crowded narrow sidewalks in glistening slickers, or huddled under umbrellas, traffic almost at a standstill, clouds dense and low overhead, and inside the car the windows half fogged over.

So it was opening at last, and in the official limousine none of us spoke as we neared the stadium.

I had been up long before dawn, unable to rest, on this first morning of play. Part of it was delayed reaction to Saturday night's events. But I would have been keyed up anyway. I showered, examined my rackets again, walked around and around my little room, fought the urge to smoke because I knew I was going to need all my wind today. Beyond my windows the sun was nowhere in sight and the drizzle came down.

Linda had been gone continuously since the bombing, answering questions from COS and God knew who-all. It was a relief when I heard her return to her room a little before seven. She immediately tapped on my door. When I opened to her, she went on tiptoe to kiss me lightly on the lips, then leaned back to look me sharply in the eye.

"You okay?" she asked.

"Hey, you're the one to be asked. I've been lying low while you dealt with the bureaucrats."

"I'm fine. Just a little tired."

The only person injured in the car-bomb explosion had been

Sean Cork's bodyguard, Weiss. Running to see why I was dragging Sean away from the car, he had caught the partial force of the blast. An ambulance had taken him to the hospital, where he was treated for multiple cuts and bruises and a concussion. He would be in there for a few days, but would be fine.

We had been very, very lucky.

Sean Cork's reaction had been interesting. After the initial shock he had gotten grim, rather than angry. Someone from the Yard suggested that he might want to withdraw from the tournament because of "security" or because the bombing might have shaken him too badly to perform well. "Bloody hell," Sean had snapped. "I won't be run off. I'm playing."

My contacts with Clarence Tune and later with J. C. Kinkaid on Sunday had been briefer. Kinkaid acted like Linda's and my saving of the Corks might almost make up for some of my past stupidities. "They'll try again," he added.

At midmorning today, after a nervous, tasteless breakfast, I had gotten into the limo with Sean Cork's dour trainer, Finneran, beside me up front with the driver, and Sean, Kitty and Linda in back. I had seen Sean only a few minutes on Sunday and he had still been badly shaken. Today, however, he looked pink and nervous, working hard on being cheerful and unflappable.

He pointed to a few drizzly raindrops on the windshield. "Rain might get worse."

"Yes."

"Think we'll get to play?"

"I think we'll play."

"Damn. The humidity is going to take some of the tension out of my strings, and I had hell getting the man to make them tight enough yesterday in the first place."

"What did you have them strung at?"

"Eighty-five."

"With that boron composite you ordered, the ball will come off like a rocket."

"That's what I'm hoping."

"Just remember to keep your elbow in."

Finneran snapped, "Sean doesn't need any extra coaching to clutter his mind up right now."

"Right," I said. "Excuse me."

"Idiot," Sean snapped. "Aren't you smart enough to know we're talking shop to blow off tension?"

Finneran's back stiffened. "Sorry."

Sean looked back at me. "What are you strung at?"

I grinned at him. "My rackets or my gut?—Ordinarily I would be at seventy. Today, against Allen, I'm using a stiff throat and extra-firm head and stringing at fifty."

He looked surprised.

I explained, "I intend to pound the ball hard when I get a chance. But if he starts charging me all the time, trying to drive me off the court, he's going to see more dinky garbage than he's ever seen in his whole life."

Sean's little grin flickered. "What court are you on?"

"Six."

"You? An honorary member? A former champion?" He was irate. "They at least ought to have you on Court One!"

"Hey," I said. "Leave it alone. Maybe if I get waxed, nobody will report it."

He didn't say anything to that. We crossed the river and drove into the narrow streets that formed a baffling maze on the way to the tennis club. Despite the hour there was already serious traffic. We passed the Southfields station of the Underground and turned onto Wimbledon Park Road about a mile from the club. As we got closer, silence fell again over everyone in the car. Wimbledon is that special.

We drove nearer, crammed inside with our rackets and duffel bags, looking out through the light drizzle at the fans lined up for double-decker buses, buying box lunches, walking around in the bleak chill as if the sun were shining, lining up for tea or sandwiches or part of the Wimbledon tradition, those fantastic strawberries and that indelibly rich clotted cream.

It was still early—play doesn't start at Wimbledon until 2 P.M.—but the sea of people was amazing: people walking, people being disgorged by buses and taxis, people picnicking behind cars parked all over the broad, grassy fields, people standing ten-deep along the sidewalks. It was to be the last year for standing room at Centre Court. Only about 11,000 could get precious Centre Court stadium tickets, with another 3,000 or so allowed to fight for a ticket that let them into a standing-room-only area where spectators were so crammed in that they couldn't change position if their life depended on it. But as usual people had slept all night on the sidewalks outside the Doherty and Perry gates, hoping for a chance to enter.

As we got closer, memory was stirred by the fantastic crush around the gates: fans, scalpers, idle onlookers, trinket and souvenir sellers, and what I thought was a markedly higher than usual number of uniformed security people.

"The people!" Sean exclaimed. "How many, do you suppose?"

"Forty thousand," I said. I had read that number somewhere.

Our limo pulled up behind three others at the gate and we went through, entering the grounds. Inside we were in a lush green world of grass, shrubbery, roses, hydrangea. Ahead loomed the ivy-covered wall of the stadium.

In the lee of the great old dark stadium structure, people wearing rain-beaded cloth coats and cheap, sturdy Hungarian workshoes looked up with interest, thoughtfully licking cream mustaches, as wealthy patrons paraded into the dark interior of the stadium, headed for their boxes. Broad American accents mixed with the clipped imprecision of native English, and you heard German, French, Dutch, Japanese—everything. The world was here.

We couldn't see all of it. The misting rain shut off horizons. The world seemed wrapped in white tissue paper, no definite sky and no distant view, just the colors of asphalt and amazing deep green grass, and the obscure grays of old trees standing perfectly still off over there . . . and over there . . . almost out of sight, and across the narrow street the church property being filled with parked cars.

At the players' gate we hugged the ladies and got out. It was cold. But that wasn't why we shivered, presenting our tickets to the old man at the players' gate.

Inside, officials gave us the word: start of play would be delayed. Weathermen said high pressure was moving in and we would see an end to the drizzle and a clearing trend. Sean seemed cheered by the news. I had heard it other years, before day-long downpours.

We went to the dressing rooms. We were assigned the best one, the one reserved for the top players. A lot of the guys were there ahead of us. Sean visited with some of them briefly, then began to change into his working clothes. He got halfway dressed and then stopped, just sitting on the bench in front of his locker. Pale, his freckles splotchy on his face, he picked up a racket and kept spanging it against his palm. He looked very much alone.

I didn't bother him. God knows he had enough to think about. The attempt on his life would have felled a lesser guy. And getting ready for a Wimbledon match takes all your psychological controls anyway.

People prepare in their own way. Some yammer, others retreat. Some of the habits are odd. I've done some strange things myself. Once before a sweltering WCT match in Dallas I sent Coke down on top of a salt pill. That was in the days when salt pills were considered a good thing when you were sweating gallons. In my case, the Coke and salt didn't mix very well at all. Maybe I would have lost that day anyway. At least I've never done some of the weird stuff Martina did during her blobbo days as a teenager in a new country. She swears she's eaten Big Macs in the locker room.

I wondered how much Sean Cork was worrying about the terrorists right now, and how much about his tennis. You couldn't tell.

If he was involved in anything right now besides beating his brains out in quest of a championship, I certainly couldn't see it. He worked with an almost frightening intensity. When you were around him and not playing tennis, he wanted to talk tennis: history, tactics, weather, opponents, brackets, equipment. He had one thing on his mind as far as I could tell, just one. His game.

In this he was like all the rest of the men in the championship. Young or old, few of them have ever had anything significant in their lives beyond bashing the fuzzy ball. They started as kids, little kids, almost all of them. When little Johnny down the street was going to the circus, our budding Rod Laver clone was at the courts with dad or a professional coach, or both. When Tommy got a bicycle, little Rod got a membership at the spa and started pumping the Nautilus machines. Jeffy got a dollar from the tooth fairy. Little Rod got a fresh can of balls. When Billy went to scout camp, little Rod was sent to Arizona to hit balls at a tennis school until his knees and elbows throbbed and the blast-furnace sun made the inside of his skull feel like fried eggs. About the time friend Biff went on his first real date with a girl, little Rod entered his first big tournament, nearly burst his heart trying to handle the taller, stronger 18-year-old across the net, and rode home in the family car, stuffing the tears, while Dad yelled at him for being a quitter out there.

Later, for the players who had achieved this level of play, the wins started to come. But nobody was satisfied, certainly not Dad, and by now not Rod, either. Because by now he had swallowed the whole sour pill. He was gifted. He owed a debt to his gift. No man (even a fifteen-year-old) could allow himself to be less than he could be. So he was blowing off school, falling behind, and didn't much understand what the other kids were talking about when they discussed the latest star on MTV. So he sometimes already felt the kind of desolate loneliness that blows like a winter wind through the heart of a person who gives up personhood in chasing a singleminded dream. So what? *So what?*

My mother used to have a favorite saying. A question, really. She always asked it with an ironic tone. But it was her favorite put-down, and she asked it too often for it not to have a genuine basis in her thinking.

"If you're so smart," she might ask my father (or me) after we had pontificated on something, "if you're so smart, why aren't you rich?"

Ah, the money. That was the other element in the equation of most players' single-faceted personalities. They might say they played for the competition, the one-on-one, the fun. Who believes that? Do they believe that? How do you say "It's just a game, after all," and *mean* it, when you're playing for $100,000? How do you maintain a balanced view of life, with tennis just a part of it, when every forehand drive, every serve, every trip to the net, is a vital part of a pattern that means *millions?*

So they start warped and narrowed, they grow that way, and the potential rewards—that glorious, mirage-like wonder-city of mil-lionairedom—gets *just possibly* reachable. And then nothing else matters. Most of them get like the one- or two-dimensional creature you hear about when someone tries to explain extra-dimensional math. If that little math-man in his flat universe were confronted with a three-dimensional object like a balloon, he simply could not comprehend it. Your tennis star is different. He knows there are other dimensions outside tennis. He just says fuck it, I'll get back to all that stuff after I've gotten really, really rich. Maybe.

So going back to Wimbledon was more than a memory trip for me. It meant immersion in that hot, intense, narrow little world.

It felt funny. But hardly unfamiliar. I had lived in it for a long time before. I think I entered world-class tennis slightly less warped than a lot of them do. For that you can credit Vietnam and a wife who metaphorically screwed me by being anything but metaphorical with a string of lovers before she finally dumped me in her garbage can of quickly forgotten memories. Even so, you don't reach the highest levels without near-insane concentration, narrowing of awarenesses. When I saw some of the guys come in off the practice court with glazed eyes, or heard them sit around all evening, talking backhand slice or Becker's net game, on a day when some maniac had bombed an airliner, killing 317, I could feel like I was on the other side of the looking glass. But I had been over here before, as a partial participant. So it felt funny, but not alien. And Mad Hatters should not throw stones.

I wondered why I could not hang onto the realistic notion that I had no chance at all in this tournament. And why did that match against Borg—my last appearance here—continue to plague me? There had been fine times. Great times. The doubles finals the year I teamed with Arthur Ashe and we simply could do no wrong. The year it rained forever, but we formed a car caravan to Covent Gardens, and then those two sisters—as whacky as they were rich—organized a party with ten of their equally glamorous and crazy lady friends, and the party went on for three straight days and nights. Another time . . . another year . . . listening to Billie Jean talk about opportunities for women in tennis, hearing her fighting talk, and getting that chill down my back as I saw that nothing was going to stop her from getting something like parity for the players we would never again dare to call "the girls." And even the year I lost early, and looked up to realize it was the Fourth of July, and felt so homesick I had to hide in the toilets a while until I got my face back together.

All the years, all the memories. Tennis is far different today, but Wimbledon is still the shrine. And I couldn't stop thinking that maybe—*maybe*—somehow I could work a miracle and do really well here.

Settle down, Smith, I lectured myself. *You're here to do a job.* But I kept thinking . . . with some good bounces and a lot of luck . . . with my draw. . . .

Only the reality of the terrorist talk kept me from going off the deep end of wishful thinking. There was Sean Cork, almost killed by a car bomb. They would try again. I had to watch everything, although I felt sure Anti-Terrorist Group and a lot of other people would now be giving Sean extra attention, too.

Was there a larger terrorist threat? The big boys thought so. I had to stay alert for something—anything—that might provide a tipoff on that, too.

And there was Linda, a comfortable part of me now, my desire for her so keen and continuous that it was a fact of my existence. And, back home, Beth. . . .

It blended, all of it. The tournament was on and I was drawn as tight as a fiddle string. My hands shook slightly and the headache felt almost normal. I wondered if the tension would make me function better, or not function at all.

Be calm, Babe, I told myself.

Sure. Right.

Later, an official came in and said it was time to start play. Sean gathered up his stuff and came over to say a word before heading out. We shook hands.

"Luck," I said.

"Yes," he said, his thin smile sickly.

He left. I hurried along with my own dressing, listening to some of the talk at lockers around me.

"These brackets are horribly unfair! Don't they know the people come to see us?"

"You think you've got it bad? There's this old fairy out there at the gate this morning. He must be a hundred. I forgot my ticket. He wouldn't let me in! Me! I'm so pissed. . . ."

"Did you guys see McEnroe snub me? Who does he think he is?"

"I'll tell you who he is. He's the guy who's going to beat your butt tomorrow."

"That'll be the day!"

"Will you look at this blister? It's these shoes. Just because they pay me to wear them, do they have to make them so they don't fit my feet? It shouldn't be hard to fit my feet. I've got great feet."

"I hate Court One. I hate it. It's unfair to make me play on it. They don't like me. They just put me there to give Penfors an advantage."

"Well, he needs it. Did you see how he looked against Arias in Paris? He looked as bad as Axley did. Axley, Axley, Axley, that's all I hear. These sportswriters are such pukes, they don't know any-

thing. Axley played over there like he had the rag on. I don't know who he thinks he is."

"Why can't we have better towels? I hate these towels! They're like burlap on your skin! Is it too much to ask, to have decent towels?"

"They think they're so great just because this tournament is the oldest. Well, I'll tell you what I think. I wish we would all boycott it—put them in their place, for a change! See how they'd like that!"

"I suppose the grass will be slick as owlshit. I wish I didn't have Maxwell. I could have beaten him at Milan, but slipped and missed that easy volley in the fifth game. I never get the breaks."

A low, growling vibration made the floor and walls tremble. Some of the conversations lapsed. Guys looked at the ceiling. It was the sound of the crowd, rumbling through the concrete and steel, making the building come alive. I don't know if most of them started talking again in a minute. The penetration of crowd roar was my signal that it was time to stop thinking about Sean Cork, about Terry Carpoman, about possible terrorism. I had a match and I was determined—regardless of everything else—not to go down like a sheep for slaughter.

With the weather improving fast, officials notified me that my court was open, and we would start play in my match in approximately forty minutes. I tightened my knee brace, checked my rackets, and carried my stuff out to Court Six.

I found Rich Allen already there. Rangy, long-haired and arrogant, he tried to mess with my mind during the warm-ups, hitting some drives out of my reach and pretending it was an accident, oh dear, he just forgot sometimes to rein in his great power and he hoped I understood.

I understood, all right. When you know each other even slightly as players, there's no reason why you can't warm each other up before a match. Generally you know what kind of shots to hit the other person, the ones he can use to get loose and ready. Of course the adrenaline starts flowing and we all occasionally blast one impolitely. But Allen practically made a habit of it. The result was that I was not as warm and loose as I would have liked when the man in the chair gave us our two minute warning and then ordered us to play.

It did not start off very well. Allen opened serving, and had two aces in the first game, which he won at love. I double-faulted my opening service. *All right, Smith, goddammit. This is Wimbledon and he's young and you're old and you've got a lot on your mind, but you'd better get with it. Now.*

I held service. He breezed again, I struggled again but hung on, and the early pattern began to assert itself. The damp grass kept the ball low. You have to move faster than I can move these days on such a surface or you hit a lot of half-volleys from near the baseline. I hit a lot of half-volleys from near the baseline.

He kept me back, counterpunching. Every time I looked up, he had taken the net. I was on my heels and feeling generally pretty sad about life into the eighth game.

At that point he was up 4-3, we were still on service, and I was up on my serve, 30-15. He slipped and gave me a short ball and I came in to hit a forehand crosscourt, but it was weak. It bounced nice and high and he went up the line with it, pulling me wildly to my backhand side. As I stabbed at the ball, dinking it back short, I saw him coming up.

I was completely out of position and he had the whole court to my right. Just as his racket came back, I saw the murderous look in his eyes and knew what was coming. He gave it everything he had, and the old man's reflexes were not quite sharp enough. The ball exploded into my chest with a velocity that actually made me black out for a split-second.

I didn't go down. I even heard the gasp of the spectators. My vision blurred just a little. It really, really hurt.

"Sorry, buddy!" Allen gasped. "You okay?"

I managed to grin at him. "Fine."

We walked back to our positions. The onlookers gave us a scattered hand. I tested my breathing and found, despite the fire in my chest, that I was fine. I was also suddenly into the match, furious with him.

It is possible to kill a person with a sharp enough blow to the chest. Something about the impact interfering with the normal electrical impulses of the heart. Just as you can sometimes make a stopped heart start beating again with a sharp blow of the fist—that's part of CPR—you may stop the heart the same way.

I don't mean good old Rich Allen, darling of the Sarasota jet set and two-time cover boy of *People* magazine, meant to kill the old fart. He was just being his normal self. Which is to say mean. He isn't the only one out there who's like that, of course. I've seen guys stand at the net and just slam it at each other, ignoring possible winners in their lust to hurt the opponent. Well, you pay your money and you take your choice. But I don't like players like that, and Allen's assholery fired me up.

Instead of blasting back at him, however, I started doing what I knew might frustrate him the most. Nerf and surf. Moonballs. Dinks. Dropshots. Lobs. Undersliced spinners. Cut shots.

And, perhaps because I was so charged, it worked. I broke him in the next game. That made him mad and he started hitting more aggressively. Wonderful. Everything I could reach, I nerfed back. Since he wasn't getting any pace from me, he had to provide it all himself, and some of his overhit shots began to spray. Unforced errors mounted up on his side. I got good and warm and actually hit some winners, too, shocking him with the occasional return that had a lot of pace on it. He had tried to mess up my mind in the warm-ups. By the middle of the second set his brains were like scrambled eggs.

My knee hurt worse. All my natural instincts said to put on the pressure now, try to blow him away. I fought the tendency. When something is working, you stay with it. A couple of times, when I stroked up a moonball and he went angrily scurrying back for it, I had so much time that I noticed a few of the spectators laughing their heads off. That made Allen madder. It didn't make me feel any better, however; for all I could tell, they were laughing at my Bobby Riggs impersonation.

Don't worry about looking good, Smith. Swallow your pride and nerf his ass off.

Which is what I did.

Finally he began to get control of himself in the third set. He broke my service and went ahead, 2-0. I didn't feel like I had a lot left in the legs, but I changed tactics and started hitting out. Sure enough, the change of pace threw him offstride again. Then, when he got still madder and started blasting back fireballs, I loaded up the marshmallows again.

I won the thing 6-4, 6-3, 6-3, and took less than two hours doing it. Linda was among the onlookers. A lot of the folks were grinning and whistling, like you would for a particularly good clown act, but she stood applauding and looking down at me with eyes that were transparent with her feelings.

My knee was killing me, but I didn't limp walking off.

Back in the locker room I looked for Sean Cork to see how quickly he had disposed of Vardas. No sign of him. One of the attendants reported Sean still out on Centre Court. That didn't sound good.

I got an ice bag and started it on my throbbing knee. After a few minutes somebody entered. I looked up, expecting Sean, but saw Terry Carpoman instead. He walked directly to me. He had a funny surprised expression.

"I caught the last set," he told me. "You didn't look too bad out there."

"Luck," I said. "He seemed to get out of his rhythm."

"Well, obviously, or somebody like you couldn't have beat him. But you still didn't look bad. If you can play like that in the doubles, we might have a chance."

"I'll certainly do my best, Terry."

"After Saturday night's heroics, you really surprised me."

"I deeply and sincerely appreciate your kind words."

His voice sharpened. "Are you being sarcastic, or what?"

I raised my head from wrapping the icepack. He had been working on being supportive and nice, for him, but suddenly the crazy anger had twisted his face, made his eyes burn. I said, "No sarcasm intended. I'm honored to play with you in the doubles, and I'll do my best."

"I never know when you're harpooning me. Just because you were a champion once doesn't give you the right to jab somebody who's giving you a chance at another trophy. Jesus Christ! If I can carry you long enough, you'd pick up your fifth Wimbledon championship. Aren't you even the least bit appreciative?"

I took a deep breath and counted to ten a couple of times. "Terry," I said patiently, "we haven't made a bad team. Don't read things into what I say, okay? You hold up your end. I'll hold up mine. I was playing in this tournament when you were in diapers."

Bang! His fist slammed against a locker, making everybody in the room jump or turn sharply. "There you go again, goddamn you! Why don't you just get off my back? Why don't you and everybody else just get off my frigging *back?*"

I had been right all along, I thought. He was on something.

Did that mean he might be so far gone that he would abet terrorists?

Ridiculous.

Or was it?

I said carefully, "I'll stay off your back, Terry. And good luck in your match this afternoon."

His lips curled in a superior sneer. "With Zelthman? I'll blow him away. The first few singles matches aren't what I'm worried about. I don't have to carry a partner in the singles."

"Terry, your confidence in me is overwhelming."

He stared, turned, and stalked out.

Wondering why I had ever agreed to get hooked up with him, I lingered in the locker area a while, treating myself to a long shower and a rubdown. The knee had begun to get a little water under what was left of the kneecap and I knew tomorrow I would have to have one of the doctors slide a large-bore needle under there again and drain off the excess. The prospect made my teeth ache. I have had

what seems like ten thousand needles but I have never gotten used
to them.

Getting dressed, I listened to players around the room. A few
had finished earlier than I had. There hadn't been any upsets yet,
but most of the big names weren't to start until tomorrow. I eaves-
dropped on a kid from Sweden and his doubles partner from Germany. They were handsome kids, tall and sinewy, with tangled
blond hair that made them look almost like brothers. After listening
to them a while, it dawned on me that brothers was not what they
were. I wished I hadn't figured that out. I am not anxiously aware
of every hint of homosexuality like a lot of people are; it just isn't
much of an issue with me. But I am too old or narrow-minded or
something to achieve complacency on the topic. I just sort of wish
they didn't act that way because I think it's dumb. Especially around
world-class tennis, where there are so many eager young women that
sometimes you get dizzy, just thinking about all of them. Why
would—well; forget it.

By the time I was dressed and ready to leave the locker area,
Sean Cork *still* was not back from his match. That meant he was
in the fifth set with Vardas. I decided to go out and see.

Thin sunshine made triangles across Centre Court. I made my
way to Melville Oldham's box and was pleased to see that it was
just him and Dacri inside, four seats vacant.

He acted happy to see me. "Sit down, Brad! Wonderful match,
here. Your young friend Cork has his hands full."

Sean was still young enough to be overawed by assignment to
Centre Court. Vardas, the wily South American, had had a ton of
matches there, and looked cool and fluid as he returned Sean's
serves. Sean looked tight and scared.

"Cork won the first set, then lost the next two," Oldham filled
me in. "He won the fourth, but it was a bitter battle."

Dacri, beautiful in a lavender sweater outfit, nodded agreement. "It's tied five-five in this last set."

"Wonderful match," Oldham added. "Wonderful." He

reached for his large, red-capped Thermos in the little picnic basket at his feet. "Here, old boy. A touch for what ails you."

He unscrewed the cap, revealing two other smaller cups nested below. Uncapping the jug, he poured two fingers of what looked like coffee into the smallest cup and handed it over.

I tasted it. "Whew!"

"My own secret formula," he told me, watching the match. "You start with rum, vodka, Kahlua and gin."

"Isn't he grand?" Dacri asked me, crinkling her eyes.

Oldham leaned his shoulder against hers, smiled wearily, and continued watching the match. The little gesture said it all. Whatever she might be, Dacri had made this man very, very happy. He adored her. I filed that verification of what I had thought earlier.

Down below, Sean served an ace to hold serve. That put him up, 6-5. He glanced up toward the box as Vardas got ready, and I winked at him. He nodded, squared his shoulders, and prepared to return serve.

The man in chair spoke into his mike: *"Quiet, please. Thank you."*

Vardas served a slice wide to Sean's forehand. He went out and got it and, holding his elbow in nicely, stroked a return up the line.

"He's been like that in the last two sets," Oldham observed. "Very controlled, very precise. Holding back his power for maximum opportunity. Very unlike him, don't you know. He often plays with such reckless abandon, hits so many out, makes too many unforced errors."

Dacri added, "He started this way. Then he sort of seemed to forget himself, and attacked too hard. But then it was almost as if he remembered something, and went back to his game plan."

I grinned. Sean already had the mistaken impression I was some kind of guru. Now, having tried it my way and done well, and tried it his old way and fallen behind, he was going to think I was a miracleworker.

We watched.

Vardas had gone over to whip a backhand crosscourt, but Sean, gliding like a deer, had gotten to net. The return was perhaps an inch higher than it might have been and Sean put it away.

Dark-faced, Vardas served from the ad court, up the middle, and Sean stroked another one deep to his backhand. It was like an instant replay, different angle. Vardas got it back, but Sean went crosscourt, hitting chalk on the sideline for another winner.

With the crowd yelling between points, Vardas netted a volley to go down 0-40, and bravely came in behind his second serve on match point. Sean threaded the needle up the sideline with a passing shot, and it was over.

Over the crowd noise I told Oldham and Dacri I wanted to go belowdecks and congratulate Sean. With Oldham's homebrew medicine warming my belly, I got down well ahead of Sean, who had been stopped by Bud Collins for brief courtside remarks that would play on the late network report back home.

He was jubilant when he came in.

"I almost forgot for a while," he told me after a big, sweaty hug. "But then I used my noodle—did what you told me!"

"I saw the last of it," I told him. "You looked great."

"I heard you put Allen away, too. Bravo!"

"Luck."

He thought a moment, his Irish mug red and happy. "Listen! This calls for a bit of a celebration this evening. Suppose Kitty and I meet you at that little hotel of yours about eight o'clock and we'll have a quick bite somewhere."

"That sounds good," I told him.

"Grand!" He did a shuffling little jig, his tennis shoes squeaking on the tile. "It'll be good not to have poor Weiss shadowing us, what?"

"You aren't going to hire a substitute until Weiss is better?"

The frown came and vanished in the afterglow of his first-round win. "I think they blew their chance, rather than me. And I'm just sick of worrying about them. I bet they're halfway across the country by now, anyway. They had their chance and muffed it, thanks to you and Linda. I don't expect any more trouble."

I shrugged again. I figured Anti-Terrorist Group, and probably one of our own FBI terrorism experts, would be on our tail anyway now, just in case the would-be killers did try again.

Good thinking, right?

Wrong.

Twenty

A THIRTY-MINUTE rain delay and some long matches moved Terry Carpoman's match with Andre Zelthman very late into the afternoon. I left the Jarryd-Sampras match on Centre Court to go out to Court No. 3 to watch. As usual there was an amazing crowd of fans out in front of the stadium, watching the scoreboard that registers every Centre Court point on the stadium wall. They were excited, just watching the score change. I went by one of the corporate courtesy tents and met Barry Rathman from ESPN, and we reviewed my tentative schedule for commentating with him.

When I finally got to Court Three, I spotted beautiful Alicia behind her large blue Revo sunglasses at once, but didn't move to join her, preferring to watch alone.

No. 3 is the worst there is at Wimbledon in my opinion, especially after rain: it's soft, and if there have been any hard matches on it at all, you get divots and funny bounces. At his best Terry could have had trouble adjusting his power game to Three. Even during the warmups he looked far from from his best, sliding around, blasting everything impatiently, angry to be there. He looked erratic, driven, crazy. I felt I could read his mind: *It's unfair to put me on No. 3, and I have to blow Zelthman away to prove I'm someone to contend with in this tournament—show them I should have been put on Centre Court.*

The match began, Terry serving. He bombed in an ace down the middle on the first point and went to the ad side talking angrily to himself as if he intended to serve out the match that way. Zelthman, a tall, skinny player who had never lived up to his early promise, jangled sadly to the other receiving court and waited, swaying right and left, sorrowfully holding his racket at ready.

Terry double-faulted.

On the third point, he served even harder. Zelthman stroked it back. Terry banged a winner crosscourt. On the next point, however, he netted a volley and then double-faulted again. Fuming, talking to himself, clearly out of control, on the next point he knocked an easy overhead ten feet over the baseline.

Zelthman, handed a break, began to look a little more cheerful. He then played a nice steady service game to go up 2-0.

In the third game, up 30-15, Terry got what might have been a questionable call on the sideline and went after the man in the chair.

His voice carried all over the place: "That ball was an inch inside!"

The umpire leaned over and I strained to hear him: "The call was correct."

Terry's face went fiery red. "You could see it. You had a perfect angle! The ball was clearly good!"

"The ball was wide."

"God damn it, the fucking ball was good!"

The umpire's face tightened under the pressure. "Play."

Terry dropped his racket and put his hands on his hips. "Are you going to reverse the call?"

"The call was correct."

"That sonofabitch back there called it wrong! This is supposed to be a class tournament. Is that call any indication of what kind of idiots you've got calling the lines?"

"Mr. Carpoman. *Play.*"

Terry stood there, glaring. His face worked. Some whistles came from the crowd. He grabbed up his racket and went back and evidently heard something in the crowd. He turned and said something I couldn't hear, and raised his hand. His body blocked my view of the gesture, too. Whistles erupted. He kicked at the grass.

"Mr. Carpoman," the man in the chair said over his microphone, "consider this a warning."

Terry wheeled around, his face demonic, and charged across the court, finishing directly below the umpire's chair. "*What?* What did you say to me?"

"You are warned for unsportsmanlike conduct."

Terry slammed his racket onto the top cord of the net. "*What* are you talking about! What kind of cheap trick is *that?* If you want to do something worthwhile, shut those fuckers up back there! This is supposed to be tennis, not soccer, you asshole."

"Penalty, one point," the umpire said, making a note on his tablet. "Play."

"*What did you say?*" Terry screamed.

The umpire looked down at him with a stony calm. Clearly he did not like this, was uncomfortable with it. Just as clearly he was going to stay in control. "Play," he said into the microphone for all to hear. "The score is thirty-forty."

Terry started to slam the net again. He just managed to stop himself. Striding back to the service line he kicked out a loose clod of grass the size of an apple. More whistles rained down. He fumed, walked around with hands on hips, kicked the ground again.

"Mr. Carpoman," the umpire said warningly.

Terry signalled for balls.

"Quiet, please."

He served, coming in behind a good, deep ball. Zelthman hit a forehand up the line that spat chalk, a clean winner. Terry looked at the sky like a man who had just been given another low blow.

After that, the first set went fast. Terry came all to pieces, making one unforced error after another. You could see Zelthman's confidence soaring. He began to thread the needle down the lines on both sides.

Watching it, I still could not believe Terry wouldn't come back. He was ranked so far ahead of Zelthman on the ATP computer that they might as well have been playing on different planets.

He had played the Frenchman six times before, and Zelthman had never won a set.

In the second set, however, there was another nasty argument early. After getting a really wretched bounce on a short ball he should have put away for a winner, Terry was still steaming two points later when he hit a volley deep to Zelthman's backhand. The gangly Frenchman went back and made a good get, scooping up a lob. Terry backpedaled. The ball hit either right on the baseline—or just beyond it.

"Out!" the back judge yelped.

Zelthman looked surprised. Terry nodded satisfaction and started back toward his backcourt.

The umpire pulled his microphone over. "Play a let."

Terry stood up straight as if he had been shot. *"What?"*

"The ball appeared to be good. Play a let."

Terry charged again, hurling his racket to the grass. "You think the lob was good?"

"Play a let."

Terry wouldn't let go. "You think the ball was good?"

"The ball appeared to be good."

"Then reverse your linesman's call, you gutless fucker! Don't call for a let!"

The umpire stared down in silence.

Terry screeched, "Either have the guts to reverse the call or let it stand. Don't call for a goddamn let!"

"Mr. Carpoman, you are warned."

Terry picked up his racket. He slammed it against the post supporting the net. The racket shattered and folded up like an accordion. He kicked one piece across the court.

The umpire pulled his microphone over. "Game, Zelthman."

After that penalty game it was never a match. Terry never got himself back together. There were more endless arguments, more challenges, more bad manners.

Give Zelthman credit, too. A lesser player might have been so shaken out of his concentration that his game would have come unraveled. You could see him frowning, looking at the ground and trying to think of other things during Terry's outbursts. He succeeded in keeping it together.

So, unbelievably, Terry went down in straight sets, 6-3, 6-3, 6-1. After the last point he treated us to a tirade against one of the men calling the sidelines on his end; then he threw his racket against the players' benches, breaking it. Then he knocked the soft drinks off the table, pulled all the towels out of the box and hurled them around, kicked his equipment bag, and stormed off, cursing and spitting in the direction of the nearest whistling spectators.

More worried than ever, I decided to get out of there. Partway out of the area, however, I heard someone call my name and made the mistake of tuning to see who it was.

Alicia Carpoman, hands and wrists ablaze with diamonds, strode up to me and whipped off her Revos to fix me with bright, excited, worried eyes. "Can't you help him?" she demanded.

"It's a little late," I told her. I knew that was cruel, but I was so angry at him for his act out there.

She stamped her foot. "He's getting worse and worse! I hoped teaming up with an old-timer like you in the doubles would provide some stability. But you haven't helped at all!"

"Alicia," I said carefully, "I didn't realize my role was babysitter. I don't do that well."

"Well, you bastard," she snapped. "Don't you see how he's wasting all his glorious talent? Don't you even *care?*"

"What am I supposed to do? Prescribe a tranquilizer?"

"I certainly don't need your sarcasm, and another drug is the *last* thing he ought to have, don't you agree?"

So there it was, the confirmation of my theory. Even though I really didn't need it.

I said, "Would you like to explain that?"

"Well," she pouted, "surely he told you about the wonderful results he's had from the stuff."

"*What* stuff?"

Her eyes went wide. "Shit. Maybe I've said the wrong thing."

I grabbed her by the arms. "Alicia. What stuff?"

"The injections!" she flung back. "The Dianabol! —What are you looking at me like that for? It's the most harmless there is . . . isn't it? Everybody uses it . . . don't they?"

I don't know how long I stood there staring into her remarkable, glorious, greedy, stupid eyes. Maybe it was quite a while. I hadn't suspected steroids. But I saw at once that they fit my suspicions just fine. They were as bad as anything else.

Steroids promote muscle development and bulk. But they also provide tremendous strength and recuperative power. An athlete on steroids may hyperventilate and look on the brink of a heart attack during a workout, but a few minutes later he may be fresher than his undrugged teammates, ready to go another punishing workout at once.

I now remembered how Terry had driven me, wanting more workouts after I was already dragging—he appearing fresh as a daisy. I also remembered how he had filled out in the months since I had seen him, how his muscles had smoothed and strengthened, and how much stronger he was.

All good stuff from steroids. Unfortunately there are the side effects: erratic behavior, heart problems, liver damage, impotence, maybe, in the longer term, death.

Too much to risk, shooting yourself with a healing agent intended for horses, betting a short-term athletic gain will not bring with it insanity or impotence or life as a cripple—or premature death? A lot of kids say the risk is acceptable.

Just go down to your local high school and watch one of the teams work out. Remember when you were in high school, and the Hulk Hogan of the squad weighed maybe 195? Check out your high school's offensive and defensive starters across the line. Do you really believe that their *average*—something like 255 from tackle to tackle—can be attributed to better Post Toasties and quarter-pounders with cheese?

Terry Carpoman had squirted the stuff into himself because he thought it would make him No. 1. He *needed* to be No. 1, be-

Jack M. Bickham

cause he had bought the story that winning is the only thing. And he *needed* to be No. 1 to keep gorgeous Miss Alicia in the style to which she intended to be accustomed all the rest of her decorative, parasitical life.

Steroids. Strong enough to make you crazy enough to do almost anything.

Crazy enough to deal with presumed supplier "friends" who might actually be terrorists?

I made a phone call and gave my anonymous contact the information straight out on the telephone on the assumption that my suspicions now couldn't wait for anything. I felt sure we had found a link.

Maybe that's a partial explanation for my failure to anticipate what happened that night with Sean and Kitty Cork. But it's no excuse. There can be no excuse.

Linda and I were waiting out front, protected from the cool drizzle by the little front porch roof of our hotel, when the Corks pulled up that evening.

"There's a place not far from here that has wonderful Indian food," Sean told us as he shifted gears. "Not very grand, but you would like it unless you detest that sort of thing." He was wearing jeans and a blue jacket, and looked more like a collegian than a Wimbledon headliner.

Kitty, looking very young and beautiful in a utilitarian pantsuit and pale olive jacket, nodded agreement. "It isn't too spicy, either. So no need to worry about tummy upset before tomorrow's matches."

From long habit, I turned partly sideways and looked through the rear window at the car lights a half-block behind us. Enough daylight remained for me to see that it was a dark gray British Ford sedan. "Sounds fine to me, guys. Linda?"

"I'm all for it," she agreed.

I said to Sean, "Are you still sure it's a good idea to be out like this?"

His jaw clamped stubbornly, showing he understood. "You sound like the police. Those cowardly terrorists won't try again. They had their chance and they flubbed it. They're probably a hundred miles from here by now."

"Do you agree, Kitty?" I pressed.

She looked worried but game. "Sean says we can't spend our lives hiding. If we do that, those people have already won."

I gave up. "It's fine with me."

Sean drove happily, a boy out on a lark. "Good matches today. One win down, several to go, eh?"

We were headed west and a bit north, driving narrow streets lined closely by old residences and taller, narrow buildings that might have been hotels like ours. Sean asked, "How's the knee this evening?"

It had been swollen enough that I had to change trousers, going to a pair with fuller legs. "Not bad," I said.

"You have Soratini tomorrow?"

"No. Not until Thursday. Terry Carpoman and I are in the men's doubles tomorrow."

"He *lost* today!" Sean's voice rose in disbelief.

"I know," I said.

"The man is a wonder. How did he lose to Zelthman? My word, he shouldn't have lost to Zelthman!"

"Well, it was just one of those things."

We turned a few more corners as Sean negotiated a maze of streets he obviously knew better than I did. He rhapsodized enough about my supposed coaching help that I felt embarrassed about it. Kitty told Linda about a late-afternoon tea tomorrow, and invited her to attend it with her. Then she told us about some of the famous people she had seen in the stands today. When told Johnny Carson had been there, Sean got as excited as a high school kid.

"Imagine that! And I heard that Andrew and Fergie will attend on Saturday! Doesn't it just amaze you, when you stop to think that *celebrities* are taking time out just to come watch you play?"

"Sean," Linda said with quiet amusement, "a lot of people consider you and Kitty as celebrities."

It seemed to shock him for a moment. Then he gestured in the air. "Oh, yes, of course. But we're just *tennis people.*"

God. It was not an act. He was as genuinely humble and down-to-earth as he sounded. I really liked this kid.

Kitty said something about the royal family that I didn't catch, looking through the rear window for the fourth or fifth time.

"—but Becker is on his game," Sean was saying. "That means trouble for anyone in his bracket."

I leaned forward. "How much farther to the restaurant, Sean?"

"Oh, about two kilometers, I would say. Of course it isn't a straight line from here, on these streets. Why? Hungry?"

Peering past him out ahead, I pointed. "You see that chemist's shop up in the next block on the left side? Could you pull to the curb there long enough for me to duck inside for something?"

"Sure. Of course. Painkiller? The knee?"

"Oh, just some aspirin. Won't take a moment."

Linda frowned at me, seeing something was going on. She didn't say anything. Sean wheeled through the intersection and pulled to the side in front of the little shop, its bright lights spilling onto the empty sidewalk.

I opened my door and nudged Linda. "You wanted to look for that lipstick. Might as well rush in with me."

"Yes," she said. "Right."

I got out and gave her my hand. "Back in a jiffy, guys."

We hurried across the wet pavement to the door of the shop and ducked inside. It was a long, narrow little place with the walls stacked to the ceiling with shelving, more counters down the middle creating aisles just wide enough to slide through sideways. The pharmacist was in the back, behind a high counter, and started toward us as we closed the door behind us.

"What's going on?" Linda asked softly.

"Car following us. Gray Ford."

"Shit. Where is it now?"

"Pulled to the curb near the corner behind us."

"What do we do? Call COS?"

"No time. You hold the owner's attention long enough for me to go out the back door of this place and circle through the alley. Give me a couple minutes and then go back out to the car and stand beside it and make up something to tell Sean and Kitty through the window. That will give the gray car something to watch."

"What the hell do *you* expect to accomplish?"

"Look. Either we nab the fuckers right now, or we wait for them to hit us on their timetable."

"Well, *you* can't stop them."

"That's what you think." The pharmacist was hustling near. "Just *do* it, Linda, goddammit."

I didn't give her time to answer. The old man reached over the counter and asked if he could assist us. I slid away, going toward the center racks of goodies. Linda stammered something about aspirin, and did he carry Kodak film. While he was answering, I sidled on to the back, patent-type medicines and rows of toothbrushes.

There was a narrow wood door, closed, beside the high counter the operator had vacated. I glanced forward and saw Linda engaging him in a discussion over boxes of film. I opened the wood door and slipped into the back.

A narrow hall led past a restroom and storage area. Farther back, overhead bulbs lighted more storage, double wood doors that had to lead outside. I pulled the opened padlock off the hasp, slid the door back a couple of feet, and stepped into the alley.

A security light gleamed mistily through the drizzle. Black cobblestones glistened wetly. Pulling my nice Clarence Tune .38 out of my belt in back, I ran to my left down the alley, headed for the side street.

At the corner I turned left again, jogging in the wet, staying close to the dim buildings. Up ahead twenty yards or so were the lights of the intersection. Unless it had moved on, the gray car would be just around the corner, nosed in to the curb beside a darkened, closed news kiosk.

I reached the corner and peered around. There it was.

The idea of pouncing on IRA assassins did not exactly thrill me. But it was this or blunder on into the night, knowing they would attack us—Linda and me and the Corks, or the Corks alone—on *their* terms and timing. I figured my having a weapon was not something they would expect, and if I moved fast I had surprise on my side.

There was no time to think more about it. I rounded the brick building corner and ran flat-out toward the little gray sedan, approaching it from an angle behind. I had a glimpse ahead: Linda standing at curbside, talking to Sean and Kitty through the opened driver's-side window. I was counting on that little tableau riveting my IRA guys' attention.

It worked. I reached the side of the car and jerked the door open. There was only the driver in the front, and he was so shocked he almost tumbled out onto the pavement. I caught him by cramming the muzzle of the .38 into the side of his face.

"Don't move an *inch*," I yelled. Youthful, chalk-colored, he obeyed. There was a sharp movement in the back seat and the second person there started forward.

"Freeze or I blow his head off!" Sounded corny even as I yelled it in my fright. But noise helps sometimes, and anything I could do to get control was bound to be wonderful.

The movement in the back seat stopped cold. I grabbed the driver by the collar with my left hand and hauled back with all my strength, unceremoniously dragging him out of the seat and dumping him onto the wet pavement. "Out of the back!" I bellowed, pointing the gun at the window.

The back door opened.

Clarence Tune, looking shocked and frightened, poked his head out.

*　　*　　*

It took me a few seconds to react. Linda was running up the
sidewalk in our direction, and Sean Cork had opened his door to
get out of his car.

Clarence wobbled to his feet on the sidewalk, hands shakily
raised. "It's *me*, sir!"

"Clarence," I groaned, "shit!"

He bent to help his younger colleague to his feet. The younger
guy had gotten pretty thoroughly drenched when I dragged him out
into the gutter. He staggered slightly, leaning against the car and
brushing futilely at his clothes.

Linda got there. "Brad—?"

"Go on back," I told her. "It's okay.—They're on our side."

"Oh, shit," she murmured, looking at them in dismay.

"Yeah. I said that. Keep the Corks up there."

"How?"

"Do it!"

She paused, then turned and hurried back the way she had
come.

I turned to Clarence and the guy I had roughed up. "I thought
you were IRA," I said feebly.

"Yes, of course, a natural mistake," the young man said in a
chill, clipped accent. "Well. With Mr. Cork's personal bodyguard
ill, it was necessary for us to tighten our security measures for him.
I have been assigned to his case from the outset, but circumstances
earlier allowed me to be more . . . circumspect."

"I feel like an idiot. —Clarence? Are you along to watch closer
after me, too?"

Tune shook his head. "Actually, sir, I joined Jeffrey outside
your hotel. My only function was to inform him of your, ah, double
identity, as it were. So I was merely riding along for a few blocks
while I did that, and until we had ascertained your destination. At
that point we separate again."

I looked back at the other man. "I'm sorry I spoiled the play-
house."

He sniffed. "Yes. Quite. That was an interesting weapon you had."

"Me?"

"The revolver you put back into hiding behind your back, under your coat, the moment you realized our identity. —Tell me, Mr. Smith: do you have any authorization whatsoever for that weapon?"

I noted Clarence's ashen expression. "We'll talk later about that," I ad libbed. "I'd better get back to my people."

"I have not released you," Jeffrey snapped at my back as I started away.

"Later," I called back, and kept going.

Sometimes, when you've made a complete ass of yourself, the only thing left to do is act confident.

When I neared the Corks' car, I saw that Linda was arguing quietly with Sean.

"Just get in and we'll explain later," she pleaded.

Sean swung around at my approach, and his eyes had a wild look in them. "What was *that* all about?"

"Let's get going, Sean," I suggested, putting a hand on his shoulder, "and I'll tell you all about it."

He violently shrugged me off. "You had a *gun* back there."

No way to lie out of what he had seen. "Right," I said. "Can we go?"

He stared at me, then at Linda, then down the street, where the agent named Jeffrey and Clarence Tune had gotten back into their car. "Who are those people?"

"Anti-Terrorist Group. For your protection."

"Then why—"

"Sean, let's go . . . okay?"

He climbed into the car. Kitty stared over her seat at us like someone who had just seen a ghost. Sean started the engine and jerked the gears, pulling away.

"Who are you?" he demanded. "Why do you have a gun? Why

did you pull it on *them,* if they're protecting us?" He turned a corner, missing his shift again, and then had another thought. "The whole thing about wanting aspirin was a damned lie, wasn't it! — You two are in it together. You lied to us."

"Okay, Sean," I said wearily. "I saw that car following us. I thought it was terrorists. I doubled through the shop to try to grab them before they could strike at us. I was wrong. I goofed."

"Why would *you* take that on yourself anyway? Where did you get the gun?" He missed another gear change, grinding a pound of metal in the transmission beneath our feet. "Who *are* you? What organization do *you* belong to?"

I looked at Linda, seeing her grim worry, and didn't answer fast enough.

Sean said tightly, "I thought it was just great good luck when you saved us from that bombing. I thought you were what you *said* you were. But it was all a damned lie, a trick. You're no friend of mine, no good guy. You're only around me because you want to use me for *your* ends in this filthy, never-ending war."

"That's not true," I said.

"You're American. You're CIA."

I didn't say anything. Bitterly I saw how balls-up I had turned the whole thing.

"Are you CIA?" Sean insisted.

"Do I look like a CIA officer?" I asked.

He drove a block in silence. We came to a traffic signal and had to wait for it. He slammed his palm onto the steering wheel. "My God! You're CIA! —I've been making friends with someone as bad as the IRA!"

Wonderful, I thought in despair. "I just tried to help you. I can't help it that I'm stupid."

"The CIA!" he repeated incredulously. "Did you hear that, Kitty? We've been buddying about with the same kind of people who overthrew the government in Chile—sponsored the mass killings in Africa—supported people like—"

"Sean," Kitty interrupted, her voice tight with pain. "These people are our *friends!*"

Sean looked back at us in the rearview mirror. "And I thought you were truly a good friend."

"I was," I told him. "And I am. Sean! I haven't done a damned thing to hurt you, or any of your people. What I just did, I did because I thought it might save your life."

He shook his head violently. "I've read about the CIA. I know some of the terrible things your people have done. You're as bad as the IRA—possibly worse, because you have the sanction of an entire government behind you."

Linda put her hand on my knee, trying to warn me to restrain myself. I tried. "Maybe we could talk about this later."

He didn't reply. We drove for several minutes in silence. I alternated between self-castigation, worry about what he was going to do or say next, and concern about what fallout there would be from my showing a gun to a young, eager-beaver operative like our friend Jeffrey. Linda moved her hand, taking mine and squeezing it between her nervous, icy fingers.

"Look," I said after more time had passed. "I can explain the whole thing to you."

Sean shook his head again, although not quite so violently. "Maybe what we need to do is just go back and drop you off at your hotel."

"Oh, Sean," Kitty pleaded, "we came to have dinner. Look: there's the street just ahead where the restaurant is. Can't we at least go on and have dinner . . . and talk it over?"

"I don't know what there is to talk about."

I said, "Let's see, anyway."

He turned the corner, downshifting expertly this time to show he had calmed down somewhat. "We can eat," he said bitterly. "We have to eat anyway."

I thought it was a hopeful sign. Linda squeezed my hand tighter, showing she thought so too.

Once inside the small, smoky restaurant, however, it began to be apparent that Sean Cork was not a man who easily shunted aside what he thought were good principles. He sat across the table from Linda and me, his chair close to his wife's, looking at me with hurt, suspicious eyes that reminded me of a small child who has just learned his best friend can be hateful.

Linda made some conversation. Kitty desperately tried to respond in kind. I put in a few words. Sean sat there, glowering, his mind obviously going a mile a minute on other matters. The waiter came and listed a lot of strange-sounding Indian dishes. I tried to make a joke of asking Sean to interpret, but he ignored me and ordered for himself and Kitty. Feeling impatient and miserable, I said Linda and I would have the same.

"I can't believe it," he said finally, looking directly into my eyes. "I thought you were a good man. You've always been one of my sports idols. Now—to find out *this.*"

It stung and I hit back: "Don't lecture me, Sean."

"Brad," Linda warned softly.

"You're just here to carry out your criminal bosses' orders," he said. "You're a lackey peddling blood, just like the radicals in Ulster."

"Brad," Linda repeated more sternly.

It didn't do any good. "Listen, Sean," I told him. "When you've taken shrapnel in one war and then seen the one person you care about more than anything in the world *murdered,* you come back and lecture me about morality."

He stiffened. "Brad," Linda said for the third time.

Kitty faltered, "Sean is an idealist. Violence of any kind—"

"I know," I said impatiently. "But sometimes when you turn the other cheek, you get your head blown off."

Sean's eyes looked like pools of mercury. "I thought you were a hero," he said quietly. "And it was all just more trickery—another faction wanting to use me for their own ends."

"Sean, that's bullshit."

We had ordered wine and it was on the table. He raised his

glass to me, his face twisted in a grimace of savage sarcasm. "A toast, then. To bullshit."

I half-expected him to jump up and charge out of there, hauling Kitty along with him. He surprised me again, lapsing into silence. After a minute or two, Kitty tried with a faint, desperate smile to talk about something else. Linda and I played along. The food came, and all of us miserably picked at it.

Later he jumped in again, the bitterness still heavy in his tone although he seemed much quieter, resigned: "Why were you assigned?"

"Hints of widespread terrorist activity," I told him bluntly.

"And your role?"

"To try to help root it out—prevent it."

"And me?"

"You're one of the obvious potential targets."

He put down his fork. "I'm going to tell everyone you're CIA," he said venomously. "I'm going to blow your cover sky high."

Linda asked, "Is that going to help anyone?"

"Never mind," I said. My patience had finally snapped. I tossed my napkin down. "Let's get out of here."

He stood. "I'll pay and then we'll take you back."

"I'll pay."

"I don't want your goddamned money, Brad. It has blood on it."

I walked out, Linda behind me. He and Kitty followed. I was hot. He headed for the car, parked half a block up, and I followed.

"Brad," Linda whispered, "ease off."

"Right," I said. "Eat shit and ease off. Right."

"He's a *boy!*"

"I'm tired, Linda, of being lectured by boys, girls, men and women alike. I'm tired of holier-than-thou critics. I'm tired of stupid idealists who don't know reality from first base. Just shut up about easing off."

We got to the car. Sean unlocked the doors on the curb side and started around to enter streetside.

Just as I held the open door for Kitty up front, I saw the small van hurtling up the street toward us. No lights. And sticking out a back window on our side, an unmistakable cylindrical object.

"Down!" I grunted, and pushed Kitty sideways, hard, making her sprawl painfully on the sidewalk.

Sean was in the street, looking up, his face slack as he turned from us to the van, now roaring down and right on top of us.

"Linda, *down!"* I said, and went over the hood of the car after Sean.

He actually, reflexively, tried to duck out of my way. I managed to catch him with one clawing arm as I tumbled over the front of the car and into the street. I hit hard on my shoulder and side of my head, but there was no time to think about the pain. All I could hear was engine roar, and I couldn't think about anything but getting us out of sight. I grabbed Sean's shirt-front and half-hauled him against the car, then got a knee in his chest and brutally shoved him half underneath the front end of the thing.

The van was on top of us. Chattering little explosions burst out over our heads. Wheels screamed and the engine howled with a change of gears and the bark of automatic gunfire pounded into my skull and shut my hearing off. Pieces flew off the top of the car and the windows of the darkened store behind us blew up in crystal shards.

Just as quickly the van was past. I rolled over, seeing I hadn't been hit—seeing Sean's saucer-sized eyes staring out at me from under the car. I staggered to my feet and looked after the van.

It had slowed for the corner, rocking almost to a halt. I grabbed out the .38, leveled it, and started firing. I knew it wasn't going to do any good. I think I was thinking, *Maybe this will surprise you bastards, to have fire returned.*

That was what I thought, perhaps—empty retaliation—and what I expected—nothing. What I got was stunningly different.

Maybe a bullet hit the gas tank. I think it was not that. They must have had plastic explosives and detonators inside, and by freak luck I hit those.

After my third or fourth shot, anyway, as the van started to career around the corner and out of sight, there was an instantaneous flowering of shocking orange—flame—and in the same moment a tremendous explosion. The top of the van went sky high, and pieces of things, maybe seats, maybe people, flew with it. The walls vanished. The concussion reached us and knocked me over on my back again.

"My God!" Sean cried, scrambling to his feet. His face, contorted by shock and horror, was crimson in the light reflected from towering flames. "My God! My God!"

I staggered around the car. Linda and Kitty, unhurt, had gotten unsteadily to their feet. Kitty leaned weakly against the car, which had some bullet holes in the top and the back windows gone, but appeared otherwise intact.

I heard the wail of a police unit somewhere. Shocked patrons were beginning to flood out of the restaurant up the street. Lights flashed on in windows above some of the dark shops farther away.

"Get in the car," I told the women, and hurried around to Sean, still transfixed in the street.

"Get us out of here!" I ordered.

He stared with sightless eyes. "What? What?"

"Do you want to spend the rest of the night talking to police?" I demanded, shaking him. "I don't! Get in the car, dammit! Get us out of here! Through the alley."

"I—don't know," he choked. "Why—should we run?"

"Because I said so, you idiot." I shoved him in behind the wheel. "Me. The bloodsucking monster who just saved your life. Now move! *Drive!* Or so help me, I'll—"

With a baffled, dazed, gargling sound, he waved me silent, shoved his key into the ignition, and turned the starter. The engine fired. He sawed the wheel hard, making a U-turn, and we rocketed into the alley, on our way out of there.

Twenty-one

SEAN CORK DROPPED us off in front of our hotel. I helped Linda out and then bent to look in through the open driver's side window. "What now, Sean?"

Bright, shocked eyes looked up at me out of a colorless face. "The police. They have to be told."

"At least let me call my man from the Home Office," I argued. "Let his outfit handle things."

Sean hesitated. Kitty said with soft urgency, "Listen to him, honey."

He surprised me: "All right—if you'll have them contact me *now.*"

"I will," I promised.

He looked at his watch. "I'll wait two hours."

"Okay. I'll tell Clarence that."

He scowled. "I am not going to protect your what-do-you-call-it . . . cover."

"Okay, Sean. Fine."

He moved the gear shifter, clashing gears, and pulled off.

Linda touched my arm. "I have to contact COS at once."

"Right."

"Brad, I think you'd better stay in your room after you contact Tune. Wait for instructions."

"I will."

With a squeeze of her long fingers on my forearm, she turned and walked up the street away from me, striding hard, in a hurry.

279

I went into the hotel and directly to my room. It was dark, and smelled musty from my cigarettes. Turning on the overhead light, I went through my billfold and dug out the piece of paper on which Clarence Tune had written an emergency number. There seemed no percentage in going outside somewhere in search of a more secure, anonymous telephone. After tonight's work, Sean Cork was probably going to blow me sky high anyway. I dialed the number from my room phone.

"Yes?" a quiet male voice answered.

"This is Brad Smith," I said. "I urgently need to talk with Clarence Tune immediately. It's an emergency. I'm at my hotel."

There was a pause. Calls so in the open were probably damned unusual for them. Finally the voice said, "I have your message, sir."

"Emergency," I repeated.

"Yes. I understand."

I hung up and waited. Looked at my pack of cigarettes—the ones I wasn't going to smoke until after the tournament. Pulled one out and lit it, taking the smoke deep. My hands shook.

It seemed like a week since I had been oncourt at Wimbledon, and since I had learned what was making Terry Carpoman so crazy. I looked at my watch and realized incredulously that I would be out there again, oncourt with him in the doubles, in slightly more than twelve hours. Everything normal in the world was going right on, smoothly, placidly, without knowledge of homicidal crazies and anti-terrorist operators falling over their own feet. I felt isolated, like a man living inside an invisible bubble, unable to discern through the iridescent layers what was reality out there, and what fantasy: swimming through a world where dimensions crossed and nothing could be counted on to be as it might seem.

I had had the feeling before. When you are operating on a clandestine basis, everything in your environment is subtly hostile. The man on the corner who looks like a retired schoolteacher may be quite someone else, and a threat to you. The wrong-number call on your telephone may not be a wrong number at all. Did I leave the magazine open on the bed that way when I left the room this morning? Was that a careless glance from that passerby, or something more? Have I—knowing that absolutely *nothing* is normal here—acted normally enough, or have I made some thoughtless, revealing error?

In the aftermath of the attack on us, my body was still coming down. I felt wobbly and almost like I had a fever. I took out my .38, dropped out the empty shellcases, and reloaded from the little plastic envelope Clarence had thoughtfully provided with the weapon. I put the spent ones in the envelope with the half-dozen fresh ones that remained. This was not done as easily as it should have because my shakes were worse.

I reviewed.

I could not see where I might have handled things much differently, but that did not hide the fact that I had undoubtedly screwed up. My cowboy act against Clarence and the agent named Jeffrey, in the car that had tailed us, was probably inexcusable. Somehow I should have been smart enough to consider that a tail represented security, and somehow I should have also been smart enough to figure out a way to check that possibility short of galloping around alleys and waving my illegal gun in somebody's face.

That had blown me with the Corks, and I did not think I had heard the end of it about the .38. Especially not after what had happened later.

I had no doubt that Sean was going to talk to the police about me, and probably to the press at the tennis club tomorrow. He was one of the true believers, one of the innocents who had all the answers, and all of them good and fine and whole and pure and true. The CIA had been in some nasty and probably stupid operations at one time or another, so it was unadulterated Evil. I could be assumed to work for the CIA, so I was evil too. Therefore I deserved no consideration.

It galled me. Maybe I had forestalled one try on his life, but there would be others, so in the long run I had accomplished nothing. As to possible broader terrorist activity during Wimbledon, I had gotten nowhere that I could see. On balance, by blowing my own cover and alerting the baddies that Sean—and others—might have security, I might have made matters potentially worse.

I looked at my watch. *Come on, Clarence!*

I was, if the truth be known, personally mortified too. Not that that seemed very important. But it was. I knew what a lot of the real pros thought of using an amateur like me. They had as much respect for me in their line of work as a tournament pro might feel facing a skinny sixth-grader off the city courts, armed with an old wooden racket with two broken strings. I simply was not viewed as in their league, and tonight's escapades proved they were probably right. I don't pretend to be as good as they are. But damn, I hate giving them proof that I'm a complete moron.

The telephone rang, startling me. I snatched it up. "Hello?"

"Mr. Smith, sir?" Clarence Tune's voice, out of breath.

"It's me, Clarence. Listen, there's been a real problem."

"I'm in Westminster, sir. Something else afoot. They caught me with the beeper. Is this of great urgency? Can you possibly tell me on the telephone?"

I just went ahead and blurted out what had happened after we had last seen each other.

"Oh, dear!" he gasped. "But where was Jeffrey in all this?"

"I don't know."

"Oh, dear, oh, dear! —Please stay in your room, sir. I will be back in touch as soon as possible."

"Sean Cork has to be contacted immediately, or he'll be at his nearest police station. You understand that?"

"Yes, sir. Goodbye." The connection broke.

I hung up my instrument and reached for another cigarette and the phone jangled again, making me jump.

"Hello?"

"Brad?—Linda."

"Yes."

"Info passed. Steps being taken. Sit tight. Do nothing. —Got it?"

"Got it."

"Brad?"

"Yes?"

"Might take hours. Try to get some sleep if you can."

"Okay."

I smoked again, then limped down the hall to the refrigerator beside the exit sign and got a pan of ice for my knee. Went back to the room, locked in, changed to a robe, and made an ice pack. The knee looked fairly nasty, with a lot of water under the remains of the kneecap, pain with any lateral flexion, a faint purple coloration on the inside, denoting some leaking blood. I lay back on the bed and let the ice work, and figured that anybody who thought I could sleep any tonight had to be crazy.

I didn't factor in a day full of excitement and the exhaustion that follows a championship-caliber match. The next thing I knew, my eyelids were heavy.

And the next thing I knew after that, somebody was banging on my door.

I sat up. The ice pack slid off my knee in a slushy, melted mess. According to my watch it was 4:30 A.M.

I swung my legs off the bed, getting a nice stab of pain in the knee in the process, and dug the .38 out of my robe pocket. "Who is it?"

"It's Clarence Tune, sir," the voice answered anxiously.

I opened up. Tune, scant hair straight on end, face the color of dirty snow, hurried in. "Please close and bolt the door, sir," he ordered crisply.

I obeyed. He went to the windows and checked to make sure the draperies were tight. Then he turned to eye me with tired sympathy. "It's a bit of a balls-up, sir, as you said."

I got a cigarette.

He said, "Perhaps I could have one too?"

Surprised, I handed him the pack. He let me light one for him, and inhaled with the luxuriant intensity of a reformed smoker.

"I am sorry to say," he said through the smoke, "my poor associate Jeffrey is dead."

"God. I wondered where he was when they hit us. What happened?"

"Found in his car less than a block from your restaurant, actually. Shot once in the brain, very close range, probably a nine-millimeter, silenced, in all likelihood, since no one reported hearing a shot."

"So they spotted him and took him out while we were eating our curry." I felt a little sick.

"The two terrorists in the van were blown rather to pieces," Clarence went on, brightening. "Identification will be most difficult. Lab says there were both plastic explosives and either dynamite or gunpowder in the back of the vehicle." He actually gave a tiny, explosive chuckle. "You shot well, Two-Gun."

"Under the circumstances, Clarence, if you call me that again, I'll stuff that Marlboro up your nose. What about Sean Cork?"

He frowned. "Yes. Quite. Well. Our people reached him prior to tracing of the rental vehicle by the police, from a witness at the scene. We are with him and Mrs. Cork at this time."

"What is he saying?" I asked. "What is he going to do?"

"An attempt, of course, is being made to keep the entire incident mysterious, as far as official reports and any publicity are concerned. My preliminary information is that he is . . . rather upset about your role in all this."

"So he's going to scream his head off about my connection," I said disgustedly.

Tune looked sadder.

I got up and walked around the room. "I might have been stupid earlier, Clarence, when I jumped you and your partner. But I did what I had to do when I saw that van coming."

"Yes, sir. Quite. The evidence at this time would surely indicate you are accurate in that assessment. But our people will have to interview you, quietly of course, within the next few hours about that."

I didn't say anything.

The little man fidgeted uncomfortably. "We have no way of knowing what your side will conclude, of course."

"Of course."

He sighed. "About the gun, sir."

I looked at him.

"I must ask you to return it to me at once," he told me. "I devoutly hope, sir, that in addition you can find it in yourself not to reveal where you got it, or where it has gone."

I hadn't thought of this. Meeting his rheumy old eyes, I saw that he was right. I didn't want to let the .38 go. But there was going to be hell to pay. A lot of people were going to be asking questions. If I didn't cooperate, somebody was sure to conduct a search anyway, whether I liked it or not. Maybe there was some obscure way it could be traced back to him.

I took the revolver out of my robe pocket and handed it over. Coloring, he accepted it and buried it in an inside coat pocket. He hesitated, then, looking embarrassed. "The ammunition and spent cartridges, sir?"

I got them and gave them to him. He continued to look uneasy.

I told him, "I got the gun from a contact I have in Soho. I won't reveal his name because I was collecting on an old favor, and he didn't want to give it to me. Last night I left the hotel again and walked a long ways and threw the gun and ammo in a sewer. I could never find the place again."

He considered it. "Flimsy."

"It's my story and I'm sticking to it."

He breathed deeply. "Thank you."

"Now what?" I asked as he got to his feet.

He went to the door, turned and looked back at me like a bird dog after you've just missed your shot. "I'll be in touch. We have a lot to sort out, here."

I let him out. He patted me on the arm the way you would console an opponent who has just had the worst day of his life out there. After watching him slouch along to the stairs at the far end of the hall, I locked up again and wondered how long it was going to be until I heard from some of my people.

It was another hour.

"Where did you get the gun?"

"From a source in Soho."

"How?"

"It's a long story. He owed me one. I browbeat him into it."

"Where is it now?"

"I took a walk—threw it down a sewer."

J. C. Kinkaid sprang out of his chair in my room and went to the window, jamming his hands in his pockets as he looked down at the sunny, peaceful street below. He had arrived angry, and my answers had not calmed him down any. His face worked as he stared outside, thinking.

Finally he turned. "I don't suppose you could lead us to the sewer?"

"No. Sorry."

"You're a lying bastard, Smith."

I didn't say anything.

"You disobeyed direct orders. You went against all the rules. If MI5 can't keep Cork shut up, you've not only ended your own effectiveness, but probably given the entire Agency a black eye."

I didn't say anything to that, either.

He gave a loud, exasperated sigh. "You're to lay off. For the moment, while we reevaluate, you're a tennis player and journalist. Nothing more. Play your matches—" Sarcasm dripped, making it sound like he was telling me to crochet—"and don't do *anything* else. Have you got that?"

"I've got it," I said.

"COS is querying Langley. He is not a pleasant person at best, and right now he's about as happy as a hungry grizzly bear. He is so pissed—" Kinkaid stopped, unable to come up with an adequate expression. He spread his arms in a gesture of futility. "I think some heads are going to roll. The *only* way you could possibly help at this juncture is by doing nothing and waiting for orders. Do you think you can do that?"

"What about Terry Carpoman?"

"We're still checking. He looks clean, as far as terrorists are concerned. Of course you probably blew our whole operation with that panic phone call in the clear."

"What about Linda?" I asked.

He studied my expression, giving away nothing in his. "She's being debriefed. COS is blaming her for part of this."

"She didn't—"

"She was assigned to you. She let it happen."

"None of it was her fault, J.C.! I'll take my lumps, but—"

"Just stay out of it!" he flared. "Just do what you're told. *For once* do just as you're told, and nothing else. Have you got it? Just. Play. Tennis. Right? Right?"

"Christ. —Yes. Right."

"You'll be contacted," he promised, and walked out.

Like many of their promises, this one didn't come true very fast.

On Tuesday the weather was marginal, but play was on. I went out alone, early, and got my knee drained. Later I was getting ready when Terry Carpoman came into the dressing room, sullen, unspeaking and bitter. I made a formulary effort to have a conversation.

"Fuck off, old-timer," he snarled.

We went out and got our heads torn off in the doubles, 6-1, 6-2.

Afterward, coming out of the shower, I almost bumped into Sean Cork. He was not scheduled, and had come to see me.

He sat on the bench beside my locker while I toweled and started to dress. Hands locked over his knee, he looked grim and miserable.

"I've told the intelligence people everything I know," he told me.

I nodded and didn't otherwise reply.

"As for the rest of it," he went on dully, "—I mean the London police, the journalists, all of that—I am clamming up."

"Clamming up?" I repeated, surprised.

He looked at me with eyes filled with resentment. "What you do is your own affair. You have to live with your own conscience. I am not taking a side. You did, after all, save our lives . . . Kitty and mine. That has to count for something. So you'll not get any bad pub from me. I've decided to hold my peace. I'll not get involved in it."

"Thank you," I said.

"Don't thank me, you bloody imposter," he snapped, and walked away.

I felt bad about that, but relieved too. Just like being through with Terry Carpoman, blood-sucking beautiful Alicia, and his steroid crazies. I waited to see what next from Kinkaid or Linda.

And waited . . . and waited.

Twenty-two
Elsewhere

London

TUESDAY EVENING. THE Soviet embassy.

"It is very difficult," young Major Kreptik said.

Mikhail Gravitch studied his aide's expression, and was reassured to see stoic realism there, with no trace of self-pity or reluctance. "Yes, Major," Gravitch said. "I have some idea of how difficult it must be. Yuli Szulc is an extraordinary man. Your difficulty in observing his movements without detection only shows us again just how difficult he has been for the West all these years, when he operated as Sylvester."

Kreptik, wearing his army uniform for this secret consultation with his KGB superior in the most secure area of the embassy, allowed himself a dour nod. He was a tall man, blond, his handsome face pocked by the ravages of a childhood illness. He was thirty-three years old, a veteran of Afghanistan, and the best Gravitch had. "We know more than we might have hoped," he said.

Gravitch looked over the typed report. "He is in Belfast?"

"That is correct, sir. His schedule is as the report outlines. His regular visits to the employment offices, the pubs, and the park are as you see it. He has made a great number of casual friends who now appear to accept him as one of their own. Away from these contacts, he eats alone and is solitary."

"The Belfast-London shuttle has been under constant surveillance?"

"As you ordered, sir."

Gravitch closed the report and placed thick hands on top of it. "Now as to his interest in Wimbledon."

Kreptik nodded. "He has been observed closely studying the early results in the newspapers. In a visit to a bookstall, he purchased a copy of a souvenir book on the history of this tournament. As the report says, we also procured a copy. Included are area street maps and charts showing the location of all courts, as well as seating areas inside the stadium."

Gravitch took a deep breath. "I am assigning two more men to you. I would assign more, but there are *not* any more."

Kreptik's eyes widened slightly, betraying his surprise.

"I know, I know," Gravitch said impatiently. "Our manpower is stretched to the breaking point. However, this confidential investigation must continue to be given top priority. And remember, Major: *no one* outside of those assigned to the investigation is to have any hint whatsoever that such work is in progress."

"Yes, sir."

"*No one*, Major. You understand?"

"Yes, sir."

After the meeting, Kreptik departed via the back way, using the exit shared by the electronic data intercept group. Every paper and computer file relating to him here said he worked in that office, rather than for Gravitch.

So far, the worm Lemlek appeared to be entirely fooled.

Gravitch knew Lemlek had better continue to be deceived. The swine could raise an unholy row about assignment of so many of their limited KGB pool to what amounted to spying on one of their own. Lemlek would also howl that following Szulc, alias Sylvester, properly fell under his auspices of internal security.

The risks had to be taken. Although Sylvester's conduct had appeared to be exemplary since Gravitch had ordered surveillance begun, Gravitch was not satisfied that it would remain that way. The American Brad Smith had won one singles match at Wimbledon. He played again the day after tomorrow—on Thursday—and, if he won then, again on Saturday or Sunday.

Gravitch was no great sports fan, but he had studied the newspapers enough to realize that Smith might not win again. He had already lost in the men's doubles, and was in no other brackets. So Thursday could mean a defeat, and the end of him in this year's play. If he won Thursday, then his weekend match would almost certainly spell his ouster: for then he was likely to meet the great John McEnroe.

Which meant, Gravitch thought, that a clock was ticking for Sylvester. If he intended to make a move against Smith, it had to be soon; otherwise the American might no longer be in any predictable place at any known time.

That was why the KGB Resident had just committed the rest of his available manpower. If Sylvester was to move, he would move very, very soon. And Gravitch had to know the moment he started to go out of line.

Reading

Jack Blake and Jana Murnan arrived first at the house, driving up at dusk under their cover as the married couple who had rented the place. They carried some cartons and potted plants in from their battered old Volkswagen microbus, just as any couple might in the early stages of moving in. Perhaps a few neighbors in the poor neighborhood noticed them, but no one took serious note; transients were common enough in this depressed section.

About ten o'clock the same night, Squirrel Henry limped up the street, rapped on the door, and joined them inside. Within the next thirty minutes, Mack and Taylor arrived by bus, and Hennigan walked in, using the sooty alley. Francis Moriarty was next, a little after eleven. By that time the shades had all been drawn, and sentry duty assigned at the doors, with Henry pacing the darkened second floor, peering vigilantly from first one window, then another.

At midnight Terrence Dean came. All doors were then locked, and Taylor, the swarthy steelworker, was ordered to join Henry on the upper floor as a second lookout.

The others sat on the floor of the dusty living room amid the boxes and dying potted plants: Dean, their leader, small and slight, the lamplight glinting off his school-teacherish wire-rimmed glasses; Moriarty, the thickset, dark-haired subgroup chieftain; Hennigan, thin, bloodless, with his fringe of pale red hair and the perpetual faint odor of fish; the silent, beetle-browed Mack; blond-bearded young Blake, and his supposed wife, Jana, who sometimes traveled in other circles under the name of Rebecca Mavson.

Dean stared at them in sullen anger. "Whoever the idiots was that tried to kill Sean Cork, they made this a lot harder for us. Does anybody have any idea who they were?"

The terrorists looked around at one another. Nobody spoke.

"Bastards failed, and in the process got every agency in London on highest alert," Dean said, gritting his teeth. "No matter. Saturday is the day. Three days from now, boys and girl. You understand? You're all ready?"

No one spoke.

"All right, then," Dean said. "We'll be brief as can be, here." His thin little hands fluttered. "The truck is prepared and ready?"

All eyes turned to Blake. He nodded. "Ready and waiting."

"It will be moved to the nearer location Friday?"

"Yes."

"And from there to the church property parking?"

"Yes. Understood," Blake said.

"You will drive," Dean told him, soft voice underlaid by steel. His eyes swiveled around the room to the pale-faced Hennigan. "You in the other side, and to set the timer on the valves."

"Aye," Hennigan croaked.

"You have rehearsed?"

"Four times more, Terrence. And I got the big spanner to break off the nozzle in case of some last-second mess-up."

Dean nodded. "Good. The exact time will come by radio."

"Aye."

"I'll be on the site, in charge of creating the diversion. That will give you time to get the gas masks on and do your work in the confusion." Dean turned to the hulking Moriarty. "You will be inside, with the trigger."

Moriarty grunted understanding.

"The explosion will be very powerful," Dean told him intently. "You will be on the opposite end, but even so there could be flying debris—pandemonium. You understand how to position yourself near the exit, then allow yourself to be carried out through the exit with the crowd when it stampedes."

Moriarty gave a mocking half-salute. "And drop the camera underfoot, where it gets smashed and can never be traced to anybody."

Dean's teeth clicked with a sound like an animal trap. "Right." He turned to Mack. "I'll talk again with you and Taylor and Squirrel. It all depends on your making a clean job of it with the girl."

"Won't be no problem," Mack said, scowling under the shelf of his bushy eyebrows. "We already got the key to the back door, and we got the sedative. We go in after midnight, with the car runnin'—"

"There's no need to repeat it all," Dean said impatiently. "I know you know it. Right now we need Henry and Taylor upstairs, on watch, so we can't discuss your plan as a group anyhow. But like I said: we'll get together later. There's time."

"After we nab her," Mack insisted dully, "we go up through Cambridge."

"Right. Right. Just like it's laid out."

"Then we meet—"

"Right."

Mack frowned, worried. "But what happens to the girl after it's all over?"

Dean's lip curled, and his eyes so changed and chilled that it was as if a fierce blue light rayed out of them. "That's not your worry, sir. The girl will be taken care of. Your team just has to get her as far as the rendezvous, and you don't have to think about beyond that point."

"Yessir," Mack said hurriedly. "Right!"

Dean continued to fix his henchman with that bright, baleful stare. He held the gaze so long that several in the room stirred uneasily. There was not a person here who had not seen and caused and experienced bloodshed. But Dean was capable of frightening any of them.

The terrorist leader finally broke off and swiveled his eyes again, this time to the pretty, dark-haired young woman, Jana Murnan. "Now as to you, Jana, m'luv," he said almost good-naturedly.

"Yes," Jana chirped. Her body canted slightly toward Dean; her voice sounded huskier than normal, and her eyes warmed. "I'm ready to move in when ordered."

"Good, good. You'll be notified at your standing place, where you're to be constantly from tomorrow afternoon on. Understood?"

"Yes, Terrence."

"After Mack and his team have nabbed the girl, a telephone call will be made. In about five hours' time. We'll then watch and observe the telephone tap to make sure he don't go wild, call the police or nothing like that. He won't, he'll be too scairt about the girl. Once we're sure about that, we contact you. Then you move in."

Jana nodded. "I understand."

Dean leaned forward intensely. "Jana, luv, you've got to load the stuff. You've got to place the wire and set the receiver. You might not have a lotta time."

"I've done it a thousand times in practice, Terrence. I can do it in my sleep. I can do it inside ten minutes anywhere, anytime."

"It'll be taken in and then you'll have to arm it and make your departure."

"I understand."

Terrence Dean stared at her. The sexual tension between them was thick in the room, a stark animal presence. Jana's eyes danced with life and fire and something akin to amusement. Dean's eyes held that underlying chill, the seriousness of feeling love and staring into the skull-face of death.

Finally he broke the spell by slapping his knee. "We may not meet again, all together. Certainly not before the operation . . . and maybe never.—It's a nasty business we're in, here." He paused as if finished, then raised his hands, fluttering, almost like a priest in the parish church at home at the time of the *Dominus vobiscum.* His voice choked. "We owe this to our families . . . friends . . . the history of our country. We have got to do it. We have got to strike back, make them pay. —Boys and girl, we have never planned to do a finer thing."

He paused, swallowing with difficulty. The room was so silent that all could hear the faint creaking of boards in the ceiling as one of their sentries above paced from window to window, always watching.

"Are there any final questions at this time, then?" Dean asked at last.

There were a few—minor details. All were dealt with efficiently, carefully.

Finally there were no more.

"We're adjourned," Dean said then, standing. "Tell the lads upstairs, make sure the coast is clear for us to be leaving. —Remember: lay low, do your work, be ready. The clock is ticking, boys and girl. Unless there's a rain delay, it happens Saturday. We got a lot yet to do in the three days left to us."

Twenty-three

WEDNESDAY DAWNED COOLER, with drizzle. I expected to see Linda, who had not been near her room, and to hear from J. C. Kinkaid and Clarence Tune. Instead I was startled to get an early call saying Terry Carpoman was downstairs.

I went down. Alicia was nowhere to be seen. Terry paced like a caged creature, a facial tic leaping under his eye.

"I just wanted you to know," he growled. "We're cutting out." He paused, seemingly fighting to say more. Then: "Sorry about the way things turned out."

"Terry, I am too," I told him.

"I'm heading back stateside. Seeing a doctor."

I put a hand on his shoulder. "That's the best news I've heard out of you in a long, long time."

He shook me off and glared into some private space. "There are new ones. The one I've been taking has these side-effects. The doctor I've heard about in Mexico has some different, newer ones. A few days of intensive treatment, and then I can do them myself."

"God, Terry!"

He looked at me, surprised. "What?"

"Don't do any more of the damned things. Please!"

"But of course I'll do more," he shot back, the anger flickering in his eyes. "Look at my performance here! I need more stamina. More strength. I've got to *double* my practice time . . . handle my emotions better. I can do that. There's nothing wrong with steroids. I've just been on an old-fashioned one too long. A new one—"

"Terry, you're going to kill yourself!"

"Look! I didn't come by here for a stupid morality lecture! You don't understand the pressure I'm under. My expenses are running ahead of my income. This loss here screws me out of a wonderful endorsement contract I had working. My agent says I've *got* to start winning, or I'm finished!"

"Terry, I know a doctor. Let me give you his name. He can set you up at a place where you can get some rest . . . unwind . . . have a clearer view of things in a few weeks."

"Bullshit! I've got to get with the program and start *winning* again! I can't afford some fancy shrink, and I don't need one anyway. I'm fine. Just fine. I'll just economize in the meantime, but I've got to get back on track in these tournaments. I've been losing to people that shouldn't be on the same court with me. Alicia and I are going to stop off in Houston—there's a hell of a buy down there on a Spanish-style house on twenty acres—and then we'll take my jet on down to Mexico City. Within two weeks I'll be a new man, once the dosage gets regulated."

"Terry—" I began in dismay.

He clapped me on the back. "Good luck here, old-timer! Watch for me at Flushing Meadows!" And he was out the door before I could think of anything useful to say.

It further depressed me. By noon, when Linda still hadn't shown up or called, I began to feel like a tanker on a reef.

I went out to the tennis club alone. Steffi and Martina won their matches easily, but Zina had to go three hard sets, and stave off four match points, before finally defeating a Bulgarian girl named Stovanich.

The papers Tuesday had made a big deal of the van explosion, but Wednesday saw only the follow-up articles on inside pages, quoting Scotland Yard as saying they had no new information to release. True to his word, Sean Cork hadn't uttered a peep in public. From all appearances, it was to become another in the endless string of random violent acts that defied explanation. London's newspapers, like most of ours back home, no longer had many real journalists—

people who would look behind the obvious and dig for the truth. Even the editors appeared to have gone brain dead or given up in quiet despair. So once the sensational photos had been run, and the scare headlines written, the guardians of the democratic process seemed content to sit back and await the latest handouts.

Handouts were not likely to be forthcoming. I was cut off from all my sources of information, but I could imagine what had happened. The Home Office and every other clandestine organization involved had issued a spate of misleading statements, then stonewalled it. Everybody was looking at his hole card. You could be sure that new security agents had been assigned to Sean Cork and his wife, and maybe even to me. But I had screwed up—been an embarrassment—and suddenly was just another outsider, not to be told anything.

I did two interviews and wrote them up, and worried what was going to happen next. If I had been taken off Sean Cork, that was fine; others might handle it better next time. If my maverick actions had sent London COS and the boys at Langley back to the drawing board, that was okay too. I hadn't done anything I probably would not do over again.

Clarence Tune and Linda, however, worried me more.

I really had expected the sad-eyed little guy to show up again long before this. It had dawned on me slowly that assignment to me had probably been in the nature of scut work, and my screwups—especially having a gun—would reflect badly on him, get him in worse favor with the powers that be. I didn't feel good about that.

As to Linda, it was more personal. Much.

I missed her a lot. More than I would have guessed. It hadn't been that long, but since her assignment to me she had hung around on a fairly continuous basis. Her cover as my tournament lady had been successful, accepted unquestioningly by most of the other players and wives. A couple of the guys had made mild, jealous remarks about how an old guy could get so lucky. Kind of flattering, and I had just smiled.

But now she was nowhere in evidence and I realized she had

helped keep me on an even keel. Not only was she my contact—
my bridge to the boss-man—but she helped keep me focused on
the job at hand, and out of too sickly a preoccupation with the tennis.

She had, I realized now, missing her, bewitched me . . . a little.
Being bewitched had not felt bad. It had kept me from brooding
too much about Beth and her bitter opposition to my life choices,
and her surfer-boy legal colleague. Whether Linda approved of me
had simply not been an issue; we were in the same line of work.

But it had become more than that. I simply enjoyed the day-
lights out of her. She looked the part of a player's special friend.
She wore the right kind of clothes: pretty dresses with bare legs,
sweaters thrown over bare shoulders against the chill, her hair loose
and natural. Or flattering slacks and bulky wool sweaters on the
colder days, with a pretty little gold rainshawl. She had been there
a lot, even watching practices with a real interest. Sometimes when
I did something well, I glanced her way and saw her expression of
approval. Other times, after a bad move, I also registered her reaction. Some of these oncourt things were very subtle; the average devoted fan would probably have missed them. She noticed.

Offcourt, our accepted role-playing had required us to be an
item, and under all the circumstances I had enjoyed that, too. When
one of the London scandal sheets ran a photo of us coming out of
somewhere together, it had given me a faint but definite twinge of
anachronistic male pleasure. SMITH STILL A CHAMP WITH THE LA-
DIES, it said. That had been enough to get many of London's other
so-called journalists going, so that in the interview room I had had
all the routine, predictable tennis questions, and then some others
that would have irked me no end if they hadn't been sort of flattering: *"Is it true you're planning wedding bells along with Breakfast
at Wimbledon?"* and *"Has the lady an engagement ring?"* and *"How
does it feel, making love to a girl young enough to be your daughter?"*
(Lot of class, those guys.)

Now, however, she had just vanished. I kept looking around
for her and not seeing her. Her absence focused all my other feelings

of sudden isolation. It also made me wonder—damn, damn, damn!—hadn't she actually had some feeling about me, too, beyond the assignment parameters? Even if she had been pulled, couldn't she at least call?

Late in the afternoon I pulled myself out of disgusted lethargy enough to get the knee drained again—not much fluid this time—and then work out for about forty minutes with a young Scot home for the summer from his college in the United States, where he was the team's No. 1. He had a big serve and moved me around, got the adrenaline going a bit, the heart action stimulated. All my shots dropped in and I had no idea why. *We might have lost the doubles but I'm still in this thing . . . I can do it, maybe, with enough luck. . . .*

Then, when I got back to the showers, I found a message saying Mr. Kinkaid was waiting for me outside.

"Well, we'll go over here to a place I know and have a spot of tea."

"Fine," I agreed.

He had a car. Driving through the heavy southwest London traffic, he looked tired and strung out.

"What's the story?" I prompted.

"Let's get to the tea shop," he suggested.

"Now," I said.

He set his jaw. "COS is pissed."

"Well," I said lamely, "I imagine."

He maneuvered a busy intersection and went along in the traffic. "You should never have gotten that gun, Brad."

"Maybe," I conceded. "But one guy had already tried to take me out and—"

"It was against every fucking rule in the book!"

I didn't say anything.

"There's a certain amount of reluctance to use somebody like you anyway," he added. "Back home, I mean. You've done some fine work for us. But you have a reputation as a vigilante-type anyway: the way you freelanced your own solution in Belgrade that time, the way you went off to St. Maarten on your own after you were told to stay out of that one."

"I didn't ask for this assignment," I pointed out. "As pitiful as it may have been, my effort here has been right down the line, except for the gun."

"You weren't current. Your request for a weapon was reviewed and denied on that basis. Then you went out and got one on your own, against orders. As a result, MI5 is having an intensive inside investigation, Washington has had a strong protest from the British government at the highest possible levels, your effectiveness is zilch, and every one of us who backed you and trusted you has egg on his face. The FBI's counter-terrorism group over here is screaming that you—and us—should never have been involved in the first place. You've given the whole agency a serious setback."

I thought about it. We rode along without conversation. He reached the cafe he had mentioned, and parked in its narrow back lot, silencing the engine.

"So what's the bottom line?" I asked.

He turned to face me, and I could see both the anger and the frustration. "You're relieved. As of now."

I had almost expected it. But it still made me feel sick at my stomach. "Meaning?"

"Meaning just what I'm telling you. You're off the case. You're relieved. You have no further status and will make no further contact." His chest heaved. "I am instructed to tell you that you will be paid in full on your contract, as agreed at the beginning. Your return travel voucher will be honored. You will receive additional standard per diem through the end of this week."

I turned to look out through the dirty, sun-brilliant windshield. A squirrel had wandered over from the little park across the street, and was rummaging around among the trash cans against the pink brick back of the building. I was aware of my pulse and the way the squirrel picked through the debris and how the feeling reminded me of a time in high school, when a linebacker gave me a cheap shot and my lungs would not draw air.

"What, uh, about Linda?" I asked after a while.

"I don't have that information," he told me tonelessly. "Somebody is going to be assigned to stay around you until you leave the country. There is some thinking that you might have made yourself a terrorist target, if anybody on the other side had made you before you blew up the van."

I struggled to sort things out of the disappointment. "I'll probably, uh, stick around through the weekend. It's likely I'll lose in the singles tomorrow, but I've got some commitments for TV commentary that might last another couple of days after that. I'll . . . uh . . . I don't know. I've got to think."

He popped the car door on his side. "Let's have some tea or something. There's a paper I've got that you have to sign: acknowledgement of the termination of the contract, et cetera."

I didn't budge. "I think I can sign that right here, J.C."

His face twisted. "Well, let's have the tea anyway."

"I think I don't want any tea. Let's have the paper. I'll sign it right here, right now."

"Come on, Brad."

"Just let's sign the goddamned paper, J.C., okay?"

With another disgusted sigh he pulled it out. I read it and signed it and handed it back. He folded it, replaced it in the original envelope, and put it in his inside coat pocket.

"Suppose I could hitch a ride to my hotel?" I asked him.

He looked at me. Clearly there were other things he wanted to say. A minute or two passed. Then he put the key back in the ignition and started the car again.

"Sure," he said.

He backed out.

"Shit," he said, and we pulled away.

Back at the hotel I paced my floor and then took a short walk around the neighborhood and came back, expecting to have had telephone calls from *someone*, but didn't. I went back upstairs, smoked, and opened the door that led to Linda's adjoining room.

The door on her side was closed, locked. Foolishly I knocked and of course got no response.

Out came the lap computer and I tried to brush up one of the article outlines I had been working on. My mind felt scattered and useless, I couldn't concentrate, and I got so distracted and angry with myself that when I closed my working file, I mistakenly quit-abandoned it rather than quit-saved it, which meant I had trashed the whole thing.

I was smoking another cigarette when the phone rang.

"Yes?"

"Hi." It was Linda's voice, recognized instantly. "I'm down in the lobby. Can you come down and meet me in the coffee shop?"

"Would you rather come up here, Linda?"

"No." That was firm. "Will you come down?"

"Sure," I told her.

Going down the stairs, I was aware of a stirring excitement that she was here, and I got to see her again. But it mixed with an almost sick anticipation of what she might be ready to tell me. I had to remember I was not only in the doghouse now, but in real disgrace.

Still, when I walked into the little coffee shop and saw her— ivory linen dress that bared her throat and arms, and long legs crossed beside the table—I felt a jolt inside that surprised me. My God, this lady could really move me. But I still dreaded what she might have to say.

I walked to her table. At this hour, nobody else was around.

"Brad," she said, her voice and expression strained.

"Missed you today," I said, sitting across from her.

She ignored that, and we ordered drinks from the waiter who had appeared. She traced an invisible pattern on the tabletop tiles until he had gone away again. She was keeping busy not looking me in the face.

She said, "I heard about your cancellation. I'm sorry."

"Yeah. Thanks. Me too."

She met my eyes. Her caring shone in them. "You saved Sean Cork's life. You should be proud of that. You couldn't have done it, probably, if you hadn't found yourself a gun. Their reaction is just more of their assholery."

"Right."

She resumed avoiding my gaze . . . made her voice brisk. "Here's the deal. Since I already have the cover established, I stick around until you head home. I hear that's probably this weekend?"

"Probably. What do you mean, 'stick around,' Linda?"

Her face was so tight with control that she almost looked like a store mannequin. "I keep the room. I stay close, in case you actually have become a target for others in the terrorist organization. If you want to have dinner or have me go with you to the matches or anything like that the next couple of days, that's in the job description."

"What," I asked bitterly, *"isn't* in the job description?"

Her eyes flashed upward to mine. "Goddamnit, Brad, this is hard enough."

"You've got to do this," I told her, "but you've got orders not to get *too* close to the pariah, and for God's sake don't tell him anything. Right?"

She stiffened, angry now. "I'm going for some instructions right now. But I will be back later, or tomorrow. What's happened is the pits. We'll still have some time together, as part of my assignment. We can iron out the details later, if we have to."

The waiter came back with our drinks and left again.

I said, "If you get back tonight, we might have dinner later."

"I'm not sure I'll be back in time for that," she told me.

"Well, some conversation in our rooms, then."

"Look," she said. "We might as well be clear about that. I've already been told to make sure that door between our rooms stays closed."

"Is that the way you want it?" I asked.

"What I want or don't want isn't at issue, Brad."

"Look. I've been fired and now you tell me you've been given the onerous assignment of making sure I don't get myself killed— or do any further meddling into things that are none of my business—before I skip the country. That's all well and good. I'm just clumsily trying to explore the boundaries, here.—Weren't we having some fun, Linda? Wasn't it getting to be a little more than assignment? Does that have to go down the tubes?"

She shook her head. "I don't know." Then she looked over my shoulder, toward the entrance behind me. "We'll have to talk later."

"Why?"

"Look."

I turned and looked. A doleful Clarence Tune had just entered, and was headed our way.

"Damn!" I said.

Linda stood. "Later."

"When?"

"I don't know." She started to turn away.

I reached out and caught her wrist. "Wait a minute."

As I spoke, a violent shock, like heavy-voltage electricity, flowed through our touch. It jolted me even more violently than the other time it had happened.

She looked down at my hand around her wrist, then brought her eyes up to mine. Her eyes were different. She had felt it too.

"Later," she repeated.

Mutely I let her go. She turned away from me and strode briskly across the shop, meeting Tune halfway.

"Hello again!" I heard her say cheerily, and then she went on out.

Tune came over. He looked paler and shakier than I had ever seen him. "Hello, sir. Sorry to interrupt with the lady. If I might have a word, sir? It's very important, actually."

"Sit down, Clarence."

He sat in the chair Linda had vacated. His shoulders slumped. He looked like he had not had any sleep lately. His smell of defeat curled around us like the air in a mortuary.

He said, "I *am* sorry about interrupting, sir."

"What's on your mind, Clarence?"

"Well." He fidgeted with his old-fashioned self-winding wristwatch. "I am given to understand that you have been, ah, relieved of your operational responsibilities."

"You guys work fast. I found out only a couple of hours ago myself."

"Yes. Well, actually, there was an official communication of some sort."

"I see. I guess nobody wanted your people thinking I might still be running amok with official sanctions of any kind."

He actually colored. "I am sorry it turned out this way, Two-Gun."

"Clarence, for the last time—"

"Sorry! Sorry!" He grimaced. "A feeble attempt at humor. At times such as this—"

"Sure. But tell me: if your people know I've been fired, what are you doing here?"

"Well, sir, under the circumstances—which is the real reason I am here to see you at this time—it was decided that I should remain on station, as it were, with you until your departure."

"Your people also figure I might have been so obvious that somebody could now be after me?"

"It's . . . more complex than that, actually."

I saw for the first time that he was operating under some new pressure that made him fidget and squirm. The poor little guy was practically writhing in embarrassment.

"Clarence," I said, "they didn't figure out about the gun, did they?"

He heaved a sigh. "They have no proof. Of course I know nothing of what you're talking about."

"Yes. Of course."

"I believe, however, unfortunately, the commander has drawn his own conclusions. I have been informed that I am to complete my assignment *in re* your stay in England, and after that time my retirement papers will be processed immediately."

I stared at him while it sank in. He looked back at me directly and tried to smile, but his lip trembled. He was having a very hard time of it.

"Clarence," I said, "I am so sorry."

"Not to worry, sir. The retirement will be . . . honorable."

"But you weren't ready for it."

He looked off into some private world. "I was hoping to complete this five-year period. The retirement pay goes up considerably at that time. And of course there is the matter of what is obvious to people on the inside . . . the disgrace."

"Isn't there some kind of appeal procedure?"

"Not in my case, I suspect." He shrugged. "My service time is extensive as it is. They count military service, you see, and . . . special work done long ago. So I am far over time in grade, so to speak. The younger men press for advancement. People like me stand in their way. Relics. Dinosaurs. It's assumed we don't understand modern techniques, the latest methods. I. . . ." He stopped and looked back at me. "I am a holder of the Military Medal. Twice . . . long ago . . . I received commendations handed to me by the Queen herself." A smile quirked at his liver-colored lips. "But a few years ago there was a most difficult assignment. I volunteered. Three of us did the job. The other two were killed. I was in a coma for six weeks, and took a long time recuperating. Reports were written while I was unconscious. Someone had to be blamed. It was not my fault, but someone had to be assigned responsibility. I'm sure you are familiar with how these things work, Mr. Smith. It's like aviation accidents: fate or bad luck—or faulty design—can never be blamed; if the weather can't be blamed—or a broken piece of equipment that can be held up and shown to the press—then the cause must be assigned to 'pilot error.' "

Tune sighed. "I had a friend once, long ago. He was directed to fly an incoming vector through a violent rainstorm. He asked for different vectors and was refused. Low on fuel, he flew the assigned routing. Downdrafts smashed him into the earth a mile short of the runway. The official judgment was 'pilot error.'

"After our group was sent into a . . . shall we say . . . impossible situation with inadequate intelligence, I was the only survivor so the blame had to fall on me. It was not my fault. *It was not my fault.* However, the project director placed a letter of reprimand in my file. In order to close the case, don't you see. Since that time, assignments have been small . . . routine. We are evaluated on results. When you are given routine assignments that cannot possibly show major results, and then evaluated on quality of results, a low effectiveness rating is a foregone conclusion. Rather amusing, when you stop to think about how it works."

He looked off somewhere again.

"So," I said, "you get a bad rating, so you're given a thankless assignment that can't produce a good rating next time—and when the inevitable new bad rating comes down—"

"Precisely. Wonderful system, no?"

"Clarence, I would say I would put in a good word for you, but in my present configuration that would just be another black mark against you."

He surprised me by snorting a mirthless laugh through his nose. "Please don't do me any such favor, sir!"

"I wish I could do *something*, Clarence!"

"I almost made it," he said so softly I had to lean closer to hear. "I was promising. I tried as hard as I knew how. I was . . . almost a success."

I had heard men speak of themselves in the past tense before. It never failed to twist my guts and send a nasty shudder down my back. "It isn't over yet, Clarence."

He waved a pudgy hand. "It isn't significant, sir. What I really came here to tell you is . . . perhaps . . . sadly . . . vastly significant. Although we have no way of knowing."

"You mean there's more?"

"I'm afraid so, sir. Some very bad news, I am sorry to say."

"Worse than this?"

"It's . . . most embarrassing . . . unpleasant."

I watched him. He looked grimmer, tight-mouthed, hurting. You could see the toughness beneath the layer of defeat and resignation, the stuff that had gotten him through. But I saw that he had had to build himself up to whatever information he had for me now.

"Say it," I told him.

His eyes drooped in their watery sockets like the eyes of dead fish in the bin at the market. "You remember our visit to the mortuary."

"Sure. Of course. What about it?"

"It seems there has been a missing persons report."

I chilled. "On *Sylvester?*"

"The international system. A Swiss citizen. Missing several days. Enquiry by his landlord and part-time employer. Also a half-sister. Such reports circulate throughout the Common Market community through a computer system. Our computers automatically compare incoming and logged data against reports of homicides, suicides, and so forth."

"Get *on* with it, Clarence."

He sighed. "The missing Swiss citizen matched the input data on our man at the mortuary. Very precisely. Height, weight, evident age, old gunshot wounds and reconstructive surgery. It seems he had been in a car wreck—"

"Are you telling me the man we looked at was *not* Sylvester?"

"In such cases, of course, blood type information and genetic coding data are recorded prior to disposition of the body." He studied me sadly. "I fear the evidence is incontrovertible. Our accident victim was a man named Pierre Motard, age 47—"

"Clarence, Jesus Christ!"

"He left his apartment two days prior to the time he was found dead here. A ticketing agency has been located which shows Eurorail ticketing to the French coast. Evidently he entered this country via ferry or hoverboat, probably from Calais. Beyond that we have no information."

"So it was a mistake," I said. "All a mistake."

"I am very sorry, sir. I know this has been a very unpleasant day for you already. But we felt you should have this information at once."

*   *   *

Climbing the stairs to my room, my legs started feeling like somebody had poured concrete in them. Most European lifts scare the bejesus out of me, and the ancient contraption in this hotel was worse than most. It shook when you got on and trembled when it started and made whooping cough sounds all the way up or down. So the stairs were better.

Also, the feeling in my legs had nothing to do with the stair-climb or even my earlier workout.

Clarence Tune's news, on top of everything else, had hit me hard.

I tried as I climbed the stairs to think about everything that had happened during the day *except* Tune's news. Because I knew that when I started facing the real identity of that body in the morgue, I was also going to have to try to deal with what had started coiling like a snake in my guts.

And before I had reached the upstairs landing, there it was: disappointment turning to dibelief turning to a blind, yammering mixture of anger and fear that made me feel like somebody had pumped the blood out of my veins and refilled them with sludgy, half-frozen puke.

There hadn't been any guarantees that the corpse was Sylvester, and I had told myself I was maintaining a disbelieving attitude of wait and see. But each passing day had dulled my cynicism. The rat-like watchfulness had retreated out of its customary corner of my mind; the little niche where the hate squirmed, demanding revenge for both Danisa and Beth, had begun to get dusty. I had begun to concentrate on life here, *now*, without the sense that one day I would look up and he would be there again, and I might have one second to do the right thing and kill him at last, or stare into the black void and enter it for all time.

I had known I should be less ready to accept the incredible good luck of his death. But I had wanted to believe it much more than I had allowed myself to realize. We should not grasp at straws. But when we're desperate we welcome them, we fabricate them from the flimsiest materials, we adore them, we make them our religion. The rush of recent events had made the job easy for me.

But no more straws. Not now. The man in the morgue had not been friend Sylvester. I was back to square one. Kinkaid and the boys would say they had no evidence that Sylvester might be in England—or that he even existed any more. They had said that before and they would say it again. I had not believed them before and I would not be able to make myself believe them now. So I was simply back where I had been before as far as the endless fear and hate of Sylvester was concerned—no better, no worse.

Which was a lie. I felt immeasurably worse. Because I had had some hope—a sense of liberation from the anger-fear, and now it was back. The weight of it—back again—felt ten times worse than it had before. And I had been cashiered out.

Reaching the door to my room, I stood to the side while I unlocked. A man might hear the key in the lock, don't you know, and fire through the door. I went in, moving quickly to the side and closing the door quickly behind me. Kept moving. Crossed the room as well out of the opened draperies as I could get, and corded them fully closed. Looked around. Same pale wallpaper, same rug, same old furniture, same lamp. But all different.

I poured some brandy and lit a cigarette and tried to think. It was too much too fast.

All right: *One,* I was fired, on my own, disgraced, waiting for the formality of my elimination from the tournament so I could go home. *Two,* Linda would be around—on orders—keeping her distance, making the need that gnawed at me seem a dirty, furtive thing. *Three,* poor Clarence was going to be forced out of his service under the guise of early retirement—finishing in disgrace—at least partly because of me and the gun deal. *Four,* Sylvester was alive . . . might be in Moscow, or might be anywhere.

Oh, and add *five:* I felt stupid, angry, frustrated, guilty, mortified, shaken, scared.

I lectured myself: the news about Sylvester was really not that big a deal. He had been alive in recent days when I was fat and happy, thinking him dead. He could have struck if he were around. He had not struck. Therefore he must not be around. So nothing was different except my perception of it. Also, you could not live your life in fear. You had to keep on going. If I allowed the constant apprehension to put boogeymen in every corner of every day, that would be worse than if he had already killed me. If part of my mind coiled around the hate I felt for him all the time, I was already partly dead. There is no past. There is no future. All any of us has is right now. This minute. We've got to live that. Looking back or forward takes from us the *now,* which is all in the world we ever have.

Right.

When I was a kid, sometimes when I was scared of some other boy in the neighborhood, or worried about being spanked for something, or just felt like the world was too much for me, I used to go out into a corner of the big garage and crawl inside an old refrigerator carton that my father kept standing there. He kept it because he used it once a year to hide our Christmas tree between the time he bought the tree and the time our family myth said Santa Claus brought it on Christmas Eve. (We all knew Pop bought the tree, hid it in the box, and set it up, but we always pretended otherwise. In my family we were awfully good at knowing one thing and pretending another.) So the carton sat there all the time, and it was a good thing for a kid: it could be a cabin in the mountains when you were playing cowboys, or a rocket ship, or a submarine, or anything you wanted. But best of all it was simply stout, big, black, secure. You could hunker down in there.

Grownups have a lot of big cartons: booze, gambling, smoking dope, affairs, buying sprees. Even suicide is a carton, although you never climb back out of that one. I felt like I needed a carton badly right now. But I couldn't think of one. What I needed to do was to *do* something. But I couldn't think of anything useful to do, either.

Tomorrow, early: Sebastian Soratini on Court 14. *Concentrate on that,* I lectured myself.

Didn't work.

Twenty-four

I LOOKED HARD at the spectators around the player area Thursday morning, but Linda was not among them. I would have spotted her if she were. Ah, well. To business, Smith.

Sebastian Soratini was twenty-three years old and he came from Milan, Italy. He had never attained really top ranking on the computer, but he was a steady, hard-pounding baseline player with a good forehand and a beautifully classic backhand that he could hit with overspin or underslice. When his serve was on, it was effective. He liked to serve aces and tended to get upset when his service game failed him.

My plan against him was to refuse to get sucked into long baseline rallies. I knew I couldn't win that way. The idea was to come in behind my serve whenever possible and force the action. Any time I could hit deep into either corner, I would come in behind that, too. On his second serves I would blast the ball right at him, and charge.

He was a nice, dark-complexioned kid with a big smile and the kind of Roman features that make the girls palpitate. He was polite and attentive during our warmups, and sweetly wished me good luck as we got set to begin play.

I held serve, moving to the net on three of the four consecutive points I won, Soratini netting a spin second serve at 40-0 to hand it to me. My knee felt achy and stiff, but I got a couple of short balls from him during his first service game, and barrelled in to take the net on those, too. I could tell he hadn't expected it from the old-timer. He didn't like it, either. But he held serve.

My second service game went tougher but I hung on after he had a break point. He also held, and then I held again to go up 3-2, and the match had begun to take on a pattern, he sitting back and rallying, me doing my kamikaze act at every opportunity. It was a thinly clouded, chilly morning and I couldn't seem to get warmed up right.

During my next service game, going wide to my left for a sliced backhand, I slid awkwardly on the moist grass and went down, sort of doing the splits. The knee twisted despite my heavy, ugly brace. It felt like somebody had stuck a red-hot screwdriver blade in there, and when I rolled over and got up, beads of cold sweat had popped up all over my body.

Trying not to limp, I went back to play and promptly double-faulted. That made it 15-40, and my next serve, bringing weight on the throbbing knee, sat up for him. He picked on it, drilled it down the line for a clean winner, then held on to win the first set, 6-4.

Another glance around showed Linda still hadn't shown, and I knew now she was not going to. It felt sort of lonely without her there. I did spot Melville Oldham and his friend Dacri, watching intently. Oldham, I thought, was perceptive enough to understand something about what had just happened.

I was still not sure exactly how bad it was, but it was bad enough: I could feel the knee starting to puff and swell under the brace. During the next break I loosened the brace cords slightly to give the swelling more room. I couldn't tell how much damage I had done. I decided to lay back a few games—despite my earlier strategy—and see how the knee would hold up during lateral movement.

To my surprise it seemed to hold up pretty well. There was a lot of pain, but nothing that couldn't be handled. You do not block out that kind of pain. People who talk about such a process are talking nonsense. You can get a good adrenaline flow, and that does mute pain a little. You can get so deeply into the zone, thinking of little else beside the point in progress, that you don't think much about the pain. But the pain is always *there*, and so is the body's primitive defense system, which sometimes makes you pull up a bit short, or fail to shift your weight for maximum effectiveness, because *the body knows*—or thinks it knows—that the movement would cause new damage. So you play with the pain and you fight your own fundamental reflexes. Anyone who thinks this process is "blocking out" has never gone through it.

Halfway through the second set, I experimentally took the net on a couple of points again. On both occasions I slammed good volleys for winners. It seemed to shake Soratini up a little, and before he could get himself collected again I had eked out a service break. After that we seemed to be at deuce a dozen times in every game, this way and that way, with long, punishing baseline rallies. I was hurt just enough that I couldn't seem to blast one quite hard enough to take the net and end the point, one way or the other, and he kept stroking them back to me right at the backline. I never hit so many half-volleys in my life. But somehow I hung on, 6-4, so we were tied after almost an hour and a half oncourt.

In the third set, Soratini suffered one of those baffling breakdowns we've all suffered more times than we want to remember. His serve abandoned him and he seemed to be simply careless as he made one unforced error after another. I extended the set by fluffing a great many at the net and missing a crucial topspin lob. It took almost another hour for me to win this one, again 6-4.

Up two sets to one now, with a dull fire burning all the way up my thigh from the squishy hot knee, I glanced at the clock during our next short respite on the sidelines and saw that we had been out here now for two and a half hours. That was far too long. My brilliant strategy had called for *blitzkrieg*, win or lose inside two hours.

Well, I was still in the match anyway. And might surprise a lot of people—myself included—by winning. If I could hang on long enough.

So Soratini started right off by breaking me to go up 2-0. Then he held easily and I was down 0-3 and beginning to see the spectre of losing this one, then having to play still another set. *Christ!* It was not just my knee now, although that was far and away the worst of it. My thighs felt shaky, on fire from lack of quick-recovery oxygen, and I couldn't seem to get fluid in fast enough to replace what I was practically spurting from every pore. My skull throbbed. A faint nausea tugged in my stomach. When I sprinted for a wide ball, my legs felt like wood—simply refused to move as fast as I ordered.

Soratini saw it, too, and started cutely playing the long-term game: stroke it wide right, stroke it wide left, dink up a nice little lob when the old fart approaches the net.

He had chances at clean winners if he had hit out, hard. But he was smart. He had this set in hand, it looked like, and there was no sense taking chances when he could use the remainder of it to run my legs to stumps, setting me up for annihilation in the fifth and final.

Sluggish, hurting far more than I ever like to, I surprised myself by holding my next serve and then getting to the net on a couple of his. *I might still win this.* But I played in a daze, going on automatic pilot, entering that weird dreamworld where your conscious mind doesn't seem functional and you are just doing things, stimulus-response.

The sun came out and went away again and we played and took a break and the knee hurt far worse.

Then I sort of looked up and saw that he was serving at 5-3, and was up 30-0, and when I dinked my return into the net he had three set points.

He tried for an ace on his first ball, missing wide. I thought what the hell and stepped into the next one, a short ball, taking it dangerously early and smashing it crosscourt. He didn't get near it. Then, still down 40-15, I surprised myself again by reaching a fireball down the middle, and he was as surprised as I was, so surprised, in fact, that he hit the bad bounce clear into the gallery.

Waiting for his next serve at 40-30, I saw the expression that scuttled across his dark eyes, almost hidden beneath the wet shelf of his bushy eyebrows. It was the gnawing rat: the one who slips in and bites deep with sharp little teeth into your nerves just when you don't expect him. The thought: *I can still screw this up if I think about it and I'm already thinking about it but I have to stop but how?*

Despite the rat's sudden rush into his eyes, Soratini hit a fine service. I drilled it back. He returned to my backhand. I got back a weak one, short.

He dumped it into the net.

Walking back to receive serve at deuce, I made damned sure not to limp, as I might have been doing on a few previous points. Waiting, I even did a little dance, trying to look light-footed and encouraged. *Hey, pal, look at me, I'm twice your age and fresh as a daisy.*

And you just blew three set points, pal old pal.

He double-faulted to give me an ad. I netted an easy one to go back to deuce. He aced me. I hit a crosscourt winner. He hit a lob long by an inch after I had given up on trying to get back for it. He missed with his first serve and I hit my best shot of the day down the line to break and make the score 4-5.

It seemed to take something out of him. He played the next game like a sleepwalker. It began to dawn on me through the discomfort that I had this thing if I could just take it. So I took it, breaking him again and then holding again, 7-5.

He shook my hand graciously at the net, his forced smile failing to mask the disappointment. "Fine match!"

"Thank you, Sebastian. It was tough."

We shook hands with the judge and hiked to the lockers, where I took off my brace and felt things wobbling around inside the joint.

The doctor examined me with careful, gentle hands. His face got darker and darker and he made little clucking sounds. When he seemed through, I sat up on the side of the table, swinging the good leg—relatively speaking—but not the one with a blowtorch in it.

"Mr. Smith," he said, "I strongly recommend against further abuse of this knee at this time."

"I'll rest it all day tomorrow," I told him.

He clamped his lips together and shook his head, staring at the leg.

"Are you going to take off some of that fluid now?" I asked.

"I recommend ice, and a cast to immobilize it."

"Doctor, I've been through this before. Let's drain it."

"Mr. Smith. Each aspiration inevitably causes further subtle degradation. In the strongest possible terms, I—"

"Doctor. Shoot it. Then drain it."

Sick sweat filmed my face, making me feel chilled and shaky, when I hobbled back out more than an hour later. I had a hot drink and a sandwich, then made my way to Oldham's box. He and Dacri were there, having returned from the outer courts where I had played. I looked for Linda, but she still hadn't shown up. Boris Becker was on Centre Court against Haiti's Ronald Agenor, and was already up one set.

I slid in beside Oldham and Dacri. He looked shockingly gray and grim.

"Hello!" he muttered, eying me closely. "Good match. Fine comeback.—How's the knee?"

"Better now," I told him.

He wasn't fooled. "Painkiller?"

"A touch."

He reached for the everpresent Thermos jug. "Do you think a touch of Oldham's remedy would go down well, or might there be a reaction with the shot?"

"Let's try it and see."

He poured. I drank the foul brew down and thought I might start feeling better.

"Is your friend around?" Dacri asked.

"She had to work part of the day," I lied.

Oncourt, Becker finished off the second set with two howitzer aces. The crowd spattered applause.

"I suppose you'll have McEnroe on Saturday," Oldham observed. "He plays Steed here next, you know."

"I imagine that's right," I agreed.

Oldham leaned back, scowling. "I have McEnroe to go to the finals. I'll be rooting for you, old chap, but I thought you ought to know where my money has been placed."

I grinned at him. "Never let sentiment get in the way of good gambling judgment."

"Quite right!" He smiled for the first time, the kind of smile you see on survivors' faces at a funeral.

I had to like the man. The newspaper stories about the bombing of his factory in Belfast had made it clear that it was a devastating blow to his idealistic plan for manufacturing a new sportscar in Northern Ireland. I wondered how even a man of his resources absorbed a multi-million-pound loss like that. Because the factory was a pilot operation not under way yet, and thanks to Northern Ireland's record of violence, nothing had been insured. But here Oldham was anyway, his gorgeous American girl close beside him, thinking tennis, and probably a fifty-pound bet.

We watched Becker finish off poor Agenor, who did his damnedest but still went down in straight sets. Dacri oohed and aahed with the best of us. She knew tennis, and her comments to Oldham showed she liked him, a lot. I began belatedly to realize that she might be a flirt, but their relationship had real substance. Probably it wouldn't endure. But right now it meant a lot to both of them, despite her risk-taking. I wondered if her presence helped Oldham maintain his composure when things like the factory-bombing happened.

After a short break between matches, McEnroe and West Germany's Carl-Uwe Steed came out. I watched this one with interest. McEnroe was on his best behavior almost all the time, and beat Steed 2-6, 6-3, 7-6, 6-1, totally dominating at the end.

"I would say your work is cut out for you, Brad, eh?"

"I'll show up," I said ruefully.

"We'll have a brew for you afterward, win or lose, right, Dacri m'luv?"

Dacri cooed and nestled her face against his, and he looked almost happy.

The painkiller was wearing off by this time, and I left them and went by the players' box, where I got the usual cracks about getting a lube job on my wheelchair before Saturday. Martina was among the spectators and I got the usual wide grin from her by saying "Good day to you, Ms. Navratilova!", pronouncing it right—Nav-RAH-tee-low-VAH—rather than the way so many people mistakenly say it.

"You hung in there today!" she observed, giving me a triumphant fist.

"How about coming out to help me Saturday?"

"You can do it.—How's the knee?"

"A little sore but okay."

She studied me with sober, knowing eyes for an instant, clearly realizing it wasn't true. But she let it go.

Within another few minutes it was my appointed time to go upstairs for one of my contract stints with ESPN, and at once there were more knee questions from commentators Fred Stolle and Cliff Drysdale. I faked it cheerfully enough. Then they let me do some commentary on the Forget-Arias match and a taped headshot soliloquy about Wimbledon and what it means to the players. After that I excused myself, found four extra-strength Tylenol, and got a taxi with two other players back to the hotel neighborhood. They had both lost, so there wasn't much conversation. I limped inside alone and ordered up two buckets of ice.

Evening came, and no word from anybody. I took a few more pills, went downstairs and ate alone, and returned to my room after dark. Sylvester spooks stood in some of the shadows of the hallway. I went in and locked up quickly, and pulled the shades. The door to the adjoining room had been neatly closed and re-locked. The maid had turned down my bed and left me a chocolate on the pillow. I ate the chocolate and chased it with some gin. *My God it's sore, but it's been sore before and I'm still in this thing. I could play six miles over my head and get the bounces. . . . Sylvester doesn't have to be anywhere close. . . . Screw COS and all the rest of them. . . .*

A little later, I heard sounds in the hall, and then, to my great surprise, a noise that definitely signalled the door to Linda's room being opened and closed again. I heard the bolt being secured. Waited. Probably not Linda, I told myself. Probably re-rented. Or the maid or somebody.

New sounds came: the door on her side being unlocked and opened.

Then a tap on the door on my side.

I put down my latest glass of gin and went over. "Yes?"

"Brad?" Her voice, tight and nervous. "Open up."

My hand shook a little as I complied. It dawned on my stuporous mind that I had had this fantasy about sixteen trillion times—she opening on her side, knocking, telling me to unlock mine. And then—

I swung the door back. She stood there, the light from her side framing her in a soft, fuzzy gold coloration. She still had her raincoat on. Little drizzle-drops glittered on its shoulders and in her hair, too.

"I just learned about the Sylvester thing," she said.

"Oh," I said. "Yes." Her expression, so fiercely intense, so centered on me and filled with feelings I could not read, puzzled me. "No problem, I guess."

She came into my side, brushing past me as she removed her coat. She tossed it at a chair and missed. It fell to the floor. I went over to pick it up.

"Brad," she said. "Will you leave the goddamned coat, please?"

I turned to look at her. She stood halfway between me and my bed, and she had never looked more fervently alive.

She told me, "Maybe you screwed up with the gun. Maybe you were right. Maybe they were even right to take you off this thing. Maybe they weren't. But they weren't even surprised when the report came through that the body wasn't Sylvester after all. I don't think they ever thought it *was* Sylvester. The bastards just let it go—conned you."

"Well," I said, puzzled by the passion of her outburst, "maybe they know something else as well. Maybe he really is in Moscow or someplace."

She stamped her foot. "Goddamn it, Brad! They've screwed you six ways from Sunday on this deal. Here we've been, being a good little boy and girl, and what have we gotten for it?"

I managed a smile. "I dunno, keed. A nice couple of afternoons?"

Her eyes—her parted lips—showed she did not even hear my words. She asked huskily, "Do you want me?"

"Want you?" I repeated idiotically.

"Because if you do," she whispered, "I want you, too. Right now. No more fooling around, wondering about what's best for COS or any of that shit. No more *any* of that."

I just looked at her, and I had never seen anyone so wonderful.

"Well?" she said, exasperated, after a long time. "*Well*, Brad? *Well?*"

I went across the space between us and took her in my arms. With a moan of need she moved against me, sweet curve of thighs molding her against me. She raised her mouth toward mine. Her mouth was a volcano.

Twenty-five
Elsewhere

Langley, Virginia

SIMON BIXBY HAD a bushel of high-priority TWXs on his desk when Tom Dwight walked into his office Friday afternoon in response to the call. Bixby looked flushed, pressured and irritated.

That was unusual for the top administrative aide to CIA Director Jeremy Malcomber. Bixby, fifty-three, was a career man *par excellence*, a former case officer who had lost his left hand in a car bombing in Beirut years before. When you have lost a hand and almost your life in a fiery car explosion, office pressures and red tape seldom have the impact they might on men with more placid backgrounds.

"Sit down," Bixby told Dwight peremptorily. He pointed at the mountain of paperwork. "London messages, mostly. MI5 got a report on a known URA terrorist named Cruickshank spotted in London yesterday. By the time they got some people there, he had blown the place. Car found abandoned near Reading. Identified as stolen. Two people saw the man who drove it away after hot-wiring it in broad daylight three days ago. They gave a perfect description of Francis Moriarty."

"Jesus Christ," Dwight grunted. "If he's that close—"

"Rumors are flying through Anti-Terrorist Group's usual sources. People say Terrence Dean is supposed to be in London. Talk about a big shipment of plastique. The Brits are putting every available man and woman out on the streets, doubling up everywhere."

"They think the fears about something at Wimbledon are looking worse, then?"

Bixby's good right hand slammed on top of the papers, making a couple jump off onto the floor. "Goddamned Smith won again yesterday. I suppose you saw that?"

"Yes. I even caught a couple of highlights on the late sports wrapup last night."

"I wanted him out of there and on the way home," Bixby grated. "We've all got enough to do without him on the scene, maybe presenting another target."

Dwight concealed his amusement. "I don't suppose we can hold it against him, that he's trying to win."

"The sonofabitch at least ought to have the decency to lose and get out of there!"

Dwight kept his face straight. "Yes, sir."

"Of course," Bixby fumed, "we've got somebody tailing him. I've seen her file. She's all right. But goddammit, we could use her on Cork if Smith wasn't still around, muddling up the works. What a mess!"

London

"Good afternoon. The women have their day today at the All-England Tennis Club, site of the Wimbledon championships. In early matches, Pam Shriver defeated Stacy Martin of Largo, Maryland, 6-3, 6-4; Germany's Steffi Graf easily eliminated Carling Bassett-Seguso, 6-1, 6-1; and Zina Garrison eliminated fellow American Susan Sloan, 7-5, 6-3. After early rain delays, matches are now beginning to get back on schedule. In other news. . . ."

Belfast, Northern Ireland

Sylvester left his flat late in the afternoon and, by long-ingrained habit, followed a torturous route, doubling back on itself several times and using three different taxis, before finally taking the bus to the airport.

He had timed his arrival very closely, and just had time to purchase a ticket and board the next shuttle flight for London Heathrow.

His precautions had succeeded in losing the man assigned to follow him in Belfast. Another agent, however, recognized him and picked him up the moment he reached the airport. His departure was observed and the flight noted, and this information was telephoned to London.

London

Sylvester's flight landed at Heathrow shortly after dark. Two men waited to follow his every movement. Routinely, Sylvester collected his bag, then had a cup of tea at a stand-up counter. He next entered a men's rest room which had two doors, one at either end of the area.

An agent watched each.

After fifteen minutes, one of them started getting distinctly uneasy. He went into the restroom and looked around.

Sylvester was gone.

Which was impossible, but he was gone just the same.

One of the unlucky men got to call Mikhail Gravitch.

Gravitch screamed for Major Kreptik. "Assign the best man available to follow Smith *everywhere,*" Gravitch ordered. "Nothing must be allowed to happen, I do not care what it takes to make sure of that!"

"What about Sylvester?" Kreptik, pale, demanded.

"Find him!" Gravitch bellowed. "Find him! Find him!"

Wimbledon

Dacri crept out of Melville Oldham's bedroom in their temporarily rented house shortly after midnight. Behind, Oldham snored contentedly. Dacri smiled to herself in the dark. He was a dear man and she really did like him. It was her idea that they seldom spent the entire night together. His snoring was simply too much for her to take. A girl needed her beauty sleep.

For someone of Oldham's importance, Dacri thought, he was very trusting. Which allowed her the luxury of an occasional more virile lover, and Oldham never suspected a thing.

There would be no extra lover tonight, however. The old man had been quite wonderful, and Dacri stifled a yawn as she headed for her own bed, content.

The door to her upstairs bedroom stood ajar. The thinnest shaft of moonlight made the room silver-pale. Yawning again, Dacri padded across the bare wood floor, slipping out of her robe.

A sudden slight movement behind her startled her. With the beginning of a gasp, she started to turn. A hand went around her face, shutting off her mouth so she could make no sound. She struggled. A cloth—foul, sharp, rank medicine odor in it—went over her nose. She gasped and lost consciousness.

Croydon

Terrence Dean sat in the dusty little rented room, staring at the telephone through Friday night. Hours passed. He did not move.

The first streaks of Saturday's dawn began to appear beyond the filthy window.

The telephone rang. Dean snatched it up instantly.

"All is well, all is well," the voice said. It was Squirrel Henry's voice.

"Understood," Dean said, and hung up.

He looked at his watch. His mind raced into high gear, calculating movements, arrangements, timing. He felt very nearly sick with excitement. He forced himself to think more slowly, making certain nothing had been overlooked.

Reassured, he made his first call.

"Yes," the voice said. Moriarty.

"Today," Dean said, his voice thick with emotion. "Seventeen hundred hours."

"Seventeen hundred hours."

"Right. Five o'clock here, noon in New York. Smack in the middle of their live television coverage. It's the start of their long July Fourth holiday, you know. 'Independence Day.' We'll show them a real blow for independence. They'll give us maximum coverage, maximum effect."

Moriarty replied, "They call that show *Breakfast at Wimbledon,* over there in America."

Dean chuckled. His nerves made the chuckle sound high-pitched, almost girlish. "I wonder what they'll be calling it after today."

Twenty-six

THE RAIN STARTED around 3 A.M. Saturday, but by the time the first hints of daylight streaked my hotel window, it had stopped. I turned carefully in the warm deeps of the bed, Linda's firm-sleek contours close against me. As I moved, she murmured in her sleep and then roused sweetly, putting a bare arm and leg over me. "Whasa?"

"Time," I said, stroking her shoulder.

She opened one eye. Her pelvis insinuated gently against me. "Right now?"

I disengaged. "Afraid so, babe." I got out of bed, testing the knee and finding the dull pain right there in its usual place.

She sat up, hair loose on her shoulders, and stretched her arms toward the ceiling. The covers tumbled off her breasts, making me start to reconsider the time schedule. But before I could get any further she tossed the covers back and swung gleaming long legs out of the bed to climb to her feet. She came around the bed and moved into my arms, nuzzling. "Morning."

I grinned at her. "Morning yourself."

She padded into her own room, a vision. In a moment I heard her shower start.

From the window I could look down onto the street and over the roofs of the buildings across the way. Low dark clouds scudded along, but they looked thin. I thought the sun was going to burn them off. Which meant today's matches would run more or less on schedule. Starting times had been moved earlier to make up rain-postponed matches.

328

The new schedule called for me to face John McEnroe at three. We would be on Centre Court, a place I hadn't played in more than ten years. The assignment was merited by John's No. 4 seed and had nothing to do with me. We were scheduled to start after the conclusion of the Sean Cork-Jimmy Maxwell match, which people were saying would be one of the best of the tournament. My only hope was that the knee would hold up, and I could play well enough to make my match with John not one of the worst.

You always harbor a distant hope, and I had a plan for the match. But McEnroe was on top of his game again and my knee was worse than I was letting on. Friday's drainage procedure, while not producing too much new fluid, had hurt like hell, and the constant ache set my teeth on edge. Under the best of circumstances I couldn't have taken someone of John's caliber to five sets. Things being as they were, my realistic goal was avoidance of disgrace. I kept struggling against my win-it-all fantasy.

I went into my shower and let the hot water bash against my face. I tried not to look directly at the feelings of sadness, of failure.

Friday had been a very strange day. Awakening with Linda nestled beside me, after the night we had had together, gave me a small stab of guilt about Beth, so far away. Linda's insistent hands and tongue had made me forget those thoughts very quickly. She was a dream in bed. Teasing, murmuring, demanding and giving equally, she was funny and passionate, skilled and yet mysteriously shy at times, electric in her response to me. There was no awkwardness when we finally left my bed, and no talk about what-might-have-beens. Or even what was to be.

We left the hotel separately, she to check in for possible orders or information, me to meet briefly with poor Clarence Tune, then make a series of telephone calls, trying to book a flight home early in the week. Clarence had no news, except reports of possible terrorist sightings in the city which had yielded no arrests. Flights to the states were filled. I put myself on three standby lists.

Trying to rent a shotgun, on the basis of a story about trap shooting, was just too complicated. Carrying a loaded shotgun around town was not acceptable behavior anyway, especially for me. I settled for a store that sold tools, selecting a nice, heavy crescent wrench that just fit my inside coat pocket. Maybe Sylvester was far from here, I reassured myself. And maybe if he was a lot closer, he would be stupid enough to let me reach in my pocket and pull out my nice new spanner, and brain him with it.

Right. . . . But any fantasy in a storm.

Later Friday Linda came back and we went to the club and watched some of the women's matches on outer courts. She said her assignment to watch over me was still in force, and everybody down there seemed far too busy to worry about details. We had dinner together that evening at a small French place I knew not far from the Gloucester, where so many of the players were staying, and it was nice: I heard about her parents, and her growing up, college, her recruitment into the Company, what she thought of London, some of the things she hoped one day to do, some of the places she wanted to see, how she felt about a lot of things. She asked me some questions about Vietnam, about tournaments back in the days when I thought I could beat anyone and often did. Later we danced a little bit. She was a good dancer, too, but my knee wouldn't let me do a lot of that. And so home, as the estimable Mr. Pepys might have said, and to bed, and the slow, crescendoing repetition of the previous night, but with greater knowing, the different kind of urgency that grows out of an increase in trust, certainty, caring.

Now: It was past nine when I left the shower and began hacking at my whiskers, a half-hour later when, dressed and ready, I started collecting rackets and other gear for the trip out to the club. Linda came in from her side, gorgeous in mauve slacks and matching sweater, with a bright scarf around her neck. We went downstairs and had the continental breakfast, then took her car south, across the river, to Wimbledon.

Weaving expertly through the clotted traffic, she got me close to the players' gate. "Jump out, darling, and I'll go find a place to park this thing."

I leaned through her window to kiss her. "Meet me at the Oldham box?"

"Great." She frowned. "Are you sure that knee is all right?"

"That knee," I told her, "feels fine. You didn't hurt the knee, hardly at all."

Her eyes laughed. "Go." And pulled out toward the traffic again.

After showing the old man my ticket, I went to the players' area and left my equipment in safe hands. Then went back into the stadium and made my way toward Melville Oldham's box. The crowd was already in a lather, cheers racketing around the old stadium after many points. Sean and Maxwell were oncourt, going after each other, and the scoreboard showed Jimmy ahead 4-3 in the second set, on serve, after Sean had won the first set, 6-4. Sunlight flooded through breaks in the clouds, showing the effects of constant play on the old court as the first week neared a close: the grass, despite the showers, had worn thin up the center on both sides of net, and it had started to take on that sickly yellow hue it gets by the time of the quarters. It looked nice and firm, however, not too badly chewed up, and the ball seemed to be bouncing better than one might expect at this stage.

I got to the right section for Oldham's box and started toward it. I spotted him in his usual corner seat, but when I looked at Dacri I got a surprise. It was *not* Dacri. The girl seated beside him was the one he had been so mad at the other night at his house here: Rebecca something. She looked crisp and striking and happy, and Oldham looked like a man who had just looked into his own coffin.

I made my way over there. The girl glanced up at me with sharp curiosity—and possible worry?—but Oldham kept staring sightlessly at the match going on below.

"Morning!" I said fatuously. "Mind if I watch a few games with you?"

Oldham started violently and turned to look up at me, standing there in the aisle beside him. "Oh. Smith. Right. Of course." He gave the girl a murderous glare. "Move over. Let Brad sit next to me."

She beamed fondly at him. "Of course, sweetheart, whatever you say." She scooted over one chair. I slid in between them. She offered a pale, slender hand. "Hi! Remember? Rebecca Mavson." She was wearing black slacks, a bulky white cotton sweater, and a little cap that resembled a beret. She looked smashing.

"Sure, Rebecca," I said, shaking her hand. "Nice to see you again."

"I'm so looking forward to your match!"

"Right. I remember you're quite a fan."

"Oh, golly yes!"

But maybe thirty years behind on who the players were, I remembered. I turned to Oldham. "Good match here?"

"What?" He frowned. "Oh. Yes. Quite. Sean seems to be having the better of it, but you know Maxwell. He would charge a tank if he thought he could get a winning volley against it."

His raincoat, umbrella and ever-present Thermos were on the vacant chair in the box. He glumly gestured toward the Thermos, offering me a drink, but I shook my head. He made no gesture toward having one himself. I gave up trying to get him to talk, and watched some of the match.

Oldham had been accurate. It was a good one. Maxwell was hammering everything on both sides with everything he had, as always, and I saw that Sean was patiently playing a baseline game, coming in only when he felt sure he had a ball deep enough for a a definite advantage. He was playing within himself, elegantly controlled, moving with the grace of a champion yet always ready for one of his shockingly quick darts to the net.

Oldham watched, I noticed, but did not seem to react to some great points. He applauded a few times, half-heartedly, as if remembering he should. On my other side, Rebecca clapped her hands when she saw others doing so. Once or twice she squealed appreciation when nothing much happened, and during an especially long and brilliant point, finally won by Sean with a buzzing topspin lop over Maxwell's head, she was looking out *over* the court, as if searching the crowd for familiar faces.

I wondered where the hell Dacri was. Maybe she and Oldham had had a falling-out, I thought. Which would make Rebecca his consolation—or revenge. In which case I didn't want to ask.

Sean broke again in the tenth game and then held on to win the second set. The crowd applauded insistently as Maxwell prepared to serve for the first time in Set No. 3. Most of them were for Sean Cork, but nobody liked a short blow-away match, and Maxwell had a lot of sentimental backing because he was the "old-timer." I would have some of that kind of support against McEnroe.

Linda appeared and joined us, and Oldham, usually animated around a beautiful woman, was no more cheerful with her. Rebecca chattered about how wonderful this all was. She did not seem at all stupid to me, but she had as much business at a tennis match as I might at a kayak race. She simply had no idea of things.

Puzzled, I concentrated on the match below. Cheers racketed over the wall, coming from the Agassi-Noah match on Stadium Court. Below, Maxwell got a break up on Sean in the third set and grimly hung on, 6-4. It was now past noon.

Despite the early hour, the stadium was not only packed but overflowing. Between the third and fourth games of the fourth set, the crowd began buzzing. Prince Andrew and Fergie had entered the royal box, with its fluttering canopy of purple and green, the club colors, along with a couple of people I had no way of identifying. Fergie was easy to spot in her shocking pink linen outfit with a straw hat wide enough to use as a parachute.

Oldham leaned forward and gave Rebecca a look that would have melted lead. She smiled back at him. "Doesn't Fergie look cute?" she trilled.

"Is this what it's about?" Oldham snapped.

"Now you just watch the great tennis!" Rebecca replied blithely, and leaned back, seemingly unfazed by his killing glare.

Linda caught the interplay, of course, and gave me a questioning look. I shrugged. It made no more sense to me than to her.

A little later, with the players on serve, it was time for me to go and start getting ready. I had already stayed up here longer than I should have. Promising to be back after my match, whatever the outcome, I told Oldham I thought his wager on McEnroe was quite safe, and headed for the lockers.

Cheers rumbled through the structure, or maybe through the earth itself, while I changed and got ready. John McEnroe and I exchanged dubious glances from opposite ends of the long room, but didn't speak. This might be his last Wimbledon, too. I wrapped my knee with a big Ace bandage and then had trouble getting the lacing of the brace right because the knee was so puffy. I tested the flex, relaced again, and did a few mild bends and stretches. I was so tight I hurt.

An official came in and told John and me to stand ready. I glanced at the TV set in the players' lounge long enough to see Sean was up a break in the deciding set. Then I joined John at the far end of the room and we carried our bags out.

Leaving the dressing rooms, we entered the main lobby of the All-England Club. Members were milling around on the far side, and nearer we were squired along by uniformed military volunteers, some with impressive medals. We turned left, John preceding me, and went down the short flight of stairs. On one side were cases displaying all the fine old cups and plates that would never leave the premises, and on the other side the gold-lettered names of all the champions since 1877. Without slowing I looked for my name, just like I always did, and found it. *They can't take that from me.*

Going under the old overhead signboard with the Kipling quote, we went through double doors into a small foyer, and through this to the left again into the waiting room. Austere, with its wicker furniture and pictures of some former champions, it had never seemed friendly to anyone who ever waited in it. John sat down and rested his elbows on his knees, his eyes going far off somewhere. I did deep breathing.

After an interminable time they came for us. We grabbed our bags again and went out through more double doors into a narrow rectangular courtyard behind the south wall of the enclosure, and, I knew, under the royal box. Turning left again, we walked about thirty feet, then went right, through the opening to Centre Court.

Walking out of the tunnel-like opening gave me a lung-rush of something like agoraphobia. The first impression was of the dark stands, the vast sky funneled down by the structure, the building waves of applause that beat against the body like feather hammers. We walked to the service line and turned to the royal box and bowed, feeling awkward and silly as always, and went to the players' benches to get out rackets and get to work.

You are given fifteen minutes to warm up on Centre Court. John was withdrawn, professionally hostile, and scrupulously polite, hitting me the shots I needed. We rallied, starting slow and adding pace. It was not warm but I began to sweat. Maybe the knee would loosen up. The dark maw of the stadium loomed around us, the sky a bright patch at the top of peripheral vision. I glanced at Melville Oldham's box once or twice, and Linda waved. Oldham sat like a granite statue. Then I concentrated on getting as loose and ready as possible.

The man in the chair called us to be ready in two minutes, and then he called on us to play. John was to serve first. I glanced at the clock. Past 3:00.

"Quiet, please. Take your seats, please. Gentlemen?—Play."

John served me four straight balls I couldn't handle to go up 1-0 in the first set. To my considerable surprise I also held serve and the knee began to feel like it might warm and loosen. We started deeper into the match and I played a lot on instinct, getting into the zone, no longer thinking in any usual linear way.

In the fifth game he hit a couple of loose shots and I got a break point, could not follow up on it. In the sixth game he broke me to go ahead, 4-2. The crowd rumbled a little. I was having trouble moving to my left, but my knee was not hurting unbearably.

Glancing at Oldham's box during the next changeover, I registered Linda's bright, worried smile of encouragement and Rebecca's blank and uncomprehending stare. Oldham seemed to be looking off at a corner of the court where the most exciting thing happening was a ballboy scratching his rear end. We resumed play.

What's his problem? I thought, going wide to my right and flipping a forehand up the line. John glided over to the ball and returned crosscourt, a wicked angle. I hurried. *Come on, legs! Oldham is a tennis freak, but he doesn't even seem to be paying attention, he's not here. Why?* I made a good get, but John had sneaked in to the net for a winning volley.

Each of us got a bad bounce. I netted a forehand that should have been a winner for me. The first set went down the tubes.

And where's Dacri? I managed to reach a short lob and put it away with a solid overhand, getting a ripple of appreciation from the crowd. Trying for a change of pace, I hustled in to the net twice in the next game, and was rewarded with the sight of magnificent passing shots crackling past, out of my reach. Then I hit a couple of good shots myself, and the thing began to settle down into a war of attrition. We went back and forth, deuce and ad, deuce and ad, seemingly every game taking an incredible amount of time. This kind of match could only benefit John, but I couldn't break out of the pattern that was established.

I checked the clock again. *4:15,* and I was starting to get tired. The second set was starting to go the way of the first. In his box, Oldham continued to sit like a zombie. *Something has happened to him, something else, bad.* I hit a winner crosscourt. *What?*

John served. I returned down the middle. He stroked it back, adding more pace. I took it early and went wide to his left. He jackhammered a forehand to my left. Preoccupied, I rushed over and slid into the shot and my foot went out from under me. The ball went to the ground at the same time I did.

The knee exploded.

For a second or two I didn't know how bad it was. The flash of pain was extraordinary. I might have blacked out for a few seconds. The next thing I knew was, I was rolling onto my side, tasting the bitter taste of grass or mud in my mouth, and my entire left leg felt like it had been run over by a steamroller. Over the roaring in my ears I heard the vast, deep silence of the stadium.

Well, this was ridiculous, I decided. My racket was just beyond my outstretched hand. I picked it up and rolled over and started to climb back to my feet. The damned knee did not buckle, exactly, but the agony made it impossible for me to put all my weight on it. I sort of tumbled back onto my rear end.

Cold sweat burst out all over me. I was by God not going to retire from the match. No, sir. I tried again—got to my feet this time, brushed myself off while my stomach threatened to send up breakfast. The crowd applauded appreciatively.

John was standing near the net, his forehead mightily wrinkled in concern. I waved at him and limped back to receiving position. Pulse-waves of pain came up out of the knee. My left foot had no feeling in it, but the pain coming up out of the knee was really extraordinary. I was definitely going to be sick pretty soon.

I stalled a few seconds, toweling my face. Linda remained standing in the Oldham box, her face graven with worry. Rebecca sat in the next chair, looking blank. Melville Oldham's seat was empty and he was nowhere to be seen.

Tossing the towel to one of the boys, I returned to the line. The knee felt like someone had a blowtorch inside, trying to burn their way out.

I waited for John's serve. He fiddled around, giving me an extra few seconds to collect myself, and then his arm went up in his motion.

He served into me and when I moved to try to get it I went down again.

That was it. The chair called a time out. Some people—a doctor and a linesman and John himself—came over. I could not get it together. *God damn it,* I thought, trying again to put weight on the leg, *you are not going to end like this, Smith.* But I could not get through the pain.

Fifteen minutes later, polite and sympathetic applause washing over me, I headed down the tunnel, out of it. *McEnroe, U.S., def. Smith, U.S., 6-4, 5-5, withdrew.*

What a way to end it. But until the doctor gave me the pain injection into the joint and it began to take effect a few minutes later, I didn't even much think about the disappointment.

I glanced at my watch: let it be noted that the old man finally began to see that it was over for him at exactly 4:35 P.M.

Twenty-seven
Elsewhere

A BLOCK FROM the stadium, Jack Blake nudged the nose of the bulky gasoline truck out of the side street and into the slow-moving traffic. Up ahead, taillights flashed red as the line of cars stopped and started, inching along. It was 4:35 P.M.

"C'mon, c'mon," Blake muttered nervously.

In the right-hand seat, Hennigan straightened up from arranging the gas masks on the floor. His Remington shotgun lay across his knees. "We're on schedule, lad. There's five minutes or more built in fer the traffic." The words were calm, but his voice sounded hoarse with excitement.

"Gimme my mask," Blake grunted.

Hennigan handed it over. Blake put it on his lap, moving aside the handle of his Armalite rifle, stuck between his knees. The cars ahead stopped again. Blake could see a bobby in the street, stopping this line of traffic to let a few cars inch out of the parking at right angles. The sidewalks teemed with tennis fans of all ages, descriptions and nationalities. Blake's gut felt like somebody had tied a knot in it.

"Cruickshank better be over there yonder with that car," he said.

"He will be, he will be," Hennigan replied.

Up ahead, the bobby stepped back and signalled, and the gasoline truck's line of cars began to inch forward again. Blake slowly released the clutch and the truck moved closer to the point of attack, now less than forty meters ahead.

339

"When the smoke goes," Blake said, nervously repeating instructions that were not necessary, "I go out and open the bonnet."

"Just do it," Hennigan said. Then his voice finally cracked under the tension. "Do it an' run, an' I do the same. It'll be a piece of cake, lad."

The line stopped again for a moment,

"Goddammit!"

"Calm yerself."

The cars ahead moved. The gasoline truck inched past a news kiosk, stands of vendors selling everything from photographs to tea to strawberries and cream. Some people on the sidewalk were leaving, carrying away blankets, coats and umbrellas. Others, clad in short-sleeved clothing more appropriate to the clearing sky overhead, hurried in the opposite direction, intent on finding standing room.

Ten yards.

Then they were close enough—almost opposite the driveway that fed the parking on the far side.

"Ready?" Blake rasped.

"Ready," Hennigan said, and reached for his gas mask.

Blake reached down, grasped the loop at the end of the wire that extended through a hole drilled in the firewall to the engine compartment, and pulled it sharply. There was a sharp bang and the smokebomb under the engine cover started belching dense gray smoke.

Standing on the side of the street with Supervisor Simley, Officer Hedges was startled by the sudden loud popping noise. He turned and saw the hulking white petrol vehicle stalled just a few meters to his right, dead in the center of the street, blocking everything. The pop had come from the truck, and now clouds of choking gray smoke boiled out from under the bonnet and bottom of the vehicle, enveloping other cars and people on the sidewalk in the densest fumes.

"Here now!" Supervisor Simley barked. "See that that is

cleared immediately!" He raised his Motorola radio unit and started barking orders to other officers nearby.

Officer Hedges tooted his whistle for fire assistance and started down the street toward the offending vehicle. Out of the corner of his eye he saw three of the security forces—one soldier and two plainclothesmen he judged to be Anti-Terrorist Unit—coming from other directions.

Ahead, both occupants of the fuel truck had bailed out of the cab. One ran to the front of the vehicle and tried vainly to get the bonnet open. The other man ran around in little circles as if confused and frightened (poor bugger, Officer Hedges thought), and then unaccountably leaped up onto the security railing around the bulbous rear section, putting a foot on the little ladder that led to its rounded top.

"Here, now!" Officer Hedges called. "If the vehicle is on fire—"

He stopped right there.

Because the man on top of the fuel tank had suddenly hunched down—was pulling something out from under his filthy jacket—was pulling it on over his face. *A gas mask.*

"Stop that!" Officer Hedges yelled. He pulled his club and raced ahead, intent on dragging the man off there. He heard other shouts, more whistles.

The man at the front of the truck suddenly turned. From under his coat *he* pulled a mask, too—snapped it over his face and adjusted it. But before Officer Hedges could react to that, the man on the ground swung toward him and he had something—a rifle of some sort—in his hands.

He fired it.

A terrible impact hit Officer Hedges in the chest. The next thing he knew, he was on the ground. He looked down at himself and he was bleeding. There was a hammering noise. He realized the noise was gunshots—many gunshots. Through blurring vision he saw some of the plainclothes men kneeling, firing at the truck through the smoke. *Where had their guns come from?*

*   *   *

A half-block away, Sylvester heard the initial pop too. Trying to see over the crowd that jammed the sidewalk, he heard a woman scream and men shouting, and then the ugly, familiar sound of automatic weaponsfire.

"Pardon me, please—pardon me—" Sylvester took advantage of the milling confusion to fight his way curbside so he could lean out and see.

A bobby was down, others were running from all directions. Several—four, perhaps five—men in suits had dropped to the pavement around a smoke-streaming old fuel truck, and were firing into the murk. Out of the smoke, muzzle-flashes showed return fire. Sylvester saw stampeding bystanders go down, and others scurry wildly.

A man wearing a gas mask rushed out of the smoke. He had what looked like an Armalite rifle, spraying bullets at the security people. A siren started somewhere. Weapons spat response. The man in the mask was blasted by a dozen or more hits, jackknifed, tumbled forward on his face onto the pavement.

Sylvester clung to a utility pole to keep from being swept away in the stampeding sea of people running from the scene. The smoke around the truck began to clear. He looked through the smoke and saw a second man up on the side of the cannister section. He was upside down, splayed grotesquely, an ankle caught in the narrow ladder that ran up the side. Blood ran down off his head and torso, staining the white side of the truck. Sylvester thought of the Tarot deck's hanged man. The dead man in the gas mask on the side of the truck looked like that.

Inside the stadium, the sounds of gunfire and screaming penetrated. Some spectators panicked and there was a rush for exits. Some of the smoke drifted inside and some women started screaming that the stadium was afire. An official quickly got on the public address and started announcing that there had been an accident outside, but there was no problem now, no need to panic. Gradually, peace began to be restored.

Linda Bennett, waiting in the Oldham box for Brad's return from the lockers, recognized the sounds for what they were. "I'll be back shortly," she told Rebecca, and hurried up the aisle.

Clarence Tune, standing near the players' tunnel, also knew something serious was happening. He ran for the nearest exit.

Jana Murnan, alias Rebecca Mavson, sat right where she was, the raincoat, Thermos and umbrella on the empty seat beside her. She looked far across the playing surface at an oblique angle and thought she could make out Terrence Dean's figure, up in the standing room, unmoving. Her heart speeded. She felt nauseated with excitement. With her toe she touched her large canvas purse, reassuring herself that the other jug was still there.

Francis Moriarty got back out of the way when people started rushing for the exist. He cradled his precious camera against his chest. Nothing must harm the camera now.

Twenty-eight

THE DOCTORS WANTED to put me in the hospital, but I couldn't allow that with nothing solved. Grumbling, they built a plastic knee cast around the injury, gave me a shot and some percodan, and added dirty looks.

"It can collapse again, Mr. Smith, I suppose you know that."

"Okay, doctor, I know. But I can walk on it if I take it real easy, and I'll see a doctor just as soon as I get back to the states."

Disgusted look. "Very well, then. Please wait. We have one more item for you." And in a moment they came back with an old-fashioned wooden cane, very heavy, with a brass cap on the curved top.

I slid off the examining table. "I don't need a cane."

Then I put weight on the leg, and stifled a gasp.

I said, "Okay, I need the cane."

I hobbled out of there and was back in the dressing rooms, clumsily trying to shower without soaking the knee brace, when somebody started yelling about trouble in the street out front. I limped out, toweled off, and got to the TV lounge to watch.

The room was already jammed. Guys were talking excitedly and others yelling at them to be quiet so we could hear the television. On the screen, the scene was of the street outside: smoke drifted across stalled cars, appearing to emanate from a white gasoline truck dead in the middle of the pavement. There were police and security people all over the place. An armored car had already pulled up, although I couldn't for the life of me see how it had gotten through

344

the tangle. One body—covered by a blanket—lay on the pavement beside the truck. Another, not yet draped, sprawled a few yards in front of it. A third and maybe a fourth could be seen on the edge of the picture, out of focus, nearer the curb. A lot of the men around the truck had automatic weapons.

Someone turned the volume on the set higher, making the announcer's voice crash through the room: "*—at least two apparent terrorists, wearing gas masks and carrying weapons. Both were shot down and can still be seen in this picture. At least one police officer and six onlookers have been shot—killed or wounded. Ambulances are on the way. First word from officials below say no more terrorists are at large, and whatever this bizarre incident represents, the threat is ended. The amazing sequence of events—*"

I had heard enough. I retreated and limped back to my dressing area. Throwing my clothes on as fast as I could, I gathered up my gear in one hand and my jacket in the other and got out of there, heading toward the stadium entry and Melville Oldham's box.

Reaching one of the entry portals, I found myself caught in a gentle wave of excited, chattering spectators jostling to get back inside. Apparently a lot of them had broken for the exits when the excitement started, and were now returning reassured but still on edge and talkative.

Inside, Centre Court lay deserted. For whatever reason—some rule, maybe, saying what they should do whenever play was interrupted—groundskeepers had put half the covering over the court. Now they were in the process of removing it again. No players were to be seen. The royal box had been vacated. It looked like the stadium was about three-quarters full, and more milling in every second.

The scoreboard clock showed 4:55 P.M. If the mess in the streets outside had been the best the terrorists could do, Wimbledon would suffer no more than a half-hour's setback to the regular playing schedule. I had been here some years when the rain set us back days.

Using the cane to allay some of the pain leaking past the shot the doctors had given me, I made my way around the higher level of the seats, trying to pick out Oldham's box. I finally got close enough to spot it, but saw that Linda was not there. Rebecca Mavson, Oldham's raincoat, umbrella and Thermos on the empty seat beside her, sat alone.

When I thought about it a second, it figured. Linda would have gotten into motion the moment all hell started outside. For all I knew, she might have a backup emergency assignment in case of trouble. If what the TV man had said was true, she ought to be coming back before long.

Down below, the groundspeople finished removing the tarp material. I spotted signs of activity in the tunnel, and then some of the linespeople and ballboys started coming out. A ripple of applause greeted them. I saw two uniformed ushers come out of the portal just ahead of me and resume their stations on the aisles. Business getting back to normal.

So the terrorist threat had been real, I thought. And now it was over. A lot of to-do about one abortive attempt. But Christ, no telling how much harm that truck might have done if security hadn't been ready to head it off.

I became aware that the letdown had started for me. I felt shaky after all the adrenaline, and with the pain spreading despite the shots, I was in for a real downer. *Dr. Needham is going to be so happy to see you again. He probably has another new cutting technique he's just been itching to try on somebody.*

Hurting fairly seriously, I sidled along the metal railing, headed for the aisle that led to the Oldham box. Whatever had happened in his life, I expected him back soon too. Linda would be able to provide some kind of preliminary wrapup on what had really happened outside. That taken care of, I thought it was time to try to pump Oldham . . . find out why he looked so out of it today. It was no longer my job. But I might get something out of him anyway when most people couldn't.

The stands continued to fill as if by magic. From the tunnel emerged Ivan Lendl and Peter Lundgren, who had been in the middle of their first set when things started happening. Both of them looked a bit shaky and I could hardly blame them. It isn't every day you hear shooting outside the courts, and officials order play suspended, everybody out of sight.

The players started warming up again. I glanced down at Oldham's box, wishing somebody else would show up. I didn't relish the idea of sitting there, an ornament for the ignorant Rebecca. Now, instead of watching the warmups, she was bent over, rummaging through her big, floppy purse.

She puzzled me. What the hell was she doing here? Did she really have something on Oldham? The idea that he had her here by choice, as revenge against Dacri, just didn't hold water. And where was Dacri anyhow? And what had taken Oldham himself away on the biggest day so far?

Down at one of the court-level gates, a familiar figure appeared: walking slowly, as if the world's weight were on his back, lost inside his trenchcoat, poor old Clarence Tune. I saw him look up toward the Oldham box, then frown and say something to one of the security people standing courtside, against the wall.

It dawned on me that Tune's assignment was me. When things started to happen, he must have rushed to the players' area to check my safety. But by the time he had gotten there, I had left by the other set of doors. Standing down there now, he looked bereft, worried. I saw him say something more to the security man, then anxiously scan the rows of seats.

I waved but he didn't see me.

Well, all right. Swinging my bad leg down first, then supporting as much weight as I could on the heavy oak cane, I started down the steps to get to the box and wave at him from there.

Going down behind a clot of other people, I looked ahead again at Rebecca, alone in the box. She had the Thermos upright, and was turning the top. A small toddy, Rebecca? I wondered how Oldham would like that.

She removed the cap. Inside was another. She started to unscrew that. But instead of unscrewing it, she used an unusual hand-motion that for some reason caught my attention. Instead of turning the inside cap counter-clockwise, the way I knew it unscrewed, *she turned it first to the right, then to the left, then to the right again.*

I stopped. Looked harder.

The Thermos in her hands had a bright red top. Oldham's had had a dark red top. Then I saw something that startled me: Oldham's Thermos, still on the folded trenchcoat on the seat beside her. *What the hell?*

The girl stirred. From a pocket of her jacket she removed something. At first I couldn't see what it was. She paused, holding her hand over the throat of the still-closed Thermos, and looked hurriedly around.

She almost saw me, but her eyes swept too swiftly. I had time to see her expression, however, and it jarred me.

It was fear.

She turned her attention back to the Thermos.

I hobbled painfully down more steps, getting some irritated comments from fans I jostled aside. I could now look across the rows and see what Rebecca had in her hand. It was a short, thin length of wire.

"I say there!" a bulky, gray-mustached man protested as I shoved him rudely aside.

"Sorry!" I managed to climb over an empty seat and lurch on downward. In the box, the girl bent over slightly, shielding her actions from all but the most intense scrutiny. But by this time I was icy inside, and had forgotten all about my knee, and was watching nothing but her and the Thermos.

She made a quick little thrusting movement with her right hand.

Inserting the slender wire down through the top of the Thermos.

Which—Jesus Christ—was no Thermos at all, in any ordinary sense.

"Clarence!" I yelled, and rushed across the row as best I could.

Below, Tune showed no sign of hearing me. A security man

standing at the head of the aisle asked for my ticket. I knocked him aside and kept right on going. Below me, Rebecca Mavson—or whoever she really was—carefully set the new Thermos upright in the empty stadium chair beside her. She started to leave the box, going in the direction away from me. She still hadn't seen me.

Forgetting the pain in my knee, I reached the pipe railing and climbed over it. She saw me, then, and started to bolt out the other side, into the far aisle. I went over the pipe and snatched at her and missed. She reached for the Thermos, got it in her hand, and reared her arm back. She was going to throw the damned thing.

All I had was the clumsy oak cane. I raised it. *Can I really bash her over the head with this thing?*

I could. The cane whistled through the air like a golf club on the downswing and hit the back of her head solidly. She started to keel over. I caught the Thermos as it dropped. She slumped against the seats and slid onto the deck. People in the seats around jumped to their feet, yelling. The security man, already after me, vaulted the railing and closed in.

"Clarence!" I yelled again. *"Clarence!"*

He turned, scanned, finally found me.

"Here!" I yelled, holding up the Thermos. *"Quick!"*

His face went blank and then focused and he came through the gate and up the steps at an amazing clip. The security man came crashing across seats, his face a thundercloud. "See here, sir! What have you done here? You'll have to come with me!"

I brandished the cane, which had an appalling amount of blood on it. "Stay back!"

A woman behind me cried, "He's killed that poor girl! Arrest him!"

I glanced down and saw the thin wire—*maybe an antenna*—sticking out of the top of the Thermos cap. But it was not a Thermos cap at all, but some kind of knurled knob. I dropped my cane and reached down and jerked the wire out of there.

The guard grabbed me, driving me painfully backward against

the seats. His uniform smelled of mothballs. "That will be enough out of you, sir. Now come quiet, or—"

Tune struggled into the box.

"Clarence," I choked, held down by the guard's angry weight. "This is it!" I gave the guard a knee in the groin, eliciting a painful squeal and an instant's breathing room. I held the Thermos out toward Tune. "Get it out of here, Clarence! *Get it out!*"

Clarence, bless him, registered shock only long enough to reach out and grab the thing out of my hand. Then he turned and fled up the steps with it clutched against his chest, and my angry guard knocked me off the side of the seat and all the way onto the dirty pavement floor, where he started pummeling me with his fists.

Twenty-nine
Elsewhere

Wimbledon

FRANCIS MORIARTY WATCHED transfixed for a few seconds when the man charged down the aisle and approached Jana Murnan. Moriarty had the camera out on the neck strap but had not opened the leather case yet. It was three minutes before he was to activate the trigger.

Moriarty saw the man grab at Jana—saw her turn—then saw the man swing at her with something bright in the pale sunlight, hitting her on the head. She crumpled.

Moriarty's internal alarm systems all started howling. He fumbled at the snaps of the camera and got the front open, revealing the toggle switch and pushbutton protruding out of the holes drilled in the top of the case. He pulled up the flimsy four-inch antenna and glanced nervously across the way. There was a melee in the Oldham box. A uniformed usher or guard was attacking the man with the weapon. Jan was down, out of sight. The man with the weapon also now had the bomb. Moriarty saw another man—short, slight, dumpy—rush across to the box. The man who had attacked Jana tossed the bomb to the little man, who started up the steps with it, running.

Moriarty did not understand anything except that it was going all wrong. He flicked the toggle switch on top of the camera-transmitter, took a shuddering breath, and pressed the firing button.

Nothing happened.

"Shit," Moriarty moaned, and jabbed the button again. And again. But still nothing happened—either his transmitter was failing

351

or the bomb device was somehow not receiving the signal to deto-
nate.

He jammed the button twice more. Still no response. Looking
around wildly, he saw a couple of spectators staring incredulously
at him.

Letting the false camera drop onto his chest on its strap, Moriarty turned into the mouth of the exit tunnel and fled down the
ramp.

Halfway around the stadium, Terrence Dean saw what was
happening in the Oldham box. He swung around with his little bin-
oculars and found Moriarty, in position at the mouth of the tunnel.
Fire it, you fool! Fire it now!

Dean clearly saw Moriarty try to trigger the radio device. He
braced himself for the blast. Nothing.

Lowering his glasses, the terrorist leader turned his gaze back
toward the Oldham box. The little man with the Thermos bomb
had now vanished up the top of the steps. The guard was dragging
the American, Smith, up off the pavement. People all around the
section were on their feet gawking.

Dean swallowed bile. So carefully planned . . . so close to perfection. And now, failure.

Bitterness made him reach into his coat pocket, where his fingers found the cold curvatures of the tiny plastic gun. He was twenty
meters from the royal box. The young couple and three of their reti-
nue had returned. He could perhaps get off two shots. He wanted
to do that. His frustration said to do that, and if he died now what
did it matter.

Dean almost did it.

But then he remembered his practice with the little plastic gun.

Dean was an extraordinarily good shot. But the plastic weapon
was an extraordinarily inaccurate piece of equipment.

Fire at them? he thought frenziedly. Almost certainly miss?
Die for a stupid one-in-a-thousand chance?

Terrence Dean was ready to die. He had come here today,

knowing he might do just that. But he was also a realist. As acid as this failure tasted in his mouth, he was better off to fight another day, and on terms more to his liking.

Grinding his teeth in revulsion, he turned and started working his way slowly—casually—toward a gate that would lead him out.

London

Mikhail Gravitch sat in the unmarked embassy car with Major Kreptik, listening to the radio account of what had happened at the All England Tennis Club.

"Bunglers!" Gravitch rasped. "Amateurs! Fools! What good would it have done their cause to kill thousands of innocents at Wimbledon?" With an angry gesture he turned the radio off. He motioned at the stolid, sweating Kreptik. "Call for a report."

Kreptik nodded and produced a small, hand-held radiotelephone from the inside pocket of his dark wool suit, which was much too hot for today's temperature. He punched in a code. The device rewarded him with a beep. He punched five buttons, sending tones.

"Yes?" a male voice said.

"Reports on search?" Kreptik said.

"Negative."

"Out," Kreptik said, and snapped the device off again.

Stewing, Gravitch thought about his options. Brad Smith's loss, in conjunction with the aborting of the terrorists' plot at the tournament, meant he might depart the area at any time. If the latest information was correct, and Smith had truly been taken off assignment, his departure might come as early as tonight. Sylvester was in the London area somewhere. Gravitch thought that could only mean the madman meant to make an attempt on Smith's life. Sylvester could reason timetables and options as well as anyone else. QED, Sylvester had to have come to the same conclusion as Gravitch, that time for an attack was fast running out.

If Sylvester meant to attack Brad Smith, he was going to have to try it very, very soon.

"Sir?" Kreptik prompted nervously.

"All men are in place?"

"Yes, sir."

Gravitch nodded, making his decision. "Call Report. We will station ourselves near the players' gate and watch Smith when he leaves the grounds."

Kreptik again reached for the radiotelephone. "At once, sir."

Less than four miles away, Sylvester walked up to the taxi stand in the deep, pleasant shade of the trees lining the park. Smiling, he peered through the driver's-side window at his newfound friend from the pub.

"Hello!" Sylvester said heartily. "I see you wait exactly where you described for me!"

The driver looked up, wrinkled his nose in a surprised grin, and nodded. "Aye, like I tole you, Ben, it's a dandy place to set an' relax, an' there ain't much walk-up business if you're feelin' like a spot of loaf."

"Would you mind if I set a spell with you?" Sylvester asked.

"Why, I'd be pleased fer the company! Come on around!"

Sylvester walked around the car, his eyes taking in every inch of the long, deserted sidewalk ahead of and behind the taxi, the similarly vacant walk across the way, the old woman waiting to cross with the light a half-block away. He opened the passenger-side door of the taxi and climbed into the front seat beside his friend.

"Why," he said, closing the door, "it's downright pleasant in here, ain't it!"

"Sometimes I hustle," the driver said, yawning. "But sometimes I don't. Right now, I'm enjoying my break."

Sylvester leaned across the seat, pointing out through the windshield toward the trees. "Is that a thrush, there, or what is it?"

His friend cocked his head and leaned sideways toward him slightly, seeking a better angle through the glass. "Where? What?"

Sylvester moved swiftly. He drove the long, tempered steel needle in under his friend's sternum, tilting the thrust upward to find the heart. He felt the tougher gristle of the heart muscle make the deadly needle vibrate in his fingers, and he twisted, cutting, side to side. His friend stiffened, gasped, made a wet coughing sound, and fell limp onto the steering wheel, quite dead.

Sylvester got out of the taxi, walked around to the driver's side, and climbed in, shoving the dead man across the seat and onto the floor. He reached inside the pocket of his gray jacket and pulled out the ugly red wig, which he quickly tugged over his skull.

He glanced at himself in the rearview mirror. A shaggy, red-haired Viking stared back.

Sylvester started the car's engine and engaged the gears to pull away from the curb. The fake hair started itching. Sylvester mentally cursed shoddy British workmanship.

The little old lady ahead was just now crossing the street. Sylvester waited for her, waving heartily. She waved back, evidently cheered to meet such consideration from such a nice man.

Thirty

EARLY EVENING, and rain spattered against the high, frosted windows of the room inside the stadium. Melville Oldham, his face gaunt with worry, looked up at me from the cheap plastic chair in which he had been hunched for hours.

"What's *taking* them so long?" he demanded hoarsely.

"Lots of questions," I told him. "Lots of inter-agency red tape."

He groaned and buried his face in his hands.

It had been raining for two hours. But the rain didn't matter; the day's play had been cancelled for security reasons immediately after we got the Thermos from Rebecca Mavson, and Anti-Terrorist Group figured out what was going on. Except for the dense bustle of security people from a half-dozen agencies, the entire club had been cleared.

Oldham and I sat in a small concrete room with a low ceiling and ugly red tile floor. The furniture consisted of a shiny tan plastic couch, four equally unattractive plastic straight chairs, and two battered pine end tables. There had been considerable traffic in the room earlier: Clarence Tune and several of his colleagues, London police, people from Anti-Terrorist Group, the Yard, a man who showed me FBI credentials. Oldham and I had been alone now for what seemed a long time. Nursing the pain in my knee and a throbbing headache, courtesy of the stadium usher/security guard who had bopped me a couple of pretty good ones, I tried to be stoical.

356

The British have always done stoical better than I can, and underneath I was feeling as twitchy as my companion.

Somewhere beyond the tomblike walls a door could be heard slamming. Oldham looked up sharply, an expectant expression tightening his features. Then, when our door didn't open, he slumped again.

"This is unconscionable," he told me. "We've been sitting here for hours, as if *we* were the prisoners!"

"They've had a lot to handle, Melville."

"Does this mean they haven't heard anything about her even *yet?*"

"I'm sure they're looking."

He wrung his hands. "Poor Dacri. My God. All I knew was that the terrorist bastards had her. I didn't know what they planned."

"I know. They counted on that."

"They called. It was just like I told you before. She was *gone*, and then they called and said they had her. They said I was to attend today's play as if nothing had happened—take their bitch, Rebecca, along with me. I thought she was just going to keep an eye on me, make sure I was following orders. They said I was to leave my seat at 4:30, leave the stadium, get to the Albert Memorial. They said I should wait . . . a car would appear with a man inside who would hand me an envelope with my instructions in it." Oldham raised his face to look at me. "I didn't *know.*"

"Nobody could have guessed," I told him.

"You must understand. I was crazy with worry. I really thought there would be a man in a car there. I thought they wanted ransom for her."

"Nobody is blaming you, Melville."

"But my God! All they really wanted was to get me out of the box so that horrid girl could plant a bomb in a vacuum bottle. I would *never* have gone along with it, if I had had an inkling."

"They were counting on your not thinking very straight," I said. "That's how they operate."

"Did you hear what that inspector said the bomb squad reported? That damned device could have killed half the people in the stadium! An explosive in there, and some kind of nerve gas—what did they call it?"

"They called it GD," I said.

"GD? What's that?"

"I don't know," I replied wearily.

"Who makes it? Our side or theirs?"

"Does that matter?"

"Can you really get enough of it into a vacuum bottle to do that kind of harm?"

"Oh, we're very clever at these things, Melville."

"What kind of monsters *are* these URA people?"

"The same kind," I told him, "who blew up your factory in Belfast."

Mention of that earlier disaster seemed to stiffen him. His jaw set and his eyes took on some angry fire. "If Dacri is harmed . . . if they do anything to that girl . . . I'll spend the rest of my days helping to track them down."

"The interrogators have had Rebecca in a very small room for a long time now," I pointed out. "I think her head must be hurting real bad by now and she must be getting pretty tired. They're pros. They'll get something out of her about what the plan was for Dacri."

Oldham slammed his fist into his palm. "They should never have let the slut be seen by a doctor before they began questioning her. That wasted precious time."

"I hit her hard. If she had had a skull fracture out of it, we might have had to wait a lot longer."

"The little bitch! *Twice* they put her into my household with their threats. I thought she was merely a message-carrier. To think she had that bomb-bottle in her bag all the time, and wasn't to arm it until two or three minutes before the radio signal was to be sent! If you had not had the presence of mind to pull the wire out of the top, it might have been detonated anyway!"

"Well, we got lucky," I said. "They—"

The dirty white door in the concrete wall opened, interrupting me. J. C. Kinkaid came in, trailed by Clarence Tune. They both looked rumpled and worn, Tune of course much more so.

Oldham rose to his feet. "Have they found out about Dacri?"

"They're still working on the girl, sir," Clarence said solicitously. "I believe one of the investigators will be in shortly to talk with you."

"They've got to find her!"

"Yes, sir, quite. We realize this has been a dreadful experience for you. We are deeply sorry for delays in taking your statement, but as you can imagine, there has been much to do . . . all available manpower has been used."

Clarence's groveling seemed to give Oldham more backbone. He straightened, muttered something under his breath, and got some color in his cheeks. "Well, you're absolutely correct that it has been dreadful, and my patience is nearing an end." He thought about that. "It is *very* near at an end! I demand to have information on the status of the investigation. A girl's life is at stake here. I am not without influence."

Clarence gave me a despairing glance and then practically writhed in apology. "Yes, sir. Quite, sir. If you could just be patient a little while longer, I am assured someone will speak with you shortly."

"See here! I want a better answer than that!"

I had never seen Oldham's bullying side before, and it was not flattering. I was torn between telling him to shut his mouth and forgiving him on the theory that he wasn't himself at the moment. Before I could do either, however, the door at the far end of the room opened again and a large, handsomely distinguished man of about sixty, wearing an expensive gray suit and bow tie, strode in. He took us in quickly and marched up to Oldham. "Mr. Melville Oldham?"

"Yes?" Oldham snapped. "And you are—?"

"Commander Fairchild, sir. I have just been informed that you were still waiting here. I beg your pardon for the gross oversight."

Oldham's face worked. He appeared impressed. "I demand to know the state of your investigation. I wish to have my statement taken down. I can furnish the name—although it may not be the actual name—of a damned terrorist minion who has made my life miserable for months!"

"Of course, sir," Commander Fairchild said smoothly. He turned to Clarence. "I should have been informed hours ago."

"Yes, sir," Clarence said. "I thought—"

"We shall discuss this later," the commander said brusquely, and put a solicitous hand on Melville Oldham's arm, starting him in motion toward the door. "Please accompany me, Mr. Oldham. I believe we can find more suitable quarters for you. You certainly have every right to be informed of the present state of the investigation, and I can assure you—" The door closed behind them, cutting off his words.

Clarence stood still, looking like all the air had been let out of him. Kinkaid offered me a cigarette, which I gladly took. We lit up. Clarence eyed us mournfully.

"Want one?" Kinkaid asked, and offered the pack.

"Yes, thanks," Clarence said. He removed a cigarette, tapped it on the back of his hand, and accepted a light. He took the smoke in with the greedy pleasure of an addict.

"Nice guy, your commander," I observed.

"He is very efficient, sir," Clarence said.

I turned to Kinkaid. "Is Linda okay?"

"She's fine. She's back at the . . . office. They wanted a complete report as fast as they could get it, and she saw more of what happened than anyone else we had."

We looked at each other a moment.

I said, "I devoutly hope COS will forgive me for swatting the girl with my cane and taking the radio bomb from her. I had to use the cane because I'm not current with a handgun, see, and I had to make an instant decision that it would be okay to try to prevent blowing up the stadium even though COS had deactivated me and told me to cool it."

"Okay, Brad, okay. I get the message."

"Maybe if you were to put in a good word for me, J.C., then COS won't put another letter of reprimand in my file—"

"*Okay, Brad!*"

"Sorry," I said. "My knee is killing me and I've got a headache from where that cop socked me in the eye, and you guys have let these pricks keep me sitting here almost three hours, cooling my jets and not knowing anything that's going on.—What are you here for now, J.C.? Do you want me to issue an official apology for an American mucking into Britain's internal security?"

"Brad, Jesus Christ, will you ease off?"

"Will you tell me what's going on beyond that door?"

"The bomb people have the fake Thermos jar in a secure place."

"It had an explosive and nerve gas in it?"

"That's what they think so far. They haven't opened it. They're still doing X-rays or whatever they do. They can see a tiny electronic gadget, probably a radio receiver and relay device, plus what they think is some kind of explosive—not much, it doesn't take much to disseminate the stuff—and a cavity that seems to be filled with the fluid."

"Radio controlled, then."

"Sure. Apparently there were other terrorists inside the stadium, or close outside. The experts figure somebody, maybe the trigger man himself, could see the girl. When you started rassling with her, the man with the transmitter didn't want to key it off and get her, too. What they aren't quite sure of is why the trigger man didn't blow it when Mr. Tune, here, was running up the steps with it."

"They might get an answer to that question," I said, "if they would ask me."

"You think you know?"

"Yes. The bottle's triggering device didn't get the signal."

"Right. How did you know that?"

"Because I pulled the antenna out of the goddamn thing."

Kinkaid blanched. "You could have detonated it!"

"I screwed up again. Tell COS. It ought to go in my file."

The door opened again, and back came Commander Fairchild, steaming. Clarence Tune hurriedly put out his cigarette in the tin ashtray and snapped to attention.

The commander towered angrily over him. "Dammit, Clarence! This was a *terrible* breach of etiquette! Terrible! Melville Oldham is a powerful and influential man!"

"I've been with the bomb squad most of the time, sir," Clarence said meekly.

The commander glowered. "Yes . . . yes, of course. Good bit of work, that . . . taking the bomb away and finding assistance. Of course I understand it was a dud anyway, couldn't be fired. Of course you had no way of knowing that, did you, Clarence? —But then you turned right around, Clarence, and completely failed your obligation to debrief Mr. Oldham at once. He may have invaluable information that will help us trace and apprehend those kidnappers who have the young woman."

The commander sighed. "You do one good thing, and then you negate it entirely by failing to use your head in the least! —Ah, I know it was a touchy bit of work with the device, Clarence, but then you turn right around and create a problem through routine oversight! Well, that's sort of the story, isn't it, Clarence? One good thing, and then something else that simply spoils it all. As we discussed just the other day."

"Yes, sir," Clarence said. "I'm very sorry, sir." I thought he was going to cry.

The commander looked down at him and then gave him a quick, fraternal pat on the shoulder. "Well, we do as good as we can do, eh, Clarence? Thank goodness I had the foresight to have the bomb squad on call! My staff assignments placed help within moments of your reach, as well, I am pleased to note. I believe I am safe in saying we have handled most phases of the crisis admirably . . . admirably. My emergency planning has paid off in a splendid way. —Well. —Staff appraisal at twenty-two hundred, the office. A late hour, but I believe in efficiency. Do try to be on time, Clarence, eh? Carry on." He rushed back out of the room and the door slammed again.

Kinkaid and I looked at each other. He said, "Once you're out of here, COS wants to see you at the, uh, office."

"Thrilled, I'm sure," I said.

"The guys here have assured us that they want to take a formal statement from you and ask a few more questions, and then you'll be free to go. Unless you want me to stick around, I'm going to head back ahead of you."

"Before you go," I told him, "you might fill me in on the real state of the search for Oldham's girlfriend. She's an American, you know."

Kinkaid's forehead got a hundred wrinkles in it. "We know. —Well, there are roadchecks set up all over England. Oldham found a picture of her and it's already being sent to every city and town. SAS is having a maximum effort along the border of northern Ireland, in case they get that far with her and try to slip across. All the planes are being watched, of course, and Anti-Terrorist Group has people at the harbors."

"But it was a long time between her kidnapping and the alert," I said.

"I'm afraid it was."

"What do you think?" I asked. I turned to Clarence. "What do *you* think?"

Clarence sighed. "We can always hope they will simply see that her usefulness to them is over, and drop her off somewhere."

"Sure," Kinkaid said. "Just dump her out, make better time without her."

"Alive?" I prodded.

"Ah," Clarence murmured sadly. "That is an entirely different question."

I glanced at Kinkaid.

"I hope they drop her alive," he told me.

"Do you think they will?" I countered.

"No. She'll have seen their faces. So—no."

Much later, two of Clarence Tune's younger, better-dressed, more socially acceptable colleagues interrogated me. I didn't figure I had anything left to hide, so I told them what I knew. They had a stenotype reporter take it all down. I signed something.

"Did you catch any of them?" I asked when we were finished up.

"I'm sorry, sir," the thinner one, with a beautiful hairdo, said solemnly. "All information relating to the matter is classified."

"Thank you very much."

We went out into another room, where Commander Fairchild stood with Clarence, waiting for us.

The commander shook my hand and gave me his handsomest smile. "Your assistance is appreciated, Mr. Smith. Dreadfully sorry about how you were forced to withdraw from the tennis earlier today."

Despite the pain, I had almost forgotten that. "Thanks."

He turned to Clarence. "Please deliver Mr. Smith to his hotel. Clarence. Then hurry right along, and try to reach the offices in time for that meeting."

"Yes, sir," Clarence said quietly.

The commander turned to the younger men. "I believe we have time to consider our findings, gentlemen, and then off we go."

Clarence silently walked with me and a security guard through the tunnels and walkways to another guard station, where they were holding my duffel bags and rackets. I signed a form and got them. They gave me back my cane, too. Then the guard escorted us outside.

Dark was coming on. Cold drizzle. The street looked strange, alien, almost deserted as it was. The parking across the way was already gloomy, empty.

"I parked in the security area," Clarence said, and turned south.

I limped alongside him, careful with the cane on the wet pavement. There were no cars along this section except for one lone taxi parked a few yards ahead of us and another car far down the street, obscure in the darkness. Clarence was too quiet and I sensed that despite the day's events he was feeling low after his brush with Commander Fairchild.

"You'll get another medal, Clarence," I said.

"Oh, no, sir," he murmured. "A letter of commendation, perhaps."

"They'll keep you on now."

"No, sir," he said more firmly. "The commander has already made that point clear. It's a nice point on which to go out, was the way he put it. He will overlook my balls-up in keeping Mr. Oldham waiting, he said. With a letter of commendation on top of my file, I retire in honor, was how he said it."

We had halved the distance between the gate and the lone taxi. I could see now the vague silhouette of the driver, forlornly awaiting a fare that was not likely to come. I wondered why he persisted in waiting in such an isolated place. Maybe, I thought, he was having a snack.

I asked, "Do you *want* to retire, Clarence?"

"There are younger men, sir. My retirement will make room on a promotion roster, don't you see."

I didn't see, but I have never understood bureaucracies. I decided to change the subject. "What about Oldham's girl?"

"Well, sir, as was said before, she does have a chance."

"What do you really think her chances are?"

Tune turned sad eyes toward me. He didn't have to say a word.

We neared the dark taxi curbside. As far ahead as it had to be to Clarence Tune's car, I wished I could just hop in this vehicle and save more wear and tear on the knee. Clarence seemed unaware that I was in pain, however, so I gimped along.

"I suppose, sir," Tune said, brightening, "we should be extraordinarily pleased with ourselves. Perhaps you would like to drop off someplace with me for a quick nip, eh?"

"You're on a tight time schedule to get to your meeting with the Commander, Clarence."

He chuckled softly. "Be good for the pompous bastard if I'm a few minutes late."

"Clarence!" I said in mock dismay. "You shock me!"

As I said this, we walked alongside the lone taxi. The driver leaned across the seat inside and popped the front door open for us.

"Oh, no," Clarence told him. "I have a car—"

The driver stuck his head out—bushy red hair and a dark beard, and something in the eyes that struck the first chill into me.

"So, Brad Smith," the driver said.

I knew the voice instantly. Every cell in my nervous system started screaming. No one else had a high-pitched voice quite like that.

For an instant I simply froze, and time froze with me. It was the stuff of nightmare, repeated a thousand times: I was totally off-guard and helpless, and there was no time whatsoever to think.

Sylvester moved again, and stuck something—a handgun—out through the open door of the taxi.

In a spasm of shock, I jerked to the side. My cane slipped, my knee failed, and I staggered, then went down to the filthy wet pavement. Sylvester extended his arm. The gun was a snubby semiautomatic with the long snout of a silencer—

"*No!*" Clarence squeaked in alarm. And jumped between me and the taxi.

The gun made its *pfftt! pfftt!* sounds, two, close together. I heard the bullets hit Clarence in the chest and he was hurled backwards, sprawling over on top of me.

Headlights flashed to life up the street somewhere. Sylvester started out of the taxi. I rolled away from Clarence, going over and over, looking for cover. The gun made its ugly little spitting sound again and a slug smashed the pavement beside my head, showering me with hot fragments that dug into my face. I got to the front of the taxi, still rolling, and Sylvester came around its side, moving deliberately along the sidewalk to get a better angle. I heard the sound of a car engine roaring. I rolled over again, knowing it was absolutely hopeless.

There were a couple of tall trashcans on the sidewalk, back against the high fencing. I crashed into them and they fell over on top of me, showering me with wet trash. Frantic, I tried to burrow into the stuff.

Brilliant light—car headlights—emblazoned everything. I saw Sylvester between me and the onrushing brilliance, a twisted silhouette. I think he fired again.

Tires screamed and there was a hell of a clattering noise. The headlights blinded me for a second and then I saw a big car hurtle up, bouncing front wheels over the curb, skidding to a halt. Sylvester's silhouette whirled to face it. The doors of the car swung open while it was still in motion. I caught a blurry glimpse of men jumping out on both sides.

Sylvester yelled something. His gun sputtered again but now he was firing at them. Out of the blinding headlight glare came an incredible explosion of return fire—muzzle flashes, flare of smoke, pounding staccato roar that instantly shut my ears down.

The bullets hit him everywhere. He jerked upright, twitching under multiple impacts, and then half-twirled and buckled at the waist, taking another dozen or more hits. Stuff sprayed. He tumbled to the pavement. One of the figures in the headlights fired again. A long, deliberate burst, aiming down from the hip at point-blank range. Hosing him down. His body jumped and lurched with the multiple hits.

For a second I thought I was next. Then, stunned, I realized the firing had stopped. The figures obscured by the light-glare jumped back into the car. Doors slammed. The car engine roared loud enough to get through my numbed hearing as a distant hum. The tires spun, this time in reverse. The big car bounced back off the sidewalk and into the street, the wheels pivoting, going into forward gear. The car rocketed past the taxi, barrelling on up the street in full flight.

One glance told me Sylvester would never hurt anyone again. I crawled on past him to the side of the taxi, where Clarence lay sprawled on his back in the rain.

His eyes were open. So was most of his chest.

He looked up at me, recognition clear through the pain.

"Oh, Clarence," I said. "Oh, Clarence."

His grayish lips curled in a little smile. "I think they got me, Two-Gun," he whispered.

"Just take it easy," I said. "Don't talk."

He nodded. Then the life went out of his eyes.

In the distance, police sirens warbled. I knelt there, holding him, trying to shield his face from the rain.

Thirty-one

SUNDAY'S NEWSPAPERS WERE full of the Wimbledon violence. Propped up in bed with a mighty achy leg, I had to search the back pages to find Sylvester. The small item said an attache for cultural affairs at the Soviet embassy had fallen prey to what police termed random street violence by unknown assailants. There were no details.

I had to search the agate to find one paragraph on Clarence Tune. It identified him as "a career government employee." As usual the media guardians of our right to know had missed the boat: cause of death was not listed.

On Monday I saw the doctors with the knee and they clucked and re-cast it, and I promised to be a good boy and hurry right home to my own orthopod. Then I limped over to see Commander Fairchild. He did not want to see me but I made myself unpleasant until he did. We had a nice little chat. He let me know that he did not like implied threats. I threatened.

Later, COS sent J. C. Kinkaid by to let me know that I had been far out of line, going to see the commander that way. I said COS should get stuffed.

"You're overreacting again," Kinkaid told me.

I ignored that. "Who killed Sylvester?"

He shrugged. "Every indication points to his own people."

"Why?"

"Evidently he was out of control. —Sort of how you get sometimes."

I ignored that, too. "I can't believe they would kill him."

"Oh," Kinkaid said, "I'm sure they would express horror if the idea was proposed to them. But the bullets the coroner dug out of him were 7.62, Russian manufacture. He *was* working out of their embassy, although we hadn't known that for sure. He had a used ticket stub in his coat pocket: the Belfast-London shuttle, so he was probably supposed to be up there for them. Our analysts think he must have come down here on his own, unauthorized, personal vendetta, and the KGB Resident picked up his trail, followed him, and took him out to prevent his doing something that could have damaged Soviet-American relations."

"Namely, killing me?"

"How does it feel to be an international trading chip?"

I didn't reply. The killing had left a vacant feeling in my middle. I had lived with the anger and fear for so long, it would take a while to learn to live without them. If people can't fill their life with happiness, they learn to fill it with feelings that aren't good for them, then grow so accustomed to the bad that it feels normal. I had never liked the damned black shadow of Sylvester over my life, but without it now the sunshine felt abnormal.

On Tuesday I went out to watch the women play. Melville Oldham was not in his box when I arrived, but he came in and sat down, alone, during the first set of the Maleva-Garrison match. I went around and limped down to join him.

"Care for some company?" I asked.

He looked up, startled, and motioned to the seat beside him. I sat. Up close he looked worse than at a distance: gray stubble showed on his cheeks, he had not carefully brushed his hair as usual, and the open collar of his wool shirt looked wrinkled and dingy, like he had worn it before. Ghosts looked out of his eyes.

I didn't want to ask, but had to. "Any news?"

"Yes," he said. The word came out a wet croak. He cleared his throat and frowned in the direction of Centre Court. "I had a call very early this morning. They were spotted, somehow, up near Liverpool. Police surrounded their flat. Called on them to surrender. Bastards started shooting, police returned fire. Killed all three men in the flat, the terrorists. Killed—" He stopped. A choking sound burst from his throat.

I squeezed his arm.

He seized cold control of himself, his face becoming a gray mask. "She was . . . they tried to use her as a shield, apparently. I'm told it must have been instant, don't you know, no pain, they said."

The fans around us roared suddenly, making me feel like we were sealed in some kind of invisible bubble. Oncourt, Zina had just ended a long, lovely rally with a spectacular get. Oldham was staring at the scene, his eyes screwed up tight. His throat worked.

"All the dead," he said in disbelief, "Why? For what? Who gains?"

"I don't know."

"She was a lovely girl. She cared more about me than anybody I ever knew. I think we would have married. —You knew she was rather wild, and probably would never have been really faithful to me. You knew that, didn't you?"

"I had no way of knowing anything like that," I lied.

"It didn't matter. We had talked about it. I didn't want to hedge her freedom. She would have been true to me . . . most of the time. She was kind. She would never have scorned me . . . talked about me to . . . others. She really did care about me. She cared nothing for my money. She only cared for me. —Imagine that? A wondrous girl like that, caring for an old blighter like me?"

Below, Zina hit a fine passing shot to even the game. The crowd cheered.

Oldham got his Thermos off the pavement. "Care for a touch?"

"It's a little early for me, Melville, and I'm on these painkillers."

He nodded. "She was so wonderful. She would never have hurt me. She loved me for *me,* and truly."

There was nothing I could say to that. He hugged the Thermos to his chest and sat there watching the match, one tear-track running down his cheek and chin. I felt very sorry for him. But he was lucky, too. This way he could always have the illusion.

On Wednesday, in a rainy little cemetery near Coventry, Clarence Tune received full military honors. A uniformed guard carried the casket to the gravesite and stood at attention. Air Force. I had never suspected Clarence might have served in the Air Force. I wondered what kind of plane he had flown.

Besides Linda and myself, there were only five onlookers: a tiny old woman who had been his landlady, Commander Fairchild and two of his dark-suited toadies, and off to one side, by himself, a sad-eyed, raincoated elderly man no one seemed to know.

Looking across the gravesite at the old guy, I had one of those little fantasies: After the ceremony he would walk over to me and introduce himself and say he had known Clarence for almost fifty years. *"Yes, we were in the RAF together during the Battle of Britain. He was a child, of course. But he was a stout little lad and he lied about his age, and of course we needed pilots very badly back then. We were in the same squadron. Spitfires. Did you know he went down in the Channel? But he got three of them before he was done. . . ."*

The weather worsened, the rain pelting harder. The minister gave a short, standard prayer. The honor guard stood at attention, rifles at order arms. Their noncom removed the flag that had draped the coffin and then, to my great surprise, marched over and handed it to me.

Afterward, Clarence's landlady came over and patted my hand. She thought I was Clarence's son. She wanted to know what to do with his cat. She said she would keep it if I liked. I said that would be grand. She said he had been a nice man and I agreed.

I looked around for the elderly man who had stood alone, sad, during the ceremony. He had gone. So I would never know who he was, what the real story was. It made me think again of Melville Oldham. Maybe, like him, I was luckier with the fantasy. The reality so often is less satisfactory.

Commander Fairchild walked over, stiffly handsome and military in his reservist uniform. He was icily in control. "I trust that was satisfactory?"

"Yes," I said. "Quite."

"Good." He started to turn away. He was very angry.

"There's the matter of the medal," I told him.

He looked back at me, red splotches appearing in his cheeks. "The medal has been authorized. Orders have been issued. The medal is to be delivered to our hall of fame, where it will be permanently displayed along with those of other men who have died in the line of duty."

I held eye contact with him. In a spiteful way I was almost enjoying this. "And the news release?"

"Damn you!" he whispered explosively.

"What?" I said.

He regained control. "The news release has been issued. It is for publication this date."

"Clarence's record is included?"

"Yes."

"His medals?"

"Yes."

"It's made clear that he served with great honor and distinction?"

"Yes!"

"Thank you, commander." I turned the knife. "That will be all."

You could see my brusque dismissal go in like a harpoon. If he had had less control, he might have hit me. Instead, after a fraction of a second, he gave me a single killing look, wheeled, and stomped back to where his aides stood waiting, unhappy and windblown in their expensively nondescript dark suits.

Linda linked her arm through mine as we went back through the rain toward the car. "What was *that* all about?"

"The commander doesn't like being pushed."

"Some of these honors . . . this service. Your idea?"

"Not at all," I told her. "I just pointed out to the commander, the other day, that Clarence died a hero. I pointed out that, if he did not receive a thorough and proper sendoff, the scandal sheets might have a field day with my story of how the service screwed such a hero, and even refused to honor him after a martyr's death. I also pointed out that a number of MI5 operational secrets might be compromised in the process of my telling the papers everything I knew about how Clarence had been screwed."

Linda looked up at me, her eyes crinkling. "You wouldn't have."

"Think not? I'm a loose cannon, remember?"

"Wow. You can really be a bastard, can't you."

"Thank you."

On Thursday, in the last of the rain-delayed quarterfinal matches, Sean Cork beat Michael Chang in five hard sets. But I didn't see it.

"Take care," Linda told me in the special Concorde lounge. She was smiling a lot and pretending her eyes didn't look the way they did.

I hugged her. "Hey, when you get home on leave this fall—"

"Sure. I will."

"Call me, I mean."

"Right." The brightness of her smile was as artificial as a sixty-watt bulb.

Behind me, people filed onboard. Almost all of them had entered the jetway.

"Better hustle," Linda told me.

"Right." I collected my duffel, picked up my cane.

She said, "Listen, give that surfer girl of yours a kiss and try to make her see it your way, okay?"

"Okay."

She leaned forward and gave me a kiss, very quick and very brief. "Bye." Before I could respond, she was hurrying out of the lounge.

I got onboard. The crew went through their Concorde orientation nonsense. The engines thrummed and we taxied out and held for quite a long time, and then the engine note changed, becoming an intensity that communicated into the bones, and we rolled.

The pilot jacked it up and out of there. Night had come. We thundered northwest, over scattered starlit clouds below, and then over a vast darkness punctuated by tiny, jewel-like points of brightness: the lights of Northern Ireland. What had Oldham said? *So many dead.*

For me it was over. But for them down there maybe it would never be over. I thought about that as the Concorde climbed higher, leaving the lights behind.